JAX

J.L. PERRY

hachette
AUSTRALIA

WARNING: This book contains sexual content, coarse language and some violence. It is recommended for persons over the age of 18.

This is a work of fiction. Names, characters, places and incidents are the product of the author's imagination or used fictitiously. Any resemblance to actual events, locales, or persons, living or dead, is entirely coincidental.

hachette
AUSTRALIA

Published in Australia and New Zealand in 2016
by Hachette Australia
(an imprint of Hachette Australia Pty Limited)
Level 17, 207 Kent Street, Sydney NSW 2000
www.hachette.com.au

10 9 8 7 6 5 4 3 2 1

National Library of Australia
Cataloguing-in-Publication data:

     J. L., 1972– author.
     L. Perry.

     0 7336 3586 1 (pbk)

     fiction, Australian.

     image courtesy Rafkat Shakirov
     images courtesy Dollar Photo Club
     design by Soxsational Cover Art, www.facebook.com/SoxsationalCoverArt
     10.8/14.2 pt Cambria by Bookhouse, Sydney
     bound in Great Britain by Clays Ltd, St Ives plc

This book is dedicated to Anna and Mellena –
the Twisted Sisters.
Thank you for inspiring me to write Jax's story.
I hope I do him justice.

To Candy, Rachel and Sophia, from the bottom of
my heart, thank you! I'd be lost without you.

BOOKS BY J. L. PERRY

My Destiny – Book 1
My Forever – Book 2
Damaged – Jacinta's Story – Book 3
Against All Odds – Angel's Story – Book 4

•

Bastard – Book 1
Luckiest Bastard – The Novella – Book 2
Jax – Book 3

•

Hooker
Nineteen Letters (coming soon)

*Sometimes the one thing you need to feel
complete is right there in front of you
. . . just waiting for you to realise.*

ONE

JAX

The past...

'WHERE DO YOU THINK YOU'RE GOING?' MY FATHER SNAPS AS I walk down the stairs, heading for the front door.

'Out.' I'm nineteen and an adult. I don't have to tell him jackshit.

'Not dressed like that you aren't.' He waves his hand up and down at me in disgust.

Here we go a-fuckin'-gain. Is this man ever going to let up? I've lived my entire life doing what he's asked, and I'm tired. I can't be the person he wants me to be anymore, I just can't. I'm not cut out to be a politician. That shit may be running through his veins, but it sure as hell ain't running through mine.

I scoop up my skateboard from beside the front door, tucking it under my arm. Out of the corner of my eye I see him storming towards me. I know exactly what he's going to do, he's done it a million times in the past, and that shit is getting old.

'Get that fucking thing off your head!' he screams, reaching for my baseball cap.

I manoeuvre my head to the right and then back to the left, avoiding his attempts to snatch it. There's a murderous glare in his eyes as he tries one last time.

'You're an Albright, not some common thug. I won't have my son walking the streets dressed like that.'

'It's just a hat. Get the fuck over it.' I've never spoken to my father like that before, I've always managed to bite my tongue. When I reach for the doorhandle, he roughly latches onto my arm, tugging me back.

I think the fact my father's long awaited plan is finally coming to fruition is the reason for my bad attitude. In two days, I'll be heading to university. Of course he's making me study politics, which is the last thing I want. I don't know why I crave their acceptance so much, but I do. I feel trapped in a world I hate, far removed from the person I want to be. The only plus is I'll be getting out of this godforsaken town and away from him—away from my whole family. My mother and brother aren't much better. Sometimes I swear I'm adopted. How can we have the same blood in our veins, yet be nothing alike? Why can't my father see I'm nothing like him, and no matter how hard he tries, I'll never be?

I hate my life.

'You're an adult now, when are you going to start acting like one?' he sneers. His fingers dig painfully into my arm.

'One day . . . maybe.' I snatch my arm away.

'I'm not finished with you, boy.'

He may not be finished with me, but I'm sure as hell finished with him. I make a hasty retreat out the door and down the front steps. I drop my skateboard onto the concrete and place my foot on it.

'I don't know why I wasted my money on that damn car!' he yells as I skate away.

When I graduated high school last year, my father asked me what type of car I'd like. All my parents' friends were buying their kids cars, so naturally we had to keep up with the Joneses. He was persistent, so I told him I wanted a classic, something cool like a 1967 Mustang. I don't know why he even bothered asking, because he bought me a brand new Alfa-fucking-Romeo. I don't drive it because it's the same type of car he has, the type made specifically for pole-stuck-up-their-arse showponies. It just screams, *Look at me, I'm a pretentious dickhead.* That's not who I am. Give me my skateboard any day.

I don't mean to sound like an ungrateful prick, but material things have never meant much to me. I'd prefer my parents' love and affection any day. Regardless of what they believe, you can't buy your kids' love, or their respect. It needs to be earnt.

Without even thinking I head to the one place I don't have to try to be someone I'm not: Candice's house. She's not only my Candylicious, blonde, blue-eyed bombshell, she's my best friend, the only person on this earth who truly gets me. We're kindred spirits. Like me, she's a social outcast, and the daughter of a single mother.

I've had a secret crush on Candice since the first day we met. Keeping my hands to myself has been a constant struggle, but I'm not the commitment type. She deserves someone better than me, we'd never last. I'd rather have a life-long friend than a fleeting good time. I'd never want to lose what we have. Candice is the only one who keeps me sane in the fucked-up world I exist in. I honestly don't know how I'm going to survive the next few years at uni without her.

'Jesus Christ, Sophia, give it a rest. It's only hair. It's not the end of the world!' I hear Candice yell after I knock on her front door. Sounds like she's having a similar day to me. *Who invented parents anyway?*

'Whoa!' I blurt the second she appears in the doorway.

'Great. Not you too.' Her shoulders slump.

'Hey. I like it,' I say as my eyes move down the length of her long, very pink hair.

'You do?'

'It's very Candylicious. Very . . . you.' I smile when I see her face light up. I love seeing that look. It never gets old.

'Come in, you dork,' she says with a light-hearted laugh, reaching for my arm and dragging me into the foyer, 'and stop calling me that.'

'What, Candylicious?' I chuckle when she playfully elbows me in the ribs. I'm the only one who's ever gotten away with calling her by that name. I watched on in amusement when one of the preppy guys at school groped her arse and called her Candylicious: she swung around and grabbed hold of his crotch, hard. I almost pissed myself laughing when his eyes rolled back into his head as he fell to his knees in agony. She's a top chick, just don't mess with her.

'Jax. Thank God you're here.' Sophia sighs as she rushes into the foyer. 'Look what she's gone and done.' I see tears glistening in her eyes as she points to Candice's hair. Since Sophia is a model, appearance is extremely high on her agenda. She's constantly having work done to maintain her beauty as she ages. So much so, she could easily pass as Candice's sister, instead of her mother.

'I like it,' I say, winking at Candice before looking back to Sophia.

'Great. Of course you would,' she cries, throwing her arms in the air in defeat. 'I should've known you'd stick up for her. You always do.'

And that will never change. I'll always have her back, just like I know she'll always have mine.

'It's just hair.'

'Fucking pink hair!' Sophia screams before covering her face and sobbing. She's a little on the dramatic side, but she has a good heart. She's also a great mum. I wish my own mother was more like her.

'I honestly don't see what the big deal is.'

Candice shakes her head, giving me a look that has me closing my mouth and not speaking another word. When Sophia lets out a howl, I'm glad I stopped.

'Come,' Candice says, reaching for my hand and dragging me towards the staircase. 'I'll show you what the big deal is.'

'I'm making a hair appointment for you tomorrow, young lady,' Sophia says as Candice pulls me up the stairs.

'Fine. Make an appointment,' Candice replies, sarcasm lining her voice, 'good luck getting me to go.' Candice not only inherited her mother's beauty, she also inherited her pig-headedness. They have a fantastic mother–daughter relationship on the whole, but when they have a disagreement—well, let's just say, it's explosive.

'Where are you taking me?' Usually we hang out in the games room, or by the pool. An image of Candice's body in one of those tiny bikinis she wears enters my mind. Do you know how hard it is to be best friends with someone you carry a permanent boner for? *Torture* is the first word that springs to mind.

'To my room,' she replies.

'Hell no,' I say, tugging my hand out of hers. That's dangerous territory. Me in Candice's bedroom? Not happening.

'Get over yourself. I just want to show you something. You're delusional if you think I'm going to attack you or anything.'

When she puts her finger in her mouth and fakes a gag, I lunge for her, throwing her over my shoulder.

'Jax, put me down!' she squeals.

'Not until you take that back.'

'Take what back?' She laughs as I run up the stairs with her.

'That gag.'

'Never,' she says through her laughter.

'Take it back,' I demand, bringing my hand down on her arse. It only seems to make her laugh harder. When I get to the top of the landing, I slide her down my body before pinning her to the wall. 'Take it back.'

'Make me.' She has that stubborn look in her eyes, and I already know I've lost.

Growling, I bring my face close to hers. Big mistake. We always muck around with each other, but never this up close and personal. Her intoxicating apple scent envelops me, and I can feel her sweet breath on my skin. My heart starts to race. We're both breathless, and the moment my eyes lock with hers, something shifts between us. The mood goes from playful to serious in a millisecond.

My face involuntarily moves towards hers. I hear her breath hitch just before our lips connect. Christ, hers are just as soft and sweet as I'd imagined they'd be.

Reality hits like a bolt of lightning. What in the hell am I doing? Pushing off the wall, I take a step back.

'Fuck. I'm sorry,' I whisper. 'I don't know what came over me.'

I swear I see hurt flash through her eyes, but it's gone as quickly as it comes. 'Don't be,' she says with a shrug as she walks away, heading to her bedroom. 'Are you coming or what?'

I pause. This is a bad idea, but I don't want things to be weird between us. That's the closest we've ever come to crossing the line. *We can't cross that line.* It's too risky. And if I walk away now, that's exactly what it will be—weird. Sighing, I follow her. I don't have a choice.

'What the?' I say the second she opens her door. Her bedroom is very pink, just like her hair. But that's not what surprises me: it's the huge display cabinets running the entire length of the far wall. Rows and rows of trophies line the shelves. 'Did you do a ram-raid on a trophy factory?'

'Very funny,' she says, nudging my shoulder. 'No, I won them.'

'What? How?' I approach the cabinet closest to me and read the inscription on one of the trophies. *Fuck me.* 'You're a beauty queen?' I ask in amazement, swinging around to face her. How did I not know this? That's when I spot all the sashes proudly displayed along the wall above her bed.

'Yes,' she says. 'My mum wants me to enter the Miss Australia pageant, but I'm not cut out for this kind of thing, Jax. I hate it.'

'Then why do you do it?'

'Sophia,' is all she says, letting out a deflated breath. I still find it weird that she calls her mother by her first name. Apparently, being called 'Mum' makes Sophia feel old.

'Oh.' I get that. My dad has been controlling my life for as long as I can remember.

'This is why she freaked out about my hair,' she says, gesturing around the room. 'The Miss Australia pageant is only weeks away. This crap means everything to her. It's what skyrocketed her model-ling career, but it's not for me, Jax.'

'To be honest, it's not something I ever imagined you doing.' I'm shocked by her revelation. My Candylicious is a beauty queen. Sure, she's got the looks for it, she's a babe, but the Candice I know is far from that type of girl.

'Exactly. You know me better than anyone. This is not who I am.'

She's always so bubbly and outgoing, so I hate seeing her so deflated. I want to pull her into my arms, but I can't—*dangerous territory*.

'Did you tell Sophia?'

'Yes. I've been telling her for years. I don't know,' she says, 'I guess she misses her old life, so she's trying to live vicariously through me.'

'That's fucked up.'

'I know, right? Welcome to my life.'

'You know, mine's not much better. I wish our parents would just let us live our lives the way we want.'

'I'll drink to that.'

She crosses the room and my eyes follow. Her sweet apple scent lingers in the air as she breezes past me. I'm addicted to the way she smells. On any other occasion, I'd probably be checking out her arse, but our little encounter in the corridor has me spooked. When she bends over to retrieve something out of a drawer, I quickly divert my gaze to the ceiling.

'So how long have you been doing this beauty thing?' I ask, trying to pull my thoughts out of the gutter.

'Since I was four,' she replies with a roll of her eyes.

'I can't believe you never mentioned it.'

'It's not something I'm proud of.' The sadness in her voice tears at my heart. 'Here.'

When she passes me a shot glass, I raise it to my nose, inhaling. The strong scent of aniseed invades my senses. Sambuca. Nice.

'Bottoms up,' she says, holding her glass in the air. 'Or should I say, penises up.'

My face screws up at her comment, then I look at the glass in my hand. Why did I not see that before? It has a tiny penis handle, and the words *I Love Peckers* written in bold letters across the front.

'No fucking way.' I shove the shot glass into her hand before frantically wiping my fingers down the front of my jeans to remove any trace of the pecker germs. 'What the hell is wrong with you? I'm not drinking out of a cock cup.'

Candice throws her head back and laughs. I'm glad she finds this amusing. 'It's just a glass, Jax, get over it.'

'A glass with a cock on it. Would you drink out of a vagina cup?' I ask, smugly.

'Um, yeah. It's just a damn cup. The shape or design holds no significance.'

How did we go from talking about beauty queens to genitals? I rub my hands over my face. Christ, I really need to get out of her room before I do something I'm going to regret for the rest of my life.

'It does if you're male and it's shaped like a cock,' I say.

'Fine. More for me.' She downs her shot, quickly followed by mine. Clenching her eyes shut, she shakes her head slightly as she swallows the liquid. I grin as I watch her. She's like no other girl I know. I think that's the thing I love most about her. When her eyes spring open, she looks at me sceptically.

'When did you become a homophobe?'

'I'm not a damn homophobe. I have no problem with a guy drinking out of a cock cup, as long as it's not me.'

When she laughs again, I swear I hear her mumble 'pussy' under her breath.

I'll give her pussy.

Stalking across the room, I grab the open bottle of Sambuca off her dresser and bring it to my lips.

••••

Two hours and an empty bottle of Sambuca later, it's safe to say we're both drunk. We're sprawled out on her bed, lying side by side and staring at the ceiling. Being on the bed with her is a bad idea, but the alcohol seems to have robbed me of my common sense.

'I'm going to miss you while you're away,' Candice whispers, reaching for my hand. I'm gonna miss her too. My chest aches just thinking about it. 'Oh, that reminds me, I got you a present.' Sitting up, she leaps off the bed.

'It's not cock paraphernalia is it?'

'No, you dork.' She laughs, coming back to sit down on the edge of the mattress. 'Here.'

I look at the parcel in her hand. 'You shouldn't have,' I say, rolling onto my side and propping myself onto one elbow.

'I wanted to. I hope you like it.'

I'll like it just because it's from her. When she extends her hand, I take the present before pushing myself into a sitting position.

'Candice,' I whisper when I see what's inside.

'I know you're not studying art at uni, but one day you'll get to fulfil your dream. In the meantime, you can keep all your sketches in there.'

A lump rises in my throat as I gaze down at the black leatherbound sketchpad. It has *Jax's Dream* embossed in silver across the front, and the words *Wicked Ink* curved around an image of a skull and crossbones underneath. This gift signifies so much. Candice is the only one who's ever supported me. I love her for that alone.

'Thank you,' I say as my eyes meet hers.

'You *will* open your own tattoo parlour one day, Jaxson Albright, I know it.' I love the conviction in her voice.

A sudden wave of sadness washes over me. 'How am I going to survive the next few years without you?'

She sighs and looks down at her hand as she swirls a figure-eight pattern in the comforter.

'Hey,' I say, placing my finger under her chin and dipping my head to make eye contact with her. When I see tears pooling in her baby blues, it's like a sucker-punch to the chest. I pull her into my arms. 'Hey, don't cry.'

'You're the bestest friend a girl could ever ask for,' she sniffles.

'And you're the bestest friend a guy could ever ask for.' Shit. Did I just utter those words? That would have to be, hands down, the unmanliest thing I've ever said. I hear her chuckle through her tears, and I know she's thinking exactly what I am—*I'm a pussy*.

'When am I going to see you again?'

'There's a spare room in my apartment in Sydney. Once I'm settled, you can come and stay some weekends.'

'I'd like that.'

My thumb sweeps across her cheek, wiping away her tears. It kills me to see her upset. I wish I didn't have to leave her behind.

Her eyes lock with mine, and just like in the corridor, something shifts. It's like the universe has suddenly stopped spinning. I'm frozen. When her gaze flicks down to my mouth, and her tongue darts out to moisten her lips, my need to kiss her again is almost my undoing. I've gotta get out of here. I'm trying to be the good guy.

Before I get the chance to react, she leans towards me as her eyes drift shut. The moment our lips connect all my resolve vanishes. My fingers thread through her hair as I draw her closer, deepening the kiss. I'm so lost in this moment, I'm powerless to stop it.

'Jax,' she whispers against my mouth as she pushes me back down on the mattress. The second she straddles my lap and her sweet lips meet mine again, I know I'm a goner.

'Candice,' I breathe, trailing my fingers up the length of her legs, my hands coming to rest on her arse. This is my wildest dream and my worst fucking nightmare. I've longed for and dreaded this moment since I first laid eyes on her.

She's my kryptonite.

I groan into her mouth when she rotates her hips over my rock-hard cock. I need to put a stop to this, but I can't. I crave her too much.

When she abruptly pulls out of the kiss, I'm filled with mixed emotions. I'm thankful that, unlike me, she has the strength to stop this, but I'm gutted too.

She manoeuvres her body down mine, sliding her hands underneath my T-shirt as she goes. Maybe I misunderstood.

When she runs her tongue across my abdomen before raising her face and giving me a mischievous smile, I *know* I've misunderstood. Sweet Jesus, have I misunderstood.

I swear my heart skips a beat when her fingers move to the waistband of my jeans. Is this really happening? I can't tell you how many times I've jacked off to the image of her lips wrapped around my cock.

She makes easy work of undoing the buttons, which is unnerving, although I'm not naive enough to think this is her first time. I know it's not.

Candice was dating one of my brother's loser mates when we first met. They were all hanging around by the pool, so I decided to go for a swim. It was only to piss my brother off. He and his preppy mates have always thought they were too good for me, and I get pleasure out of riling them. They were playing some pansy-arse game of water polo or something, so I ran out onto the back deck and did a mother of a bomb right in the middle of it. I hadn't even noticed Candice sitting on the edge of the pool until I heard her sweet laugh when I broke the surface.

My brother and his mates screamed profanities at me, but I only had eyes for the pretty blonde sitting a few feet away. She was fully dressed and soaked from the splash, but surprisingly, she was smiling. It was a beautiful smile too. I've never been a believer in love at first sight, but, fuck me, if I didn't fall a little in love with her in that moment. If it had been any of the other stuck-up bitches my brother hangs around with, all hell would've broken loose.

A few weeks later, I ended up beating the crap out of her boyfriend in our kitchen after I heard him bragging about her exceptional oral skills to my brother and his dickhead mates. Thankfully, Candice saw the light and broke up with him a week later. We've been inseparable ever since.

I'm pulled back into reality when her hand slides inside my boxer briefs, causing me to inhale sharply. I'm torn. I want this more than I want my next breath, but it's what comes after that petrifies the hell out of me. I can't lose her.

'Holy crap,' she whispers once she's freed my cock. 'I had no idea you were packing this monster in your pants. This thing should come with a warning label.'

I laugh. 'You're not the first person to say that,' I reply. When her eyes slightly narrow and her grip on my cock tightens, I get the impression she doesn't want to hear about the other girls I've been with. I don't blame her.

I'm positive that's one of the reasons I beat up her ex—because he was disrespecting her by telling his mates how well she sucks cock. And also, the thought of them together like that really messed with my head. I hadn't even known Candice very long at that stage, but that was irrelevant; she'd already captured my heart. The day we met, when my brother and his mates moved their pansy-arse party inside, she stayed out the back. We sat on the patio and talked for hours. I've never clicked with anyone the way I did with her. She was like nobody I'd ever known, or am likely to know again. She ignited something in me that day, which only seemed to grow brighter the more we were together.

I take a deep breath and hold it as her lips inch towards my cock. Part of me is screaming, *stop this before it goes any further!* But I can't. Maybe the alcohol coursing through my veins is affecting my rational thinking, or maybe it's because all the blood in my head is now rushing to my cock.

The second her sweet mouth wraps around the head, every ounce of fight leaves me. 'Candice,' I moan as my hands grip her hair. *'Fuck.'* My eyes roll back in my head as my hips involuntarily thrust towards her mouth. She takes me deep into her throat, palming my balls in her hand at the same time. I bet you a thousand bucks one of those trophies in her cabinet says: *Blowjob Queen—Candice Crawford.* If there isn't one, there should be.

I bask in her magic mouth for a little while longer, before putting my hands under her arms and dragging her up my body. It's not fair that I'm the one getting all the pleasure.

When her mouth crashes into mine, I flip her over, covering half of her body with my own. 'It's my turn.'

'Jax,' she whispers when my fingers trail up her inner thigh and under that sexy little denim skirt she's wearing. I groan when she parts her legs for me, allowing me better access. I'm still unsure about this but my resolve is slipping with every second that passes.

The moment my hand runs between her legs and over the soaked fabric of her lace panties, all my indecision vanishes. I need her—*more than life itself.*

Sliding my hand into her underwear, my fingers glide through her heaven. I groan again when I feel how wet she is for me. 'I need to taste you,' I say, pulling out of the kiss and making eye contact with her.

'Please,' she whimpers.

'Are you sure?' I ask, hoping she has the sense to stop this, because I sure as hell don't.

My hopes are dashed when she nods before uttering, 'Yes. I've never been surer.'

There's no way I can deny her.

Sitting back on my haunches, I glide her pink lace panties down her legs. She lifts her torso away from the mattress, pulling her shirt over her head, and removing her bra while she's at it. She's beautiful. Surely she didn't need all those trophies to tell her that? My eyes rake over her luscious body. She takes my breath away.

I'm so fucking hard my cock aches.

She moans the moment my mouth bears down on her and her fingers clutch my hair. Christ, she tastes just as sweet as I knew she would.

It only takes me minutes to have her coming undone. I reach up and place my hand over her mouth when she screams out in pleasure. Her mother's downstairs—I don't fancy facing Sophia's wrath if she finds out what we're up to in here.

Taking my time, I kiss my way up Candice's body until my mouth covers hers. I know the day will come when I'll regret doing this, but right now I'm too lost in her to care. My body is nestled between her legs, and my need to be inside her is so strong.

'Fuck me, Jax,' she breathes as her fingers skim down my back. Did she just read my mind?

'Candice,' I murmur. The moment I slide the tip of my cock inside, I throw my head back and groan. She's so tight. She feels *amazing*.

My mouth hungrily captures hers as I push my hips forward, filling her completely. I hear her breath hitch as her body stiffens.

'Shit. Are you okay?' I ask.

'I'm perfect.'

'Do you want me to stop?' *Please don't say yes*.

'No. Just give me a minute. You're hung like a horse, remember?' I chuckle. She has no filter whatsoever. I love that about her.

Stilling, I give her body time to adjust. My mouth meets hers again, but this time my kiss is a lot softer. I stay buried inside her for the longest time, while we make out until my need to move becomes too much.

Drawing my hips back slightly, we moan in unison when I slide back in. Soon I'm moving at a steady pace, thrusting into her little slice of heaven over and over. Rocking her hips, she meets me stroke for stroke. What I'm feeling for her in this moment scares me. It's like nothing I've ever experienced.

Flipping over onto my back, I bring her with me. 'You've never looked more beautiful than you do right now,' I say as she straddles my hips and sinks down onto my cock.

She rewards me with a smile. 'I've never felt more beautiful.'

My fingers dig into her hips as I lift her before drawing her back down. I watch as her eyes flutter shut and her mouth parts as she sweetly moans. Lowering my gaze, I stare at her pussy tightly wrapped around my dick. It's a perfect fit. Then my heart sinks.

'Fuck,' I grate out, pulling her off me in a panic.

'What?' she asks, confused.

'I forgot to put a rubber on.' I've never gone bareback before. 'Shit,'

I say, looking down at my cock. Is that blood? That's all I damn well need. 'Fuck. Please don't tell me you're a virgin.'

'Okay, I won't,' she whispers as she draws her legs up to her chest and wraps her arms around them.

'You won't what?'

'Tell you,' she replies, turning her face away from me.

Christ. How could that be? I never would've let this go so far if I'd known.

The moment I go to stand, Candice grabs for my arm. 'Don't go,' she begs. 'I've mucked around with guys before, but I've never gone all the way. It's no big deal.'

Running my fingers through my hair in frustration, I turn to face her. 'It's a huge fucking deal, Candice.'

When I notice the tears pooling in her eyes I pull her to me.

'Why didn't you tell me?'

'Because I know the type of person you are, Jax. You never would've gone through with it.'

She's right, I wouldn't have. Too late now, the damage is done.

We're both silent for the longest time, before she finally speaks. 'Please don't leave me.'

I don't reply because truthfully, I don't know what to say. I'm not sure if she's talking about this moment, or me going away to university. The thought of leaving her and not seeing her for God knows how long is tearing me up inside.

'I need you, Jax,' she says, sliding her leg over my lap and strad-dling me again.

My entire body comes back to life the moment she sinks down onto me.

'I need you,' she repeats.

When her lips meet mine again, I'm lost. I fucking need her too.

'Wait. Let me wrap it,' I say, pulling out of the kiss. 'You know how I feel about having kids. I'm not cut out for shit like that. I'm not taking any chances.'

When I attempt to reach down for my jeans, she stops me. 'I'm not ready for anything like that either, Jax. Christ, I'm only eighteen. Sophia would kill me.'

'She'd kill me too.'

'But I want to feel all of you. Can't you just pull out when it's time? It'll be safe, right?'

My common sense screams, *don't be a fool, wrap that fucker*, but my heart tells me to give Candice what she wants. My heart will always win out when it comes to her.

Holding my orgasm back, I drag this out as long as I can. I don't want our time together to end, because I know it'll be our last, our only.

The second I feel her muscles clench around my shaft, I can no longer stop the inevitable. Quickly pulling out, I stroke my cock a few times until I'm coming all over her silky soft skin. It's a beautiful sight.

In this moment, I know I'm ruined. I'll never again experience anything remotely close to what I just did with her. *Never.*

••••

When I wake, the room is bathed in darkness, and my head hurts like a bitch. I lay there for a few minutes, trying to get my bearings. Then it hits me like a ton of bricks—Candice.

Please let this be a dream.

Turning my head, I see her beautiful profile illuminated by the moonlight shining through her bedroom window. Christ. It's not a dream.

Throwing my legs over the side of the bed, I sit up, clutching my pounding head in my hands. What have I done? A lump rises in my throat as the enormity of everything I've just risked hits home.

I'm suddenly feeling like I can't breathe. I need to get out of here. I blindly feel around the floor, searching for my pants. 'Fuck,' I murmur to myself as I slip into my jeans. 'Fuck, fuck, fuck.'

Once I'm dressed, I make the heart-wrenching decision to walk away. It's gonna kill me, but it needs to be done. I can't face her in the morning. I just can't.

'I love you, Candice Crawford,' I whisper as I lean down, gently placing my lips on hers. I've never uttered those words before—my family doesn't do love. But I've been in love with Candice for a long time, last night just confirmed it.

She stirs briefly before releasing a cute snore. Even though my heart is heavy, it brings a smile to my face. I walk to the door, glancing over my shoulder as I go. This may be the last time I ever see her.

I selfishly put my wants before my needs, and I hate myself right now. I've always wanted her, but more than anything I've needed her. I always will.

I fucked up.

I've ruined everything.

TWO

CANDICE

'UGH!' I MOAN, THE MOMENT I WAKE AND TRY TO SWALLOW.
My throat hurts so bad. Come to think of it, so does my head. I feel like I've been hit by a freight train. I roll onto my side, tucking the blankets around my chin. Why am I naked? My brain seems foggy.

'Jax,' I breathe as my eyes spring open. I groan from the pain as I quickly roll over. My heart drops when I see that the spot where he was lying last night is now empty. *He's gone.*

Groaning again, I hastily throw back the blankets and get out of bed. Shit. I'm never drinking again. 'Clothes, clothes,' I mutter to myself, spinning in a circle and scanning the floor. I can't go downstairs naked.

Scooping up the denim skirt and pink singlet I wore yesterday, I quickly dress before hurrying out of my room. I cup my bouncing boobs in my hands as I run down the stairs. This is an emergency—there was no time to put on underwear.

Maybe Jax is having coffee in the kitchen with Sophia. Please let him be having coffee with my mother. He's stayed over countless times when we've fallen asleep watching movies, but last night was the first time he's been in my bed. I know my mother well enough to know she'll think nothing of it. She knows we're just friends, or should I say were. I have no idea what we are now, but I hope it's something. *Please let us be something.*

From the second I laid eyes on Jax, I knew he was special. He's like no one I've ever known. We fit like two pieces of a puzzle. I've secretly wanted more since the day we became friends, but until last night, he never seemed interested in me in that way.

'Morning,' Sophia says when I rush into the kitchen.

'Is Jax here?' I ask in a panic.

'I haven't seen him.'

Shit. My heart drops. Breaking into a run, I head for our usual hangouts.

'Don't forget your hairdresser's appointment today,' Sophia calls at my retreating back. She's delusional if she thinks I'm going.

When I enter the games room, I find it empty. *God, please be here somewhere.* If he's left without so much as a goodbye after what we did last night, I'll be crushed. He has a bit of a reputation with the ladies; I hear all the girls raving about him at school. I hate it, but I guess I have one thing they'll never have: his friendship.

Crossing the room and pushing open the French doors that lead to the back patio, my shoulders slump when I find no sign of him.

'Shit,' I mumble as a sick feeling settles in the pit of my stomach. He's really gone. He fucked me and left. How could I be so stupid? I should've left things the way they were. Now I've ruined everything. *What was I thinking?*

'Is everything okay?' Sophia asks when I walk back into the kitchen. 'You look like someone's kicked your puppy.'

'I don't have a puppy,' I snap.

'It's a figure of speech, honey.'

'I know.' I slouch onto one of the bar stools and bury my head in my hands.

'Hey, baby,' she says with concern. 'What's wrong?'

'Nothing,' I lie as the tears start to fall.

Sophia comes to stand beside me, her hand tenderly rubbing my back. 'Did you two have a fight?'

'No.' *We had sex*. But of course I don't say that part.

'Well, what's with all the tears then?' she asks, cupping my face. 'Is this about him going away to university?'

'I don't want him to go.' It's the truth, but it has nothing to do with my tears. I can't tell her what happened last night. She's a pretty cool mum, but if I tell her what Jax and I did, she may not let me go and visit him while he's away at uni. Actually, I can practically guarantee it.

My birth not only robbed Sophia of her youth, it ended her high aspirations for a successful modelling career. She wouldn't want the same fate for me. Before I was born she was on her own. She had no support, and nobody to reach out to. My grandmother tragically passed away in a car accident when Sophia was only nine. If that wasn't bad enough, her life changed dramatically when her father remarried. She never got on with her stepmother, and over the years she managed to drive a huge wedge between my mother and my grandfather. Sophia was kicked out of home when she was seventeen years old, and has had no contact with them since. Thankfully her modelling jobs paid enough to support her.

Sophia was only nineteen when she fell pregnant with me. My father—or, more accurately, sperm donor—was the CEO of a large mining company. They met on the set of a modelling job she was hired to do for his firm. He apparently swept her off her feet, showering her with expensive gifts and exotic weekends away. She was besotted. Their tumultuous affair lasted three months, and ended abruptly the moment my conception was discovered. He'd forgotten to mention the fact that he was already engaged to be married to a rival mogul's billionaire daughter. News of his affair and my impending birth would've ruined his chances of merging their thriving corporation with his own. He has provided for us financially over the years. We wanted for nothing. He even bought us this big-arse house. It wasn't because he cared though. It was more like hush money, to keep my mum quiet. As much as I've struggled to come to terms with our circumstances over the years, I know deep down we're better off without him. But I'm not gonna lie, it hurts me deeply to know my own father wants nothing to do with me.

'It's not the end of the world,' Sophia says, pulling me into her arms and stroking my hair. 'You'll still get to see him on holidays and weekends.'

'It's not the same, and you know it.'

'You have other friends . . . what about Jasmine and Bianca?'

'They're stuck-up bitches. I can't stand them.' We were friends before Jax and I started hanging out together, but I never truly fitted in with them. That was my fake life. The true me didn't come out until I met Jax.

'Since when?'

'Since I realised how shallow and self-centred they are. They're nothing like me. I don't fit in with them . . . I'm different,' I ramble. 'The only person who gets me is Jax.'

'I always thought there was something special between you two. You seem like the perfect match.'

Her words only break my heart further. We are perfect for each other, but he obviously doesn't see it that way. The fact he's not here speaks volumes.

I feel like such a fool. I've stood by for years watching Jax pick up, screw and then discard other girls, but I never thought I'd be one of them. In my heart I thought going all the way with him would change things between us—move our friendship to the next level. I was hoping he'd finally see me in a different light. Not just as his buddy, but something more.

Maybe I disappointed him.

Maybe he just doesn't want me in that way.

Maybe the whole stupid beauty pageant thing turned him off. *I wish I hadn't confessed that now; he probably thinks I'm conceited like all the others.*

••••

I spend the rest of the day locked in my room, beside myself with worry. I must've checked my phone a thousand times, hoping to see a message from him, but there was nothing. Everything in me wants to text or call him, but I don't think my heart could survive another blow today.

By late afternoon, I can't take it anymore. He leaves for uni tomorrow and I have to see him before he goes. I want to know where we stand, but more than anything I need to know we're okay. I don't want to lose him.

After showering and dressing in a pair of cut-off denim shorts, a white fitted tee and my favourite pink Converse sneakers, I drive over to his house. My stomach is in knots by the time I arrive. I rarely come here, because Jax prefers to be at my place. His family are weird, so I totally get that.

My hands are shaking when I knock on the front door. *Please don't let things be awkward between us.* I don't care if we forget last night ever happened. I just don't want to lose his friendship. I couldn't live without it.

'What the fuck did you do to your hair?' Jax's brother, Brent, says when he answers the door. I've never really liked him. He's a pretentious prick, just like the rest of his mates. I can't believe he and Jax are related. 'You look like a damn Easter egg.'

'Yeah, well if I had a face like yours, I'd sue my parents.'

'Ha ha,' he says sarcastically. 'My brother has turned you into a weirdo, just like him. You used to be cool.'

'It's a good thing that I don't give a flying fuck what you think then, isn't it?'

'You can pretend you hate me all you want, but we both know that's not true.'

'I'm not saying I hate you, but I would unplug your life support machine to charge my phone.'

'Bitch.'

Hands on hips, I stare him down. I refuse to let this jerk get the better of me. 'I bet your arse is jealous at the amount of shit that comes out of your mouth.'

'Very funny, freak.'

I could stand here all damn night and throw insults at the douche—it's actually kinda fun—but he's not worth the breath. Besides, the only freak here is him; there's nothing wrong with me, or Jax for that matter. He's just as beautiful on the inside as he is on the outside. He has a unique style, which, sadly, is frowned upon in our circle. I love him for his individuality: his dreamy chocolate-brown bedroom eyes, his just-fucked messy brown hair and panty-melting smile. Every girl at school wants to bed him, and I hate to admit that, unfortunately, most have. I'm pretty sure the disdain Brent holds for Jax is ninety-nine per cent jealousy, because as much as he tries, he'll never hold a candle to his brother.

I take in Brent's perfectly styled, slicked-back hair and stupid polo shirt. His facial features are similar to Jax's, but their personalities are miles apart. Brent is a cocky, stuck-up dickhead who thinks he's better than everyone, and Jax is just . . . sweet, nice and the essence of cool.

'Is Jax here or not?' I snap.

'Not,' he replies, folding his arms over his chest like the smug arsehole he is.

'Do you know when he'll be home?'

He chuckles. 'In about four years.'

'What? He's left for uni already? He wasn't supposed to go until tomorrow.'

'He packed his things into his car this morning and drove away. You probably scared him off with that ridiculous hair. Good riddance, I say.'

I could seriously slap this guy right now. I've always hated the way Jax's family treat him. He's too good for them, and they could learn a thing or two from him if they just gave him half a chance.

'Great brother you are.'

'You don't need someone like him in your life. The sooner you learn that, the better off you'll be. Tell you what, I'm home alone . . . you're more than welcome to come inside and suck my cock if you like.'

I take a step in his direction, and I see a smile play on his lips. He really is up himself if he thinks I'd even entertain the idea. 'Suck on this, arsehole,' I say as I grab hold of his crotch and squeeze with all my might. 'You'd be lucky if you were half the man your brother is, and by the feel of it, you're not even a quarter.' I release him from my death grip when he lets out a high-pitched squeal. That'll teach him for thinking he can speak to me like that.

Turning, I run down the stairs. Tears cloud my eyes as I head for my car. I refuse to break down in front of that cocksucker.

I'm hurt and angry. I feel used and dirty.

My heart is completely shattered.

How could Jax leave without saying goodbye?

THREE

JAX

One month later . . .

I HATE MY LIFE.

University has finally started, and there's only one word to describe it—*hell*. It's been a week and I already feel like I'm suffocating. I knew I was going to hate it, but I wasn't prepared for just how much. It's bullshit. This isn't me. I'm only doing this because I crave my parents' acceptance. That's all I've ever wanted. I'll never understand why I'm not enough for them.

As soon as I enter my apartment, I drop my backpack on the floor, kicking it in frustration. I feel lost . . . trapped. In a world I despise. I exhale forcefully as I flop down onto the sofa. How am I going to survive four more years of this bullshit?

My thoughts move to Candice. My pink-haired angel. I need her. I miss her so much I ache. Pulling my phone out of my pocket, I scroll through my contacts for her number. I've done this a million times since I left—it's a constant battle not to contact her. Not a day passes that I haven't wanted to speak to her. I yearn to hear her voice. I've written countless texts, but haven't had the guts to send any of them. What can I say? *I'm sorry I left the way I did . . . I'm sorry I never said goodbye . . . I'm sorry I'm such an arsehole?* She deserved so much better than that. So much fucking better.

My finger hovers over her number, but, like always, I can't go through with it. I'm a gutless prick. Flicking my thumb across the screen, I move down my list of contacts until my parents' number appears. I've had no word from them since I've been here. They were probably glad to see the back of me.

This time I don't hesitate. My mother picks up after three rings.

'Hello, Mother.'

'Oh . . . Jaxson. Hi. How's university?' The unenthusiastic tone in her voice lets me know she's not over the moon to hear from me, her own son. I don't know why I let this bother me, but it does. It always does.

'Honestly, I hate it.'

'What? Why would you say that?'

'Because it's the truth. I'm not cut out for this life, Mum.'

'Jaxson,' she sighs. 'When are you going to grow up? You're an adult now, act like one. Your father and I have bent over backwards to give you and Brent a good life.'

'Yes, you've bent over backwards to give me the life you want me to have, not the life I want. There's a difference.'

'We've given you everything—a nice home, a great education, a future—and this is the way you repay us?'

'I appreciate everything you've given me. I just wish I had a say in what I study. I'm not cut out to be a politician. It's not what I want.'

'Huh. What you want. Enough with this constant whining! Your father is a politician, and a damn good one. Is it too much to ask for his sons to want to follow in his footsteps? You should be proud. You should aspire to be the type of man your father is.'

'What? A bully?'

I hear her gasp. But it's true, my father is a bully. I would never aspire to be anything like him.

'How could you say such a thing? You ungrateful—' She pauses. I don't know why, I'm not unaccustomed to her insults. 'Where did we go wrong with you, Jaxson? You're a constant disappointment.'

I'm a disappointment. She always has to throw that in. My parents may be disappointed in me, but it's a two-way street. 'Thanks. As always, your compassion and belief in me is astounding. I've gotta go.'

I end the call without waiting for her reply. I was stupid to think I could talk to her, or that she'd understand.

I toss my phone onto the coffee table. I've done everything they've ever asked of me. I worked hard at school and always received good grades. I tried my best to stay out of trouble. I attended all their fucking functions with a smile, albeit a forced one. I even wore a damn suit and tie and acted like the perfect son as expected. So how am I a disappointment?

I need a fucking drink.

I grab a glass from the kitchen cupboard, and my bottle of Jack Daniels off the benchtop. Unlike my parents, good old Jack never lets me down. We've become very well acquainted since I've moved here. Especially in the first few days. It almost fucking killed me to get in my car and drive away from Candice after our night together. Probably the hardest thing I've ever done. But in the end, I knew it was what I needed to do.

Filling the glass halfway, I down the whiskey in two gulps. I welcome the burn of the amber liquid as it slides down the back of my throat. I don't hesitate in refilling the glass—I need to be numb. I don't want to feel anymore. It hurts too much. I have studying to do tonight, but fuck it, it can wait.

I lean back into the sofa, resting my head on the cushion. There's got to be more to life than this.

When my phone dings, it startles me. Nobody texts me anymore.

I reach for my phone and see Candice's name on the screen. My heart starts to race as a smile tugs at my lips. My angel. She has no idea how much I need this right now.

I open her text straightaway, but as soon as I do, my heart sinks.

> Candice: I'm so disappointed in you, Jax.

Whoa. That's not what I needed to hear. Is this some kind of sick joke? I double check the number to make sure it's really her. That's something my mother would send, not *my* Candylicious.

There's no mistake, it's from Candice all right. I sigh as I flop back into my seat. We've had no contact in over a month and this is all I get? I guess I deserve it after what I did.

> Me: It was only a matter of time before that happened.
> Disappointing people is what I do best.

As soon as I hit reply, I reach for the bottle of Jack. This time I don't even bother with the glass. I can't believe out of all the things Candice could've said to me, she chose that. Maybe they're all right. Maybe I am a disappointment.

When my phone dings again, I'm hesitant to read her reply.

> Candice: Wow. I hear nothing from you for all this time,
> and that's the response I get?
>
> Me: Yep. That's the best I got. I don't have time for
> this bullshit.

I press send, feeling sick. As if things weren't already bad enough. I want to punch myself in the face for sending her that. What in the hell is wrong with me? This is not how I wanted my first contact with her, after all this time, to go down. A few seconds later my phone dings.

> Candice: Fuck you, Jaxson Albright.

'Fuck!' I scream as I throw my phone across the room. 'Fuck, fuck, fuck!'

••••

Two weeks have passed, and I've heard nothing more from Candice. I sent her a text the day after she contacted me that simply said, *I'm sorry*. She never replied. I don't blame her. She has every right to be disappointed in me. If I hadn't gotten off the phone with my mother just minutes prior to receiving Candice's text, I would never have replied the way I did. But that's no excuse.

After class, I head to the supermarket to pick up some groceries. As I'm passing a jewellery store, a necklace in the window catches my eye. The bottle-shaped pendant has a pink-jewelled heart inside. Not only does the colour of the stone remind me of Candice—her hair, her Converse sneakers, her bedroom—but the heart in the bottle symbolises so much more to me. My true feelings for Candice are something I've always kept bottled up deep inside me. This necklace is an omen, the push I need to make things right between us again. Without hesitation, I go into the store and buy it. If nothing else, I want her to have it. It's important that she knows just how much she means to me.

Putting myself out there isn't something I've ever done, so I end up carrying the necklace around in my wallet for almost two more weeks. It taunts me the entire time, to the point where I can no longer take it. That's when I decide to write her a letter. Originally, it was just going to be something along the lines of, 'Hi, I've missed you. I'm sorry I left without saying goodbye . . .' but once I put pen to paper, I end up pouring my heart out. I tell her everything. My feelings, my fears, my insecurities. I'd never been so open and honest with anyone, not even myself.

It takes me another few weeks to gain the courage to post the letter, but when I finally do, I feel lighter than I have in years. *I have nothing to lose and everything to gain*.

Well that was what I was stupid enough to believe. The letter arrives back two weeks later with a cross through her address and the letters *RTS* written across the front of the unopened envelope. I'm shocked. I can't believe that she's returned the letter unopened. I can't even put into words how that makes me feel. It's definitely not the response I'd hoped for, but it tells me everything I need to know. We're finished. I've lost the most important person in my life. I'm not gonna lie, it almost breaks me. To say I'm crushed, devastated, even heartbroken, would be an understatement.

As much as it kills me, I know I have to forget her, and try my best to move on. I hate myself for the way things have turned out. One incredible moment has ruined the best thing that has ever happened to me: *Her*. My angel, my Candylicious.

At least I got to love her the way I wanted to, even if it was only for a few hours.

FOUR

JAX

Two years later . . .

AS I HEAD BACK TO MY PARENTS' HOUSE, MY STOMACH CHURNS.
It's a three-hour drive to Canberra from Sydney, so I have plenty
of time to think about what I'm going to say when I get there. My
parents moved to the capital when my brother and I were small. It's
where Parliament House is, so naturally it's where my father wanted
to be—since he lives, eats and breathes fucking politics.

It's the first time I've been home since I left to go to uni. I've always
made excuses not to go home for the holidays—there was nothing
left for me there. Not even Candice. My family certainly didn't give
a shit. Each year, my mother simply said, 'Have a nice Christmas,
Jaxson,' and a week later she'd deposit some money into my bank
account: my present. At least I took the time to buy them all gifts
and post them home. I never got a thank you though. *My family suck.*

My younger brother, Brent, started at the same university as
me last year, but I never hear from him. I've seen him a few times
on campus and the cock just nodded his head as he passed. What's

with that? We may be different, and have never been close, but I'm his flesh and blood. He thinks more of his pansy-arse mates than he does of me.

As I pull into the driveway of my parents' estate, all I can think about is Candice. I should be worried about what I'm about to face, but she's only a few blocks away, and this is the closest I've been to her in two years. Two years ... it feels like an eternity. I've slowly gotten used to not having her in my life.

Who am I kidding? I still struggle. I'm hurt by the way things played out between us, but my feelings for her haven't diminished in any way. I'm still hopelessly in love with her.

Pushing all thoughts of Candice out of my mind, I climb the front stairs before raising my hand to knock on the door. Although this is supposed to be my home, I've never truly belonged here and I don't feel comfortable using my key.

'Jaxson,' my mother says in a surprised voice when she opens the door. 'What are you doing here?' I roll my eyes when she gives me an air kiss. She's never been the maternal type. I used to love watching Candice and her mum together when I'd hang out at her house. I always found myself wishing my mum was like that with me. Sophia was a touch dramatic on occasions, but she's a good mum. There's no denying she loves her daughter.

'Hello, Mother.' Nervously sliding my hands into the pockets of my jeans, I give her a pleasant smile when our eyes meet. 'I came to speak with Father. Is he home?'

'Yes, he's in the study.' She steps aside so I can enter, and it doesn't go unnoticed that she doesn't even ask how I am, or how I've been. Figures. 'Is that an earring in your eyebrow?' she cries when I pass.

'Yes.' She may not like the person I've become, but I'll never be ashamed of who I am.

'Are they tattoos on your arm?'

'They are.' I love my ink. It's a true expression of me.

'Your father was right; you won't be satisfied until you ruin the Albright name. How do you expect to ever get elected into parliament

looking like a thug?' She shakes her head. 'You're such a disappointment. Where did we go so wrong?'

It's nothing I haven't heard a thousand times over. Ignoring her
comments, I make my way down the long corridor to my father's
study. Nothing seems to have changed in this house since I left; it's
more like a display house than a real home, something to show off
to all their guests when they have their stupid dinner parties: *Oh
look at us . . . see how rich we are*. It's sickening how they carry on
sometimes.

I roll my shoulders and take a few deep breaths when I reach
the door. I knock once before entering. My father is sitting behind
his desk. He's on the phone and eyes me sceptically as I stand in the
doorway, waiting for him to finish. He doesn't look pleased to see
me, but I kind of expected that.

'I'll call you back,' he says abruptly before ending the call.
'Shouldn't you be in Sydney?' he snaps at me.

'I'm heading back to my apartment tonight, I just needed to speak
with you in person.' I should've just called and given him the news
over the phone, but that would've been the coward's way out. I'm
man enough to do this face to face.

'About what?' he asks as I take a seat.

'I've dropped out of uni.' No point sugar-coating it. It is what it
is. I'm done. This man can no longer control or dictate my future.
I'm twenty-one years old, for Christ's sake. My life is my own, and
that's exactly how I intend to live it from now on.

'You what?' He bangs his fists on the desk as he stands. There's
a murderous expression on his face as he leans towards me.

I don't budge. I refuse to let this man intimidate me anymore.
'I quit. I'm not cut out to be a politician. I never have been. I tried
to be the person you wanted me to be. I gave it two years of my life,
but I can't do it anymore.'

'I don't give a damn what you want,' he spits, fisting my shirt in
his hands before pulling me off the chair and towards him. 'Get your

fucking arse back to that university now.' His face is bright red and I can see a few veins protruding on his neck.

'I'm sorry, I can't do that.' He can't control my life. My mind is made up. There's no turning back.

'Don't screw with me, boy.'

Prying his hands from my shirt, I step away from the desk. 'This isn't the life I want. This isn't the person I want to be. Why can't you see that?'

'What you want to be!' he screams as his face turns even redder. 'I don't give a shit who you *want* to be, this is about who you're *destined* to be. Politics is in your blood. You're my son and you don't have a choice in the matter.'

I shake my head as disappointment fills me. I was kidding myself if I thought he'd understand. He's too selfish to ever see past his own wants and needs. 'That's where you're wrong, Father. I'm twenty-one years old and you don't have a say in my future.'

'If you want to be a part of this family, I do.'

Family? What a joke. 'This family doesn't give a shit about me.'

'What a load of crap.'

'Really?' I snap. I'm trying to keep my cool here, but failing miserably. 'It was my twenty-first birthday last week, do you even know that? Do you even *care*? My so-called family didn't even call me to wish me a happy birthday.'

He falters slightly but recovers quickly. 'Well, I'm too busy to worry about things like that—that's your mother's department.' He flicks his wrist, dismissing the subject.

It may be nothing to him, but it was a huge wakeup call for me. Not one person wished me a happy birthday, not even Candice. I've never felt as unloved or unimportant as I did that day. I think that's the moment I finally decided that enough was enough. If I wanted happiness and acceptance, I needed to go out and find it. I certainly wasn't going to get it from my family.

'This family revolves around your stupid career. That's all you ever talk about. There's more to life than damn politics.'

'My career means everything to this family, you ungrateful little prick.'

'Not to me.' Turning, I head for the door. 'Goodbye, Father.' I've got everything I needed from this visit—confirmation that in the grand scheme of things, I'm nothing to them.

'If you walk out that door, you're dead to me,' my father hisses.

But I leave anyway.

I grab my backpack and other stuff out of my car then put the keys to the Alfa Romeo in the letterbox and walk out the front gate, ready to start my new life. A life without my family. A life alone.

Walking away with nothing is the only way—I don't want to be indebted to my parents. They paid my way while I was attending uni, so I saved every cent I earnt while working part time in a local tattoo parlour. I also have a small trust fund, left to me by my maternal grandmother; she was the only decent family member I've ever known. She passed away when I was twelve, but I couldn't access the trust fund until I turned twenty-one. And while I'd prefer to do this on my own, the money is there if I need it.

It was no secret my grandmother wasn't fond of my father. She never condoned the way he bullied me and tried to turn me into a carbon copy of him. I was just a kid, but even back then she knew how unhappy I was. I know she'd want to see me use that money to follow my dream.

Slinging my backpack over my shoulder, I pull my baseball cap out of the back pocket of my jeans and put it on. I exhale slowly as I make my way down the street. I'd be lying if I said I wasn't hurt by the way things had just gone down, but in my heart I had no expectations of a good outcome. My father's a selfish prick, and my mother is his puppet. It's always been his way or no way.

Well, no more. From now on it's going to be my way. I'm going to be the man I *want* to be, the one I was *destined* to be.

Despite everything, I'm looking forward to my new beginning. I have a fresh start. I may fall flat on my arse, but at least this time it will be my choice. Something I haven't had until now.

••••

I had no intentions of seeing Candice before heading back to Sydney, even though the thought did cross my mind a million times on my drive down here, but that's exactly where I head. *Old habits die hard.*

I'm gutless, though. I'm not going to knock on her door. She's already rejected me once, by returning the letter I wrote her, and I'm not going to give her the chance to do it again. I'm just going to walk past her house on the way to the bus stop. It will be for the last time, because I won't be coming back here. If lady luck is on my side, I may see her.

Who am I kidding? Shit like that doesn't happen to disappointments like me.

Besides, seeing Candice again is only going to dredge up all those feelings. But I hate that this is what we've become and I miss her, so I'm willing to take that chance.

I want to know why she returned my letter. It's something I've struggled to wrap my head around. Despite everything that's happened, I honestly thought our friendship meant something to her. Yes, I fucked up, but when I tried to make things right, it was too late.

I'm doing my best to get on with my life, but I still think of her often—I'm constantly wondering how she is, and what she's up to. I even followed the Miss Australia pageant, although I was stoked to see she wasn't in the running. She's so much braver than I am. She knew what she wanted, and did what she needed to do to make it happen. Wondering if she still has her pink hair brings a smile to my face.

Running my sweaty palms nervously down the front of my jeans, I turn into Candice's street. It's funny, I'm more worried about possibly seeing her than I was about breaking the news that I'd quit uni to my father. My heart beats faster the closer I get. When I'm a few houses away, a silver Mercedes-Benz passes me, slowing down to pull into her driveway. The windows are tinted so I can't see who's inside. Neither Sophia nor Candice drove a car like that before I moved, but things change.

I reach the bottom of the driveway just in time to see a man in a suit get out of the car. Who is he? Candice's boyfriend? He looks too young to be Sophia's. My heart sinks.

My questions are soon answered when the front door opens and a small boy and a woman leave the house. 'Daddy!' the kid squeals as he runs across the front lawn towards the man.

'Hey, buddy,' the man replies, ruffling the kid's hair. He slides his arm around the woman's waist, drawing her in for a chaste kiss.

'Dinner's almost ready,' I hear her say as the three of them turn and head inside.

My shoulders slump as disappointment floods me. They must've sold their house. They never mentioned anything about moving. *She's gone.*

A crushing pain settles in my chest as I shove my hands into my pockets and continue down the street. It's like déjà-fucking-vu, the exact feeling I got last time I was here—the night I realised I was hopelessly in love with Candice.

The same night I lost the best thing that's ever happened to me.

FIVE

JAX

One year later . . .

'SIGN HERE, MR ALBRIGHT,' THE REAL ESTATE AGENT SAYS, passing me a pen. I can't describe the feelings I have right now. I finally did it. A year after I walked away from my parents' house, my dreams are finally coming true. I've just purchased a small building in Newtown, and in a few short weeks I'll be a business owner when my tattoo parlour, Wicked Ink, opens. I chose Newtown as the place to start my new life because I fit in here. I can be myself without fear of retribution. This is where I want to work, and live; the only place that's ever really felt like home.

Newtown's close to the University of Sydney, so there's a lot of students, but it's also home to people with artistic flair. There's a higher than average population of gay, lesbian, bisexual and trans-gender people living in the area. Give me any one of these people over the pretentious fuckers I grew up with. Candice would fit right in here. Especially with her pink hair.

I don't know why I keep torturing myself by thinking about her. I'll always regret losing her, but it's times like this that it hurts the most. She was the only one who ever believed in me, and encouraged me to follow my dream. I wish she was here to share this moment with me.

At least I have the satisfaction of knowing I've done it all on my own. I've worked my arse off for the past year, saving every penny I could. It was a struggle at times. I went without so much, including decent meals; I've been living off baked beans on toast, two-minute noodles, and toasted cheese sandwiches for far too long. Tonight I'm gonna celebrate with a motherfucking steak. In the end, all my sacrifice has paid off. I had enough money saved for a deposit on this building, as well as some left to buy the equipment and fittings I'll need to get my shop up and running. It will probably take me the rest of my life to repay the loan I had to get from the bank, but I'm willing to work hard to see that happen.

My only regret is I have no one to share my success with.

When I first arrived back in Sydney, the weight of losing not only my family but Candice as well hit really hard. I truly was all alone. They were dark days, but I realised that giving in was only letting those fuckers win, so I used all the negatives in my life to inspire me. I was going to succeed or die trying.

It took about a week for me to get my shit together, and the first thing on my agenda when I did was finding somewhere new to live. My parents had bought me the apartment I was living in, so I had to go. I packed up my stuff and moved into a run-down one-bedroom shithole, but it was cheap, and it was mine. It was also a long way from where I'd come from and what I was used to, but my freedom and independence were worth it.

The move was liberating. I posted the keys for my old apartment back to my parents. They'd stolen the first twenty-one years of my life, and I flat-out refused to let them take one more second of my future. I wanted to show them that despite what they thought, I would go a long way without them.

After securing full-time work in a popular tattoo parlour in Kings Cross, I set my plan in motion. I took the time to ask a lot of questions so I could learn everything there was to know about running a successful business. My new boss was very forthcoming with information. He was not only impressed by my eagerness to learn, but my natural artistic talent as well. It helped to propel me forward at a rapid pace. I continued working weekends at the place I'd worked while I was studying, and I took in all the after-hours cash jobs I could. I had no life and was exhausted, but in the end I knew it would be worth it.

Being so busy also helped to keep my demons at bay.

Six months later . . .

It's just after seven pm when I finish with my last client for the day. Some nights I'm here until midnight. I've been working seven days a week since I opened five months ago, but I love it. Besides, I have nowhere else to be. Nobody waiting for me at home.

I'm not the only tattoo shop in Newtown, but it hasn't affected business—it's booming. In the beginning it was just me and a casual artist I called in when I needed him. Within two weeks I already had more work than I could keep up with. Now we're booked out weeks in advance. I've taken on three full-time employees: Gus, Shane and Mandy, the receptionist.

After sterilising my equipment and packing it away, I turn off the lights and lock the door to my studio. I groan to myself when I see Mandy sitting behind the front counter in the reception area. She's supposed to finish at five-thirty. I told her to go home over an hour ago.

'I thought you'd already left,' I say. She looks up from her phone and smiles at me sweetly. I ain't falling for that shit. There's nothing sweet about this woman. She's pretty in an overly made-up, Barbie-doll kinda way, and has a great set of tits, but she's trouble with a capital T. She's been openly flirting with me since the day she started

JAX

41

working here. For the most part I ignore it, but that doesn't seem to deter her. If she wasn't my employee, would I fuck her? Hell yes, but that's all it would be—a quick fuck. I'd have no desire to see her again, so having to see her at work would just make things uncomfortable.

'I thought since it's the end of the week maybe we could go and get a drink.'

'I'm fucked. It's been a long day, so I'm heading home,' I say, trying to be polite. It may be the end of the working week for her, but I still work weekends.

'We could always grab a bottle and head back to your house,' she practically purrs as she stalks towards me.

'Look, Mandy,' I say, when she comes to a stop mere inches from me. 'We work together—this isn't a good idea.'

'It's just a drink.' She gives me a flirtatious smile and flutters her eyelashes as her fingers twist in the front of my T-shirt.

I've seen that look hundreds of times. *Just a drink*, my arse. I know exactly where it will lead. Does she think I'm stupid?

'No,' I snap, taking a step back when she doesn't seem to get the message. I'm a guy and I have needs, but even I know sleeping with her won't end well.

'Fine. Your loss.'

I sigh with relief when she turns in a huff and storms back to the counter to grab her bag.

'Enjoy your weekend . . . *boss*.' The sarcasm in her voice doesn't go unnoticed, but frankly I don't care. She might be good at her job, but she's not irreplaceable. I'm her employer, and she needs to remember that.

••••

I wake Monday morning feeling somewhat human again. I went out for a few drinks on Saturday night and ended up picking up some random brunette chick at a bar, who I banged into the early hours of Sunday morning. The lack of sleep and a monster hangover meant I struggled through yesterday's shift. The brunette's name was Kate?

Kristy? Or was it Kim? I'm pretty sure it started with a K. I try to stay clear of blondes. There's only one blonde in this world for me, and since I can't have her, I'm not interested in the others.

I'm standing at the front counter going over my appointments for the day when Mandy arrives. I have a busy day ahead, so it's gonna be another late night. Thankfully, I love what I do.

'Morning,' I say, glancing up.

'Hi,' she grunts, slamming her bag onto the shelf behind the counter. She usually greets me with a smile and a takeaway coffee from the café down the street, but not today. I guess she's still pissed at me for knocking her back on Friday night. I'm inclined to say something to her, but decide against it. I'm not in the mood for her crap today.

As the day progresses, so does her attitude. What's this chick's problem? She's lucky that her bitchy attitude only seems to be directed at me—if she was rude to my clients I'd kick her arse out of here in a flash. I wouldn't put up with that shit.

It's around one pm when I finish up with a client. I have a short window of time before my next appointment, so I decide to go and grab something to eat. Usually, I'd get Mandy to duck out for me, but I'm not asking her to do shit for me today. She'd probably try to poison me.

'I'm going to lunch,' I say as I pass the front counter.

'Oh . . . you don't want me to grab you something?' Mandy asks.

'Nope.'

'Sure. Okay.' I can hear the surprise in her voice as her tone softens. 'Your next client is at one-thirty.'

'I know,' I snap, pushing through the door. Now she wants to be normal with me? I swear I'll never understand women. Mandy's behaviour only makes me miss Candice more. She was always easy-going and drama free. I've never met anyone who can hold a candle to her, and I doubt I ever will.

Shoving my hands into my pockets, I head down King Street. I walk straight past the café I usually eat at—don't ask me why,

I guess I just need some fresh air and time away from Moody Mandy. I don't know what to do about her—I'm too busy to look for another receptionist right now, but on the other hand, I hate feeling uncomfortable in my own place. Hopefully her attitude will improve. At least she seems to have gotten the message loud and clear: we're never going to happen.

I end up at a takeaway joint not far from where I live. I flat-out refused to use any of the money my grandmother left me to start the business—that was something I felt I needed to do on my own—but I did use my trust fund to buy a two-bedroom terrace house a few blocks from my shop. The apartment I'd been living in was practically falling apart around me. My place is only small, but it's enough for me. I have my bedroom, and a weights set and punching bag set up in the spare room. I've never been a big fan of sports, but I do like to stay in shape. The previous owners had a modern kitchen and bathroom installed before I bought the place. Apart from a fresh coat of paint on the walls, I didn't need to do anything to it when I moved in.

'Afternoon,' the shop assistant says as I approach the counter. 'What can I get you?'

'Just a burger, thanks.'

I walk to the back of the shop to grab a bottle of water from the fridge while I wait. After placing it on the counter, my eyes drift across the street. I see a homeless man sitting on the footpath, holding up a cardboard sign that says *I'm hungry*. Poor bastard. I hate seeing shit like that. As I stand watching, I see hordes of people just walk past him like he doesn't even exist. One incredibly insensitive lady even shakes her head in disgust as she does a detour around him. That's something my mother would probably do. Where's their compassion?

'Hey, can you make that two burgers?' I grab another bottle of water, and after I've paid, I cross the street. 'Here you go, buddy,' I say to the man.

His blue eyes light up when I pass him one of the burgers and a bottle of water. He looks to be in his sixties, possibly older, with long, dirty, greying hair and a big bushy beard. He's in desperate need of a shower and clean clothes.

'Thank you, young man,' he replies, placing the bottle of water on the footpath beside him, before quickly unravelling the paper on the burger and taking a large bite. I pull a twenty out of my pocket and shove it in the tin can sitting beside him. When I straighten, I'm surprised to see tears in his eyes.

'Jax,' I say, extending my hand to him.

He looks bewildered as his gaze moves between my hand and face before eventually taking hold. 'Brian,' he replies. I get the impression it's been a while since someone has taken the time to talk to him, and that thought tugs at my heart.

'Enjoy the rest of your day, mate.'

He nods before taking another bite out of his burger.

I turn to head back to work, but I'm suddenly frozen to the spot. I swear my heart skips a beat as I blink a few times to make sure I'm not hallucinating. The girl, or should I say woman, who has haunted my dreams for the past three and a half years is standing before me like a goddamn apparition. Her mouth is slightly open and she looks just as stunned as I feel. She's just as beautiful as I remember, if not more so. She still leaves me breathless.

'Jax,' she whispers before launching herself into my arms.

Relief floods through me. After our last exchange, I was half expecting her to go all ninja on my nuts.

'Candice.' Even though my hands are full, I wrap my arms around her waist, using my forearms to hold her tightly against me. My hurt and anger immediately vanishes. It all seems irrelevant now. 'I'm sorry.' Fuck, am I sorry. I feel like I've waited an eternity to say those words to her. I stupidly let her go once, but fate has brought us back together. If she'll have me, I won't make that mistake again. I smile to myself as I inhale her sweet apple scent. I haven't been able to even look at an apple since I lost her, which is ridiculous.

'For what?'

'For everything. The way I left . . . the way I replied to your text . . .'

'I'm sorry too,' she whispers as her hold on me tightens. She has nothing to be sorry for. She did nothing wrong. The responsibility falls squarely on my shoulders. We cling to each other for the longest time, like our lives depend on it.

'What are you doing in Newtown?'

'I've been working here,' she says drawing back to look at me. I can see tears glisten in her eyes, and the corners of my lips curve up. I was right, she is happy to see me. 'Mum and I moved to Sydney three years ago.'

'What? You've been living here for that long?' My thoughts instantly move to the letter. Is it possible she never got it? Had they already moved away when I sent it? I decide not to mention it, just in case. There's no point dredging up the past. If this is our chance to get back the friendship we lost, then I'm gonna take it. I'd rather that than nothing at all. Truth is, I'm miserable without her.

'Yes,' she says, nodding at the same time.

'I can't believe it. Where are you working?'

'In the beautician shop. Just there.' Turning her body slightly, she points to the shop a few doors down. I pass this joint regularly. We've been working on the same street. I shake my head. My angel has been within reach this whole time.

I take a step back. 'It's so good to see you.' I didn't mean to voice that aloud, but it's true. 'I thought I'd never see you again.'

She reaches out and grabs hold of my wrist. 'Same.'

'So you ended up going to beauty school after all?' I knew that's what Sophia wanted for her, but I'm surprised she actually went through with it.

'Yeah.' She smiles, but it doesn't quite reach her eyes.

'Is that what you wanted, or what your mum wanted?'

Shrugging, her gaze drops to the footpath. Her reaction concerns me. She has never mentioned *her* aspirations, but I know her well—this isn't what she wants.

I use this time to take in her appearance. She's different from the Candice I remember. She looks grown up and sophisticated in the tailored white jacket and matching slacks she's wearing. The company logo on the breast pocket tells me it's a uniform. Her hair is slicked back into a tight bun that sits on top of her head; she has beautiful, soft hair and I much prefer it when it falls free. I smile when I see her familiar pink Converse sneakers. It makes me happy because I know the girl I love is still buried in there somewhere.

'She's made a lot of sacrifices for me over the years, Jax. It was the least I could do. Plus, I kinda ruined her plans for me to follow her into the modelling world.' She points to her pink hair. I'm so glad she kept it. 'How have *you* been? How's uni?'

'I dropped out.'

Her eyes widen in shock. 'What? When?'

'Eighteen months ago. I gave it my best shot, but it was too much. I couldn't do it anymore. I felt like I was suffocating.'

Her grip on my wrist tightens. 'Politics was never you. How did your family take it?'

'They disowned me.' I still find it hard to believe myself.

'What! Oh Jax.'

I can see the pity in her eyes, and I hate that. I don't want people feeling sorry for me. It is what it is. At least Candice gives a shit—she's the only one who ever has.

'I'm fine with it,' I say with a shrug, which isn't exactly true. I've become accustomed to it, but I'm definitely not okay with it. My parents haven't even tried to contact me since I walked away from them. I'd never admit it, but it stings.

I can tell by the look Candice gives me that she has reservations about what I've just said, but I'm grateful that she doesn't call me on it.

'If you're not going to uni anymore, what are you doing with yourself?'

'I opened my own tattoo parlour.'

'You did not.' She playfully pushes my chest and I chuckle.

'I did. It's just down the street if you'd like to come and see it.'

'Jax!' she shrieks as she throws her arms around me again. 'I knew one day you'd do it. I'm so proud of you.'

A lump rises in my throat when she says that. I knew in my heart she'd be happy that I've accomplished my dream. Her unwavering belief in me is what gave me the courage to even believe it was possible. I'm so glad to have her back.

'Oh my God. Jaxson Albright,' I hear someone say from behind me.

When I let go of Candice and turn around, I find Sophia standing there with a stunned look on her face. But what shocks me the most is the small child she's holding in her arms. My heart starts to race—is she Candice's child? Though I guess Sophia is still young enough to be a mother. *Please let her be Sophia's.*

'Sissy!' the little girl squeals, holding her arms out to Candice, and relief floods through me. The thought of Candice being with another man in that way is something I don't want to consider. It's selfish of me to even think that because I've certainly had my fair share of other women since her, but in my heart she'll always belong to me and I don't want to share her.

I watch as Candice peppers kisses all over her sister's face. It's a beautiful sight and you can easily tell they're related. Apart from the different eye colour, they have the same sweet facial features.

'Hi Sophia,' I say, tucking the bottle of water under my arm and holding out my hand to her. I'm taken aback when she ignores it, stepping forward and hugging me tightly instead.

'It's so good to see you again, Jaxson,' she says.

'You too.'

When she lets go and steps back, her eyes travel down the length of my arm. 'Look at you, all grown up. I love your ink.' Sophia's always been a cool parent. I wish mine were more like her.

'Thanks.' They're only the visible ones. I have a lot more. I love them and each one has a special meaning. Especially the tiny image of a piece of pink candy that sits right over my heart. I'm the only one who knows the true meaning of that tattoo. It was my way of ensuring I'd always have a piece of my Candylicious with me. I'm going to need to be keeping my shirt on around her.

'Jax has his own tattoo parlour now,' Candice says. Her face lights up as she speaks and I'm trying hard not to stare, but I can't seem to take my eyes off her.

'I'm happy to hear things are going well for you. You were always a good kid.'

I nod, giving her an appreciative smile. 'And who do we have here?' I ask, turning my attention to the child.

Candice's eyes dart to her mother.

'This is my daughter, Maddison,' Sophia says.

'We call her Maddie,' Candice adds.

Maddie has a little Snoopy stuffed animal tucked tightly under her arm. Its worn condition tells me it's extremely loved.

'Hello, Peanut,' I say, extending my hand to her. She's only a toddler, so I doubt she'll get my Charlie Brown reference. She giggles as her chubby little fingers curl around mine. 'My name is Jax.'

'Jax,' she says as her free arm reaches out to me.

Shit. Does she want me to hold her? I've never held a kid before. I give Candice a look that hopefully conveys I'm not comfortable holding her sister, but when the kid leans her torso towards me and extends her arm further, I'm left with no choice. I begrudgingly take her out of Candice's arms. I can see she's already inherited her mother's and sister's stubborn streak.

Even with Snoopy tucked under her arm, she manages to raise both hands, and places them on my cheeks. Turning my face to hers, she studies me.

'Hi,' I say.

'Hi,' she replies as her cute face scrunches up in a toothy smile. She has the biggest brown eyes. These Crawford women are bewitching.

Reaching up further, the kid removes the cap from my head and places it on her own. I chuckle when she turns it backwards, just like I had it. 'Hat,' she says proudly.

'Yes. That's Jax's hat, bubba. You need to give it back,' Candice replies.

'No.'

I chuckle when she purses her lips. There's that familiar stubborn streak again. How do these three live together without killing each other?

'Are you joining us for lunch?' Sophia asks.

'I can't. I have a client in about ten minutes,' I reply, looking down at my watch. 'I guess I should be getting back.'

'Do you have to?' Candice asks. I can tell by the tone of her voice that she's disappointed and that pleases me. I'm not ready to let her go either.

'Why don't you drop past my shop after work? I'd love to show you around.' I need to see her again. *Please say yes*.

'I'd really like that,' she answers. I can't tell you how happy that makes me. 'We'd better be going too. I have to be back at work soon. My boss is a tyrant. If I'm late she'll be pissed.' Candice rolls her eyes as she speaks. Even if it is to please her mother, I hate that she's working somewhere that obviously makes her unhappy.

'It was nice seeing you again, Jax,' Sophia says, taking the kid out of my arms. Candice scoops my hat off Maddie's head and passes it back to me.

'Hat!' Maddie screams. When she reaches for it, Sophia turns and starts walking down the street. I feel bad when I hear her start to cry. It's my favourite hat, but I probably would've let her keep it if I'd known she was going to get upset.

'So you'll drop by later?'

'Of course.' The beautiful full smile Candice gives me when she says that, reignites the flame that once burnt brightly within me. She makes me feel alive. Fuck, I've missed that feeling. 'My shift finishes at five-thirty. I'll come over then.'

'Great.' I pull a business card out of my pocket, passing it to her.

She smiles as she gazes down at it. 'Wicked Ink,' she whispers as her fingers skim over the surface of the card. The logo on the card is identical to the one she had embossed onto the sketchpad she bought me.

We stand there in silence. I don't want to leave. 'I'm glad I bumped into you.' It's made my day. Who am I kidding? It's made my fucking year.

'Me too.' Stepping forward, she hugs me once more. 'I never stopped hoping this day would come. I've been lost without you, Jax.' Her words make me smile. She's just the lift I needed. She'll always be my happy place . . . the light in my darkness.

'Me too. I've missed you so much. Never let anyone dull your sparkle, Candice,' I whisper as I hold her tight.

SIX

CANDICE

'IS IT ALL RIGHT IF I LEAVE NOW?' I ASK MY BOSS. I ALREADY know the answer, but for once she may surprise me.

'No. You were late back from your lunch break, again, so you can sanitise all the manicuring equipment and sweep the floor before you leave. I'm running a business here, not a charity.'

'But I've already sanitised all the equipment.' I was only a few minutes late. She never takes into consideration all the times I've arrived early, or stayed back. God, I hate working here.

'Well, re-do them,' she snaps.

'Bitch,' I mumble under my breath when she storms to the back of the shop. I know what I'd like to do with all the nail files and clippers—shove them up her arrogant, unreasonable arse.

It's almost six by the time I finally arrive at Jax's shop. I practically run all the way because I'm worried he'll think I'm not coming. Seeing him again is all I've thought about the entire afternoon. Regardless of what's happened between us, I need him in my life. Truth is, I'm miserable without him. Jax's parting words from earlier are stuck in my mind and I have a feeling my sparkle will return now he has.

I'm relieved when I see the lights inside are still on and I spend a minute or so catching my breath before entering. I use this time to take in the shop front. My heart swells with pride—I knew he'd follow his dream. He's always been driven. I wish I could say the same thing for myself. Things changed dramatically for me after he left. The last few years I've struggled, to the point where some days I even found it hard to breathe without him. All my dreams were squashed. Even though I had no real aspirations when I was at school, I hate where I've ended up. I think it's more my boss than the job itself though. I actually don't mind that part.

Pushing through the front door, I see a blonde behind the front desk. She's extremely attractive—just Jax's type. I wonder if he's been with her too. I hate the jealousy that rises within me. My head knows what happened between us was a mistake and we'll only ever be friends, but my heart hasn't gotten to that place yet.

'Hi,' I say as I cross the shop floor.

She smiles, but it's forced. 'Hi. We're getting ready to close; can I help you with something?'

'No. I'm actually here to see Jax. He's expecting me.'

The smile drops from her face as her eyes narrow. She looks down at the appointment book in front of her.

'Do you have an appointment? There's nothing in the book. He asked me to cancel his last client.'

I wonder if he cancelled it because of me. That thought makes me deliriously happy. I can tell the exact moment his receptionist has the same thought because her lips purse and her face turns red with anger.

'I'm not here to get a tattoo.'

'Then why are you here?' There's venom in her voice. Maybe I was right in thinking there's something between them.

'Is he here or not?' I don't owe this bitch an explanation. Whether they're a couple or not, Jax is my friend and I have every right to see him.

'Take a seat. I'll see if he's free.'

When she flicks her hand at me, I have to bite my tongue as I turn and walk to the black leather L-shaped sofa by the far wall. Before I'm even seated I hear Jax's voice behind me.

'You came.'

I face him and my stomach does a flip-flop as soon as my eyes lock with his. It's been years since I've had these feelings. Is it possible that he's grown more handsome? Because I'm pretty sure he has. Don't even get me started on those sexy-as-hell tattoos of his. He was a dreamboat back in high school, but now he's all man. His badass look is so hot.

'Of course I came.' The shy, boyish look that appears on his face is something I've missed. As handsome and confident as he is, that childlike expression he gets occasionally has always been endearing. He steals another piece of my heart every time I see it.

'I'm glad.' He gives me a brief hug before turning his attentions to the bitchy blonde. 'You can leave now, Mandy.'

'What?'

'You can leave. Your shift finished half an hour ago.'

I have to suppress my smile at the way he's speaking to her—she deserves it after the way she treated me.

'Sure,' she says, trying to act unaffected, but I can see straight through her. Snatching her bag from behind the reception desk, she storms to the exit. 'I'll see you in the morning, Jax.' She gives him a weak smile as she glances over her shoulder. When her eyes move to me, her dislike shows. I'm not usually the nasty type, but for this woman, I'll make an exception.

'Bye,' I say, smiling sweetly, giving her a little wave.

She grunts as she opens the door. It slams closed behind her.

'What's the go with psycho Barbie?' I ask.

'Psycho Barbie.' He chuckles. 'That name suits her perfectly.' Sighing, he removes his cap and runs his hand through his thick brown hair. 'She's become a thorn in my side. I think it's time I found a new receptionist.'

'So she's not your girlfriend then?' The words are out of my mouth before I even realise.

'Hell no.' He laughs. 'You know me better than anyone, I'm not the girlfriend type.'

Forcing a smile, I try to act unaffected by his admission. I'd be lying if I said his words didn't sting, because they do. He crushed me when he left.

'So your place looks great,' I say, changing the subject. I'm not ready to hash our past out with him just yet. The day will come though—he seems oblivious to the heartache I've had to endure since he walked away and didn't look back.

'It does look great, doesn't it? I fucking love this place,' he says, beaming. He has every right to be proud.

He slides his hands into his pockets and, out of the corner of my eye, I see him watching me as I walk around the reception area. The walls are painted a deep red and the furnishings are black. There's large, colourful, framed prints of heavily inked bodies hanging on every wall.

'Come out back and let me show you my studio.'

I feel giddy as I follow him down the corridor. I can't help but smile the minute I enter. I've never been inside a tattoo parlour before. Everything is set out meticulously. The walls are a sterile white. There's a black reclining chair in the far corner, with a matching stool sitting beside it. On the adjoining wall is a bed, similar to the ones we use at the beautician salon. The row of cabinets are stainless steel. It looks like Jax has the best equipment money can buy. I'd love to get him to give me a tattoo, but I'm too afraid to ask. Sophia would probably freak anyway. It took her months to adjust to my pink hair.

'I'm so proud of you,' I say as I turn to face him. 'I knew you'd do this one day. I didn't doubt it for a second.'

'You're the only one who ever believed in me. Your unwavering faith is what gave me the courage.'

I hate that his family has never supported him. The fact that he's accomplished this all on his own makes it so much more inspiring. My heart skips a beat when he reaches for my hand. The effect he has on me is still so strong. Electric—that would be the best way to describe it. I often think about that night we spent together—the night I gave him my heart. The same night he crushed it into a million pieces. It's still so raw, I'm not sure if I'll ever completely recover from it.

I turn my head away, trying not to let him see the hurt that still lingers. 'Oh my God. You still have the sketchpad I gave you,' I say when I notice it sitting on the bench by the wall. I pick it up and flick through the pages, admiring all the drawings inside.

'I've kept everything you've ever given me.'

I glance at him over my shoulder. 'Everything except me,' I want to say, but there's no point dredging up the past. We're back together again, and that's all that matters. I think we both know that we can't go there again. It's what tore us apart. We have a second chance to get this right and I'm going to try my hardest not to screw it up.

JAX

I'm grinning like a damn fool as I watch Candice move around my studio. In all honesty, I never thought I'd have her here. I'm so glad I was wrong.

'Do you have any dinner plans?' I ask. I'm going to drag out my time with her as long as I can. We have so much to catch up on. I have no idea what her life's been like since I left Canberra. It's something that's weighed heavily on my mind. I want to know how she ended up here, and what she's been up to. Has there been anyone else since me? Does she have a boyfriend? Okay, maybe I don't want to know the answers to the last two questions, but on the other hand I need to.

She smiles. 'No. Not really. I was just going to go home and eat with Sophia and Maddie. Do you want to come with me?'

I would've liked to take her out somewhere nice, but it's been years since I've had a home-cooked meal, and Sophia is an amazing cook. Hanging with Candice, at her house, was something I always loved doing.

'Sounds great.'

Ten minutes later we're heading to my terrace house to pick up my car. We haven't stopped talking the whole time. I love how we've instantly reverted to the way things used to be between us. There's no awkward silence or forced conversation. I'm so comfortable around her.

'So this is where you live?' she asks when I unlock the front door.

'Yep. It's not much, but it's home.'

'It's really nice,' she says after I give her a quick tour. 'I'm glad things eventually worked out for you. Are you happy, Jax?'

'Define happy.'

'You know, with the way your life panned out?'

I shrug. 'I have a few regrets. The biggest one being how I left things with you, but yes, overall I'm happy.'

'I guess running into each other today was fate. Our second chance.' She smiles as she runs her hand down my arm. The feeling goes straight to my cock. 'I've really missed our friendship, Jax.'

'I've missed it too.'

Fuck how I've missed it.

••••

I'm smiling to myself as I lock the front door and head down the path on my way to work. It was close to midnight when I got home last night. Dinner with Candice and Sophia was just like old times— *amazing.* Being around Candice and her mother again lifted me in ways I hadn't realised I needed. It forced me to see how I've just been existing for the last few years, going through the motions of life alone, and not really living. I've had nobody to share my successes, my daily highs and lows with. The feeling was bittersweet. But Candice and Sophia were sure to rectify that over the course of the night. They both seemed interested in me, my life, my shop; the questions never stopped coming. It was nice. I got to share all my accomplishments with them and there's no words for how that felt. Just to know they're proud of me meant the world.

And then there's Maddison—Maddie. My little Peanut. I've never been around small children before, and never felt the least bit interested in being so, either, but that kid is a gem. There's something about her. I can't quite put my finger on it, but she's so damn entertaining.

After we'd eaten, Sophia took Maddie upstairs for a bath and to get her ready for bed. She looked so sweet when she came back down in her pink PJs, sucking a dummy and carrying her Snoopy under her arm. I'm learning fast—that toy goes with her everywhere.

'Nye-nye, Sissy,' she mumbled around her dummy as she climbed onto Candice's lap for a kiss.

'Goodnight, baby girl,' Candice replied before hugging Maddie tightly and placing a lingering kiss on her cheek. 'I love you.' Hearing her say those words so freely made me smile. I've only ever said them once. That was the day I walked away from her, and she wasn't even awake to hear them.

The way Candice doted over Maddie at dinner tells me she'll make a great mother one day. Although it was nice to see, I felt like a knife was being plunged into my chest as I watched them together. One day Candice will probably meet the man of her dreams, settle down and have kids of her own. Where would that leave us?

Once Candice put Maddie down, Maddie headed straight for me. I was taken aback, but helped her up as she attempted to climb onto my lap. 'Nye-nye, Jax,' she said as she slid her chubby arms around my neck to hug me. She smelt so sweet, like baby powder or some shit like that. I wrapped my arms around her middle and held her tiny body against mine. I was surprised by the lump that formed in my throat. Settling down, and becoming a father, is not something I've ever wanted, but in that moment I realised that maybe one day I'd like to have a child of my own.

'Night, Peanut,' I whispered.

When she finally released me, she pulled her dummy out of her mouth and placed a wet, sloppy kiss on my lips. I'm not ashamed to say it melted my heart. That was until she shoved Snoopy in my face.

'Tiss Puppy,' she said.

I can't believe I actually kissed a stuffed toy. When my eyes moved to Candice, I was expecting her to make a smart remark, or laugh. But instead I was surprised to see tears in her eyes.

'You're very sweet with her,' she said, smiling. 'She's not usually good with strangers, but she really likes you.'

'She has good taste,' was my only reply. What else could I say?

SEVEN

JAX

STOPPING AT THE BAKERY, I ORDER A BLUEBERRY MUFFIN AND
a coffee. I can't rely on Moody Mandy to bring me breakfast anymore.
While I wait, my gaze moves down the street towards Candice's work.
I know it's early and her shift doesn't start for another forty-five
minutes, but it still doesn't stop me from hoping that I might catch
a glance of her. I've arranged to have lunch with her today. I'll need
to shift a few of my appointments around when I get to work, but
I'll make it happen. I'm not going to miss the opportunity to spend
some more time with her.

As I approach my shop, I see Brian, the homeless man from
yesterday, hobbling out of the park across the street. He's carrying
a large striped bag that I presume holds all his worldly possessions.
Poor guy. That must be where he sleeps. Checking both ways for
traffic, I quickly cross the road.

'Morning, Brian,' I say when I approach him.

'Good morning, young man,' he replies with a smile. How can he
smile so freely when his life is so shitty?

'Here,' I say, holding my muffin and coffee out to him. He needs it a hell of a lot more than I do.

'Thank you.' Placing his bag on the footpath, his shaky hands take them from me.

'I've gotta get to work . . . have a good day.' I turn and head to my shop. I wish I could do more for him. I wonder how he ended up on the streets. I suppose if I hadn't had a job to go to and money in the bank when my parents disowned me that could've easily been me.

I'm standing behind the front counter, seeing how I can rearrange my appointments for my lunch date with Candice, when Mandy enters. 'Morning,' I say.

She doesn't speak until she's standing beside me. 'Did you have fun with that pink-haired bimbo last night?' she spits as she shoves her bag under the desk.

'Excuse me?'

'Is that the type you prefer?'

Her comment instantly gets my back up. Candice runs rings around this bitch. 'What do you mean by "type"?'

She pauses briefly. 'Weirdos? What's with the pink hair? I can't believe you'd pass up this—' she runs her hands down her body as she speaks '—for that.'

I go from reasonably calm to angry in a millisecond. I won't have her disrespecting Candice. There's nothing weird about her, not even her hair. It's cool. She's a stunner, and has a room full of fucking trophies to prove it.

There is so much I'd like to say in response to Mandy's comment, but I need to remember I'm her boss. I have to keep my head and act responsibly. So I do the only thing I can; I storm down the hall to my studio. I need a few minutes to calm down.

I slam the door and remove my cap, throwing it across the room. Pacing back and forth, I run my fingers through my hair. This narrow-minded bullshit is what I've fought against my entire life. You can't judge a person by the colour of their hair. That's fucking ludicrous.

Mandy's got to go. I can't work with her any longer. I'd rather no receptionist than this crap. And I don't want her making Candice feel uncomfortable whenever she comes here.

A few minutes later, I unlock the safe and take out my cheque book. After filling out a cheque, I head back out to reception.

'Here's a cheque for one month's wages.' In my opinion, it's more than she deserves. 'I'll no longer be needing you.'

'What?' she screeches. 'You're firing me?'

'Looks that way.'

'You can't do that.'

I take a deep breath and pinch the bridge of my nose as I try to calm myself. 'I can, and I just did. Not only has your behaviour recently bordered on sexual harassment, this is my shop and I won't have you disrespecting me or my friends.'

I feel bad when I see her shoulders slump and tears well in her eyes, but that doesn't last long. She takes her bag from under the desk and storms towards me.

'You're an arsehole,' she snaps as she snatches the cheque out of my hand. 'You're going to regret this.' Her eyes narrow as she stares me down.

I don't take well to threats. 'You know where the door is,' I say as I turn and head back down the hall to my studio.

••••

'You fired her?' Candice gasps as we sit in a booth at the café. 'Why?'

'Things weren't working out,' I reply with a shrug. I'm not going to go into the details. It'll only upset her.

'Wow. What are you going to do?'

'Look for a replacement, I guess. Not much else I can do. It's already been a shit fight today without her.'

'If there's anything I can do to help, just ask.'

'Do you want a job?' I laugh like it's a joke, but I'm deadly serious. I'd love to have her working beside me. Having her so close could get complicated, but being near her all day certainly wouldn't be a hardship. She'd brighten anyone's day with that smile of hers.

'Gee . . . really? I'd love nothing more than to come and work for you, but I can't leave my job. I don't want to let Sophia down.' She gives me a pained look. 'Shit, I don't want to let you down either.' She takes hold of my hand across the table. 'I made a promise to Sophia a few years ago. If she let the whole beauty pageant thing go, I'd go to beauty school like she'd hoped. She paid a small fortune for my course.'

'It's okay. I totally get it. I'll find someone. I can put a sign in the window when I get back.' It was worth a try. I'm happy just to have her around again.

'I'm sorry, Jax.'

I can see the disappointment on her face. 'You have nothing to be sorry about.'

We fall into easy conversation after we order and wait for our food to arrive. As we eat, we talk about everything and nothing. It's just like old times. I feel lighter than I have in years.

'Shit,' Candice cries when she looks down at her phone. 'I'm late. Like really late. My boss is going to kill me.'

I look down at my watch and see that we've been here for almost an hour and a half. It's funny how it only seems like minutes. My time with her is never long enough.

Quickly gathering her things, she stands. 'I've gotta go.'

'Okay.'

'Oh, Sophia asked if you want to come over for dinner again tonight.'

'Sure, I'd love to.'

She leans across the table and plants a soft kiss on my cheek. 'Great. Can I get a lift with you again?'

'Of course.'

She smiles. 'As soon as I finish I'll come to the shop. Bye, Jax.'

'Bye.'

She rushes out of the café. I just sit there smiling like a damn idiot. I put my hand over the spot she just kissed. I'm pathetic. It was an innocent peck, but a kiss nevertheless.

I'm only back in the shop twenty minutes when Candice comes barrelling through the door. My heart drops the second I see tears streaming down her beautiful face.

'Christ. Are you okay?' I ask as I round the counter towards her.

She falls into my arms and sobs against my chest. 'My boss screamed at me in front of my client for being late back from lunch. I just lost it, Jax. She's such a cow. I'm sick of the way she treats me, so I told her to shove her job up her arse and walked out.'

I have to suppress my smile when she says that. I run my hand down her back to comfort her while she sniffles.

'Do you still need a receptionist?'

'Hell, yes.' This time there's no stopping the smile from forming. I hate that Candice's boss upset her, but things couldn't have worked out better if I'd planned them myself.

EIGHT

JAX

'YOU NEED TO TAKE AT LEAST ONE DAY OFF A WEEK,' CANDICE says as I look over the diary: 'You work too hard, Jax. I'm worried about you.'

Her comment makes me smile. She's been working here for almost two weeks now, and I couldn't be happier. Candice has slotted in perfectly, just like I knew she would. *My trusty sidekick*. She runs rings around Moody Mandy. My other employees and our clients all love her, which doesn't surprise me in the slightest. She's an easy person to love.

Sophia blew a gasket when we arrived home for dinner the night Candice quit, but calmed down once Candice explained what happened. She hadn't realised how horribly her boss had been treating her. That's when the mama bear reared her head.

'Is that why I have a clear calendar on Tuesday?' I ask, grinning.

'Uh huh. As of next week, Tuesdays will be your day off.'

'Is that so?' She's been looking after me from the day she started, and I gotta say, I love it. It's nice to have someone care for you and look out for your wellbeing. It's not something I'm used to.

'It'll do you good. You can take up golf or something.'

'Golf? I don't think so. You'll never catch me in a pair of those ridiculous pants.'

She snickers from beside me because she knows damn well that's not something I'd ever be interested in. It'll be good to have some time off, though. I can sleep in or catch up on the things I never find time to do.

I place a chaste kiss on the side of her head. 'Thank you.'

'You're welcome.'

My gaze moves to the door when the buzzer chimes. It's Jason, my next client.

'Hey,' I say as he approaches the counter.

'Hey, Jax.' I've been working on his full-arm sleeve for over a month. He's a bit of a wuss, so I can only do a small patch at a time. It's going to look wicked once it's finished.

I get instantly annoyed when his gaze moves to Candice—I know that look.

'And who do we have here?' he asks, extending his hand.

'I'm Candice, Jax's new receptionist,' she replies, reaching across the desk to shake his hand.

Is it wrong that I want to pry their hands apart? I'd be naive to think guys wouldn't hit on her—she's beautiful. Having to witness it though, and pretend I'm not affected by it, is gonna be tough. In my heart, Candice still belongs to me. Maybe having her here isn't such a brilliant idea after all.

'Well ain't you a pretty little thing?'

I clear my throat when Candice drops her head and a blush creeps onto her cheeks. He used the same line on Mandy when she was working here, but it didn't bother me in the slightest. This does. A fucking lot. I don't mind Jason, but to be honest, he's a bit of a tool. He's always big-noting himself, bragging about all his connections and female conquests. He never stops talking about himself, actually. I usually tune him out before our session is over. I'm certainly not one to judge him on his philandering ways, because I sleep around too, but I've never been the type to kiss and tell or brag about it.

Jason finally lets go of her hand, but leans into her. 'Please tell me you don't have a boyfriend.'

I've never been a violent man, but in this moment, I seriously want to knock him the fuck out.

'Yes, she does,' I cut in before Candice has a chance to answer. She gasps as her head snaps in my direction, but I resist the urge to look her way. I know her well enough to realise she's unhappy with my comment, but I don't give a shit. There's no way in hell I'd let her go out with this guy. Not only is he a manwhore, he associates with bikie gangs. Well, he says he does. He could be full of shit, but that's a chance I'm not prepared to take. I give him a look that says, *shut the fuck up*. I'm relieved when he doesn't say another word.

There's an amused smirk on his face as his eyes lock with mine. 'Are you ready for me, boss?'

'Yep.' I'd love to smack that look right off his smug head. It's the first time I've ever had violent tendencies towards one of my clients. Why does this woman bring out the best and absolute worst in me?

I see him wink at Candice out of the corner of my eye when I turn to walk to my studio. *Fucker*. I may have to press extra hard on the needle today.

••••

'What the hell was all that about today?' Candice snaps the moment we lock up and head down the street to my place. They're the first words she's spoken to me since the incident with Jason. She obviously waited until we were alone so she could serve me my balls on a platter.

I've been having dinner at her house every weeknight since she started working for me. When we finish up for the day, we walk back to my place to collect my car. Candice, Sophia and Maddie live about a ten-minute drive away, in Ultimo.

'I don't know what you're talking about,' I reply, shoving my hands into my pockets.

'Bullshit, Jax. You tried to cock block me.'

She's right, I did. But her comment infuriates me nevertheless. The thought of her even wanting to be with someone in that way messes with my head. I have no right to stand in her way, but she can do so much better than that cockhead.

Inhaling a frustrated breath, I stop walking and face her. 'He's not the right guy for you, Candice.'

'Really?'

'Yes, really.'

'Since when did you become the boyfriend police? You had no right to say what you did today.'

'I was only looking out for you. Can we just drop it?'

'No. I won't drop it. You can't tell me who I can and cannot go out with, Jaxson Albright.'

Oh shit. She usually only uses my full name when she's really pissed.

'He's a cock. He treats women like shit, plus he has connections. I don't want you involved with a guy like that.'

'What type of connections? He didn't seem like the "connections" type.'

I almost want to laugh at her comment. Is there such a thing as a *connections* type?

'Just connections, all right? You don't need to worry about it. Just stay the hell away from him.'

Her eyes narrow as her hands bear down on my chest, shoving me. 'Connections, my arse. You're just making that up.'

'It's true.' Sure, there was an ulterior motive for what I did today, but I *was* looking out for her as well.

'Bullshit. The only connections he has is at McDonald's—when he's connected to their free wifi.'

As mad as I am, this time I do laugh. Candice has always been quick-witted, with the best comebacks.

'It's not funny, Jax. This is my life you're fucking with.'

When I see the tears glistening in her eyes, I feel like an arsehole for making light of the situation. This whole friendship thing is going to be harder than I thought. I was a fool to think things could go back to the way they were.

'I'm not trying to fuck up your life, Candice, I'm looking out for you. There's a difference.' I turn and continue walking down the street. I can't have this conversation with her—it would only end badly.

No words are spoken the rest of the way, not even once we're in the car heading to her house. I ended up buying my dream car—the 1967 Ford Mustang I'd always wanted. It's a fucking gem. I love it. It needed a bit of work when I got it, but it went for a good price. A steal actually. The old guy I bought it from had no use for it anymore. To him it wasn't a classic, it was just an old car. One of my clients is a mechanic, so we did a trade. I did his ink for free, and he got my baby running in tip-top condition. I had all the interior re-covered. All it needs now is a shiny new paint job, and it'll be as good as new. When I have some spare cash, I'll get it done.

My head is spinning on the drive to Candice's house. I love having her with me during the day, and then playing happy families with her, Sophia and Maddie at night; they've welcomed me back into their lives with open arms. For my own sanity though, I think I need to put a bit of distance between us. If I don't pull my head in, I'll end up losing her again. I can't let that happen.

She's still staring out the window when we pull into her driveway. I have to make things right. When I see her reach for the doorhandle, I place my hand on her knee.

'Candice, wait. I'm sorry.'

Turning in her seat, she faces me. The hurt I see in her beautiful blue eyes tears me up inside.

'I shouldn't have said what I did today.' This is going to be hard for me to say, but it needs to be said. I take a deep breath before I continue. 'I know we're just friends and I have no right to interfere, but please not with Jason. You deserve better than a guy like him.'

It would be selfish of me to stop her from finding happiness. I only wish I was that type of guy to give her that, but I'm not. I'd only end up disappointing her, like I did my own family, and like I did when I left her without saying goodbye. It's what I do best. I've never been with the same girl more than once, and I'm pretty sure I don't have it in me to commit, so I'm not about to risk everything with Candice again on an uncertainty.

She sighs, and her gaze drops to her lap. When I see her wipe under her eye, I know she's still upset. Everything in me wants to pull her into my arms, but we need distance—that's the only way we'll survive this. Comforting each other was what got us into this mess in the first place.

I wait for her reply, but it never comes. Reaching for the door-handle again, she gets out of the car. 'Are you coming in?' she asks.

'I don't think it's a good idea. Tell your mum I'm sorry.'

'Fine.' She slams the door before running across the lawn towards the house.

I sit there and watch until she disappears inside.

'Fuck.' I bang my hands on the steering wheel. I hope I haven't ruined things again.

••••

I feel like shit when I leave for work the next morning. My head hurts like hell. After leaving Candice's, I had a meeting with my old friend Jack Daniels. I polished off three-quarters of a bottle before I eventually crashed. I needed the escape—reality can be a bitch sometimes.

When I arrive at the shop, my shitty mood intensifies when I see someone has sprayed *Arsehole* across my front shutters. I know Candice would never do something like that. Well, I hope she wouldn't. It could've been that psycho Moody Mandy. She did call me an arsehole the day I fired her.

'Fuck,' I mumble under my breath as I scrub my hand over my face. I don't need this shit today.

I google a local graffiti removal company on my phone when I get inside, jotting their number down on the notepad on the counter. I'll get Candice to call them when she gets here. That's if she shows up.

Thankfully, a few minutes later she pushes through the front door. I feel immediate relief.

'Morning,' I say, giving her a look that hopefully conveys my apologies for yesterday.

'Morning.' She gives me a weak smile in return as she stows her bag under the counter. It's not the greeting I'd hoped for, but she's here and that's a start.

'Can you give this number a call after nine?' I ask. 'Someone spray-painted "Arsehole" on the front shutter last night.'

'What? Who would do that?'

I shrug, because I have no clue.

'Do you think it was kids?'

'I doubt it. They usually use a tag.'

'Guess I'm not the only one you've pissed off recently then.'

'Guess not,' I reply dryly.

Candice pulls her purse from her bag. 'I'm gonna go and get a coffee, I'll call them when I get back. Do you want one?'

'I'd love one.' I pull my wallet out of my back pocket and hold out a twenty-dollar note, but she waves it away.

'I think I can afford to shout you a coffee, Jax.'

'Candice,' I call out when she reaches the door. 'Are we okay?'

'We will be, as long as you don't pull another dick move like you did yesterday.'

'I can't make any promises, but I'll try.' That's the most honest answer I can give her. I'll always protect her, because she means the world to me. If a situation arises and I need to step in, you can be damned sure I will. I see a smile tug at her lips before she turns and goes out the door.

As the day progresses, nothing much changes. Candice is polite, but it's plain to see she's still pissed off. *Women.* I don't think I'll ever understand them.

I'm in my studio when she knocks on the door at the end of the day.

'I'm heading home. I'll see you tomorrow.'

'You don't want a lift?'

'No. I've asked Sophia to come and get me.'

I give her a casual smile, trying not to let her see I'm hurt by her brush-off. 'Oh. Okay. I'll see you tomorrow.'

'Bye, Jax.'

'Bye.'

Fuck. This is worse than I thought.

NINE

CANDICE

'HEY SWEETIE,' SOPHIA SAYS WHEN I CLIMB INTO THE CAR.

'Hey.' I give her a weak smile before turning and reaching into the back seat, running my hand affectionately down Maddie's leg. 'Hey, baby girl.'

'Jax!' Maddie screams as she points out the window at the tattoo parlour.

Turning back around in my seat, I look out my window. He's standing behind the glass door, watching us. His hands are shoved in the pockets of his jeans, and the look on his face only serves to make me sadder. I feel bad about the way I've been acting today, but I'm hurt. I'm not even interested in stupid Jason. What upsets me the most is the fact that Jax doesn't want me, but he doesn't want anyone else to have me either. That's so unfair. I turn away from the window.

'Take me home.'

'Are they tears in your eyes, baby?' Sophia asks as she places her hand on my leg. 'Did you two have a fight?'

'No. I've just had a crappy day.' I didn't tell her what happened yesterday, I lied and said Jax had to head back to work, and that's why he couldn't make dinner.

'You didn't say anything to him, did you?'

'What? No, of course not. There's no point. Things are best left the way they are.'

She gives my leg a comforting squeeze before putting the car into drive and pulling away from the kerb.

'Jaaaax!' Maddie screams.

Damn this whole situation to hell. Reaching into the back seat, I gently rub Maddie's leg to soothe her as I clench my eyes shut, trying to stop my own tears from falling. Poor Maddie. I can't believe how quickly she's taken to him. She's not usually good with strangers, especially men. Being surrounded by only women will do that I guess. What is it with Jaxson Albright and his spell on us poor unsuspecting Crawford girls?

After we eat, I give Maddie a bath. She always makes me smile. I'm not sure how I would've survived the last few years without her. She's my happy place.

'Read, Sissy,' she says once she's dressed in her pyjamas. Toddling to her shelf, she grabs her favourite book, *The Very Hungry Caterpillar*, and hands it to me. I've read it to her so many times she knows it off by heart.

Lifting her off the ground, I nuzzle her chubby cheek. 'Let's go downstairs and say goodnight to Mummy, and then I'll read to you.'

'No Mummy—Phia.'

'Yes, Sophia.' I laugh. There've been times over the years when I've wished Sophia would let me call her mum, but it's just a title. Sophia's a mother in every sense of the word—she's proved that over and over again. There's nothing she wouldn't do for me, or for Maddie.

••••

I step off the bus and head down King Street towards the tattoo parlour. I choose not to drive to work. Finding somewhere to park in Newtown, is pretty much impossible. If I don't get a lift home with Jax, Sophia picks me up. She's not comfortable having me travel on public transport at night.

I made a decision as I lay in bed last night; it's time to let this thing with Jax go. The look on his face as we drove away last night hurt my heart and I haven't been able to get it out of my mind. I don't want to put a wedge between us. I've let him suffer enough. When and if I'm ready to start dating, he needs to respect my wishes.

As long as my heart still pines for him though, I can't see that happening.

It's going to be a good day, I tell myself. Positive thoughts and all that. I love my new job, but more than anything I love being around Jax.

I get that familiar flutter in my stomach when I see Jax ahead. I stop walking and hide behind a street pole to watch him cross the road. I feel like a stalker, but I'm curious to see what he's up to.

I grin when I see he's heading towards the homeless man I saw him give food and money to the day we reconnected. I place my hand over my heart and sigh when he passes the old guy a takeaway coffee cup and a small paper bag. This is one of the reasons why I can't help but love him. He has a beautiful, kind soul.

I wait until he's entered the shop before I make a move. He's a modest man and would probably feel uncomfortable if I made a fuss over what I just witnessed.

Jax is standing behind the front counter counting out the float when I walk through the door. 'Morning,' I say in a chirpy voice.

He looks up, and the beautiful smile that crosses his face takes my breath away. He always seems genuinely happy to see me. It's surprising how one look from him can affect me as much as it does.

'Morning. You're here early. Did you wet the bed?'

I laugh 'No. I came in so we could talk.'

'About what?' he asks, giving me his undivided attention.

'Us.'

'Shit,' he mumbles as he walks around the counter, guiding me to the black leather sofas. 'You're not quitting are you?'

'What? Of course not,' I say, taking a seat on the sofa and tapping the space beside me. 'I love it here.'

'Thank Christ. Because I love having you here.'

I place my hand on his leg once he's seated. 'Jax, you know you're my best friend, right? That will never change.'

'I know.' He sighs and looks at the floor.

'I don't want either of us to do anything that will jeopardise that. I don't want to lose you again. I couldn't stand it.'

'Me either.'

'Well, maybe we need to set some ground rules.'

'Such as?' he asks, and his gaze moves back to me.

'I wasn't going to bring up . . . you know . . . that night, but maybe I should. I think we need to clear the air and get it all out in the open.'

'What night?'

'The night you left.' *And crushed my heart into a million tiny pieces*, I want to add, but I don't.

'Oh . . . that night,' he says as he removes his cap and runs his fingers through his hair. 'That's one of the biggest regrets of my life.'

'What do you mean? Walking away, or what we did?'

'Both.'

I have to fight back the tears when he says that. I had contemplated telling him everything I went through after he left, but now I know there's no point. It wouldn't do any good. I don't regret one second of that night. I hate that it tore us apart, but it was one of the best experiences of my life. I'll never regret him being my first. It was everything I'd hoped it would be. There's been nobody else since him. I was so busy with beauty school and helping Sophia with Maddie that there wasn't time for men. To be honest, I wasn't interested anyway.

Jaxson Albright owns my heart. I wish he didn't, but he does.

We need to be on the same page if our friendship is going to survive this. I was good at masking my true feelings for him before we crossed the line, and I'm pretty sure I can do it again.

'I care about you, Jax.' I pause, I'm afraid my voice is going to crack. I don't want him to see how much he's upset me. 'A lot, but you're right. What we did was a mistake.' Those words taste so bitter in my mouth. 'We're friends and that's all we'll ever be. If I want to see other people, you need to respect that. And I'll show you the same courtesy. Okay?'

He rises from the sofa and starts to pace, fighting some kind of inner battle. He pauses and goes to say something, but then thinks better of it. I sit there in silence as he continues walking back and forth. It makes me feel uneasy. When he eventually stops, his eyes meet mine.

'Okay.'

Geez. All that for one word?

'Great.' When I go to stand, he holds out his hand and helps me up.

'So, we're okay now?'

I place a soft kiss on his cheek. 'Yes. We're okay, Jax.'

••••

Over the next few days everything goes back to the way it was. Well, kind of. Jax still isn't coming over after work, for dinner. He hasn't mentioned it, so I haven't either. He's been totally normal with me, but I get the feeling he's trying to put some distance between us. Maybe it's for the best. Pretending I'm not hopelessly in love with him all the time is hard work.

I'm sitting behind the front counter when a pretty brunette enters the shop. She's dressed to kill and doesn't look like the type who would be interested in getting a tattoo, but I could be wrong. We have a lot of clients who I wouldn't have picked for the tattoo type. Last week we had a sixty-five-year-old grandmother come in to get her first-ever tattoo, a tiny dolphin on her hip. I thought it was pretty cool.

'Hi,' the brunette says when she approaches the front desk.

'Hi. Can I help you?'

'I'm looking for Jax. Is he here?'

'Do you have an appointment?' Looking down at the diary in front of me, I see his next appointment is with someone named Matthew. It's safe to say that's not her.

'No, I don't. I just wanted to see him quickly . . . if he's free?'

'He's with a client, but if you want to take a seat, I can let him know you're here.'

'No, that's fine. I, um . . . I don't want to disturb him. Can you give him this for me?' She plonks her designer handbag on the counter and her perfectly manicured hands dig around inside before retrieving a man's black leather wallet. 'He left his wallet at my place last night. I found it this morning on the floor next to the bed. It must've fallen out of his jeans while he was getting dressed. I thought he may need it.' She laughs nervously as she passes it to me.

I force out a smile as my already battered heart tears in two.

'Sure. I'll give it to him.' What I'd really like to do is ram it up his double-standard hypocritical arse.

JAX

I follow my client, Brad, out to reception once we're done. I've spent the last three hours putting the finishing touches on the large eagle that's spread across his back. It's taken me five sittings to complete it, but it was worth the time that I put in—it looks amazing. I made sure to get a photo before he put his shirt back on. I love seeing the look of satisfaction on my clients' faces once the job is complete.

'I wanna get my kids' names on my arm next,' he says. 'I'll need a few weeks to save up the cash though.'

'No problem. Just speak with Candice, she can slot you in when you're ready.'

'Thanks again, mate,' he says, extending his hand. 'I'm in awe of your work.'

'You're welcome.' When I let go of his hand, I turn my attention to Candice. 'I'm gonna head out and grab something to eat. You want anything?'

'Nope,' she says without making eye contact with me. 'Oh, you'll need this.' She slaps my wallet down on the counter.

I scratch my head as I walk over to pick it up. 'I was wondering where I put that. Where did you find it?'

'I didn't.' She looks at me briefly before lowering her eyes, continuing to flip through the diary in front of her. 'You left it on the floor beside some girl's bed last night. She dropped it off earlier.'

I hear Brad chuckle from beside me, but I'm not amused. I went out for a few drinks to drown my sorrows and ended up going home with some chick. Not because I was attracted to her—the total opposite. I just needed to forget Candice for a while. *She's consuming me*.

The crazy thing is, I thought of Candice the whole time. I even closed my eyes and pretended it was her so I could blow, which is so messed up. But just like the others, last night was all in vain. My heart won't stop pining for the one person I know I can never have again. I'm a lost cause.

Picking up my wallet, I leave Brad with Candice as I head out into the street. I hate that she knows what I got up to last night but there's nothing I can say to undo what happened. I shouldn't be concerned about it, but I am. Candice made it quite clear the other day that we're only friends, and that's all we'll ever be. But the last thing I want to do is rub my conquests in her face. If the shoe was on the other foot, I know I'd hate it.

When we talked the other morning, I almost professed my love for her. Thankfully I had the sense to shut my mouth before the words fell out—it would've only made this awkward situation worse. I could never give her what she wants. I'd only fuck it up and ruin everything we have. I refuse to let my feelings get in the way of our friendship.

Candice is quiet for the rest of the day. She's still talking to me, but she's not her usual bubbly self. I'm not stupid; she's hurt, or maybe just angry. She probably thinks I'm a hypocrite for the way I carried on about Jason.

I'm cleaning up after one of my clients when she knocks on the door. 'Hey,' she says, 'can I come in?'

'Of course.' Initially I think she's going to bring up the wallet, but she doesn't. She's a better person than I am.

'Sophia wants to know if you're coming over for dinner tonight.'

I grin. 'Do you want me there?'

'I'm asking you, aren't I?'

'Okay, I'd love to.' I'm relieved that we're all right.

'Great, I'll let her know.' She turns to leave, but then stops. 'I'm right to get a lift home with you then?'

'Of course. It's pointless getting Sophia to come all this way when I'm going to your place anyway.'

She glances over her shoulder and smiles before disappearing down the hall. I'm grateful she's at least trying to keep things normal. I pray in time it'll get easier for us both.

It has to.

TEN

JAX

THE NEXT FEW DAYS ARE UNEVENTFUL. THAT IS, UNTIL I WALK
out into reception one day to find Candice missing. Shane, one of my
artists, is sitting behind the counter in her place. 'Where's Candice?'
I ask, thinking she may have stepped out for a minute.

'She's with Gus. He's popping her cherry.'

'He's fucking what?'

'Calm down, man. She asked him to ink her. He's popping her
tattoo cherry, not her, you know . . . *cherry* cherry.' He chuckles.

I'm not amused, I can tell you. Like hell Gus is inking her. She
never mentioned getting a tattoo to me, and there's no way I'm letting
anyone else put their hands on her. I'm confused. I'm her best fucking
friend for Christ's sake. Why wouldn't she ask me to do it? I can't
even put into words how much that hurts. I spin around and storm
down the corridor to his room.

I open the door without knocking. This is my business, so I can
do whatever the fuck I like. 'What the hell, Candice?' I say, stalking
towards the reclining chair where she is sitting. Gus's surprised

eyes meet mine. I'm relieved to see he's still putting the transfer on her arm and hasn't started inking her yet. Thank Christ it's just her arm—if it was anywhere else on her body, I may have completely lost my shit.

Candice eyes me sceptically when I come to an abrupt halt next to the chair.

'What the fuck are you doing?'

'What's it look like?' she replies. 'I'm getting a tatt.'

'Why?'

'Um . . . because I want one?'

'Don't be a smartarse, Candice. Why didn't you ask me to do it?' I see red when she shrugs her shoulders. Is she for real? This may not be a big deal to her, but it is to me. 'If you want a tattoo, then you'll be getting it from me. End of fucking story.'

'Easy there,' Gus says, rising from his stool.

He's twice my size and built like a brick wall, but I'm not backing down here. I can't wrap my head around the fact she didn't ask me. I give him a look, warning him not to push me—I'm already teetering on the edge.

'Butt the fuck out, Gus,' I snap when he opens his mouth to say something more, before turning my attention back to Candice. 'I want to know why you didn't ask me to do this?' *No, I need to know.* I'm not good with rejection. I've had to deal with it from my family my entire life. I never thought I'd have to face it from her as well.

'Because . . .' She pauses before releasing a defeated breath.

I stand there and wait for her to continue but she doesn't. Her eyes dart between Gus and me and I get the impression she doesn't want to tell me her reasons in front of him. I reach for her hand. When she stands, I pull her from the room and towards my studio. I need to get to the bottom of this.

'You can do my two o'clock appointment, Gus,' I call over my shoulder, as Candice tries to tug her hand out of my iron grip.

As soon as we're inside my room, I close the door and stand in front of it, blocking her escape. She's feisty when she's mad, and the look on her face tells me she's about to let me have it. *Bring it on, my little spitfire, bring it on.* I'm angry too.

'Why did you embarrass me like that?' she says as she takes a step towards me, pushing my chest. 'You had no right.'

'Why didn't you ask me to give you a tattoo?'

'You can't answer a question with a question, Jax.'

'I can do whatever the fuck I like.'

'Fuck you.'

'Fuck you too,' I say.

What in the hell is happening to us? We've never been this volatile before.

'You had no right to do what you just did.'

She's right. I didn't. I'm acting like an arsehole. 'Fine,' I eventually say. 'I may have overreacted slightly, but in my defence, I'm hurt that you went to someone else.'

'Slightly . . . huh,' she scoffs. 'Overreacting is where you've moved to apparently. What happened to the easygoing Jax I once knew? Who replaced him with this . . . this . . . overbearing, controlling . . . jerk?'

'I'm supposed to be your best friend.'

'So?'

'So how do you think it makes me feel knowing you don't want me to do your tattoo? That's like me going to see someone else to get a stupid facial.'

When she laughs my anger spikes.

'I can just imagine it. Your face covered in a pore-reducing mask, sliced cucumber placed strategically over your eyes.'

Like that's ever going to happen. 'Shut up and sit.'

'What if I don't want to?' she says, folding her arms over her chest. 'And don't tell me to shut up.'

I sigh. 'Please, sit.'

'Fine,' she says with a huff.

Fuck me. Wonders will never cease. I wasn't expecting her stubborn arse to give in so easy.

Taking a seat on the stool beside her, I look over the large transfer of a hibiscus flower that Gus placed at the top of her arm. 'What colour do you want the flower?' I ask as I grab the equipment I'll need out of the drawer beside me.

'Pink,' we say in unison, followed by, 'Jinx.' We laugh. We've always been in sync like that. It's not unusual for either of us to finish each other's sentences, or think what the other is thinking.

I can feel her watching my every move as I mix up the colours and get everything ready. I like that.

'Ouch. That hurts,' she whines the minute the needle connects with her skin.

'You didn't think it was going to tickle did you?'

'I guess not,' she says with a shrug.

'Stay still.' I use my free hand to stretch the skin tight. When my eyes dart up to hers I find her studying me intently. 'What?'

'Nothing.'

There's a comfortable silence between us as I outline the first few petals of the flower.

'I'm sorry I didn't ask you.'

'I'm sorry too. I shouldn't have acted the way I did.' It was only because I was hurt, but I'm not going to tell her that. 'Are you going to tell me why you didn't come to me?'

'Because we're friends.'

What does being friends have to do with it? 'What the fuck is Gus then?' If she says they're more than friends, I'll crack it.

'A friend.'

'Well?'

'Well . . . Gus and I don't have a history.'

'Oh.'

'Yes, oh.'

'It's just a tattoo, Candice, it's not like I'm going to jump you or anything.'

'Don't I know it . . . been there, done that.'

There's sarcasm in her voice, and her words sting. I wish she'd stop saying things like that. She's nothing like the others—they don't hold a candle to her.

I go back to working on her arm. 'Next time just come to me, okay?' I can't stay mad at her. She had her reasons.

'Okay.' When I glance at her face, she smiles. 'I wanna get my whole arm done, maybe even both,' she says excitedly.

I'm not even finished and she's got the tattoo bug already. She's going to rock these tatts. As if she's not already sexy enough.

'Well, let's tackle one thing at a time. I can't do all that in one sitting.'

'I kinda figured that.'

'You know Sophia's gonna freak, right?'

'Probably, but it's my body. There's not much she can do about it now. It's not like this thing is going to wash off.'

I chuckle. I'm sure I'll get a lecture tonight when I go over for dinner. It'll be worth it though.

I love that my Candylicious is going to be inked.

One month later . . .

As I'm approaching my shop early this morning, a car parked across the road catches my eye. It's a classic, a red 1975 Holden Monaro. It needs a bit of work, but it's a nice-looking car. It appears to be all original as well. You don't see many of them around anymore.

After giving it a once-over, I notice the driver inside, resting his head against the steering wheel. He looks troubled, but I don't think much of it. I'm not one to get involved in other people's business. We all have shit to deal with. Turning away, I crouch down to remove the padlock on the metal shutter.

Minutes later, I find myself standing at the window, watching the guy across the street again. Don't even ask me why I'm concerned about him, but I am. He's now resting his head back against the seat. He's young, possibly in his late teens, or early twenties.

'Morning,' Candice says with a smile as she comes through the front door. 'Whatcha doing?'

'Just watching that guy.'

'What guy?' She looks across the street. 'Oh, nice car.'

'It is, isn't it?'

'So what's the go with him? Is he acting suspicious or something?'

'No, nothing like that. He was parked there when I arrived an hour ago. Not sure how long he's been out there.'

Shrugging, she turns and heads to the counter. Things have been going well for us—we've fallen into an easy routine, and despite these feelings I still battle daily, things are good. I've been working on her sleeves whenever I get some free time. They look amazing. The original version of Candice was hot, but the tattooed version is smokin'.

'Do you want one of those pastries with your coffee this morning?' she asks. I still buy a muffin and coffee for Brian on my way to work, but I've stopped getting one for myself. Call me selfish, but I love having Candice look after me. She found a small cake shop nearby that sells the best damn pastries I've ever eaten and now I'm hooked on them. I pull a fifty out of my wallet and pass it to her.

'Sure. That would be great. Grab a few for the guys.'

'Right,' she says, laughing. 'That's if you don't eat them first.'

As the morning wears on I find myself being drawn back to the window, and the guy across the road. My concern for him is escalating. He's left the car and is sitting in the park under a tree. He appears to be drawing in a sketchpad. It reminds me of the one Candice bought me before I left for uni. It could just be my imagination, but he seems like he has the weight of the world on his shoulders. When I look at him, I see myself, the guy I was before I got Candice back. *Lost and alone.*

I have an overwhelming compulsion to go and ask him if he's okay, but I have no clue how to do that without looking like a crazy stalker. What if I'm wrong about him? His body language tells me I'm not.

I'm distracted by Gus escorting his client out to reception. She's a pretty blonde, and, after she pays Candice, she turns and thanks Gus before heading to the door. Gus comes to stand beside me, throwing his arm around my shoulder, as we watch her make her way down the street.

'I just inked a caricature of a devil on her arse. Fuck me, what an arse. I wanted to bite it.'

His comment makes me laugh. 'I don't blame you man, it's a nice arse.'

'You guys are pathetic,' Candice spits.

When I glance at her over my shoulder, she rolls her eyes and shakes her head in disgust.

'Well, she's mine,' Gus says. 'You can look but don't touch. You already have more than you can handle, Mr Chick Magnet.' He slaps me on the back and laughs. 'I aspire to be just like you one day, boss—the world is your oyster with your endless supply of pussy.'

I wish he'd stop talking. Before Candice started working here, the boys and I went out occasionally for drinks. They were always astounded by the number of women who would hit on me, so they started referring to me as Mr Chick Magnet as a joke. At the time I thought it was funny, not so much now.

In an attempt to avoid Candice's glare, I take a step closer to the window. Shoving my hands into my pockets, I look across the street to the park. I watch as the guy lights up his umpteenth cigarette for the day. He's definitely stressing about something. Nobody smokes that much—well, they shouldn't. If he keeps going like that, he'll be dead before he's thirty.

That's when I get an idea, the perfect excuse to approach him. 'Hey, Gus, can I bludge a smoke off you?'

'What?' Candice says. 'You don't smoke.'

'Yeah, boss, what's the go?' Gus chimes in, giving me a confused look.

'I smoked for a while when I was in high school.' I only did it to rebel against my parents, but it also helped calm me. Their constant demands used to stress me the hell out. 'I still have one occasionally when I drink, or if I'm stressed.'

'It's 10.30 am. It's a bit early to be hitting the bottle.' He laughs.

'Just give me a damn smoke,' I snap, holding out my hand.

Gus pulls a packet out of his shirt pocket and hands me one. 'Do you need to borrow my lighter?'

'Nope.' When I turn to Candice her brow is furrowed. She's obviously surprised that she didn't know this about me. It's not the only thing she doesn't know. *Like my obsession with her.* 'If my next client shows up, tell him I'll be back in five.'

I head for the door before she has a chance to speak. My concerns for this guy may just be my overactive imagination, but there's only one way to find out.

Crossing the street, I head towards the park. The guy's so engrossed in what he's drawing, he doesn't even notice me approaching.

'Hey, buddy. Got a light?'

Looking up from his sketchpad, he makes eye contact with me. 'Sure,' he says. He picks his lighter up off the grass beside him and tosses it to me.

'Thanks. I left mine at the shop.' Once my cigarette is lit I hand the lighter back. I have the urge to cough as soon as the smoke slides down the back of my throat, filling my lungs. It's been a while since I've had one. My eyes move down to the open pad on his lap. He has a real talent. 'Hey, did you draw that?'

'Yeah.'

'That's pretty good. Mind if I take a look?'

'Sure, knock yourself out.'

He's trying to act like he doesn't give a shit that I've taken an interest in his work, but I saw the way his face lit up when I complimented his drawings. My admiration of his talents only grows as I flick through the pages. He's damn good.

'That would make a fucking awesome tatt. Ever thought of selling these?'

'Nah. I just do it for fun,' he answers with a shrug.

'I own the tattoo parlour across the road.' I point to my shop. Flicking through the rest of his drawings, I smile. To be honest I'm quite envious of his work. I can draw but nowhere near as detailed as this. I want to own these. 'Fuck, these are wicked.'

'Thanks, man.' He smiles for the first time since I approached him. Even his body language has changed. I'm glad I came over here now. I know how fucked up alone feels.

'I'm serious. I'd love to buy some of these.' Truth is, I want them all. Except the few he's drawn of some chick with her dog. I won't be able to use them. 'I'm always looking for new designs. You wanna sell them?' I pause. I don't feel comfortable leaving him here alone. 'Do ya wanna come and check out my shop?'

'Sure, why not,' he replies, standing.

'Jax,' I say, extending my hand.

'Carter.'

He follows me across the street and I grin when I see his face light up once we enter. His eyes are everywhere. I love people's reactions when they enter my shop for the first time; it doesn't look like much from the street, but it's pretty impressive once you step inside. I put a lot of thought and time into getting the place just the way I wanted it.

As I approach the counter with Carter in tow, I see a smile tug at Candice's lips. She looks him up and down. I can't tell you how much that annoys me. It's the first time I've ever noticed her openly check someone out. I don't like it one little bit.

'Candice, this is Carter,' I say, trying to keep my composure.

'Hi, handsome.'

What the fuck? I have to bite my tongue when she winks at him. What in the hell is she playing at?

'Hey,' Carter says, nodding.

I'm grateful that he doesn't reciprocate the flirting. If she's doing this to piss me off, it's working. What if she's actually interested in this guy? Maybe that's why I've been so drawn to him—is he my fucking karma?

'Check out these drawings,' I say, passing the sketchpad to her. I'm trying my best to act cool. Pretending I'm not in love with her and trying to accept the fact that she's free to be with any man she wants is torture. I hope this gets easier with time, because right now I'm struggling.

'Wow, these are amazing. Did you do these?' Candice asks. He nods. 'They're great. Oh, I'd love this one on my arse.'

I see a smile tug at his lips when she points to the image of a skull on a bed of roses. As much as I'd like to, I don't think I could handle tattooing her arse, but there's no way in hell I'd let one of the other guys do it.

'I'll give you a hundred and fifty dollars,' I say, trying to defuse whatever the hell is going on between these two.

'I guess,' Carter says, shrugging.

'All right.' I flip through the sketchpad and count how many drawings there are. 'Fifteen,' I say, leaning over to pick up a calculator off the counter. 'That's . . . two thousand, two hundred and fifty dollars. You happy with that?'

'You're paying me a hundred and fifty dollars per drawing?' he asks in disbelief.

'Yeah. Did you think it was one-fifty for the lot?'

'I did.'

I laugh, shaking my head. This guy really underestimates his own talent.

'These are good man. I'll make more than my money back in one sitting. They're going to sell well. I already know a few guys who are gonna love these.'

'Shit.' He smiles. It's a big improvement on the sombre face he's been carrying around all morning. Mission accomplished. If I've helped brighten his day, even slightly, then I'm happy.

'I've got a client coming in shortly. I've gotta go set up. Candice will fix you up with the cash. It was nice meeting you, man,' I say, extending my hand to him once more. 'If you have any more drawings you wanna get rid of, you know where to find me.'

'Thanks.'

'No, thank you. Catch ya on the flip side,' I say, turning away. I don't want to stick around to hear the rest of their conversation.

Unfortunately, I'm not quick enough. Candice opens the register and starts counting out the money.

'There you go, handsome.'

'Thanks.'

I pause. I don't want to listen, but I feel compelled to. Apparently I like to torture myself. *Please just take the money and leave.*

'Here. I wrote my number inside. If you ever want to hook up, give me a call. I'd like to see what else you can do with those hands of yours.'

My heart sinks. Christ, why didn't I keep walking?

Carter chuckles before replying. 'Sounds like a plan.'

With that, I continue down the corridor. I've heard enough. What I really want to do is turn around and tell Carter to stay the hell away from my girl. But she's not my girl—she's my damn infatuation. Nothing more.

I close my studio door and rest my head against it, taking a few deep breaths, trying to calm myself. Witnessing her openly flirt with Carter has really messed me up, but if I'd reacted like I did with that fucker, Jason, it would've only damaged our friendship further. I look down at the tattoo on my forearm.

A moment of patience in a moment of anger saves you a hundred moments of regret.

I've had this for a few years now. It was one of my first tattoos. I had Candice in mind when I got it. If I'd had this when she first texted me after I left, maybe we wouldn't have been apart for so long. I take a few seconds to let the meaning behind the quote sink in. They're wise words. After the way I've been acting towards her lately, this may be the only thing that helps me get through this clusterfuck.

I need to let this infatuation with her go once and for all.

ELEVEN

CANDICE

THE MOMENT CARTER IS OUT THE DOOR, I SLUMP DOWN ONTO my stool and bury my face in my hands. What in the hell is wrong with me? Sure Carter was hot, but my show was purely for Jax's benefit. It was a shitty move, but his and Gus's conversation earlier cut me to the core. I'm not naive enough to think Jax isn't seeing other women—the woman who dropped off his wallet was all the proof I needed. What upsets me most, is knowing I'm not enough for him. *Why am I not enough for him?*

I'm not even sure why I handed over my phone number to Carter like that. Jax had already left the room. Maybe subconsciously it was the push I needed to move forward? There's been no one else since Jax, but I can't keep waiting around for something that's never going to happen. Friendship is where our relationship began and where it ends for us.

Jax's silence for the rest of the day is unnerving. Apart from escorting his clients back and forth, I barely see him. Is he angry with me, or is it my imagination? I shouldn't have flirted in front of him. Two wrongs don't make a right.

By late afternoon, it gets the better of me. Heading down the corridor to his studio, I knock before entering. 'Hey,' I say, popping my head just inside the door and smiling.

'Hey.' He briefly looks up at me before returning to what he's doing.

'You okay?'

'Yep. What's up?'

'Sophia wants to know if you're coming over for dinner tonight.' That's a big fat lie—I want to know. Plus, Maddie's been asking for him, but I'm not about to guilt him into coming over by saying that.

'Sorry, not tonight. I have other plans.'

'Oh, okay. I'll let her know.' My heart is heavy as I turn and head back out to the reception area. He can deny it all he wants, but he's shitty with me. This back and forth bullshit is doing my head in. Why can't either of us let go and move on? I don't want to hurt him, and I know Jax well enough to know he wouldn't want to hurt me either. But that's exactly what we're doing to each other.

••••

Jax is always pretty easygoing—he never stays mad for long. So when I head in to work the next morning, I'm ready to start the day fresh, to let go of what happened with Carter. But the shop is still locked up when I get here. Jax is always here before me, so I'm concerned. I have keys, but I only bring them with me on Tuesdays. Ten minutes pass, and just as I pull out my phone to call him, I see him approaching.

The first thing I notice is he looks like shit. Then I smell the alcohol—he reeks. Why would he be drinking on a weeknight? That's not like him, and it concerns me.

'Morning.'

'Morning,' he groans as he digs his keys out of his pocket. Despite how he's obviously feeling, he smiles as he holds the door open for me, and that tells me we're okay again.

Well, we are until Gus walks through the door five minutes later.

'I'm not worthy . . . I'm not worthy,' Gus chants as he crosses the shop floor and bows down before Jax. Gus is a good guy, but can be a bit overbearing sometimes. He's like a gentle giant, prankster and big kid all rolled into one.

'Fuck off, Gus,' Jax snaps. 'I'm not in the mood for your shit today.'

'Man, I saw those two babes you left the club with last night. Fuck me.' He reaches over the counter and playfully punches Jax in the arm. 'You need to give me some pointers—how do you do that shit night after night? You're like a real-life Arthur Fonza-fucking-relli, from *Happy Days*. They just flock to you.' He lets out a boisterous laugh because he thinks he's funny. Neither of us join in. In Gus's defence, he has no idea about the history between me and Jax. I'm pretty sure if he did, he'd stop saying stuff like that in front of me.

Jax gives me a pained look, like he's trying to convey a silent apology. There's no need—he's free to screw whoever he wants. I go back to counting out the float, trying hard to will the tears away. I can't believe I felt sorry for that jerk a few minutes ago.

'Stop being a dickhead is a good start,' Jax snaps at Gus, before going to his studio.

I flinch when I hear his door slam.

'What did I do?' Gus asks, looking at me dumbfounded. He definitely doesn't have the brains to match his brawn.

I just shake my head.

Thankfully, the rest of the day is uneventful, well except for my personal pity party. Jax has remained quiet except for an occasional word here or there. To be honest, it pisses me off. Around four pm, when he walks into reception to see his client out, my phone rings. It's a number I don't recognise.

'Candice speaking,' I answer.

'Hey, Candice, it's Carter. I was in there the other day—'

Oh shit. With all this other crap going on, I'd totally forgotten about him. I take a deep breath for courage before I speak. It's now or never. This may be the chance I need to get Jaxson Albright out of my system once and for all.

'Oh, I know who you are. You have the kind of face a girl would never forget. Have you decided to take me up on my offer?'

As soon as those words are out of my mouth, Jax's head snaps in my direction.

'Yeah. You still up for it?' Carter asks.

'God no,' I want to scream, but I don't. *I can do this*. No, correction, I *have* to do this.

'Of course. Name the time and place and I'll be there, handsome.'

Jax doesn't even try to hide the fact that's he's eavesdropping on my conversation.

'Tonight?'

My eyes lock with Jax's before I reply, 'Tonight sounds perfect.' When Jax narrows his eyes, I divert my gaze to the floor. What am I doing? *I'm moving on*. 'I get home from work around six. How about I meet you at eight?'

'Great. I'll text you my address.'

Carter sounds just as apprehensive as I feel, and that calms me somewhat. 'Looking forward to it.'

My heart is beating out of my chest when I end the call. I take my time bending down and putting my phone back into my bag before I straighten and make eye contact with Jax again.

'Who was that?' he asks.

'None of your damn business.'

'Don't fuck with me, Candice,' he snaps as he closes the distance between us. 'Who were you on the phone to just now?'

'A friend.'

'Male or female?' Here we go with his double standards again.

'Like I said, none of your business.'

When Gus and his client enter reception, Jax moves behind the counter and grabs hold of my hand, forcefully guiding me down the hall, towards his studio.

'Let me go, Jax.'

'No . . . I'm not having this conversation with an audience.'

As far as I'm concerned there's no conversation to be had. He went home with two women last night, so if he thinks he's going to put a stop to my date, he's mistaken.

'What conversation?'

He doesn't reply until we enter his room. 'Do you even know this person?'

'Obviously, he called me, didn't he? Do you really think I'd go out with a guy who got my number off the back of a toilet door? Give me some credit.'

'Don't be a smartarse,' he snaps. He's clearly angry, but so am I. He has no right to carry on like this.

'Well, stop meddling in my life.'

'Is that what you think I'm doing?'

He runs his fingers through his hair when I say yes.

'There's a difference between meddling and caring. How well do you know this person?'

'Well enough.'

'How well, Candice?'

'It's Carter.'

'What? The kid from the other day?'

'Yes. And I wouldn't exactly call him a kid. I'm going, Jax, and nothing you can say will stop me.' Actually, there's a lot he could say to stop me, but I already know he won't say the words I'm so desperate to hear. *He'll never say them.* I need to accept that he just doesn't want me the way I want him.

Turning away, he exhales forcefully. 'Fine. Don't do anything I wouldn't do.' The venom in his voice doesn't go unnoticed.

'Thanks. That pretty much frees me up to do anything I like then, arsehole.'

My heart's beating rapidly as I walk back into reception and grab my bag from under the counter. I don't officially knock off for another hour, but I'm giving myself an early mark. Fuck him. If Jax doesn't like it, he can fire me. I can't be around him right now.

Hypocritical jerk.

••••

After picking at my dinner, I help Sophia get Maddie ready for bed. My stomach is in knots, but I'm forcing myself to go ahead with tonight. It's time to get back on the horse. It's been years and I'm in the prime of my life. It's just what I need, or so I keep telling myself.

'You look lovely, sweetheart,' Sophia says when I walk into the kitchen after showering and changing.

'Thanks.'

'Are you going out tonight?'

'Yeah. I'm going out with someone I met at work.' It's not a lie, I did meet Carter at work. I know she wouldn't care if I told her that someone was a male, but I'm not in the mood to go into details with her. She's being bugging me to start dating again for months now.

'I wish you'd put on a top with longer sleeves.'

'I love my tatts. I'm not covering them up.' Both arms are complete now, done by Jax of course.

'Fine,' she says, rolling her eyes. 'As you've pointed out numerous times, it's your body.'

'That's right.' Looking at my watch I see it's just after seven. I didn't realise Carter lived so far away until he'd texted me his address, so I have to get going. He's expecting me at eight. I kiss Sophia goodbye.

'Have fun, baby.'

'Thanks.'

'Hey,' she says as I turn to leave. I glance at her over my shoulder. 'It's good to see you getting out again. You're young, you should enjoy your youth while you still have it.'

My sentiments exactly. My mum has given up so much to raise me, then Maddie. She still models occasionally, but only takes local jobs so she's around for us. She doesn't do it for the money, we have more than enough of that thanks to my father, but she loves what she does. The rest of her time is spent caring for us. She never dates, or goes out with her friends. I can't help but feel guilty for everything she's sacrificed for us. The least I can do is start living again.

'I will. I love you,'

'I love you too.'

After entering Carter's address into my GPS, I drive the forty minutes to his house. The closer I get, the sicker I feel. What was I thinking? This isn't even a date, it's more like a booty call. Talk about jumping in head first, or should I say vagina first.

When I turn into his street, I pull over to the kerb and take a few deep breaths. Carter asked me to call him when I was close. God only knows why. I hope it's not so he can sharpen the knives he's going to use to hack me into little pieces. Jesus, why did I let my mind go there?

I grab my phone and dial his number.

'Hey,' he says when he answers.

'Hey. I've just pulled into your street. I'll be there in a few minutes.'

'Okay. Don't knock on the front door, just come down the side of the house.'

That instantly makes me wary. 'Why can't I knock on the front door?'

'Because I live with my mum and her fuckwit of a husband. My bedroom is towards the back of the house. The one with the light on. I'll wait for you by the window.'

Great, he still lives with his parents. I can't really hold it against him I suppose—I still live with my mum. In a way it's a plus. If he tries to kill me, I can always scream out for help. I'm pretty sure he's not that type of person, but you never know. I consider texting Carter's address to Jax, just in case I don't turn up at work tomorrow, but I can't do that.

When my phone dings, I jump. I'm surprised to see it's a message from Jax. Did he read my mind? This connection we sometimes have is freaky.

> **Jax:** I'm not going to tell you to have fun tonight because
> I just can't bring myself to say that. But be careful, and
> if you need me just call. I mean it Candice.

Tears fill my eyes when I read his message. Considering what happened this afternoon, I'm touched he cared enough about me to text.

> **Me:** Thank you. Hope you have a good night. Enjoy
> your day off tomorrow. x

Butterflies churn in my stomach as I walk down the side of Carter's house. I'm not even sure if I can go through with this, but I'm going to give it my best shot. I jump and clutch my chest when I hear a loud bark from a dog, coming from next door. I relax a little when I see Carter's handsome face leaning out a window and smiling down at me. He's gorgeous. His hair and eyes are brown, just like Jax's. But sadly there's one major difference—he's not Jax.

Without speaking, Carter hauls me into his bedroom. Once he places me on the floor, I adjust my top.

'Fuck. You didn't tell me you still lived at home with your parents. How old are you anyway?'

'I'll be turning eighteen soon.'

'Shit. You're still a kid.' That would make him four years younger than me—a baby. Great, I'm a damn cradle snatcher. I should've asked him how old he was before coming here. I just presumed he was older. He certainly doesn't look seventeen. I was around his age the first time Jax and I got together. I'll die if he's a virgin. I've only been with one man, and that was Jax, so I'm not what you'd consider an expert in the sex department. This could get awkward.

'I'm not a fucking kid,' he snaps.

Well, technically, he's not an adult either. My common sense tells me to turn around and go back to the car, but I came here for a reason; to move on.

'You look older.'

'Are we going to do this or not?'

Wow. Talk about getting straight to the point. I know that's why he invited me over, and I wasn't expecting a candlelit dinner or anything, but he could at least offer me a drink or something.

I take a deep breath as I try to psych myself up. I need to jump in before I talk myself out of it, it's the only way. Stepping forward, I wrap my arms around his waist.

'Calm down,' I say, pressing my body against his. 'I didn't say there was a problem with it. I'm just surprised, that's all.' Closing my eyes, I kiss his neck. God, he smells good. Not as good as Jax does, though; his scent is my drug. Trailing kisses across Carter's strong jawline, my mouth eventually meets his. Carter wraps his arms around my waist, drawing me closer. He can kiss, I'll give him that, but surprisingly I feel nothing. Not a damn thing.

Letting go of Jax is going to be harder than I thought.

Pulling back suddenly, Carter's troubled eyes look down at me. 'I'm sorry, I can't do this,' he mutters.

'What? Why? What's the problem?'

He gazes out the window, looking at the house next door. Releasing his hold on me, he takes a step backwards before moving across the room to sit on the edge of his bed. He buries his face in his hands.

'It's not you.'

Isn't that what they all say: *It's not you, it's me*? Great. I'm still reeling from the sting of Jax's rejection, now I have this to contend with. What is wrong with these people? What is wrong with *me*?

'Then what?' I ask, sitting beside him. I need to know. I've never had the guts to ask Jax why he doesn't want me. This time, I'm not leaving here until I get answers.

He remains silent as he stares down at the floor.

'Carter. I need to know.'

He lets out a deflated breath before he makes eye contact with me. 'I think I'm in love with the girl next door,' he says.

A smile tugs at my lips. I'm relieved his rejection is not because of me, but I also think his confession is kind of sweet. 'When I was kissing you, I looked over there and she was watching us—I'm sorry. Calling you and asking you to come here was a mistake. I only did it to spite her.'

'It's okay,' I say, placing my hand on his leg. *It's kind of ironic—I only came here to spite Jax.*

He scrubs his hands over his face. 'She really fucks with my head.'

Jax fucks with my head too. 'Does she know how you feel?'

He shrugs. 'I don't think so. I've been trying to fight it. We have a kind of love–hate relationship. I try to push her away, but she continues to worm her way under my skin. She deserves better than me.'

'That's pretty harsh. You seem like a nice enough guy.'

He chuckles at my comment. 'That's because you don't know me . . . I'm a bastard.'

It's obvious that Carter doesn't have a high opinion of himself, but from the little I know, he's definitely not a bastard.

We spend the next hour talking about Indiana, the girl next door. It's funny, his situation reminds me a lot of my own. I admire him for not going through with tonight. Not many guys would've knocked back no-strings-attached sex. Probably not even Jax. That speaks volumes about Carter's character. Especially considering Indiana isn't even his girlfriend.

When I finally leave, I feel a huge sense of relief. Tonight I made a connection with Carter, and not the type I thought I was going to make. Coming here may not have helped me move on from Jax, but at the very least, I feel like I've made a new friend.

TWELVE

JAX

ROLLING ONTO MY SIDE, I LOOK AT THE CLOCK NEXT TO THE
bed. It's six am on my only day off and I can't sleep—I've been
tossing and turning all night. Candice is on my mind and this date
with Carter is eating me up inside. I was tempted to drown myself in
another bottle of Jack last night, so I wouldn't have to think about it,
but I'm glad I didn't. I can't keep pissing away these feelings I have.
It never helps. Dealing with them head on is the only way I'm going
to get through this.

Every single fibre in me wanted to stop her from going, but that
would've been selfish. It's not like I haven't been with other people.

I sit up and bury my head in my hands. *Pull your shit together,
Albright. She's not yours . . . she'll never be yours.* Well, not in the way
I crave her. I need to let this infatuation go. Throwing on a pair of
sweats, I head straight for the spare room. I need to take my frustrations out on something and my punching bag is a good place to
start. I can't tell you how many times I've pounded it over the years.
One day I didn't stop until my knuckles bled. It was Christmas day,

and my frustrations were aimed directly at my family—or lack of. I sat alone in my house feeling incredibly sorry for myself. There was nowhere to go and nobody to spend the holiday with. Of course I heard nothing from my parents that day, but in all honesty I hadn't expected to. They would've been too busy throwing their showy Christmas dinner, where they invite their equally fake friends and neighbours. As much as I always hated those gatherings, imagining them all sitting around celebrating and not giving me a second thought, hurt like you wouldn't believe. Those are the days I struggle the most. Why do I mean so little to them?

Now that I have Candice, Sophia and Maddie, I'm hoping this year will be different. Maybe Candice will invite Carter over for Christmas dinner too. That will fucking suck. I hammer into my punching bag even harder.

I spend forty-five minutes on the bag before getting stuck into the weights. My knuckles are red raw, and my arms feel like jelly when I leave my makeshift gym and head for the bathroom. There's nothing like a good workout to clear the head. I'm already feeling somewhat lighter.

After showering, I dress in a pair of jeans and a T-shirt. Apart from a few errands, I have no plans for today. Entering the kitchen, I place a coffee pod and some water in the coffee machine and flick the switch. As I reach for a mug from the top cupboard, I hear a knock at the door. The clock on the microwave says it's eight-forty-five. Who'd be knocking on my door at this time of the morning?

'Candice,' I say with surprise when I see her standing on the doorstep with a sleepy kid in her arms. She looks frazzled. 'Is everything okay?' I hope her early-morning visit doesn't have anything to do with last night. I'm glad I could help Carter out, but there's a part of me that wishes I'd just left him sitting in that damn park. If I did, last night never would've happened.

'Not exactly,' she mutters as I move aside so she can enter. 'Sophia has one of her migraines. You know how she gets . . . there's no way she can look after Maddie when she's like that.'

'Okay. You didn't have to come all the way here to tell me that, you could've just called. I had things to do today, but they can wait. I'll stand in for you.'

'No, you won't, it's your day off. Plus, I have some stock arriving.'

'Someone's gotta work in your place.'

'Yes, me,' she says.

'What about Peanut? Who's going to look after her?'

'You.'

'Me?' *Hell fucking no*. Has she lost her damn mind?

'Please.'

'No way. I don't know the first thing about looking after a kid.'

'She's no trouble, Jax. You know that. Come on, there's no one else . . . she likes you.'

I roll my eyes when she gives me her pouty face. She knows I can't resist that damn face.

'It's my day off,' I say, grasping at straws.

'Well, fine, then I quit.'

'What?'

'You heard. If you can't look after her for me, then I have no choice but to resign.'

'Fuck,' I mumble under my breath, when she raises an eyebrow, challenging me. I know how stubborn she can be: she'd quit just to prove a point. I offered to work in her place. Doesn't she realise how much I need her? She makes my days brighter. She's my happy place. My trusty sidekick. 'Why can't you take her into work with you?'

'I'm going to be flat-out sorting through the deliveries, putting stock away and keeping those other two in line. You know how Gus can get.'

I'm going to regret this, but she's backed me into a corner. 'Fine. Give her to me.' I adore this kid, but I'm not sure if I'm cut out for babysitting duties. Actually, I'm positive I'm not.

Candice gives me a beautiful smile as she passes Maddie to me. 'Everything you need is in the bag. By the way, she did a shit on the way over here, so you'll need to change her nappy.'

'Sissy said sit,' Maddie mumbles around her dummy, making me chuckle.

'Like hell I'm changing her nappy.' I've never changed a nappy in my life.

'It appears you don't have a choice. I don't have time,' she says, looking at her watch. 'She's nearly toilet trained, so she doesn't wear nappies during the day, only at night. You've only got to change her this once. It's easy, you've got this, big guy.'

She pats my shoulder for good measure. Easy for her maybe, she's probably done it a million times.

'You'll need this,' she adds, shoving a nappy bag into my arms. 'I've gotta get going. She's had breakfast. There's clothes and snacks in the bag . . . oh and Puppy.' Of course Snoopy would be in there, the kid doesn't go anywhere without it. 'Call me if you have any questions.'

She kisses Maddie on the cheek. I want a kiss too.

'Be a good girl for Uncle Jax.'

I smile when she says that. Candice has always made me feel like I'm part of her family.

'You'll be fine,' she says, squeezing my arm. 'And thank you.'

'You're not welcome.'

She laughs as she walks down the hall to the front door. When she glances over her shoulder, I quickly divert my eyes away from her incredible arse. That swing in her hips is hypnotic.

'I'll see you tonight,' she says with a wink.

She fucking played me big time.

Looking down at Maddie, I find her smiling up at me through her dummy. 'Come on,' I say, kissing the top of her head. 'Let Uncle Jax clean you up.'

There better be some damn instructions in this bag.

Lying her down on the sofa, she watches me intently as I undo the buttons on her pink onesie. I awkwardly free her arms and legs from her pyjamas, leaving her dressed in just a pink singlet and nappy. Why did I let Candice talk me into this? My stomach turns when I get a whiff of what's to come. I take a deep breath and hold it in as my fingers pull on the tabs on either side of the nappy.

'For the love of all things holy,' I yell, throwing my head to the side and covering my nose with my arm. *Fuck me.* 'What in the hell are they feeding you?'

Maddie mumbles something in reply, but I don't quite hear what she says over the sound of my violent gagging. Christ, I think I'm going to throw up.

There are baby wipes in the nappy bag, but there's no way in hell my fingers are going anywhere near that. Putting my hands under Maddie's arms, I lift her off the sofa. Making sure to hold her at arm's length, I run to the back door and out into the yard. Placing her carefully on the concrete next to the tap, I inhale some fresh air into my lungs.

I pick up the hose and turn the tap handle, adjusting the flow of the water.

'Water,' Maddie squeals, removing her dummy and dropping it to the ground.

'Yes, water.'

She looks up at me and smiles as she places her hands in the path of the spray. I love the look of magic that dances in her eyes as her hands slice effortlessly through the water. It amazes me that such a simple thing can make her so happy. I smile when she starts laughing. She's so damn sweet.

'I need to clean the poop off your butt, turn around and bend over.'

She does exactly as I ask. I heave again when she leans forward and touches her toes, revealing the shit that's spread across her arse cheeks. It gives me a whole new respect for mothers. How do they do this day in and day out? She squeals with delight the moment the cold water comes into contact with her skin.

Thankfully, the poop comes off easy enough. Crisis averted. When I reach for the tap handle to turn the water off, she sits down in the puddle under her feet and starts splashing. 'Stay here,' I instruct.

'I'll run inside and grab a towel.' The yard is fully fenced, so there's nowhere she can go.

''Kay.' She's so amused by the water my bet is she'll still be exactly where I left her when I return.

Running through the house, I head straight to the linen cupboard down the hall. I can still smell the damn shit in the house as I jog back through the main room. The nappy. It's still sitting on the sofa. I start to dry retch again when I fold it and pick it up with the tips of two fingers. Fuck, that's nasty. How can something so putrid come out of someone so sweet? Holding my breath again, I run out the back door, quickly throwing it in the bin.

Maddie's still sitting in the puddle with her legs outstretched and her hands splashing in the water. She grins at me when I come to a stop beside her. Her singlet is now drenched and her lips have turned a light shade of blue. It's not winter, but there's definitely a chill in the air this morning. Hosing her off out here probably wasn't the smartest move.

Unfolding the towel, I wrap it around her before lifting her into my arms. 'Let's get you in a warm bath.' If she gets sick, Candice and Sophia will kick my arse.

••••

I chuckle to myself as I walk into the kitchen with Maddie following close behind me. She's like my little shadow. Wherever I go, so does she. I don't know what the hell to do with her. After she was bathed and dressed, I chopped her up a banana to eat while we watched some television. She squealed with delight when some stupid show came on the Nick Jr. channel. *Dora the Explorer*, or some shit like that. It was painful, but she seemed to enjoy it immensely.

'Wanna come to the shops with me?' I ask, scooping her into my arms.

'Yes,' she replies, clapping her hands. 'Puppy come?'

'Yes, Puppy can come.' I pull my phone out of my pocket and dial Candice's number.

'Hey,' she says when she answers. 'Is everything okay?'

'Yeah, everything's fine. You owe me big time for this though.'

'I know. I'm sorry for dumping her on you.'

'To be honest, I'm actually enjoying having her here. She's cute.'

'She is,' Candice replies with a sigh.

'I've gotta go and pay some bills, is it okay to take her with me?'

'Of course. Call past the shop and grab my car keys, it has the booster seat for Maddie in the back.'

'We'll walk. It's not that far.'

'Okay. Don't let her out of your sight, and make sure you hold her hand when you're crossing the road—'

'I won't let anything happen to her,' I say, cutting her off. Seriously, I'm not stupid.

After doing what I need to do at the post office and the bank, we head back home. I love the feel of Maddie's little hand in mine. It's crazy how quickly this kid has wormed her way into my heart. She's walked most of the way, but every now and then when I could see she was tired, I carried her.

'Hat,' she squeals when we walk past one of the shop fronts, which has a range of colourful caps on display in the window. She has a fascination with my cap and is always taking it off my head and plonking it on her own. When I spot a pink cap that says *Princess* across the front, surrounded by some sparkly shit that girls like, I decide to get it for her.

'You want me to buy you that hat?' I ask, pointing to it.

'Yes,' she screams, clapping her hands as her pretty brown eyes light up. It makes me laugh. I love how the simplest things make her happy. The moment I pay for it, she puts it on her head, turning it backwards like mine. I kiss her on the cheek as we leave the shop. I didn't think having her with me would be so enjoyable, but I'm loving my time with her.

Once we're outside, I put her down and she automatically reaches for my hand. This kid is making me soft.

We don't make it far. 'Rice,' she says, pointing to a picture of a bowl of rice in the window of a Chinese restaurant as we pass.

'You hungry?'

'Yes . . . rice.'

Chuckling, I shake my head. Fried rice is my weakness. I love it.

We go inside and someone comes over to seat us immediately. I've eaten here a few times and while the place isn't much to look at, with its mismatched furnishings, it's clean and the food is amazing. Once we're seated, the waiter gives us a few minutes before he approaches the table. 'Are you ready to order?'

I pick up the menu, and Maddie does the same. It makes me laugh, because not only is the menu upside down, I know she can't read. 'Rice,' she blurts out.

'Boiled or fried rice?' The waiter looks at me for the answer. I have no idea what type of rice she likes.

'Ride rice,' she says. Fried rice it is then.

'Can I get you anything else?'

'Would you like something else?' I ask Maddie, placing the menu on the table and looking over at her.

'Ride rice,' she answers with a smile. A girl after my own heart.

'Just the rice, thanks.'

I place a small amount of rice into her bowl and fill mine. Picking up my spoon in my left hand, I'm surprised when she does the same. I watch as she picks all the prawns out with her fingers, putting them on the table beside her. Seriously, I hate them too. I usually order my rice without prawns. I chuckle when she brings the spoon to her mouth and most of the rice lands in her lap.

'Do you want me to feed you?'

'No,' she says, frowning. She's stubborn, just like her sister. 'More rice,' she says a few minutes later, holding her bowl out to me. 'Ta.'

Maddie eats a total of four bowls of rice before she's finally had enough. For someone so tiny, I'm surprised how much she can eat. After paying the bill, I lift her into my arms. 'Time to go home.' At least we've wasted a few hours. I have no idea what to do with her for the rest of the day. I hope I don't have to sit through another episode of fucking Dora.

'Down,' she says once we leave the restaurant. She babbles all the way home. Although I don't understand half of the things she's saying, I still listen intently.

She suddenly comes to an abrupt stop when we reach my place. 'Puppy!' she screams.

When I see he's no longer tucked under her arm, my gaze moves to the ground around her feet. Fuck ... no dog. We definitely had him when we left the house earlier, she insisted on bringing him.

'Puppy!' she screams again as the tears start to fall.

Lifting her, I hold her tightly against me. 'It's okay ... we'll find Puppy,' I say, rubbing my hand over her back to soothe her. It doesn't help, because she's sobbing now.

'Puppy lost.'

Fucking hell. I head back in the direction we just came from. I rack my brain, trying to think of the last time I saw her holding it. I have no idea. She's still crying when we arrive back at the restaurant where we ate. I place her on the floor and she runs straight for the table where we sat. There's a pile of rice on the floor where she was sitting, but no dog. I hate to think what state she's going to be in if we can't find it. I ask the waiter before we leave if anyone handed it in, but nothing.

Next we head back to the post office, followed by the bank. Again no Puppy. She's absolutely beside herself now, and I'm starting to freak the hell out. I'm not sure how much more of this I can take. Her big brown eyes are brimming with tears and it breaks my heart. I walk up and down the street, scanning the footpath as I go, just in case she dropped it somewhere, but to no avail. *What a disaster*. I consider calling Candice, but I'm not game enough to do that. I couldn't stand dealing with two upset Crawford women.

'I'll buy you another Puppy,' I whisper.

'No ... *my* Puppy.' She cries into my chest and I feel like a prick for even mentioning it. It wouldn't be the same.

Removing the pink cap from her head, I gently run my hand over her soft blonde curls. I need to call Candice, maybe she can soothe her. I'm no good at this kind of stuff. I'm pulling my phone out of my pocket when it hits me—the store where I bought the cap. We didn't look there. We cross the street hastily.

Entering the shop, I make my way to the counter. 'Excuse me,' I say to the woman standing behind it, 'you didn't find a Snoopy stuffed toy by any chance?'

Smiling, she reaches under the counter and by some fucking miracle, she pulls out Puppy.

'Puppy!' Maddie squeals as she reaches for him. She kisses it before hugging it to her chest. 'P-p-puppy,' she whimpers, her tiny body still racked from all the crying.

'Yeah, we found Puppy, Peanut.' I breathe a sigh of relief.

CANDICE

What a day. After balancing the takings, I put the money in the safe. Gus stayed behind so I wouldn't be here on my own. As frustrating as he is sometimes, he's a good guy. 'You need a lift?' he asks.

'No, my car's parked around the back. I drove today because my mum wasn't well.'

'Nothing serious, I hope.'

'Just a migraine. I'm right to lock up, I'll see you tomorrow.'

He reaches for the shutter, pulling it down. 'I'll wait.' He holds out his hand for the keys, so I pass them to him.

His eyes widen as he looks down at his palm. 'You have a cock on your keys.'

'I know.' I shrug.

He shakes his head as he crouches down and secures the padlock on the roller shutter. At least he didn't freak out the way Jax does. That just confirms Jax is a pussy when it comes to stuff like that. It's not like it's even real.

'Can I ask why?' Gus asks, passing the keys back to me.

'I collect them.'

'Cocks?'

'Yeah.'

He throws back his head and laughs.

'I like them, they fascinate me.'

'I like you, Pinkie. You're a cool chick. For the record, you shouldn't tell a guy with a cock that you like cocks. It may get you into trouble.'

'You're safe with me, Gus, I only like big ones.'

'My cock's huge,' he says, bumping me with his shoulder.

I laugh. 'Sure it is.'

'Well, aren't you a fucking comedian.'

'Yep. For the record though, I can handle myself. I've busted a few balls in my time.'

'I bet you have. Remind me never to upset you.' He chuckles. 'Come.' He drapes his arm over my shoulder. 'I'll walk you to your car.'

'I'm fine, Gus, honestly.'

'Don't argue. This is not up for negotiation. I'm not letting you walk down the alleyway by yourself at this time of night. Plus, the boss will kick my arse if anything happens to you.'

'It's only six, Gus.'

'I don't care. It's getting dark.'

'Fine . . . Thank you.'

'Besides, if there's some poor unsuspecting guy taking a leak in the alleyway, he may require my protection from your freaky cock fetish.'

'Very funny,' I say, nudging him in the ribcage.

Once I'm in my car, Gus insists I lock my door before he leaves. He can be so sweet when he's not being a meathead.

I head straight to Jax's house. I was half expecting him to turn up at the shop today, so I was surprised when he didn't. I'd planned to call over and check on them both during my lunch break, but by the time I drove home and got Sophia sorted, there was no time.

'Jax, it's me,' I call out after knocking on the front door. The lights are on inside, and I can hear the television, so I know they're here. 'Jax!'

When I get no answer, I turn the handle and find the door unlocked. 'Jax . . . Maddie,' I say as I enter the foyer. Still no reply. Heading into the lounge room, I find them.

Jax is sitting on the sofa with Maddie curled up in his lap. They're both sound asleep. Jax's head is tilted back and Maddie has her dummy in her mouth, Puppy is tucked under her arm, and her pink blanket is draped over them both. It's the sweetest thing I've ever seen.

Digging in my bag, I grab my phone and take a picture. I don't want to ever forget this sight. Hugging my bag to my chest, I take a few moments to watch them together. I love how good he is with her, and how much Maddie adores him. He's always said he's not the parenting type, but he's wrong. You only have to see him with Maddie to know that.

I take a few steps towards them. Looking at Jax, I sigh. He's so handsome with his perfectly sculpted face, and rugged features. He has a bit of stubble going on today, and it makes him look even sexier. My fingers are itching to touch it. He looks so peaceful that I feel bad having to wake them, but we'll never get Maddie down tonight if I don't.

'Jax,' I whisper, gently placing my hand on his knee and shaking it. 'Jax, wake up.'

'Huh?' he says, opening his eyes. 'Fuck.' He reaches up and rubs the back of his neck while rolling his head around.

'You both fell asleep,' I whisper.

'What time is it?'

'Just after six.'

I see his gaze move down to Maddie asleep on his lap, and he smiles. 'How was she?'

'Great. We had fun.' I can tell he's sincere.

'I'll need to wake her, otherwise she won't go back down tonight.'

He looks down at her again. The fondness I see in his eyes tugs at my heart. It makes me doubt all the decisions I've made where Jax is concerned. But it's too late to undo all my mistakes.

'We had a big day. I didn't mean to fall asleep, but those damn kids' shows were doing my head in.'

I laugh. 'Yes, they're painful. She loves them though.'

'That Dora,' he says as his body quivers. I'm not a fan either, but it's one of her favourites.

'Maddie, sweetie,' I say softly, running my hands over her hair. 'Wake up, baby.' Her eyes flutter open before closing again. 'It's time to go home.' Leaning forward, I place a soft kiss on her cheek and tuck one of her blonde curls behind her ear. 'You need to wake up, baby.'

She grunts and a frown appears on her forehead, but she doesn't open her eyes. She loves her sleep. Pulling back slightly, I look at Jax. He's staring at me. The look on his face makes my stomach do a flip-flop. It reminds me of the look he gave me the first time we kissed. This is one of those rare moments that seem to make the world around you stand still. I watch as his tongue darts out slightly, moistening his bottom lip. My face is only a few inches away from his and I feel a desperate need to press my mouth to his, but I can't do that. My heart wouldn't survive another rejection.

Quickly straightening to full height, I lift Maddie off his lap and into my arms, breaking the spell. It wouldn't take much for me to crumble. Maddie lets out a little cry before closing her eyes and resting her head in the crook of my neck. Looking down at Jax, I see him run his hands through his thick brown hair.

'Thanks for looking after her for me today.'

'You're welcome,' he says, standing. 'I'll just get her things together.'

'Do you have any dinner plans?' I ask.

'No. Why? I didn't think Sophia would be up to cooking tonight.'

'She's not. I called her before I left work—she's still laid up in bed. I thought maybe the three of us could go out and eat somewhere . . . only if you want to.'

'You, me and Peanut?'

'Yeah.'

He grins. 'I'd like that.'

THIRTEEN

JAX

I WAS SO CLOSE TO KISSING HER, IT'S NOT FUNNY. THE WAY she abruptly pulled away makes me think she knew it too. There's something about the way she is with Maddie that undoes me. Maybe it's the thought of her one day being a mother. Christ, I dread that day. Will Candice still have room in her life for me once she's married with children? I don't even want to let my mind go there.

Candice sits down on the sofa with Maddie, giving her time to wake up properly, and I set about packing all her toys back into the nappy bag. Heading into the kitchen, I rinse her sippy-cup and refill it with apple juice.

'How did things go at the shop today?' I ask when I return to the lounge room.

'Good. All the new stock I ordered arrived.'

'Did the boys behave?' Gus is a prankster, and seems to be at his worst when I'm not around.

'They were okay.'

I pass the sippy-cup to Maddie. 'Ta,' she says, looking up at me with sleepy eyes and a small smile. Apart from the Puppy fiasco, we had a great day.

'Can you pass me Maddie's pink cardigan, it should be in the bag, and her shoes?' Candice asks. 'If we're going to get some dinner, we probably should get going.'

Handing her the cardigan, she slips Maddie's arms inside while I crouch down and slide her pink sandals on her feet. Maddie is the first kid I've ever been around, so her tiny hands and feet fascinate me. When I stand, I find Candice smiling at me.

'What?'

'I've just never seen this side of you before.'

'What side?' I ask as my brow furrows.

'The way you dote on Maddie. It's very sweet.'

Shoving my hands into my pockets, I shrug. 'I take my uncle role very seriously.'

'You're cute,' she says, putting Maddie on the floor.

'I'm not, cute.'

'Yes, you are,' she says, poking me in the side. She laughs when I slap her hand away.

Maddie runs over to the table, picking up her cap. 'Look, Sissy, hat.'

'Wow. Did Uncle Jax buy you that pretty hat?'

Maddie nods as she puts it on. Scooping Maddie into her arms I see a smile tug at Candice's lips. Passing me on her way to the door, she whispers, 'I rest my case, cutie-pie.'

'I'm not a cutie-pie,' I growl.

'Walk,' Maddie says as we head down the street towards an Italian restaurant. Candice puts her down and reaches for her hand. My heart melts when Maddie moves between us and reaches for my hand as well. I'm thankful she left the dog at home. I couldn't handle a repeat of this afternoon.

'Should we order something for you to take home to Sophia?' I ask as we look over the menu.

'No, she won't eat it. She doesn't get these migraines often, but when she does they really knock her on her arse. I made her a sandwich when I went home at lunchtime, but she didn't want it. I hate seeing her like that.'

'Can the doctor give her anything?'

'No. Bed rest in a dark room is the only thing that seems to help. She'll come good tomorrow, or the next day.'

Once we've finished eating, Candice takes Maddie to the bathroom to clean her up. She's covered in pasta sauce. She really made a mess of herself and I chuckle when I think of the piece of spaghetti that was in her hair. Usually she lets Candice feed her, but tonight she wanted to do it herself. She must've gained her independence at lunch with the rice.

The waitress approaches the table with the bill, so I pull my credit card out and pass it to her.

'Did you enjoy your meal?' she asks.

'We did. Thank you.' I look at the crap all over the table. 'Sorry about the mess.'

'It's no bother. You have a lovely family. My kids used to make a mess like that when they were little.'

I just smile and don't bother correcting her. I kinda like that she thought we were a family, which is all types of crazy. I learnt a long time ago that there's no point wishing for something you can never have. My family weren't the best role models. They certainly never inspired me to have a family of my own. If anything, they turned me off the idea.

The waitress's comment makes me wonder about Maddie's dad. Is he absent from her life, just like Candice's father? I've yet to hear any mention of him.

When we reach my place, I run inside to get Maddie's things while Candice straps her into her booster seat. Maddie made me carry her all the way home, and almost fell asleep on my shoulder. It's been a big day; she wore me out.

I pass Candice the bag and she places it on the floor inside the car.

Bending slightly, I look into the back seat. 'Bye, Peanut.'

Maddie gives me a weak smile as her eyelids slowly close. She'll be asleep before Candice even gets out of the street.

'Thanks again for today,' Candice says as she closes the back door and turns to face me.

'You don't need to thank me.'

'I do. I would've been screwed today if it wasn't for you.'

'Well, that's what uncles are for.'

She lets out a small laugh as she tucks a strand of pink hair behind her ear. She seems nervous. I hope she doesn't think I'm going to kiss her. As much as I'd like to, she knows as well as I do that's not going to happen.

'Does Maddie ever see her father?'

'What? Why would you ask that?' Her eyes widen slightly.

I shrug. 'I'm just curious. You guys have never mentioned him.'

She pauses briefly before shaking her head. I know talking about her own father has always been a sore point for Candice. 'It's a long, complicated mess,' she says as she looks away.

I don't bother prying any further, because I can see it's making her uncomfortable. It's none of my business.

'I should get going. Maddie's tired, and I still need to bath her.'

'No problem. I'll see you tomorrow.'

'You will.'

I shove my hands into my pockets as we stand there in silence. For some reason I don't know what to say or do. It's funny, ninety-nine per cent of the time we're completely comfortable in each other's presence, but then there's that one per cent, like now, when I don't know how to act. What I'd really like to ask her is how her date with Carter went last night, but I'm in no way prepared for her answer.

Stepping forward, she surprises me when she wraps her arms around my waist. "Night, Jax.'

I fold her into my arms. Closing my eyes, I inhale her sweet apple scent as I place a soft kiss on her hair. I wish I could hold her like this forever.

'Goodnight, Candice.' Letting go, I take a step backwards. She gives me a smile that almost seems sad, before walking around to the driver's side of the car.

I'm still standing on the footpath minutes after her car has disappeared around the corner. I've gotten used to being on my own, but for some reason, in this moment I feel lost and completely alone.

••••

I thought I'd have another sleepless night, but surprisingly, I didn't. I think looking after Maddie yesterday wore me out. Pulling out my phone on the walk to work, I text Candice.

> **Me:** How's Sophia this morning?

She replies almost immediately.

> **Candice:** Still not well. I was just about to call you. Can I bring Maddie into work today? I'll make sure she doesn't get in the way. Otherwise, I'm not going to be able to come in.

The tattoo parlour is no place for kids, but Maddie is family. I know she's a good kid. Plus, I need Candice there today. She keeps everything running smoothly.

> **Me:** Bring her with you. I can help keep an eye on her when I'm not with clients.

> **Candice:** This is why I love you. See you soon. x

I swear I reread her message a hundred times before putting my phone back in my pocket. I know she only said it in jest, but nobody has ever told me they loved me before. My family never did love; it was too real for their fake-arse lives.

Stopping at the bakery, I grab Brian his usual. I spot a little pink cupcake in the display case. 'I'll get one of those too, thanks,' I say, pointing to the one I want. Maddie has a sweet tooth like me, so I know she'll love it.

I head towards the shop with my purchases. I really feel for Brian. Someone his age should be in the prime of his life, not living on the streets and begging for food. Brian is usually waiting for me on the other side of the street each morning. He's become accustomed to me now, so I'm surprised when I don't see him. It's just after eight and I don't have time to wait around so I cross the road, heading into the park.

It doesn't take long for me to find him. Concern fills me when I see him sitting on a park bench with his head in his hands.

'Brian, is everything okay?'

When he looks up at me, my heart drops. 'Fuck. What happened?' I ask, crouching down in front of him.

'Some young thugs out for a good time,' he says.

Rage fills me as I look over his battered face. What sort of lowlife would do something like this for fun? He's a poor, defenceless old man. He wouldn't even have anything worth stealing.

'Jesus. Come, on let's get you looked at,' I say standing and extending my hand to him.

'I'm not going to no doctor ... I hate doctors. They're a bunch of quacks.'

'You need to see somebody.' He has a large gash on his head that looks like it's going to need stitches.

'I'll be fine,' he says, flicking his hand to dismiss my suggestions.

'I'm not leaving you like this, Brian. At least come over to my shop and let me clean you up.'

'You do enough for me already.' He looks up at me with his kind eyes—well, one of them, the other is practically swollen shut.

'I won't take no for an answer. Your cuts will get infected if I don't clean them, and then you'll be in all sorts of trouble.' Handing him the hot coffee, I use my free hand to help him off the bench. I pick up his striped bag, filled with his worldly possessions.

'Okay. You drive a hard bargain, young man.' He groans as he stands. I'm still flabbergasted that someone could do this. What the hell is wrong with people?

I open the shop and lead him straight into my studio. 'Sit,' I say, guiding him to the seat in the corner. I grab the first aid kit out of the cupboard, along with two towels. Wetting one, I start wiping the dried blood off his face. He's a fucking mess. There's so much dirt and grime on his skin, I have to keep rinsing the towel as I go. He winces a few times, but doesn't complain. He's a tough old bugger.

'Tell me to mind my own business if you like, but how did you end up on the streets anyway?'

He sighs. 'It's a long story.'

'Well, we're going to be here for a while. Those kids really did a number on you.'

He remains quiet for a short time before beginning to speak. 'My wife got sick about five years ago. She went through a number of tests, but they kept telling her she was fine when it was obvious she wasn't. She couldn't keep anything down . . . she'd lost so much weight.'

I pause and make eye contact with him.

'Months later we ended up going and getting a second opinion. I couldn't bear to see her suffering. That's when we found out about the tumour. By then the cancer had spread to her lungs and liver. She was riddled with it. The doctors had lied. Incompetent fools. She wasn't fine, she had an aggressive tumour in her stomach. If only she'd been diagnosed earlier . . .' There's disdain in his voice as he speaks, and now I understand why he doesn't like doctors. He brings his dirty hand to his face, wiping a tear from under his eye.

'Shit.' I don't know what else to say.

'We didn't have much money, but I used every cent I had trying to save my dear sweet May—she was my world. We were high school sweethearts, you know. I fell in love with her the moment I laid eyes on her.' When he pauses and I see his lips curve into a smile, I know he's thinking about her. 'She was wearing a pretty white dress the day I met her. She reminded me of an angel. When she got sick, it was hard to stand by and watch her suffering. I would've given anything to trade places with her. By the time she passed away, I had nothing left. The house, our savings . . . it was all gone.'

'I'm sorry. That must've been a hard time for you.'

Silence falls over us as I continue to clean him up. He gave up everything to save his wife, and in the end he lost her anyway. Life can be so cruel.

'The kids who did this—' he points to his face as he speaks, '—stole the only thing of value I had left. May's wedding ring.'

'What? Fuck.'

He gives me a stern look when I swear, and I bow my head. I gather he isn't impressed with my language.

'I'm sorry.'

I'm astounded that he kept her ring all this time when he didn't even have money to eat. It just shows how much he loved her. How could somebody steal from a homeless man?

I'm pulled from my thoughts when I hear a voice speaking behind me.

'Hey.' Candice is standing in the doorway of my studio. 'Oh, sorry. I didn't realise you had company.'

'Jax!' Maddie squeals, wiggling out of Candice's arms and running over to me.

'Morning, Peanut.' Picking her up, I kiss the top of her head. She's wearing the pink cap I bought her yesterday. 'Candice, come meet Brian,' I say over Maddie's head.

She walks into the room, and stops beside me.

'Candice, this is Brian. Brian, this is Candice.'

I smile when she extends her hand to him. He's filthy and he doesn't smell too good, but that doesn't seem to bother her at all. Like me, she's non-judgemental. Ninety-nine per cent of the people we grew up with wouldn't even stand in the same room as him, let alone touch him.

'Nice to meet you, Brian.'

'Likewise, Miss Candice.'

'And this is Maddie.'

'Hello little one,' he says. Maddie smiles, cowering into my chest at the same time.

'You look like you've been in the wars, Brian. Are you okay?' Candice asks. 'You should get that cut looked at, it's nasty.'

He looks a lot better than he did when I first brought him in here. Now that I've removed most of the blood and dirt from his face, you can clearly see the bruises forming.

'He was beaten up by some kids last night.'

'Oh my God.' Candice covers her mouth with her hand.

'He doesn't want to see a doctor. If I watch Maddie, do you think you could run to the pharmacy and grab some butterfly stitches? I don't have any in the first aid kit. Maybe another bottle of Betadine as well. I'm almost out.'

'Of course.'

Pulling my wallet out of my pocket, I hand it to her. 'Use whatever you need.'

She smiles before turning her attention to Maddie. 'Be a good girl for Uncle Jax, I'll be back in a few minutes.'

'Your niece has your eyes,' Brian says once Candice leaves.

I chuckle. 'She's not really my niece. Candice and I have been friends for years, so she's like family to me.' I look down at Maddie and smile as she stands beside me, watching me clean up Brian.

'Hurt,' she says, pointing to him.

When Candice arrives with the supplies from the pharmacy, she sets Maddie up with a colouring book and pencils in the corner of my studio so she can help me with Brian.

'It's almost nine, you better go get things ready for us to open,' I say to her when we're nearly done.

'Sure.'

'Leave Maddie here with me.' I glance over at her in the corner and she's happily colouring. She's a good girl.

'You like her, don't you?' Brian says when Candice leaves the room.

'Who, Candice?'

'Yeah.'

'Of course. As I said, we've been friends for years.'

'I'm talking about more than a friend. I see the way you look at her. It's the same way I used to look at my May.'

Lowering my head, I clear my throat. I can't answer that question without lying, so I don't. Instead, I busy myself cleaning up the mess I made.

'A love like that doesn't come around often you know.'

'We're friends. That's all we'll ever be.'

'Keep telling yourself that, son.'

Is it that obvious? I thought I'd mastered hiding my true feelings for Candice. He's the first person to ever call me out on it.

'Are there any shelters in the area you can stay at? It's not safe for you to sleep in the park,' I say, trying to steer the conversation away from Candice and me.

'Occasionally they have a spare bed, but not often.'

'My spare room at home is full, but you're welcome to use my sofa until you find somewhere safer to stay.' I barely know this man, but I can't in good conscience send him back out there.

'Thank you for the offer. You're a good kid, Jax, but I couldn't do that to you. I refuse to be a burden to anyone.'

Sighing, I remove my cap and run my fingers through my hair.

'What about if I make a few calls and see if I can find a shelter that has room for you?'

'No. I appreciate it, but you've done enough.' He stands and shakes my hand. 'I best be going, but thank you.'

'Listen,' I say as he picks up his striped bag and shuffles towards the door, 'there's a garage at the back of the shop. It's not much, but I never use it.' I pull my keys out of my pocket, taking the two for the back gate and garage door off the ring. 'You can enter via the laneway out back. Sleep in there at night.' I can already tell he's going to say no. 'Please, mate, it will make me feel better knowing you're safe at night.' Newtown is a great area, but like most places, it's not the best area to be in alone after dark.

He sighs as he considers my offer. 'Okay. Thank you.'

I smile when he takes the keys from me, shoving them into the pocket of his worn trousers. I see tears glistening in his eyes when they meet mine again.

'I'll never be able to repay you for your kindness.'

'There's no need. Having you safe is reward enough.'

'Bye, little one,' he says as he passes Maddie.

••••

'Nope, I think it will look better back over there,' Candice says, pointing to the spot I just had it in. She's kidding right? This is the fifth time she's got me to move it.

'It's just a fucking place to sleep, not the Ritz Carlton.'

'I know, but I want him to be comfortable.'

'The position isn't going to make a difference. Anything will be better than the park bench he's been calling home for God knows how long.'

'I know,' she says with a grim expression. 'This is a really nice thing you're doing, Jax.'

I shrug. 'I couldn't just leave him on the streets.'

'I wonder how he ended up there? He doesn't appear to be a drunk.'

'He's not. He spent every penny he had trying to save his wife when she got sick, but she ended up dying anyway.'

'Really? That's the sweetest and saddest story I've ever heard.' She places her hand over her heart and sighs, and I see tears in her eyes moments before she turns her face away from me. *Fucking women.* They're always so emotional.

'Come here,' I say, closing the distance between us and wrapping her in my arms. Resting my chin on the top of her head, I hear her sniffle as she buries her face in my chest.

'Doesn't he have any family he can stay with?'

'I don't know, I didn't ask. He mentioned something about not wanting to be a burden to anyone, so maybe. Then again, he could have a family like mine, one that doesn't give a shit. He'll be comfortable in here.'

'Ugh. Your parents suck.'

'Yes, they do. You can't choose your family, so they say.'

'You'll always have me, Sophia and Maddie. We all adore you, Jax. You know that right?' Her beautiful blue eyes meet mine.

'I know. You girls are all I'll ever need.' I use the pad of my thumb to wipe away the tears under her eyes. Her skin is so soft, just like I remembered. I'll never forget that night we spent together. It's up there with some of the best moments in my life. Who am I kidding? They were the best few hours of my life.

My eyes lock with hers and I hate the pity I can see reflecting in them. I don't want her sympathy.

I should know from past experiences that being so close to her is a bad idea, but again I seem powerless to stop the inevitable. Just like that first time we kissed all those years ago, something shifts between us. Before the logical side of my brain even registers, my face is inching towards her.

Her eyelids flutter closed just as our lips connect. The soft moan that falls from her lips travels straight to my cock. Her hands fist in the back of my T-shirt, drawing me closer.

She's still my fucking kryptonite.

Lacing my fingers through her hair, I groan into her mouth as I tilt her head back and deepen the kiss. I've dreamt of doing this again since the moment I walked away all those years ago.

'Jax,' she whimpers.

I'm not sure how long we stay lost in each other, but this kiss is scorching hot. My rock-hard cock straining painfully against my jeans is proof. It's like we're starved for each other. Every feeling from our one night together that I buried years ago comes flooding to the surface. Everything in me wants to throw her on that bed so I can devour her luscious body inch by inch, but I can't. That's exactly what got us into this mess in the first place.

My internal freak-out is the equivalent of a bucket of ice-cold water being thrown on me. In an instant, it extinguishes the flame that burns within me. I abruptly pull out of the kiss, taking a step backwards. I need distance.

'I'm sorry,' I say, 'I don't know what came over me . . . I—'

When she raises her hand, I don't utter another word.

'Don't.'

I see her deflate before my eyes. She turns hastily, as though to leave. I can't let her go. I need to know that we're okay. I hope I haven't fucked things up again.

'Candice, wait.'

She pauses but doesn't turn around. 'What?'

'Turn around and look at me,' I say. She's pissed, and she has every right to be. Why did I go there? Why can't I control these damn feelings? 'Let me explain.'

'Explain what?' she snaps as she spins to face me. 'That I'm not good enough for you, Jax? That you don't feel that way about me?'

'What? Fuck, no. Is that what you think?'

'It's what I know.'

'Well, you're wrong. If anything, you're *too* good for me. You're more than I deserve.'

I sigh as the realisation creeps back in. It's something I thought about a lot when we were apart, and even more so since Candice has come back into my life. She deserves way more than I am capable of giving her. I can't give her what she wants—I just don't have it in me. How can a person who's never known love be capable of truly loving someone else? Candice needs to be cherished, worshipped. I'd like to be that person, but in my heart I know I'm not. I'll never be. My parents' words are always at the front of my mind. *You're such a disappointment.* I'd eventually disappoint Candice as well, it's what I do best. I couldn't live with that.

'You're everything to me. Fucking everything! You're family.'

'Family, right.' The hurt in her voice tears me apart.

Okay, that didn't come out the way I'd hoped. 'You're my world, Candice. Don't you get that? Our friendship . . . it can never break up. But this,' I say, gesturing between us, 'it can. Relationships break up all the time. I can't lose you again.'

'How can you say that? How do you know we'd break up? We might not.'

'Fuck,' I say, rubbing my hands over my face. 'That might be true, but it's a chance I'm not willing to take.'

She exhales harshly.

My hand reaches out to grab hers. There's so much more I want to say, but what's the point? The love I feel for her is fucking hopeless.

'Friendship,' she eventually says.

'You're the only real friend I have—you're all I have.'

She smiles, but the sadness in her eyes tears me up inside. 'Sure. Friendship triumphs love any day.'

She sounds so bitter and I can tell she doesn't believe her own words. When her grip on my hand tightens, it feels like she's squeezing the life out of my heart.

'I don't want to ever lose what we have, Jax.' With that she releases my hand and walks away.

I want to scream.

I want to punch something.

I want to be so much more than just her friend.

Fuck my life!

••••

I steer clear of Candice for the rest of the day—as much as I can anyway. Maddie spends her time moving between my studio and reception. She's been no trouble. For the last few hours she's been with me while Candice is finishing getting the garage sorted for Brian.

I'm grinning to myself as I watch Maddie climb down off her chair in the corner before toddling over to me.

'Taoo like, Sissy?' she says, extending her arm to me.

'I can't give you a tattoo.' I chuckle as I lift her into my arms. 'Tattoos are only for big girls.'

'I big,' she says as her bottom lip starts to quiver and tears fill her big brown eyes. How can I resist that face? Talk about a heartbreaker. I pity all the guys when she gets older. They're not gonna know what hit them.

'Okay. Just a little one though.'

Her face lights up as she wraps her arms around my neck, squeezing me tight. Burying my lips into her chubby cheek, I kiss her sweet face as I walk to the reclining chair on the far side of the room. Gently putting her down, I drag the stool towards me and sit. I riffle through the top drawer of the cabinet beside me until I find a black permanent marker.

'So what kind of tattoo would you like?'

'Puppy,' she squeals, straightening her arm and holding it out to me. Of course she wants Puppy, she's obsessed with that damn thing. Prying the stuffed toy out from under her arm, I sit it on her lap so I can use it as my muse.

The moment the marker connects with her skin she squirms. 'Tickle.'

'I know it tickles, but you've gotta stay still or Puppy is going to be all wiggly.'

Her eyes move to me from where they're fixed on her arm. ''Kay,' she says.

She's so friggin' adorable.

She manages to stay reasonably still until I'm done. I draw a picture of Snoopy standing. He's holding a heart in his hands that says, *I love Peanut*.

'There you go,' I say, putting the lid back on the marker.

'Puppy,' she squeals. I can tell by the expression on her face she loves it. It does look pretty damn good. 'Taoo, Sissy.' When she holds out her arm proudly and looks at the doorway, I swing around in my seat. Candice is leaning against the doorframe, watching us.

Pushing off the frame, she walks across the room, coming to a stop beside me. She makes eye contact with me briefly before focusing her attention on her sister. Christ, I hope that kiss from earlier isn't going to make things awkward between us. Why can't I keep my hands—and mouth—to myself when she's around?

'Aww,' Candice says when she looks at Maddie's arm. 'Puppy. Do you know what that says, Maddie?'

Maddie shakes her head.

'It says, "*I love Peanut*".'

She smiles as she lifts her arm to her face, kissing the drawing. 'I wuv you too, Puppy.'

Could this kid get any cuter?

'Thank you,' Candice says, bumping my arm with her hip. When I hear her whisper, 'Cutie-pie,' I growl, and she laughs. I'm not a fucking cutie-pie.

She lifts Maddie off the reclining chair and into her arms. After kissing her cheek, she looks down at me. 'I just finished setting up the garage for Brian if you want to come take a look.'

'Okay.' This time we'll have Maddie with us, so we'll be safe.

'Jax,' Maddie says, reaching for me when I stand. I smile as I take her out of Candice's arms. She likes her Uncle Jax. This kid has good taste.

'Jesus,' I say when I walk into the garage.

'You like?'

'I do. You've done a great job.' I look at her and she's smiling. I can tell she's proud of the work she's done in here. So she should be. When I left earlier, there was only a bedframe, a mattress, a few cobwebs, and a hell of a lot of dust. In two hours, she's managed to transform it into a room. We picked up a secondhand bed on Gumtree. The guy lived locally and even delivered it for us. I gave Candice my credit card and sent her out to get whatever else she thought Brian would need. She went above and beyond. The bed now has linen, including a pillow, sheets, a blanket and comforter. She chose a dark navy colour. Considering the state of him, that was a wise choice. I wish there was a bathroom here so he could shower, but there isn't. And that's an expense I can't afford right now. There's a hand basin in the corner, so at least he has running water in case he'd like to wash.

I pray Brian turns up tonight. I don't want him out on the street. He'll be safe and comfortable here.

'I picked up the bedside table, chest of drawers and lamp at an op shop. Actually, everything's secondhand, except for the linen of course.'

Putting Maddie down, I walk around the garage, taking it all in. The bed is on the far side of the room. On the adjacent wall, Candice has hung a small mirror. Under that stands a chest of drawers that has a large metal basin sitting on top. Opening the top drawer, I find a hair brush, scissors, a razor, shaving cream, a toothbrush, a tube of toothpaste and a bar of soap. The drawer beneath houses a few towels and face washers.

'You've thought of everything,' I say, turning to face her. 'Thank you.'

'It would be cool if we could pick up a cheap bar fridge. We could stock it with food and drinks. Oh, and a kettle so he can make coffee or tea. In winter we should invest in a heater. It'll get cold in here.'

She's talking enthusiastically and I love that she's just as invested in this as I am. 'They're great ideas. That can be your job tomorrow.'

She scoops Maddie into her arms. 'Okay. We better get going—I want to check on Sophia. Are you coming over for dinner? We may have to get takeout.'

'Nah. I'm gonna stick around and see if Brian shows up. I wanna make sure he's okay, and I'd like to re-dress his wounds before I go.'

'You're a good man, Jaxson Albright.'

'You're not too bad yourself, Miss Crawford.'

I'm happy that things still seem normal between us—I was worried the kiss would make things weird. Is it possible we're finally making progress?

Heading back into the shop, I lock up once everyone leaves. Gus offered to walk Candice and Maddie to the car, which I was grateful for. After cashing up and putting the takings in the safe in my studio,

I head out the back. It's just after seven, and it's dark outside. I really hope Brian shows.

I'm rooted to the spot when I reach the garage. The door is open, and Brian is standing in the centre of the room. His shoulders are slumped and his head is bowed. I give him a moment before I enter.

'You came?'

He faces me slowly. That's when I see the tears that are cascading down his face. 'You did all this for me?' he whispers, wiping his cheeks with the back of his hand.

'With the help of Candice. Well, actually, she did most of it.'

'I don't know what to say.'

'Don't say anything. I'm just glad you're here. I can rest easy knowing you'll be safe tonight.'

'Thank you,' he says, stepping forward and extending his hand. 'And thank that little lady of yours for me too. You have no idea what this means to me . . .'

I smile as I wrap my hand around his. I only wish she was my little lady.

In my heart she always will be.

FOURTEEN

JAX

AS THE WEEKS PASS, MY CONFIDENCE IN US BEING ABLE TO get through this clusterfuck in one piece strengthens. The kiss is long forgotten, and Candice and I are getting on better than we have in a while. I'm smiling to myself as I walk into reception. For the first time in a long time, I'm happy with where we're heading.

The smile drops from my face and I freeze when I see Carter sitting on the sofa in a deep and meaningful conversation with Candice. Why is he here? Her hand is tenderly rubbing his arm as he speaks, and I don't like it. I don't like it one little bit. I'll admit I like the guy, but since he hooked up with Candice, my feelings towards him have changed somewhat. I know it's just jealousy, and he has no idea how I feel about her, but I don't want to share her with anyone. *She's mine.*

As much as I'd like to, I can't make a scene. Candice has already warned me about interfering in her life. So I take a few moments to compose myself before approaching them. They're so engrossed in each other they don't even notice me. I breathe deeply before I speak.

'Hey.'

Their heads swing in my direction, and my eyes lock on Candice.

'Don't you have work to do? I don't pay you to sit around and chitchat.'

The moment her eyes widen and her mouth gapes I know my comment has pissed her off. That went well. So much for not making a scene.

'Really?' she says as her eyes narrow.

'Yes, really.'

'This was a mistake,' Carter says. 'I shouldn't have come here.'

That's right buddy, you shouldn't have. If you want to make moves on my girl you can do it elsewhere. This is my shop.

When he goes to stand, Candice reaches for his arm. 'Don't go, Carter. Jax wasn't directing that at you.'

'It's okay. I should go.'

I can tell by his body language that something is up with him. He was like this the day we met. It makes me feel bad about the way I'm acting. So much for progress.

'Sit,' Candice demands. 'Give me a minute with Jax.' She pushes past me and gives me a look that says if I know what's good for me I'd better follow.

'Give us a minute,' I say to Carter, forcing a smile.

'What's your fucking problem?' Candice snaps the minute I enter my studio.

'My problem?'

'Yes. You were so rude out there.'

'Why, because I said I don't pay you to sit around and chitchat? News flash, I fucking don't.'

'You can be a real jerk sometimes, Albright, you know that?'

I scrub my hand over my face as I count to ten in my head.

'Do you even know why Carter is here? Oh that's right you wouldn't, because you were too busy acting like an arsehole to find out.'

'I'm not stupid, Candice, he came here to see you.'

'Wrong! He came to see *you*.' She pokes me in the chest. 'He's run away from home. He was hoping he could sell some more of his drawings so he has money to pay for a place to stay. Do you want him to end up on the streets like Brian?'

I sigh. 'No.'

'I really don't get you sometimes. You were the one who reached out to him in the first place.'

I want to say, '*Yeah, well that was before he hooked up with you*,' but I don't. I'm acting like a jealous prick, and I'm not about to admit that to her.

Removing my cap, I run my fingers through my hair. 'Fine. Send him in.'

I don't speak another word as I stalk across the room and busy myself at my work station. I don't need to turn around to see the daggers she's shooting me, I can feel the fuckers plunging deep into my back.

A few minutes later there's a knock at the door. Carter. 'Candice said you wanted to see me.'

'Yeah, come in,' I say as I face him. When I see his sketchpad in his hand, I feel like a cock. I need to get a fucking grip on this jealous streak.

'Thanks, man. I'm sorry for coming here, but I was desperate.'

'Why did you come?'

'I need money. Not charity,' he adds, quickly holding out his sketchpad. 'I have more drawings if you're interested. If not, that's cool too. I just thought there was no harm in asking.'

'Why do you need money?' I already know why, but I want to hear it out of his own mouth.

He shrugs. 'I left home on the spur of the moment, without thinking. I've got a little cash, but only enough to get by for a few days. I'm gonna look for work.'

'Sit,' I say, pointing to the chair. 'How old are you anyway?'

'I'm turning eighteen in a few weeks.'

Fuck, he's just a kid. He looks older. What in the hell is Candice doing with someone so young?

'Tell me to mind my own business if you like, but why did you feel the need to leave home in such a hurry? Are you having problems, or are you in some kind of trouble?'

'I have my reasons.'

I raise my eyebrows. If he wants my help he's gonna have to give me more than that.

'My home life kinda sucks,' he continues. 'My stepdad is a fuckwit. He's nice to me when my mum's around, but when she's not . . .'

I can relate to that, my home life sucked as well. Even though I hate the way it came about, getting out of there was the best decision I ever made.

'Where are you staying tonight?'

'My car, I guess.'

I think for a minute before I speak. 'You're welcome to sleep on my sofa until you find a place of your own.' Despite what I think of him and Candice, she's right, I don't want to see him on the streets. Besides, having him stay with me is better than him staying with her. That would really do my head in.

'I can't ask you to take me in.'

'You didn't ask, I offered. You can work here until you find something more permanent. You cool with that?'

'You're offering me a job?'

'Yes.' I hope I don't regret this. Having him here will mean he's around Candice all fucking day. 'You'll need to earn your keep. And if you're going to be working here, there'll be no fraternising with the staff, or my clients. Understand?' I throw that in because I'm a possessive arsehole.

'Of course. You don't have to do this, you know.'

'I know,' I say, 'but I want to. Don't make me regret it.'

'I won't. I promise. Thank you.' Standing, he shakes my hand.

'With your talents, I'm sure you'll do well.'

CANDICE

I knew Jax would do the right thing, he always does. He'd never admit it, but underneath all those muscles and tattoos is a big, soft, teddy bear, and a heart of gold.

Carter's been working here for a week now, and is fitting in nicely. I can tell that even Jax is enjoying having him around. They're a lot alike, and seem to have similar interests. Jax has Carter sitting in on all his jobs, and is teaching him everything he knows. I can't help but wonder if part of what he's doing is to keep Carter away from me. If only he knew. Carter has no interest in me in that way, nor I in him. He only has eyes for Indiana.

The day he arrived, I could tell he was a broken man. It hurt my heart to see him like that. Carter thinks he's no good for Indiana, and that she can do better than him. He has such a low opinion of himself. Why can't he see what a great guy he is? I know from experience how they're both feeling. I was completely shattered the day Jax walked away from me.

Yesterday, Indiana's father came to the shop looking for Carter. The horrified look on Carter's face when he saw him standing in reception told me he wasn't expecting the visit. When I overheard him say, 'How did you find me?' I understood his reaction. Indiana's father seems like a nice man and it's obvious he cares about Carter. He's made it his mission to help Carter find a place of his own, so he's not living out of a suitcase and sleeping on Jax's couch.

Sitting behind the reception desk, I'm scanning through my Facebook newsfeed on my phone when it rings. I see Sophia's name on the screen, and answer straightaway.

'Hey.'

'Candice . . . I'm so sorry,' she cries into the receiver.

My heart drops into the pit of my stomach. 'What's wrong? Are you okay? Is Maddie all right?'

'I'm at the hospital. I only turned my back for a second, I swear.'

'What happened?' I say, panicked, as I reach for my bag under the desk. 'Where's Maddie?'

'She's in getting an X-ray.'

'An X-ray?'

'Yes. The doctor thinks she may have broken her wrist.'

'Oh God.' I feel my knees go weak as I stand. 'What hospital are you at? I'm coming now.'

'I'm at the Children's Hospital in Randwick. The one we took her to last year when she had a high fever.'

'Shit. That's twenty minutes from here.'

'I'm sorry, baby.'

'I'll be there soon.'

Ending the call, I race to Jax's studio. I don't even bother knocking.

'What the hell?' he says, swinging around on his stool. He's in the middle of a job. My eyes dart between him, his client, and then to Carter who's watching on from beside Jax. 'Jesus, Candice. You're as white as a ghost.'

'Maddie's in the hospital. I've gotta go.'

'What? Is she okay?' I can hear the panic in his voice.

'I don't know. Sophia said she was in getting an X-ray.'

'Fuck.'

'I'm sorry, Jax. I've gotta go.'

'I'm coming with you. You're in no state to drive.'

I'm not going to argue with him. I need him right now. 'Okay.'

'Carter,' Jax says, turning his attention to him. 'Get Gus to finish this job. Can you watch the front counter for me?'

'Of course.'

'I'm sorry, bro,' Jax says, apologising to his client.

'It's all right, mate,' the man replies. 'It's an emergency, I understand. Hope it all works out.'

'Come.' Jax places his hand on the small of my back, hastily guiding me out of the room. The moment we're on the street, he steps towards the kerb.

'What are you doing?' I ask. 'I need to get to her.'

'Flagging down a taxi, it'll be quicker.'

'Okay. Good idea.' At least he's thinking straight. I'm struggling to hold myself together.

'Christ, you're shaking,' he says when we're seated in the back of a cab. 'Come here.' Draping his arm over my shoulder, he pulls me to him. The moment I rest my head against his chest, I start to cry. 'She's gonna be all right.'

I hope so.

The nurse lets us through the doors in emergency, directing us to the examination rooms. The moment I hear Maddie screaming, 'No, no, no!' I break into a run. I can tell by the pitch of her voice that she's hysterical. Rushing into the room, I find Sophia standing next to the bed. Her face is wet with tears. The doctor is on the other side, trying to plaster Maddie's arm. It must be broken.

'Thank God you're here,' Sophia whispers.

Reaching for her hand, I give it a comforting squeeze. I know she'd be feeling terrible.

'I'm here, baby,' I say to Maddie. My eyes frantically scan her body. Apart from the swollen wrist, she appears to be okay. It's a relief.

'Sissy,' she cries, as I put an arm around her. 'I hurt.'

'Sissy's here,' I say, kissing the top of her head. 'You're gonna be okay, baby girl.'

'What happened?' Jax asks Sophia.

'I only looked away for a second. I was replying to a text about a job, and she fell off the monkey bars. I feel terrible.' Covering her face with her hands, she starts to sob. 'I'm so sorry.'

'You have nothing to be sorry about,' Jax says. 'It was an accident, Sophia. Accidents happen. You're a great mother, your girls are lucky to have you.'

Jax is right, she is a good mother, and we are lucky. Moving closer, he puts his arm around her shoulder for comfort. I'm glad he's here to deal with her, because it allows me to focus my attention on Maddie.

'I need to apply the cast,' the doctor informs me.

'No,' Maddie screams when he reaches for her arm. The poor thing is beside herself. She's too little to understand. It's heartbreaking to watch.

'So it's broken?' I ask.

'Yes. She has a small fracture in her wrist. If I can't plaster her arm this way, we'll have to sedate her.'

I don't want them to do that. I glance over my shoulder at Sophia and Jax. I'm sure they can see the despair on my face because Jax lets go of Sophia and comes to stand beside me. His attention is focused on Maddie, but his hand reaches for mine and he interlaces our fingers.

'Hey, Peanut,' he says, softly.

'I broken, Jax.'

Aww. As if my heart wasn't already hurting enough.

'I know, but you need to let the doctor fix you so you don't hurt anymore.' Extending his free arm, he tenderly runs his fingers over her blonde curls. 'You know, when I was a little boy, not much older than you are, I broke my arm too,' he says, letting go of my hand and sitting on the edge of the bed.

Maddie stops crying as her teary eyes widen. She sits perfectly still as she listens intently.

'The doctor put plaster on my arm, just like *this* doctor wants to do to you. It will make your arm all better.'

Maddie's quiet, but I can tell when she frowns that she's not going to let this happen without a fight.

'It's just like a bandage, but it's a magic bandage. It sets really hard, like rock. I can even draw Puppy on there for you if you like, and he won't wash off like your tattoo did.'

I grin as I listen to him. Maddie was devastated when her Puppy drawing washed off a few days after Jax had drawn it on her arm, and he knows it. He's using it to sweeten the deal, but I'm still sceptical as to whether he can pull this off. He can deny it all he wants, but he's definitely a cutie-pie. He's always said he'd never have children of his own, that he isn't cut out to be a father. But watching him with Maddie tells me an entirely different story. He's wonderful with her.

''Kay,' Maddie whispers.

This time my eyes widen. I never thought she'd give in that easily. She's a Crawford through and through—stubborn as hell.

'Good girl. It may hurt a little bit, but you're a brave girl. I know you can do this.'

'Me brave.'

'Do you want to sit on my lap while the doctor bandages up your arm?' Jax asks.

I look at Sophia. She has tears in her eyes just like I do. I'm so grateful he's here.

'Maybe the doctor can put a small bandage on Puppy's arm too.'

Maddie nods before climbing onto Jax's lap. He softly kisses her hair. It makes my heart sing and break all at once.

Have I made the biggest mistake of my life?

FIFTEEN

CANDICE

'LET ME TAKE THOSE FOR YOU,' CARTER SAYS WHEN I ENTER the shop carrying the groceries I've just bought.

'It's only two bags, I can manage,' I reply with an eye roll. I love that the guys I work with are gentlemen, but I'm not a damn invalid. 'Thank you for the offer, though.'

'Give 'em here,' Carter snaps, walking around the counter and snatching them out of my hand. I've noticed he hasn't been himself today. I know he's still struggling with his decision to walk away from the love of his life, but he seems happier since her father tracked him down. 'Where do you want them?'

'They're for Brian, so out in the garage.'

I follow him out the back. 'How's your new place going?' I ask as he helps me stack all the food into the small fridge. Brian doesn't hang around during the day, but he continues to sleep here every night. He keeps the place tidy, and always makes the bed before he leaves. His mug and plate are washed in the small basin in the corner, and placed back on the shelf. What really breaks my heart though is the small pile of loose change I find on top of the fridge each day. He still spends his days begging, so he can give every cent he earns to Jax. It isn't much, but it's important to him to contribute. He's a proud man, so this situation wouldn't be easy for him.

When I first told Jax about the money Brian was leaving, he wouldn't have a bar of it. But Brian refused to take it back. That's when Jax asked me to buy a moneybox. I place the coins in it each day. Knowing Jax, he'll find a way to give it all back to Brian.

Jax has me replenish the food for Brian a few times a week with a variety of different things: fruit, bread, snacks and bottles of water; everything he needs to get him through, things he can take with him while he's out on the street. Sophia has been saving all our leftovers for him too. She even bought him a small microwave to reheat them. Everyone seems to be getting in on the act now.

'The apartment's small, but it's mine,' Carter replies. One thing I've learnt since Carter started working here is he doesn't have much to say. He's very closed off, which is sad.

'Are you okay?' I ask. He can try to hide it all he wants, but there's something up with him today.

'Yep.'

'Come on, Carter, I'm not blind. Is it Indiana? Trust me when I say she'll always have a place in your heart, but in time it does get easier.'

'You sound like you're speaking from experience.'

'You could say that.' I've never told him about my history with Jax. 'You know that night I came to your house?'

'Yes.'

'No offence, but I only came because I was trying to forget someone else.'

He chuckles. 'No offence taken. I kinda got the impression you weren't too keen on being there.'

'You did not,' I say, bumping my shoulder into his. I practically threw myself at him.

'Even though you were acting like a seductress.'

I laugh out loud. 'I was not.'

'You were so. I have that effect on people . . . I'm irresistible.'

'Whatever.'

Carter stops what he's doing and makes eye contact with me. 'You looked terrified when I pulled you through the window. You were trying to be all cool, but you didn't fool me. I hate to break it to ya, but you can't act for shit.'

'Fuck off,' I say, pushing him, and he laughs. It's good to see. He doesn't smile often, but when he does—wow.

'So tell me . . . are you over that guy yet?'

I bow my head. 'No. Not by a long shot.'

'That's fucked up.' He awkwardly taps my back in an attempt to comfort me. Carter doesn't seem like the affectionate type, so if that's the best he's got, I'll take it. When he notices me wipe a tear from my eye, he doesn't hesitate to pull me into a hug.

'I'm just as pathetic as you,' I say sarcastically, as I sniffle.

'Hey, speak for yourself. There's nothing pathetic about me.'

'Except that we're both pining for people we know we can never have.'

'That doesn't make us pathetic, Candice. It makes us selfless. If you love someone enough to let them go, and all that bullshit.'

He's quiet for a few minutes before he finally speaks. 'It's my eighteenth birthday today.'

'What? No way!'

'I've been thinking about my mum today. It would be hard for her, not having me around.'

'Are you close to her?'

'For seventeen years, we were all the other had.' He sighs. 'That was until she married that fuckwit.'

'Why don't you call her?' I suggest, running my hand down his arm.

'No. I can't go back there. Things are better off the way they are.'

'Well, that's a decision only you can make.'

Letting me go, he steps back. 'Anyway, enough about me, how's your little sister going?'

I know he's just trying to divert the conversation away from himself, but I let it be. I'm happy he opened up to me, even if it was just a little.

'She's going okay. She's a trooper. Jax has drawn pictures all over her plaster and she loves it. They struggled to get that thing on her, and now I'm starting to think they're going to have a fight on their hands to remove it.'

Every time I think about the way Jax was with Maddie that day, my heart goes all mushy. She cried the whole time, but she let them do it. Jax didn't let her go once. On the way to the car, she fell asleep in his arms. It was the sweetest thing ever.

••••

I'm standing on the footpath outside the restaurant when Carter's taxi pulls up to the kerb. It took some doing, but I managed to talk him into coming out to dinner with me tonight. It's his birthday, so he can't spend it alone.

'Hey,' he says when he gets out.

'Well, don't you look handsome?'

'Would you expect anything less?' He chuckles.

I roll my eyes. He's gorgeous and he knows it.

'Here, happy birthday.' I pass him the gift bag in my hand.

'You got me a gift?'

'Of course, it's your birthday! It's not every day you turn eighteen.'

'You shouldn't have, but thank you,' he says.

'Well, are you going to open it?' I ask as he stares at the bag in his hand. I got him a custom black leatherbound sketchpad, similar to the one I gave Jax before he left for uni. It's not as nice as Jax's, but it was the best I could do on short notice. There was no time to get it embossed, so I bought some fancy gold-leaf alphabet stickers instead. I put Carter across the top and *Indi Ink* underneath it, the words really pop with the black background.

'Fuck,' he whispers when he pulls out the sketchpad.

'Jax said you're picking things up really fast. Who knows, one day you may open your own parlour and name it after your girl.'

My heart breaks a little when he raises his hand and wipes his eye. 'Thank you,' he says, pulling me into a crushing embrace. 'For the present, for tonight, for believing in me . . . You're a good friend.'

'And you're a good guy, Carter. Good things happen to good people, never forget that.'

He gives me another squeeze before letting go. 'Enough of this mushy shit. Let's go eat.'

I smile as I link my arm through his. His birthday surprise awaits.

JAX

My eyes are fixed on the door when they enter the restaurant. Candice has her arm linked through Carter's, and she's gazing up at him. She's wearing that smile she usually reserves for me. I hate that. Seeing her so happy with another man is like a knife being plunged into my chest. Just like earlier today, when I stumbled across them in the garage, wrapped in each other's arms. It took every ounce of strength I had to turn and walk away when all I wanted to do was pry them apart. I held her just like that only a few weeks ago—and in the same fucking spot. I've been trying my best to keep them separated since Carter started working for me. And he's never been at Candice's house when I'm there, so I was starting to get the impression that whatever they had was over. Or maybe I was just hoping. That's probably what they wanted me to believe.

I've gotten to know Carter well recently and the truth is, I like him a lot. I want to hate him, but I can't. He's a good guy. He has no idea how I feel about Candice, so I can't be angry at him for having the balls to go after what he wants. Who wouldn't want her?

Despite my internal turmoil, I smile the moment he notices us. His whole face lights up. Candice worked her arse off today to organise this surprise. She got him a cake, and there's a large number eighteen silver foil balloon sitting in the middle of the table. Our work colleagues, Gus and Shane, are here, as well as Sophia and Maddie. I did invite Brian, but he declined.

'Happy birthday, buddy,' I say, when I stand and shake his hand.

'Thanks, man. I can't believe you're all here.' His eyes move around the table. 'I didn't know Candice was going to tell everyone.' He gives her a funny look, so I come to her defence.

'She just wanted to make your birthday special.'

'I know.' Lifting his hand, he ruffles Candice's hair. He chuckles when she slaps it away. I bend and retrieve his gift from beside my chair, passing it to him.

'Shit, not you too. I didn't expect gifts,' he says hesitantly, as he takes it.

'I wanted to.' And that's the truth. It's his birthday—I know what it feels like to be forgotten on your birthday. I don't want Carter to experience the sheer loneliness I felt the day I turned twenty-one. Plus, he's been working his arse off at the shop, so he deserves to be rewarded.

After thanking me, he tucks the box under his arm and makes his way around the table, shaking hands and thanking everyone for coming. I'm surprised when he seats himself with the boys instead of next to Candice. And I smile on the inside when she plonks her sweet little arse next to me. I'm in the middle of my two favourite girls, Candice on one side and Maddie on the other. Even Puppy has his own seat, on the other side of Maddie. The waitress set a place for the stuffed toy, which pleased Maddie no end. She's been giving him sips of an imaginary drink while we've been waiting for Carter to get here. I'm not gonna lie, watching her was the sweetest thing ever.

Now that the guest of honour has arrived, I order a round of drinks and some appetisers while we decide what to order for our mains.

'Open your present from Jax, Carter,' Candice calls out across the table.

I have a feeling he's going to like what I got him—he'd be crazy not to. As soon as Candice informed me it was his birthday, I knew I had to get it. Gus and Shane put in and bought Carter his own stool for the parlour, but it won't be delivered until later next week. They're getting his name embossed around the perimeter of the seat.

'You bought me my own tattoo machine?' Carter says, a shocked expression on his face.

'I did.'

'Fu—,' he starts to say until his eyes land on Maddie; she's a parrot, and copies everything. After opening the case, his face lights up for the second time. It's actually nice to see. More often than not, he's broody and serious, so I'm enjoying this more relaxed side of him.

'This is amazing.' He walks around the table and shakes my hand. 'Thanks, man.'

'Wow! A Micky Sharpz?' Gus chimes in, as he picks up the case and studies its contents. 'Fuck me. Why didn't I get one of these when I started working for you?'

'Because you're a pain in the arse,' I say, chuckling. 'If I spoil you too much, I'll never get rid of you.'

'Very funny, arsehole,' Gus snaps, and we all laugh. Gus sits there with his arms crossed and a scowl on his face. He's the biggest shit stirrer I know. He can dish it out, but he certainly can't take it.

Maddie even joins in. I'm pretty sure she has no idea what we're laughing at, but she's cracking up nevertheless. 'Arsehole,' she mumbles from beside me, but thankfully I'm the only one who hears. I've never noticed before how cool little people are. Without even trying, she entertains the hell out of me.

We stay at the restaurant for the next few hours, eating and drinking. Everyone seems to be having a good time. I've seen a different side to Carter tonight, and I like it.

'I really should get Maddie home,' says Sophia. 'It's way past her bedtime.'

'No,' she snaps, making me chuckle.

'Don't you "no" me, young lady,' Sophia says as she stands, lifting Maddie into her arms.

'Jax,' she cries, trying to wiggle out of Sophia's hold as her arms stretch out to me.

'How about I walk you out to the car?' I say, taking her from Sophia.

'Puppy,' she squeals as she reaches down to the seat where he's still sitting.

'We should hit the club,' Shane says, when I return from walking Sophia and Maddie out. 'The night's still young.'

'Fuck, yeah,' Gus agrees. 'Are you up for it, birthday boy? You're of legal age now.'

'I'm in,' Carter replies.

'Count me in too,' says Candice, rubbing her hands together. 'I haven't been clubbing in such a long time.'

I'm not really in the mood to go out, but if she's going, so am I. No way am I leaving her alone with these guys—someone needs to be there to make sure she gets home safely.

'How about you, boss?' Gus asks.

'Yeah, I'm in.'

Candice, Carter and I climb into the back of a taxi, while Shane and Gus jump in another. We head into the city to the Ivy bar. If this is going to be Carter's first night on the town as a fully-fledged adult, we may as well do it in style.

As we walk down George Street towards the nightclub, Gus comes up beside me and slaps me on the back. 'Seriously, that kid's making you soft, boss.'

The comment is annoying—there's nothing soft about me. 'Fuck off. She is not.'

He chuckles. 'Deny it all you want, but Candice's little sister has you wrapped around her little finger.' He lifts his hand and wiggles his pinkie in my face for added effect. I immediately slap it away. 'You're like putty in her chubby little hands. Maybe you should knock up one of your hot babes and have a kid of your own. You certainly have plenty to choose from.'

He laughs like he's just cracked a joke, and I want to punch him. Candice is right beside me. Why did he say that in front of her?

'Shut up, fucker. I'm not cut out to be a father—nor will I ever be. Fuck that shit.' As soon as the words are out of my mouth, Candice leaves my side and catches up to Carter. Fuck.

I smile when we enter the Ivy. I love this place and come here often. The atmosphere is always buzzing and the chicks are plentiful. Not that I'll be going there tonight, not with Candice present. We get a table by the pool and I can't help but feel disappointed when Candice sits in the spot furthest away from me. My eyes are fixed on her, but she purposely won't look my way.

I hate it when she's upset with me. Fucking Gus and his big mouth. I should tell him to watch his mouth around her, but I can't without giving my feelings for her away. That cocksucker would never let me live it down.

'Who's up for shots?' I ask loudly, so everyone can hear me over the music. I was going to take it easy tonight, but that's all changed now. When I get a unanimous yes, I stand and head to the bar. I only make it halfway before a pretty brunette steps in front of me.

'Hi, handsome,' she says, running her finger in a line down my chest. 'Are you here alone?'

Any other time I'd be all over this, but not tonight. 'I'm here with friends.'

'No girlfriend?' she asks, raising one of her perfectly shaped eyebrows.

'No girlfriend.'

'You wanna come sit with me and my friends?' She points to a group of women sitting in one of the cabanas on the other side of the pool.

'Maybe later.' I shrug. More than likely not, but I need to keep my options open.

'I look forward to it,' she whispers in my ear, as her hand comes to rest on my crotch. She gives it a small squeeze then walks away.

I briefly glance over my shoulder before I continue to the bar, and I see the boys are all talking and laughing about something, but Candice's eyes are on me. Of course she'd choose to look at me now.

'Can I get ten shots of tequila?' I ask the bartender when I reach the bar. Two shots each will help kick-start the night. I watch as she lines them all up on a tray. 'Do you have any lemon wedges?'

'We sure do,' she says, smiling. She grabs a handful out of a plastic container, placing them on top of a napkin on the tray along with a salt shaker. Handing her a hundred-dollar note, I pick up the tray and make my way back to the table.

'Ladies first,' I say, placing two shots in front of Candice. I move to the birthday boy next. I don't even know if he's a drinker. Gus, Shane and I all had a few beers with dinner, but he ordered a Coke. I'll have to keep an eye on him and make sure he doesn't get shitfaced. The last thing I need is a puking lightweight on my hands.

After handing Gus and Shane their shots, I take a seat, placing the tray with the lemon and salt in the centre of the table. Candice is the first to reach for it.

'What is that for?' Carter asks.

'Lick, sip, suck,' Candice replies.

'Sounds like fun,' Carter chuckles. I see a smirk cross his face and it pisses me off.

'Let me show you.'

I'm relieved when Candice places the salt on the inside of her own wrist. I would've lost my shit if I had to watch her lick it off him. I feel my dick twitch and I have to fight back a growl when she slowly licks a path over the salt.

'That was fucking hot, Pinkie,' Gus says.

I'd have to agree. I still remember exactly what her mouth felt like wrapped around my cock. Her oral skills are exceptional. Just thinking about it is making me hard. Christ, why did I let my mind go there?

She downs the shot before picking up a wedge of lemon and placing it between her lips. What I wouldn't give to be that piece of lemon right now. She has the whole table captivated. I don't think she realises how sexy she is.

For the next few hours, we drink and laugh. It's turning out to be a great night. Until it all goes to shit, that is. As soon as 'Low' by Flo Rida starts playing, Candice yells, 'Oh, I love this song, come dance with me, birthday boy.'

'Fuck that,' Carter says. 'I don't dance.'

'Come on, you pussy. Live a little,' she retorts.

I have to agree with Carter, I don't dance either. I save all my moves for the bedroom—that's where I perform best.

Candice stands, reaching for Carter's hand. 'I won't take no for an answer. Come on, it'll be fun.'

'I don't wanna,' he whines. I kinda feel bad for him when she tries to pull him off the chair. I know how stubborn Candice is, she won't give up until she has him on the dance floor.

'Fuck,' I hear him mumble after a minute or so of her tugging on his arm. Gus lets out a boisterous laugh as she drags Carter to the dance floor. I don't envy him.

'He's just standing there,' Gus roars, slapping his hand down on his leg with amusement.

I don't notice. I can't seem to take my eyes off Candice as she shakes her sweet arse around Carter.

'Pinkie can move.'

She can. I remember years ago, sitting in a dark corner at one of our school dances watching her all night. It sounds a little stalkerish, but I've always got a kick out of seeing Candice carefree and happy. She's like a breath of fresh air.

The moment the song is over, Carter turns and hightails it back to the table. We all laugh. Candice stands there dumbfounded for a few seconds before some cocksucker comes out of nowhere and pulls her into his arms. A smug smile appears on my face as I await her attack, but disappointment floods me when she smiles up at him instead. He draws her closer and she slides her arms around his neck. What the hell? The old Candice would've gone all ninja on him and busted his balls by now.

I swear I see fucking red when his hands move down to her arse, giving it a squeeze. My head snaps to Carter. 'You gonna let that fucker manhandle your girl like that?' I ask.

'What? She ain't my girl.'

Really? That's news to me. 'Since when?'

'Since always. Did you think Candice and I were getting it on? We're friends, that's all.'

I shrug because right now I don't know what to think. I know she went to his house, and I saw them in the garage, out the back of the shop. I'm not blind. *Friends with benefits.* The thought of Carter using Candice as a casual lay angers me even more. She deserves better than that.

My gaze moves back to the dance floor. I shouldn't watch her dancing with that cocksucker, but I can't seem to look away. He keeps whispering shit in her ear, and every time she laughs, my blood pressure rises. Why do I torture myself like this?

A few minutes later, my heart drops into the pit of my stomach when the inevitable happens. He slides his hand into her soft, apple-scented pink hair as his mouth bears down on hers. The grip on my beer tightens to the point my knuckles turn white. I'm surprised the glass doesn't shatter in my hands.

'Fuck this,' I say, pushing my chair back and standing. I've seen enough.

'Calm down, boss,' Gus says. 'She's just dancing.'

Ignoring him, I make a beeline straight for the bar. When I pass Candice on the dance floor, I have to control the urge I have to punch that cock right in his pretty-boy face. How dare he put his grubby hands—and mouth—on *my* girl.

As I'm standing in the line waiting to be served, the brunette from earlier slides up beside me.

'Are you having a good night, handsome?'

I almost say, 'Does it fucking look like it?' but I manage to bite my tongue. It wouldn't be fair to take my foul mood out on her, she's done nothing wrong. Instead, I revert back to my old coping mechanism, the only way I've been able to survive up until now. It's a pretty shitty move on my part, but if I stay here, I'm gonna end up in a fight.

'Wanna get out of here?'

'Definitely,' she answers without hesitation.

I reach for her hand. Glancing at the dance floor on my way to the door, I catch a glimpse of Candice. Her eyes follow me across the club. When her gaze moves down to my hand firmly holding the brunette's, her face drops. Really? She was just sucking face with some guy right in front of me. She has no right to be upset.

'Where to?' the taxi driver asks when we're seated in the back of the cab. I wait for her to answer. There's no way I'm taking her back to my place. I've never taken anyone back there—I don't need them knowing where I live. Even though I always make it clear that I'm not interested in anything more than one night, I still get the occasional one who expects more, like they have some kind of magical pussy that's gonna convert me. *Not happening.*

While she rattles off her address, I have a sudden attack of conscience. This tit-for-tat crap needs to stop. We're adults, for Christ's sake.

'Look,' I say, turning to her. 'I've changed my mind. I'm doing this for all the wrong reasons.' Pulling a fifty out of my wallet, I pass it to the driver. 'Take her wherever she needs to go.'

'What? No.' She reaches for my elbow as I open the door of the cab. 'Don't go.'

'I'm sorry,' I say, glancing over my shoulder as I get out of the taxi.

'Arsehole,' she snaps.

I totally deserve that. Shoving my hands in my pockets, I head down the street towards the train station. *I need a fucking cigarette.* I *am* an arsehole for what I just did. I should never have left with her. I only did it to hurt Candice and that was wrong. I can't keep using other women to help get over her.

SIXTEEN

CANDICE

'HOLY SHIT, JAX!' I SHRIEK AS MY EYES SCAN OVER THE PAGE of the newspaper. 'You didn't tell me Brent was getting married!'

'What?' he snaps as he storms towards the counter.

When I hold the paper up, he snatches it out of my hands and reads the small article that accompanies the picture of his brother and his new wife. His parents are standing on either side of them, smiling. It's front and centre of the society section of today's newspaper. I hope he doesn't read the caption under the image: *Malcolm and Penelope Albright, standing proudly with their only son, Brent, and his lovely new wife, Jennifer.*

Jax doesn't say a word, but the look on his face speaks volumes. It breaks my heart.

I gather he knew nothing about this, and I hate that his family have yet again excluded him. Without reading the whole article, he closes the newspaper and slams it down on the desk before returning to his studio.

I flinch when I hear the door of his studio slam. His family suck, and although he's so much better off without them, I can only imagine how much this would hurt. Nobody wants to be rejected, especially by the people who should care about you the most. I know that feeling all too well.

I sit there for a few minutes contemplating what I should do. I wish I hadn't said anything, but he deserved to know. Sliding off my chair, I walk hesitantly down the corridor. If nothing else, I want Jax to know he's not alone. He'll never be alone as long as he has me.

Things have been strained between us since our night out at the Ivy. We had a huge argument the following day, and he's been pulling away from me ever since. Unlike him, I didn't go home with the guy on the dance floor—I never intended to. The kiss was just that—a kiss. It wasn't planned. I'd had too much to drink, and the guy kissed me. That's it. After Jax left, I went back to the table and sat with the boys. I don't think that guy was game enough to come near me after that. We all shared a cab home, and even though I live the furthest away, the boys made sure the driver took me home first.

'Psst,' I hear when I walk past Gus's room. 'What's up the boss's arse?' he whispers.

I roll my eyes as I shoo him away with my hand. 'None of your business. Now get back to work.'

'Yes, ma'am, Pinkie.' I laugh when he salutes me.

'Jax, can I come in?' I ask, knocking on his door.

'Go away.'

I turn the handle anyway and find it locked. Ugh! 'Please, Jax.'

'I don't want to talk about it, Candice.'

I rest my forehead against the door and sigh. As much as I want to comfort him, I have to accept he wants to be alone. 'Okay. I'm here if you change your mind.' I wait for a reply, but it never comes.

My heart is heavy as I walk back to the front counter. Fuck his family. I have to control the urge to ring them and give them a piece of my mind. Jax doesn't deserve to be treated this way.

For the rest of the day, Jax avoids everyone, only emerging from his room to collect his next client. He doesn't even make eye contact with me when he enters reception. He looks totally deflated. I just want to pull him into my arms and tell him how special he is, and how much I love him.

At the end of the day, I stay behind while he cashes up.

'You don't need to hang around,' he says.

'I want to. Jax—'

'Don't,' he says, holding up his hand.

I know what rejection feels like, I've faced it my whole life with my father, but this is so much worse. This is his entire family. I'd be lost without Sophia and Maddie.

'Are you going to come over for dinner tonight?'

'Nope. Not tonight. I'm not really in the mood.'

'Please. I don't want you to be alone,' I plead, gently rubbing my hand down his arm.

'I'll be fine, honestly. I just want to be alone.'

I sigh. 'Okay. If that's what you really want.'

'It is.'

••••

I've tried my best to stay away, giving Jax the space he needed, but I can't do it any longer. He's been occupying my mind ever since I left work. 'Will you make me up a plate of food to take around to Jax?' I ask Sophia while we eat dinner.

'Of course. Why didn't he come tonight? Is he working back?'

'No, he's not working back.' I sigh. 'I'm worried about him. We saw an article in the social pages of the paper today.'

'What about? His father?'

'No, Brent. He got married on the weekend. Jax knew nothing about it.'

'He wasn't invited to his own brother's wedding?' Her eyes widen as she speaks.

'You know what his family are like.'

'Poor Jaxson. He's such a good kid. I never was able to take to his mother. She's a stuck-up bitch, and his father ... ugh ... he's an A-grade arsehole.'

'I know. I think I'll head over to his house after I shower. I don't want him to be alone.'

'Good idea. If anyone can cheer him up, it's you sweetheart.' She smiles as she stands and collects our plates to take to the sink.

Once upon a time I would've believed that, but things between us aren't what they used to be. Our friendship has become very complicated.

'Go and get all dolled up and I'll pack some food for you to take to him.'

'I'm not getting dolled up. Do you want me to bath Maddie before I go?'

'No. I'll do that. Jaxson needs you.'

••••

Butterflies churn in my stomach as I walk down his front path. Please don't let him have a girl inside. I'll die if he does. Although there's been no beauties dropping off his wallet at work lately, that doesn't mean he's not still sleeping his way around Sydney. He's never been one to talk about those kind of things, but the rumour mill was ripe when we were at school. And I occasionally overhear some of the things Gus says.

Jax's car is parked out in the street, and there's a light on inside the house, that's a good sign. I knock and wait, but when nobody comes to the door, I try again.

Just when I'm about to call out his name, I hear him say, 'Hold on a minute.'

My breath hitches the moment he opens the door. He's fresh from a shower and looking sexy as hell. His hair is wet and he hasn't shaved so there's a light stubble across his chin. He's wearing a T-shirt and a pair of sweats, and smells all manly and delicious. Shit. I'm not sure coming here was a good idea. It's one thing to be around him all day at work, but being alone together in his house when all I want to do is jump his bones is dangerous.

His face lights up as soon as he sees me. That expression will never get old. It turns my insides to mush every time.

'I thought you might like some company. Have you eaten? Sophia packed some leftovers for you.' I hold up the basket in my hand and I'm relieved when he steps aside so I can enter.

'No, I haven't,' he says, following me into the kitchen.

'Good.' I place the basket on the breakfast bar and start unpacking.

'You brought alcohol too?' he says, holding up the bottle of Sambuca.

'I did.'

He chuckles. 'I hope you left your cock cups at home.'

'Actually . . .' I pull out a cup and hold it out to him.

'I'm not fucking drinking out of that, Candice.'

'Wait,' I say, digging in the bottom of the basket. 'When Sophia, Maddie and I went to Vegas last year, I bought this.' I hold up a shot glass that has a pair of boobs on the front. 'I don't know why I bought it because you weren't even in my life then, but I saw it and immediately thought of you, of that nigh—' I stop talking. Tonight is not the time to rehash that. I came here hoping to cheer him up, not depress him further. One day I hope we can sit down and talk about it, but right now, it's still too raw.

He laughs as he picks up the shot glass. 'A titty cup. Now that's more like it. I love it.' He's smiling when his gaze moves to me. It's the first genuine smile I've seen since earlier today. 'Thank you for coming here tonight. I thought I wanted to be alone, but I was wrong. I'm glad you're here.'

'That's what friends are for right?'

His smile drops away, and he doesn't reply.

'Let me heat you up some food.'

'The food can wait. I'd rather get stuck into this, if you don't mind.' He picks up the bottle of Sambuca and removes the lid, lifting the bottle to his nose and inhaling. 'The last time I drank Sambuca was . . .'

He doesn't finish, and I know why. That damn night will forever haunt us. It was the last time I drank Sambuca too. I don't know what possessed me to buy it on the way over here. It was always my drink of choice back in the day, but I wish I'd picked something else now.

He fills his shot glass, followed by mine. 'Titties up.' He downs the liquid in one gulp and refills his glass. 'Drink up. Don't tell me you're going soft in your old age.'

'Fuck off. I'm not old. I'm a year younger than you.'

'Well, come on then.'

'I drove here. So maybe I shouldn't.' I'm totally rethinking this whole idea now. I'm not going soft, I just don't think us drinking together is a good idea. We both know what happened last time. One of us needs to keep a clear head.

'You can get a cab.'

I shrug.

'I'm not drinking on my own, Candice.' He places his shot glass on the counter.

'Fine,' I say, picking up mine and bringing it to my lips. 'Penises up.'

'That's my girl.' He refills my glass before drinking his second shot. 'Wanna go sit in the lounge room?'

'Sure. Just let me put the food in the fridge. You really should eat before you drink though.'

'Yes, Mum.'

I poke my tongue out at him as I gather up the containers. There's enough food to last him a week. Sophia always cooks like she's feeding an army.

I grab the bottle of Sambuca when I'm done. 'You can carry the glasses.'

'I'm not touching your cock cup.'

'What? Seriously, Jax, you have issues.'

'I have issues? That's rich coming from someone who collects penises. Besides, I don't want cock germs.'

'Hello, you have a cock. Or did you forget that?'

He clears his throat before snatching the bottle of Sambuca out of my hand. 'You can carry your own damn glass.'

Shaking my head, I follow him into the lounge room. 'Pussy,' I mumble under my breath.

'Hey. I heard that.'

I snicker because he was meant to hear it. Once he's seated, I take a seat on the opposite end of the sofa. Distance is always a good thing when we're alone, especially when there's alcohol involved. I've gotta say, though, it's nice to be here with him. It's just like old times.

We down a few more shots and seem to relax as we laugh and talk about everything and nothing. I've missed my best friend.

'So, I didn't know you went to Vegas.'

There's a lot he doesn't know. So much happened in the time we were separated. It was really tough.

'We spent a few weeks in LA. We took Maddie to Disneyland.' That was the excuse Sophia used to get me to go with them, but I know it was her way of trying to bring me out of the dark hole I'd fallen into. 'Since we were so close to Vegas, Sophia wanted to visit there before we left to come home.'

'I bet Peanut loved Disneyland,' he says.

'She did, but she was too young to really appreciate it. I'd love to take her back when she's a bit older.'

'You really love her don't you?'

'I adore her. She's . . .' I let my words drift off. *She's my life* is not what Jax needs to hear.

'She's cute. I bet you looked exactly like that when you were a little girl.'

I shrug and lift my glass to my mouth. 'The Crawford genes are strong.'

'They certainly are.'

'Why do you call Maddie "Peanut"?' I ask. I don't really feel comfortable talking about this with him. I have no filter when I drink, and I don't want to slip up.

'Snoopy . . . Peanut,' he replies like it's obvious.

'She loves that damn Puppy.'

'Did she tell you we lost it the day I looked after her?'

'No, she didn't. She would've been devastated.'

'She was. Worst fucking hour of my life,' he says.

I feel for him, because I know how upset she would've been.

'She did tell me that you hosed the shit off her arse though.' I laugh. 'What the hell were you thinking?'

'Seriously. What do you feed that kid? It was either hose her arse or vomit all over her. I thought the hose was the best option.'

I burst out laughing. I remember how much I struggled changing her nappies when she was first born. I got used to it over time.

'Fill me up,' I say, holding my shot glass out to him. After topping up mine, he refills his own. The alcohol seems to be working, but it's only a short-term solution to this problem. 'I'm sorry that your family let you down again.'

He shrugs. 'As far as they're concerned I no longer exist, so it doesn't really surprise me.'

'I hate them. I hate that they treat you like this.'

A sad smile tugs at his lips. 'It is what it is,' he says. 'I should be used to it by now.'

My heart hurts for him. He tries to brush it off, but I know it bothers him. Scooting closer to him, I place my hand on his leg. 'It would've been a terrible wedding anyway. Your mum, your dad, Brent, and all their stuck-up guests.' I shiver just thinking about it. 'You know as well as I do, you would've had a terrible time.'

'It would've been worse than torture,' he says, and I have to agree. Resting his empty glass on his upper thigh, he slumps back into the sofa. 'It would've been nice to be invited though.'

'Jax,' I say, sighing, 'fuck them. They don't deserve you anyway. You'll always have us. We all love you. You know that right?'

'I really struggled after I left, Candice. I was so lost without you.' When his voice cracks, I wrap him in my arms.

'I felt like that too. It was like a part of me was missing. I don't want to ever feel like that again.'

He slides his arms around my waist and squeezes me tight. 'You mean the world to me. You're all I have.'

I run my hand down the side of his face. 'You have a beautiful soul, Jaxson Albright, and if your family can't see that, then they're all fucked in the head.'

I see the corners of his lips turn up before his beautiful chocolate eyes lock with mine. My heart starts to race, because I know that look. It's the look he always gives me just before we kiss. The wise thing to do would be to pull away, but I can't. I want this so much. I haven't stopped thinking about his lips since he kissed me in the garage. He's an exceptionally good kisser. Every time his mouth touches mine, something inside me awakens. It's electrifying, sending currents shooting throughout my body, like every nerve ending comes alive.

Nobody has ever been able to make me feel the way he does. *Nobody*. I made out with a ton of guys when I was in high school, and I've kissed Carter, and that guy at the club a few weeks back, and neither of them came close to making me feel a fraction of what Jax does.

Jax's face moves closer to mine, but I don't close my eyes. I don't want to miss a second of this. I inhale a deep breath and hold it as his mouth inches a little closer.

When he freezes, disappointment floods me.

He sighs before he closes his eyes and rests his forehead against mine. 'You drive me crazy, Candice. I want to kiss you so bad right now.'

'Well, kiss me then,' I breathe.

'I don't want to lose you again,' he whispers.

'You're never going to lose me,' I say, cupping his face in my hands. 'Never. I lost you once, and I won't let it happen again. I can't live without you in my life, Jax.'

'Candice,' he murmurs as his hand slides into my hair. 'Why can't I resist you?'

I can't answer that question because he has the same effect on me. I wanted him from the moment I laid eyes on him.

For a split second I think he's going to say we can't do this, but then he surprises me by pulling my face forward. The moment our lips collide, my heart starts to sing. He groans into my mouth when I deepen the kiss. Sliding his hands down to my waist, he lifts me onto his lap, so I'm straddling him. He draws my body flush with his, and I feel his erection pressing against me. I'm filled with conflicting emotions. I've spent the last three years fantasising about being with him again, but it also frightens the hell out of me. What if he runs again? I know my heart couldn't take another blow like that.

Pulling out of the kiss, his hooded eyes meet mine. 'I want you so bad,' he says.

'I want you too, but I'm scared, Jax.'

'Don't be. You know I'd never hurt you.'

Tears sting my eyes. 'You've already done that, remember.'

'I'm sorry.' His grip on me tightens. 'Hurting you is the last thing I ever wanted.'

'If we do this, are you going to run from me again?'

'No. I need you in my life.' There is so much conviction in his words.

'Make love to me, Jax. I don't know what tomorrow will bring, but I want to feel that connection with you again.'

'I don't make love, Candice, I fuck.'

'Well, fuck me then.'

A primal growl rumbles deep in his chest as he grinds his rock-hard cock against the coarse fabric of my jeans. I slide my trembling fingers into his hair as my mouth crashes into his. Are we really going to do this? I may be making the biggest mistake of my life, but I'm not going to over-analyse the situation. I want to enjoy this moment with him, because it may very well be our last.

We make out for what seems like an eternity. Our hands, our mouths, our tongues are everywhere. We can't seem to get enough of each other.

Then he suddenly stands, lifting me with him. 'Wrap your legs around me,' he says as he carries me towards his bedroom.

I'm trembling with anticipation. His fingers dig painfully into my arse as my mouth nips and sucks on his neck.

'I've waited years to have you again, and I can't deny myself any longer. *I crave you*, Candice.' The look he gives me as he lays me down on the bed is so hot, I swear my panties disintegrate. 'By the time I'm finished with you, even the neighbours will need a cigarette.'

Bring it on, Mr Albright. Bring it on!

His warm breath dances over my skin, making it pebble with goose bumps, as his tongue travels a path up my neck. He sucks my earlobe into his mouth and I moan. 'I want you like I've never wanted anything in my life,' he whispers. I swear his words alone are going to make me orgasm.

'Jax,' I whimper as my hands fist in his hair. 'Are we really doing this?'

Drawing back, his haunted eyes meet mine. 'Please don't tell me you're having second thoughts?'

'I want this, I'm just . . . scared.'

'Scared of what?'

'It's been so long. I haven't been with anyone else since you.'

'Jesus,' he breathes. 'What about Carter, and that fucker at the club?'

'Nothing happened. I kissed them . . . that's all.'

His eyes search mine. Is he doubting what I'm saying? Just because he sleeps around, doesn't mean we're all like that.

'You really haven't been with another man since me?'

'No.'

He exhales a large breath as he pushes off the mattress and stands. 'Maybe this isn't a good idea.'

'What? No,' I say, sitting up and reaching for him. 'Please, Jax.' I can't believe I'm begging him. Why aren't I good enough for him?

'Why?'

'Why what?'

'Why haven't you been with anyone else?'

'Because the only person I've ever wanted is you.' I sigh as I look down at the floor. I can't bear to see the expression on his face.

I hadn't meant to confess that and I can't believe I'm even putting myself out there like this. I'm such an idiot. I'm only asking for more heartache. Humiliation consumes me.

'Maybe I should go.'

He pauses briefly, but when I go to stand, he steps forward, stopping me. 'Don't.' Placing his finger under my chin, he lifts my face until my gaze meets his. 'Stay . . . please.' He places his lips tenderly on mine. 'I want you to stay.' Pushing me back onto the mattress, his body settles over mine. 'I need you, Candice.'

Tears rise to my eyes when his hand caresses the side of my face.

'I need you more than I need air.'

Grabbing the hem of his shirt, I slide it up his back. I need to feel his skin against mine. He reaches around, grabbing the neck of the shirt, and pulls it over his head. Leaning back on his haunches, he sits me up and removes my top as well. I smile when his gaze moves down to my pink lace bra.

'You're so beautiful,' he whispers, placing his lips on the swell of one of my breasts. 'You have the most magnificent tits.'

My hands move to my back as I unclasp my bra. I want his mouth on me . . . all of me. 'Jax,' I whimper when he palms my breasts in his hands and swirls his tongue around one of my nipples before sucking it into his mouth. I love how he makes my body feel. Scooting off the bed and onto his knees, he reaches for the waistband of my jeans.

'Are you sure you want to do this?'

Doesn't he realise how much I want him?

'Are we still going to be friends in the morning?' I'm not sure I could stop this either way, but I need to know before this goes any further.

'Of course.'

'Then yes, I'm sure.'

'One night with no restrictions,' he says.

'One night with no restrictions,' I repeat, smiling.

'We'll worry about tomorrow . . . tomorrow.'

'Tomorrow is a new day. What's important is the here and now.' We both smile.

He brushes his lips against mine before pulling back to go to work unbuttoning my jeans. His eyes briefly dart up to mine, and the wicked smile he gives me holds so much promise.

'It's not going to be easy, but we'll find a way, we always do,' he says.

I know this is going to complicate things, but I'm willing to take that chance. I've dreamt about this moment for so long. He slides my pink Converse sneakers off my feet. My body is trembling as he peppers lingering kisses down the length of my legs, removing my jeans as he goes. When he's done, he leans back and admires his handiwork. I'm left in nothing but a tiny pair of pink lace panties.

'Do you even realise how sexy you are?' he whispers.

I use this time to drink him in too. He's so breathtakingly beautiful. I haven't seen him without a shirt on in years. His strong arms and broad shoulders are bigger than I remember. His abs are so ripped. He's all man now. Every delicious inch of him. He's perfection in every sense of the word.

My gaze moves to the tattoos across his chest. I've never seen them before.

'Is that a tattoo of a piece of pink candy sitting over your heart?'

He pauses before chuckling nervously. 'What can I say? I love pink candy.'

My heart starts to race. Does that tattoo have anything to do with me, or is it wishful thinking on my part? I want to ask him, but I'd feel silly if he said no. I'm distracted from my thoughts when his thumbs hook in the waistband of his sweats. My eyes travel down to his waist and my tongue moistens my lips as he reveals his delicious V. I gasp the moment he pulls his pants and boxer briefs down around his hips.

'Oh my God.' My eyes widen as my hand covers my mouth. 'You didn't.'

'If my memory serves me correctly, you were the one who said my cock should come with a warning label.'

I did say that, but it was in jest. Now he has words tattooed across his pelvis in fancy cursive writing: *Warning choking hazard*.

Below the phrase is an arrow pointing straight to his dick. I remove my hand from my mouth and burst out laughing.

'I love it.'

'I thought of you when I had it done. It reminded me of . . .' Again his words trail off. Why are we incapable of talking about that night? Maybe it's because it was the night that changed everything.

Jax may be the only person I've ever slept with, but I'm not completely innocent. I've seen a few penises in my time, and he really does have a spectacular example, huge and particularly beautiful. He could be a penis model if there were such a job, that's how perfect it is.

'You take my breath away,' I breathe as I scoot to the edge of the bed, placing my hands on his hips. I lick my lips and look up at him through my eyelashes. It's been so long since I've done anything like this, but I'm sure it's a skill you never forget, like riding a bike.

'Candice,' he groans as his hands slide into my hair. 'To this day I still remember what your lips felt like wrapped around my cock. I can't tell you how many times I've jacked off to that memory.'

I love that. After he left, I often thought about our night together, but in the end I had to let it go. It was too painful.

His whole body trembles when I lick a line up the length of his shaft, before circling my tongue around the crown. 'You have a beautiful cock, Jax.'

'Sweet Jesus,' he whimpers as I take him in my mouth. 'I don't even want to know where you learnt to suck cock like this.'

It's not like I took blowjob lessons. I'm just a natural.

I put everything I have into this moment as I work him over with my mouth, my tongue and my hands. Within minutes, his grip on my head tightens.

'Fuck, I'm gonna blow already.' He tries to pull back, but I hold tight. He didn't let me finish the job last time. I want to taste him.

I look up at him just as he throws his head back and groans loudly. I moan around his cock when I feel his hot cum hit the back of my throat. Pleasing him like this is such a turn-on. I don't stop until I've milked him of every last drop.

Without speaking a word, he places his hands on my shoulders and pushes me back onto the mattress. He hastily rips my panties down my legs, never once taking his eyes off me. His are the actions of a desperate man as his body moves to cover mine.

'I have no words for your spectacular oral skills.' He's smiling as he shakes his head. 'No fucking words.'

His mouth and hands are everywhere, but I'm not complaining. It's been a long time since I've felt like this. I haven't noticed just how dead I've been inside until now. With every look, every kiss and every touch, he's slowly bringing my damaged heart back to life.

'I need to taste your sweet pussy,' he says. The last orgasm I had was three and a half years ago. I'm not sure if my body will be able to take it.

He moves to the side of the bed, lifting my legs and placing my feet on each of his shoulders. Using his hands, he spreads my knees wide. There's a look of appreciation on his face when he stares down at me. It's surprisingly comforting, making all my insecurities vanish.

The moment his lips come into contact with my sensitive flesh, I'm lost. Lost in the ecstasy that is Jaxson Albright's mouth.

'Jax,' I whimper as my hands clutch his hair.

'You taste like heaven.' Drawing back, he blows hot air over my clit, and looks up at me. His eyes never leaving mine, he moves his face forward, licking a path straight up my centre. I quiver. 'Just as sweet as I remember.'

Seeing his handsome face between my thighs is a sight, I can tell you. I release a long, drawn-out moan when he slips a finger deep inside me.

'You're so wet . . . so tight,' he murmurs. 'I can't wait to be inside you, again.'

I smile, but on the inside I'm doubting his words. The last time he was inside me, he ran. Maybe it's just something he says to all the women he beds, *part of his spiel*. Does he even have a spiel? God, I hope not. I want to mean more to him than all the others. I want to be the special one.

Pushing those thoughts out of my mind, I concentrate on him. If this is our last time together, then I want to savour every second of it.

My inner thighs press tightly against his head and my toes curl. I'm already on the edge as my body climbs to a place of pure ecstasy. It's a feeling that's been foreign to me for so long, I'm not sure if I can even handle it. I hope I don't pass out.

'Jax,' I pant when he brings me over the edge, tugging roughly on his hair. 'I'm . . . I'm coming.'

I'm still reeling from my orgasm as he makes his way back up my body. I swear I'm seeing stars. 'I need to be inside you,' he whispers against my mouth.

When he grabs hold of his cock and slides it through my wetness, my whole body tenses. 'Don't forget the condom.'

I grin when his eyes meet mine. I'm trying my best to act light-hearted, but I am feeling anything but.

'Really? I can pull out like last time. You're the only one I've ever gone bareback with. I need to feel all of you, Candice.'

Lifting my hand, I place it on the side of his face. 'Please put a condom on.' I'm not getting into the reasons behind my request. He needs to wrap it, *end of story*.

'Okay.' He pushes off the bed. For a split second I think he's going to change his mind about doing this. 'I'll just grab one. They're in the bathroom.'

Relief floods through me. I prop myself up on my elbows to ogle his magnificent arse. He has nice, tight, round buns. *Perfection*.

He's already rolling the condom onto his impressive length as he walks back into the room. The second he settles over the top of me again, his beautiful brown eyes meet mine. The corners of his lips turn up as he gently brushes my hair back off my forehead. 'Are you sure about this? It's not too late to say no.'

'I'm sure.'

'Thank fuck. I was hoping you'd say that.' We both laugh as he lines himself up. When he slides the tip inside me, I close my eyes and moan. 'Open your eyes,' he commands. 'I want you to see who's making you feel like this.'

He waits until I do as he's asked. No words are spoken, but his expression conveys so much. It almost looks like love. Does he feel the same way about me as I do about him? Maybe not, but in this moment I'd say yes.

I run my hand softly over his hair. My gaze never once leaves his. *I love you with all my heart, Jaxson Albright*, I say in my head, hoping he can read my mind. I wish I could voice those words. I want him to know how I feel about him.

'Jax,' I whisper.

'Candice,' he groans, inching further inside me. I watch his eyes slightly roll back in his head the moment he pushes all the way in. It feels good, yet kinda hurts as well. Like a burning feeling. I guess when you're with someone who's hung like him, it's to be expected. I'm grateful when he stills again, giving me time to adjust. It's been a long time for me.

His lips softly cover mine. The kiss is so beautiful and passionate, like nothing I've ever experienced, and I feel tears rise in my eyes. Clenching them closed, I wrap my arms around his torso, pulling him closer. My hands tenderly caress his strong back as I allow my body to feel. There's been a piece of my heart missing for so long, but in this moment I feel whole again. Jax is the only one capable of doing that. I wish he could see how perfect we are for each other.

'Oh God,' I whimper, as he picks up the pace. Our bodies dance in sync as he thrusts into me over and over again.

His short, hard strokes become long and languid. 'Jesus, I have to slow down,' he says in a low voice. Suddenly he's gone, and there's an emptiness where he was.

'What's going on?' I prop myself up on my elbows, as he stands beside the bed, looking down at me. *God, please don't run again. My heart won't take it a second time.*

'I need to feel all of you, Candice.'

My heart drops. If he's referring to the condom, he's leaving that fucker on, no ifs or buts.

'It's selfish, but I want to stay inside you for as long as I can.' Moving to the foot of the bed, he grabs my ankles like a caveman, and slides me down so my butt is on the edge. I'm not sure what he's doing, but I like the way he's dominating me. It's hot. He kneels down in front of me, gently lifting my feet and placing my heels on the edge of the mattress. 'Leave them there,' he instructs.

I'm completely open to him, on display, exposed. 'Okay.'

'Christ, you're beautiful.' He grabs a pillow and lifts my hips, placing the pillow under my arse. 'I'm going to take my time, but I need to be deep inside you.' He pushes my legs apart and slowly guides the head of his cock into my pussy again.

'Oh shit,' I say through another long, drawn-out moan when he pushes all the way in. He's so big, and so deep . . . I may even suffer some brain damage because of it. Closing my eyes, I will my body to relax. I want to enjoy what he's doing to me.

'Keep your eyes open,' he demands.

I'm struggling. The intense, full sensation is pushing me closer and closer to the edge again. He brings the crown of his cock out, and traces it along my flesh.

'Jesus,' I whisper.

His hooded eyes are glued on mine; he's watching me as I'm watching us. This is the biggest turn on. He knows what he's doing, and it's driving me crazy.

'More,' I shamelessly beg.

He impales me in one swift movement, and my hips automatically gyrate towards him. 'Shit!' he groans. Sliding his arms under my knees, his fingers dig painfully into my flesh. He rotates his hips, creating long, slow movements I can't help but match.

'You feel so good.' I try to keep my eyes open, but the powerful draw between us is too strong. My eyelids flutter shut so I can appreciate the intensity of our closeness. It's like our two bodies have become one.

Jax's movements increase in speed. He's no longer gentle. And I love it—I love him.

'I can't hold on any longer,' he says. His face is turning red and his neck muscles are protruding from the effort of trying to hold back his orgasm. Watching him lose control because of me only turns me on more. He lets my left leg go, and brings his fingers down to my clit. His thumb roughly teases me.

My body is about to fall over the edge into ecstasy, but I try my best to hold on. I want to come with him.

He clenches his jaw tight and thrusts deep inside me. 'Fuck.'

He moves his body forward, trapping his hand between us, but still manages to make me orgasm. With one flick, I begin to fall with him.

'Oh God.' I try to be quiet, but there's no way I can. Jax owns my body, he knows it better than I do. His fingers, his mouth and his cock push me to the peak. My legs tremble as he extracts every ounce of pleasure from me.

It takes a few minutes for my body to calm.

Leaning in, he gives me a drowning kiss. One that tells me there's plenty more to come, and this was only the entrée. My fingertips draw light circles up and down his back, and the sensitive flesh between my legs cries out for more.

••••

'I'm fucked,' he says breathlessly, when he rolls off me. 'Literally.'

Makes two of us. I'm sure I'll be feeling the effects of tonight for days to come. He took me over and over again, in every way imaginable. And I'd be lying if I said I hadn't enjoyed every second of it. He's a sensational lover, but he's had plenty of practice. I erase that thought immediately from my mind, I don't want to ruin the moment.

I look over at the clock on the bedside table. 'Shit. It's four am.' My heart is suddenly weighed down, knowing our time together is almost over. Have we really been going at it for that long? 'I guess what they say is true ... time flies when you're having fun,' I say, rolling on my side to face him. What we shared was more than just a bit of fun, it was magical.

Turning over to face me, he reaches up and tucks my hair behind my ear. 'I guess we should get some sleep. We have to get up for work in a few hours.'

'I suppose.' I try not to let my disappointment show, but fail miserably.

'Come here,' he says, pulling me into his arms. 'Thank you for coming here. You have no idea what this has meant to me.'

'There's no other place I'd rather be,' I reply as my fingers gently brush over his hair. 'I'll always be here for you.'

'Thank you.'

'You don't have to thank me, Jax. You're my best friend. That's what friends do. They are there for each other.'

'Candice,' he says, tenderly cupping my face in his hand, 'I . . . um.'

'What?'

'Nothing,' he replies with a sigh. 'Goodnight.'

'Goodnight, Jax.'

His lips softly meet mine. My heart is smiling as I snuggle in closer to him. This is the first time I'll be sleeping in his arms, so I'm going to make the most of it. Placing my head on his chest, I let the steady beat of his heart lull me to sleep.

••••

When I open my eyes, the first thing I do is smile. Not only is Jax still here, but our bodies are tangled together in the same position they were in when we fell asleep. Last night was everything I'd dreamt it would be, and so much more. There's no denying we're magical together, in every sense of the word. I hate that this has to end. I should never have agreed to only one night. It wasn't enough. I have a feeling that spending every day of the rest of my life with him wouldn't be enough.

I lift my hand and gently move the piece of hair that's fallen onto his forehead, careful not to wake him. I take a few minutes to study him. He looks so peaceful when he sleeps. I'd give anything to be able to wake up next to him like this, every morning. Just the thought of it brings a lump to my throat. If life has taught me anything over the years it's that there's no point wishing for the impossible.

I place my lips softly on his. 'I love you, Jaxson Albright,' I whisper as I untangle myself from him and climb out of bed.

JAX

My heart sinks when I open my eyes and find her gone. Please let her still be in the house somewhere. We agreed to one night, but I'm not ready for it to end yet. While she's still here, she's mine. I quickly rise from the bed and head into the hallway. I don't even bother to put any clothes on. My heart is furiously thumping in my chest. Just as I pass the bathroom, the door flings open. Relief floods through me when I swing around and see Candice standing in the doorway.

Thank Christ she's still here. I thought she'd done a runner on me.

My eyes immediately take in her appearance. She's only wearing her top and pink lace panties. It makes my cock immediately come to life. She's so beautiful.

I see a smile forming on her face as her eyes travel down the length of my body. 'Is that a dagger in your pocket, Mr Albright, or are you just pleased to see me?'

I laugh. I'm not wearing pants, so I don't even have a pocket.

'I'm pleased to see you, Miss Crawford,' I say as I take a step towards her and slide my hands around her waist.

'I had a wonderful time last night,' she says, resting the side of her face against my chest and wrapping her arms around my waist. 'I hate that it has to end.'

'You're still mine until you walk out that door.' Looking up at me, she smiles. It's the kind of smile that hits me right in the chest.

I back her up against the wall as my lips meet hers. I'm gonna drag this morning out as much as I can.

SEVENTEEN

JAX

Four months later . . .

AFTER LOCKING THE STUDIO DOOR, I PULL CANDICE INTO MY arms as my lips bear down on hers. She's my drug and I'm addicted. We tug at each other's clothes in a desperate attempt to undress. It's like we're starved for one another.

Since that night four months ago this has become our regular thing: hiding away from everyone and fucking each other's brains out every chance we get. We tried going back to the way we were, just friends, but it didn't even last forty-eight hours. I'd innocently brushed my fingers across the small of her back one day as I passed her in the hallway and her breath hitched. It sent every drop of blood in me coursing straight to my cock. I knew in that moment it was impossible for me to stay away. I was consumed. I craved her too much. Without hesitation, I'd reached for her hand, leading her to my studio. Once the door was closed, I'd clicked the latch, locking us inside. She didn't have to speak a word; the look on her face told me everything I needed to know. She wanted this just as much as I did.

We've since turned from best friends to friends with benefits. In all honesty, this isn't what I'd envisioned for us. But it's far better than what we had. I finally have what I've always longed for, but I still want more—no, I need more. With every passing day, I fall deeper and deeper. Something's gotta give soon.

'Aren't you supposed to be working on my new tattoo?' she asks, when my tongue trails a path down her neck.

'Fuck your tattoo. I've got better things to do.'

'Like what?' She laughs. Is she kidding me?

'Like devouring you. Now turn around.' Like the good girl she is, she does exactly as I ask. She can drop the innocent act; she wants this just as much as I do. 'Raise your arms in the air.' I run my hands up the sides of her body, bringing her top with them. I need to feel her skin. After sliding her top over her head, I drop it to the floor. Palming her breast through her black satin bra, my other hand dips into the front of her pants.

'Jax,' she breathes as she rests her head on my shoulder and threads one of her hands into my hair.

'Come for me beautiful,' I whisper into her ear as my fingers circle her clit. I love that she's already wet for me.

'Mmm,' she moans. 'That feels so good.'

She better believe it does. Our sexual chemistry is explosive.

Within minutes I have her coming undone with my fingers. I wrap my free hand in her hair and tilt her head to the side so I can kiss her to muffle her cries of ecstasy. These walls are thin. Nobody has said anything yet, but it's only a matter of time before we get caught. The sneaking around part excites me, but on the other hand, I hate that we're hiding from the rest of the world. I want to claim her and make her mine. I'd love nothing more than to shout it from the rooftops. But this is what she wants, and I can't deny her anything.

I step forward, taking her with me, until I have her pressed against the wall.

'Place your hands on the wall,' I command. She does exactly as I ask, pushing her arse backwards. I groan when she grinds it against my aching cock. It pleases me that she wants me just as much as I want her. Hooking my thumbs in the side of her tights, I drag them down her legs. 'I like your pants so much better when they're around your ankles.'

She laughs. 'So do I, but only when you're around.'

Pulling my T-shirt over my head, I drop it on the floor with hers. I grab a condom from my pocket before I flick open the button of my jeans and pull down the zip. I rip the foil packet open with my teeth as I free my cock from my pants. I'm dying to take her bareback again, but even though she's now on the pill, she still insists I wear one of these fuckers.

I slide my free hand under the cup of her bra and roll her nipple between my finger and thumb. I can't seem to keep my hands off her when we're alone, and it's a constant struggle not to touch her when we're in public. When we're around the other staff, we act just like we always have, as friends and nothing more. I do grope her arse and tits, or steal a kiss when nobody is looking. Having her again is all I think about. *I'm obsessed.* She consumes me. Of an evening when we walk back to my place to collect my car, so we can head to her house for dinner, we just walk side by side. No hand holding, or touching. The moment we walk through my front door, though, we're ripping each other's clothes off like damn maniacs.

I use my knee to part her legs as much as the pants around her ankles will allow, impaling her with my cock in one swift motion. I use my free hand to cover her mouth as she moans. My other hand grips her hip as I draw back slightly before pushing all the way in. The feeling of her tight pussy wrapped around my cock will never get old. I don't think I'll ever get my fill.

'Can I take you out somewhere nice tonight, on a date?' I've never taken anyone on a date before, but I really want to do something nice with her. She deserves so much more than this.

'A date?' she whispers as I continue to pound into her.

'Yeah, a date.'

'I thought we were just having fun. You said you weren't capable of anything more than this.'

Her words have me stilling inside her. She's right, I did say that. Her comment pisses me off nevertheless. 'Things change, Candice . . . people change.'

Turning slightly to look at me, she places her hand on the side of my face. 'Okay, but can we go somewhere away from here?'

'Why, are you ashamed to be seen with me?'

'What? No.' She screws her face up. 'I'm just not ready to share this with the world yet. It will just complicate things.'

'How? Who cares what the rest of the world thinks?'

'I'm just not ready.'

'Fine,' I snap in annoyance.

'Don't be mad with me, Jax. We're a work in progress. You can't rush perfection.'

I know it's Sophia finding out that worries Candice the most. She goes all weird when we're together at her house, sitting at the opposite end of the dinner table, the furthest spot away from me. If Candice stays at my place, she'll drive her own car over instead of getting a lift with me, so her mother doesn't know we're actually together. Sophia even pulled me aside recently and asked if I'd met Candice's gentleman friend. *Yeah, I've met him, it's fucking me.* I don't know why Candice keeps us from her mother, of all people. Sophia likes me, and I'm pretty sure she'd be happy for us.

When I go to withdraw, Candice moves her arms behind her, wrapping them around my waist to hold me in place. 'Don't, Jax,' she pleads. 'Don't pull away from me.'

I exhale a large breath, resting my chin on the top of her head. 'Let's just drop it then. It was a crazy idea anyway.'

'It's not a crazy idea. I love that you want to go on a date with me. Really, I do.'

She could've fooled me. I thought she'd be happy, but I guess I was wrong. I swear I'll never understand women.

••••

'You look beautiful,' I say when I open the front door. I wanted to pick her up tonight, but again she came to me instead.

Candice doesn't often dress up all girly and shit, but when she does . . . *fucking wow*. She's breathtaking. Don't get me wrong, she always looks gorgeous, but it's nice to see her in a dress for a change. I'm already fighting the urge to rip it right off her luscious body and have my way with her, but tonight I want to do this right. I'm more than ready to take a leap of faith and put my heart on the line for her. It will only ever be her. I just pray she doesn't crush it.

The past few months have made me realise we could never go back to being just friends. She's mine for keeps now. I only hope she feels the same. We have nothing to lose and everything to gain by making this thing official.

'You look rather dashing yourself, Mr Albright,' she replies, sliding her arms around my waist.

I feel stupid in this damn tie, but I wanted to look nice for her. It's a thin black leather one, more me than the designer silk ties I used to wear to the political functions my father made me attend. To keep it casual, I paired it with an untucked white button-up shirt with the sleeves rolled up to my elbows and a pair of black trousers.

I smile as I push a strand of pink hair behind her ear. 'Thank you.' I place my lips briefly on hers. 'We better get going, the reservation's at seven.' I'd like to add, *'Since we have to drive three fucking suburbs away,'* but I don't. I want tonight to be special, so pissing her off before we leave isn't a wise move. Hopefully after tonight I'll be able to convince her there should be no more hiding.

'I'm looking forward to going on our first real date,' she says as we walk to my car.

'Really?' Because I'm having serious doubts after the way she acted this afternoon.

'Yes, really. I know it didn't seem like it earlier, but it will be nice to spend some time with you in public.'

Again I want to say, '*Three fucking suburbs away,*' but I bite my tongue.

I open the car door for her and she gets in. My gut churns as I walk around to the driver's side. Am I making the right decision here? There's no doubt about my feelings towards her. She owns my heart, and always will. But is laying my heart on the line the right choice? I've never thought of myself as the commitment type, but the last four months have proved me wrong. There's no way I could go back to the life I had. *No fucking way*. We've passed the friend zone and moved into some serious shit. This is where dreams come true, or hearts get broken.

'You're quiet, are you okay?' she asks on the drive to the restaurant. Reaching across the centre console, she places her hand on my thigh. I love it when she does that.

I'm quiet because I'm having an internal freak-out, but of course I don't tell her that. 'I'm fine,' I reply, turning the radio up. I'm already second-guessing myself, so if we want to make it through the rest of the night, it'd be best if we don't discuss it.

'Seriously, Jax. You're gonna turn the radio up to avoid talking to me?'

I shake my head and chuckle. She knows me too well.

'I'm waiting, Mister!'

I look at her when we stop at a red light. She crosses her arms over her chest and raises one of her perfectly shaped eyebrows. I'm instantly distracted by the way her perky tits are pushed up, so my gaze remains fixed on her chest.

'My eyes are up here, buddy.'

I lick my lips as I lean across the centre console and place my mouth on the swell of one of her breasts. 'You have spectacular tits,' I whisper, as I softly bite her nipple through the thin fabric of her dress.

'Jax,' she moans as her lips part slightly and her head pushes back into the seat. I run my hand up her inner thigh and under her dress, as my cock painfully strains against my pants. *She's addictive.* Nobody turns me on like she does. I groan when she parts her legs for me.

'You can't distract me with sex,' she practically whimpers when my finger slides into the side of her panties.

'Wanna make a bet?' I know her better than she knows herself.

She bites her lip when I slip a finger inside her. The moment her eyes flutter closed, I know she's lost.

'Shit,' I curse, when the car behind us sounds its horn, alerting me that the traffic light has turned green.

I reluctantly remove my finger from her little piece of paradise and straighten in my seat.

Candice adjusts her dress before looking over at me. 'Nice try. Now stop avoiding my question. What are you hiding from me?'

'I'm not hiding anything.'

'Yes you are, Jaxson Albright. You're weirding out on me. You better not have asked me out tonight so you can tell me you want to see other people? I swear if you did, you'd better start running.'

I squirm in my seat when her gaze moves down to my crotch.

'What? Of course not.' I sure as hell wouldn't like to be in my shoes if that were the case. 'Look, I just want to talk to you about something.'

'Shoot.'

Christ. I wanted to wait until after we'd eaten, but there's no way she's going to let that happen. She's way too stubborn. 'It's no big deal . . . it's just . . .'

'Spit it out, Jax.'

'Christ.' I try to bide some time by scrubbing one of my hands over my face. I'm not sure how to even say it. I've never asked anyone to be my girlfriend before. I don't want to scare her away.

'I'm waiting.'

'Just give me a sec. I'm nervous about asking you, okay?'

'About asking me what?'

I guess it's now or never. I can see she's starting to get impatient with my vagueness. I exhale. 'I want to ask you if you'll be my girlfriend.'

When she doesn't reply, my heart drops. I dart a quick look at her: her eyes are wide, and her sweet mouth gapes. If she gives me the, 'It's not you, it's me' spiel, I'm gonna lose my shit.

'For Christ's sake, Candice, say something.'

'You want to be my boyfriend . . . like officially?'

'Yes. Only if you want me to. I'm sick of hiding.'

I swear I'm holding my breath as I wait for her to reply. If she's trying to torture me, she's doing a good job of it.

A few seconds later, she shrugs. 'Okay.'

'Okay, what?' I ask, quickly pulling the car over to the kerb.

The second I bring the vehicle to a stop, she turns her face away from me, looking out the front windscreen.

'Candice,' I growl, removing my seatbelt. I'm starting to panic a little.

'Sure, I'll be your girlfriend,' she says, very nonchalantly.

'Wow . . . really? That's all you have to say?' I wasn't sure how she'd react, but I certainly didn't expect it would be this casually.

I see her lips curl into a smile, as she glances in my direction. She must be yanking my chain. I knew it could go either way, but I wasn't expecting this lame-arse response.

'Candice.' I can hear the pathetic pleading tone in my voice as I wait for her to say something else. I need more from her. This isn't a joke—I'm offering her my damn heart here. This is a huge move for me. One I never thought I'd take.

She finally turns her body, facing me. 'I'm sorry, but are you sure this is what you really want, Jax? You can't change your mind in the morning. Well, technically you can, but I wouldn't if I was you,' she adds, as her gaze moves back down to my crotch. 'If you catch my drift.'

I swallow nervously. I catch her drift all right, loud and clear. I've seen firsthand the damage Candice can cause. My balls are running for cover just thinking about it.

'Jokes aside, this isn't easy for me, Candice. I think you know me well enough to know I wouldn't even entertain the idea if it wasn't something I really wanted.'

'Are you sure?'

I hate the uncertainty I can see on her face. 'Never been surer.'

'Well in that case, I'd love to be your girlfriend, Jax.' This time she gives me a beautiful smile, the kind of smile that takes my breath away. 'In my head, I've been pretending we already are boyfriend and girlfriend anyway.'

I chuckle. As pathetic as that sounds, there have been times I've pretended the same thing. I pull her into my arms. I hope I've made the right decision for us.

'You know this means no more hiding.'

'No more hiding,' she whispers.

'Thank you.'

Drawing back, her beautiful blue eyes lock with mine. 'You don't have to thank me, Jax. There's no one else I'd rather be with.' Her hand gently caresses the side of my face. 'You're it for me.'

I fucking love it when she looks at me like this. It sends tingles down my spine and straight to my cock.

'Kiss me.' Reaching for my tie, she uses it to pull my body towards hers. She doesn't need to ask me twice. 'I can't wait to have sex with my sexy boyfriend when we get home.'

If we didn't have reservations, I'd turn around and head there right now. But I want this date with her. She deserves so much more than just sex.

I want to give her the world.

Pulling out of the kiss, I look at my watch. 'We should get going. I don't want to be late for my first real date with my girlfriend.'

She gives my hand a squeeze. Call me crazy, but I can already feel a difference in the air. Is it wrong to hope?

'Let me just reapply my lipdick,' she says, lifting her huge bag onto her lap, and riffling around inside.

'Hold on a minute, did you just say "lipdick"?' She has dicks on the brain.

'I did.' When she finds the lipstick in her bag, she removes the lid and extends her arm across the centre console, shoving it in my face.

'What the hell?' I say. 'Is that a dick?'

She throws her head back and laughs. 'Actually, yes. It's a lipstick shaped like a dick—a lipdick. Isn't it cool?'

'Get that fucker away from me,' I snap, slapping her hand away. I immediately scrub my hand over my mouth. I just kissed her with that shit all over her lips. 'You have serious issues; you know that right?'

'Why are you wiping your mouth?'

'I just kissed you not realising you were wearing cock on your lips.'

'It's a nice shade of cock, it suits you.'

'You're sick.'

'Maybe. But you wouldn't have me any other way.'

'I'm starting to rethink this whole idea.'

'What?' she says and her face drops. 'You don't want me to be your girlfriend anymore?'

This time I laugh. 'Of course I do.'

'You're an arsehole,' she says, punching me in the arm. 'I thought you were serious.'

'What is it with you and your fascination with penises, anyway?'

She shrugs. 'I just like them. I grew up in a house with no men. When I saw my first penis, I was fascinated. It all started from there.'

'Huh.' Her comment pisses me off.

She grabs my crotch, giving it a gentle squeeze. 'Don't worry, yours is my favourite.'

'It better be. You're mine now, and don't forget it.'

'You are, and have always been, all I've ever wanted, Jaxson Albright.'

Her words have me smiling like a fool.

EIGHTEEN

JAX

CANDICE AND I ARE LAUGHING AT SOMETHING SHE JUST SAID as we walk through the front door of her place. For the first time in my life, I'm truly, truly happy. The past few months have been rocky, but wonderful. We've finally decided to take that leap of faith. No more hiding, no more secrets, no more pretending. We are finally a legitimate couple.

She spent the night at my house last night, so we never got the chance to tell Sophia our good news. It was hard keeping it a secret today at work, but Candice wanted her mother to be the first to know. Tomorrow, I get to tell the world. She's finally mine, in every sense of the word.

I'm head over heels in love, and tonight I'm going to tell her. I'm scared I'm going to mess up, or disappoint her in some way, but I can't keep going like this. *I need her.* That friends-with-benefits shit was tearing me up inside. What Candice and I have is special. It's like nothing I've ever known, and if we can pull this friends-to-lovers thing off, it will be explosive. Just the thought of it has my adrenaline pumping.

When we enter the kitchen, I reach for her hand, interlacing our fingers. I'm surprised when I feel Candice's hand trembling in mine. Am I misreading this? Does she know something I don't? I'm not sure how Sophia is going to take the news, but up until this moment I was pretty confident she'd be happy for us. We're made for each other, there's no denying it.

I give Candice's hand a squeeze, and she smiles at me.

'Sophia, we have something we need to tell you,' she says.

Sophia turns from the stove and her eyes immediately lock on our joined hands. Relief floods through me when I see her smile.

'Oh my God,' she squeals as her hands fly up in the air. 'I was wondering when you two were finally going to see it.'

'See what?' Candice asks.

'That you're crazy about each other.' Sophia wipes a tear from one of her eyes as she makes her way towards us. 'You're perfect for each other. *This* is perfect.' She wraps us in her arms.

'We are perfect for each other,' Candice whispers, making my smile grow.

I agree, we are.

'Look, Sissy,' Maddie screams as she comes running into the room. 'I princess.'

Sophia lets us go, and we turn. The smile on Maddie's face melts my heart. She's already dressed and ready for bed, but she's wearing a tiny jewelled tiara on her head. She looks so sweet.

'You look like a princess,' Candice says, leaning down and scooping her into her arms.

'Phia made me pretty. I got new sparkly dress.' She wiggles in Candice's arms, trying to get free. The moment she places her on the ground, Maddie reaches up and grabs Candice's hand. 'Look.'

'Okay, I'll come look.' Candice laughs as she's pulled out of the room. She blows me a kiss over her shoulder just before she disappears through the doorway.

I can't explain the feeling I have inside. We're actually doing it. I hope we don't live to regret it.

'I'm so happy for you both,' Sophia says, snapping me back into reality. 'I couldn't ask for a better man for my little girl.'

'Thank you.'

'You're one of the good guys, Jaxson.'

I feel a lump rise in my throat when she wraps me in her arms again. She's the closest thing to a mother I have.

Our moment is quickly broken when Candice comes barrelling into the room. 'What the hell is this?' she screams, holding a sparkly, frilly dress in the air.

'Calm down,' Sophia says. 'It's just a small pageant. It's no big deal.'

'No big deal?' Candice yells. 'You promised me!'

I have no idea what's going on, but when I see tears in Candice's eyes, I know it's not good.

'Honey.'

When Sophia reaches for Candice, she slaps her hands away. I hear a small whimper come from behind me and glance over my shoulder to see Maddie in the doorway. She's wide-eyed as she watches Candice and their mother. It tugs at my heartstrings when I see her bottom lip quiver and a tear roll down her cheek.

Leaving those two hotheads to sort their shit out, I scoop Maddie into my arms and walk out into the hallway. When those two get going they're explosive. She doesn't need to witness that.

'It's okay,' I say as I hold her tightly and try my best to console her while she cries into my chest.

'Phia and Sissy fight.'

'They're just having a little argument.' Little argument my arse, it's a doozy. 'It'll be okay,' I say reassuringly as I place a soft kiss on her hair. And it will be. This is not their first argument, and it certainly won't be their last. They never last long. I've witnessed many fights between these two over the years. They're usually in tears and hugging each other within minutes.

'Sissy mad. Sissy hate my dress.'

I gathered that much from what I heard, but I don't think it's the dress she doesn't like, more the reasons behind it. I guess Candice is scared Sophia is going to push Maddie into the life she had growing up.

'Fuck this, and fuck you,' Candice screams as she comes storming out of the kitchen and into the hallway where I'm standing. She flings the dress and it goes flying through the air.

'My sparkly!' Maddie cries as she wiggles in my arms for me to put her down. When I do, she runs over to her dress and picks it up.

'Candice,' Sophia calls out. But Candice slams the front door as she leaves.

This is worse than I thought. Sophia rushes over to Maddie, crouching down to fold her into her arms.

I stand there stunned for a few seconds, before going after Candice. I still don't get why she's so upset over a crown and a fucking dress. I know she hates what she went through as a child, but that doesn't mean Maddie is going to feel the same.

'Candice, wait!' I yell as I see her crossing the front lawn, heading for the street. Where the hell does she think she's going? 'Candice!' When she doesn't stop, I break into a jog to catch up.

'Will you just stop,' I say, reaching for her arm and halting her.

'Let me go.'

'No.' I put my arm around her waist and pull her to me. She struggles to get free of my grip briefly, but I'm too strong for her. She exhales a defeated breath, and my heart breaks when she covers her face and starts to sob. I've never seen her this upset before. 'Come here,' I say, turning her in my arms and crushing her to my chest. 'It's just a dress.'

'It's more than the damn dress, Jax. You don't understand.'

'I think I do. You don't want your sister to go through what you went through.'

'Huh. Sister,' she says sarcastically.

Pulling back, I cup her face in my hands. 'This isn't about Maddie, then?'

'Of course it is. She promised me when Maddison was born she wouldn't do this.'

'I get that. I totally do,' I say as I wipe the tears from her eyes with my thumbs. 'But it's just one pageant. She seemed so excited about it.'

'That's because she's too young to even realise what's involved. Those pageants are vicious—psycho mothers and their equally bitchy daughters. I don't want that for her, Jax.'

'I love that you're trying to protect her, but she's not your daughter, Candice. You can't tell Sophia how to raise her.' Her passion for wanting to protect her little sister is admirable, but I really think she's overreacting here. And although my words are meant to comfort her, I can see that they're not helping.

'This is all your fault,' she says, pushing on my chest.

'What? How the fuck is this my fault?'

'Because if you didn't leave, none of this would be happening right now.'

'Why does me leaving have anything to do with Maddie entering a pageant?'

'Because she's *my fucking daughter*, Jax,' she screams, pushing on my chest again. The moment the words are out of her mouth, all the colour drains from her face. 'She's my daughter,' she repeats, in a whisper.

I must've heard her wrong. How could that be? When her words finally register, I drop my arms by my side and take a step backwards. 'What? Maddie's yours?'

Tears flood her eyes as her hands cover her mouth.

'Answer me, damn it.'

'She's not just mine, Jax, she's ours,' she says, bowing her head. 'If you hadn't left me . . .'

'*Ours?*' I take a second to let her words settle in. 'What? *Fucking what?*' I try to digest her words. She's lost her mind, I'm sure of it. I clutch my head as I try to make sense of what she just said. Maddie can't be mine. How?

The air is silent between us as I stand there and wait for her reply. My heart is beating furiously against my ribcage. She's having me on, she has to be.

A few seconds later she raises her head and makes eye contact with me. Before the words are even out of her mouth, the devastation on her face tells me everything I need to know.

'I'm sorry, Jax.'

'For what?' I need to hear her say it.

'For not telling you.'

'For not telling me what?' I scream as I reach out and shake her. My heart rate spikes to a dangerous level and I swear I'm gonna have a fucking heart attack. She better not say what I think she's going to say, or I'll lose my shit.

'Maddie is our daughter.'

'How?'

'The night we had sex . . . I fell pregnant.'

I stand there unmoving for the longest time. Please tell me she's kidding. Please tell me that the person I love, the one I trust more than anything hasn't deceived me like this. *Not my Candice*.

'Is this some sick joke?'

'It's not a joke, Jax. It's true.' She covers her face with her hands and starts to sob again. 'It's true. She's our little girl.'

'Fuck.' My head is spinning as I start to pace. How could she do something like this to me?

She reaches for my hand, but I snatch it away. I don't want her touching me.

'Please let me explain, Jax.'

I swing around and face her. 'Explain what, Candice? That I have a daughter who's almost fucking three, and I'm only just finding out about her now? How the hell are you going to explain that?'

A lump rises in my throat as the enormity of this situation sinks in. Maddison is my kid. Christ. For some strange reason, Brian's words enter my mind: *She has your eyes*. Fuck, why didn't I see that? I guess the idea never crossed my mind because I trusted Candice.

Jesus Christ. I have a little girl. I don't know whether to scream or cry.

My brief elation quickly turns back to anger. I loved this girl, I trusted her with my life. And now she's deceived me in the most unthinkable way. She not only lied to me, she robbed me of almost three years of my daughter's life. How can I be okay with that?

'I was eighteen. You left me.'

Is that her lame excuse for doing what she did? She's got to be kidding. Who is this monster standing before me? How could I be so wrong about a person?

'I went away to university, Candice. I didn't just up and leave for the fun of it. You knew I was going.'

She pushes me again. 'You fucked me and left! You snuck out in the middle of the night and didn't even say goodbye!'

Her tears continue to fall, but I feel no sympathy for her. She may see it that way, but that's not how it was. Yes, at first I ran, but I was scared. I freaked out. It still doesn't excuse her keeping this from me. I had a right to know.

'Yes, I left, but that's no excuse for keeping this from me.'

'I messaged you when I first found out and you were a cock.'

'Hold on a minute,' I say. 'You sent me a text to say I was a disappointment. At no time did you mention you were pregnant.'

'Because you shut me down before I even got a chance.'

'I messaged you the next day and said I was sorry, but you never replied. A few weeks later I wrote you a letter, but it came back unopened, with "return to sender" written on the envelope.'

'What?' she says as her brow furrows. 'What letter? I never received a letter.'

'I sent a letter to your old address in Canberra. I thought you were the one who'd sent it back.'

'I never received it.'

'I gather that now.'

She pauses as she lets this news sink in, but the silence doesn't last long. 'Letter or no letter, you still left without a word.'

'I had my reasons for leaving the way I did, Candice.'

'And I had my reasons for not telling you about Maddie,' she snaps. 'You broke my heart, Jax. It took me years to get over what you did.'

Her comment only infuriates me further. I doubt she could say anything to justify what she's done.

'So you kept this from me as some sick form of revenge? Is that what you're trying to tell me?'

'What? Of course not.'

I have no more words to say to her in this moment. Not any nice ones, anyway. I'm confused, I'm shocked, I'm angry, but more than anything, I'm broken. Turning, I head towards the car.

'Jax, wait! Please,' Candice pleads.

'Don't touch me,' I snap when she grabs hold of my arm.

'Please.'

I can hear the desperation in her voice, but for once I don't care. Whatever she needs to say she should've said years ago.

I slam the car door. I need space. I need to clear my head. I need to get a grip on the fact that I'm a father. Talk about an insta-fucking-family.

Tears sting my eyes when I think of Maddie. I'm not the only one who's been lied to. I'd love to march into that house, grab my little girl and take her with me, but I don't want to frighten her by removing her from the only home she's ever known.

Jesus. I can't quite fathom that I have a kid. A smile briefly tugs at my lips as I picture her sweet face. I've missed so much of her life already. I feel so robbed. I hate that Candice stripped me of my right to know my daughter and be involved in her life.

Once I've turned the key in the ignition, I put the car into reverse and screech out of the driveway. I see Candice drop to her knees in my rear-view mirror. I take a moment to watch as her body shudders with sobs. As angry as I am, seeing her like that breaks my fucking heart in two.

Slamming my foot to the floor, I take off down the street. My vision is blurry, but I'm not sure if they're tears of pain or happiness. I just lost the most precious thing I'd ever had, but on the other hand,

I gained something just as precious. A strangled sob bubbles up from the back of my throat as I let the tears fall freely.

I still can't believe it.

Maddie is my little girl.

••••

I drop the cigarette to the ground, stubbing it out with my foot. I bought a packet when I stopped off at the bottle shop on my way here. This is one of those stressful times that requires smokes and plenty of alcohol. I'll take anything I can if it helps calm me the hell down.

I knock on the door. 'Who's there?' I hear Brian call from the other side.

'It's me, Jax.' Don't even ask me why I'm here, but I had nowhere else to go. I need someone to help me wrap my head around this clusterfuck.

'Jax,' he says when he opens the door. 'Is everything okay?'

As shitty as I'm feeling, I smile when I see he's wearing the striped flannelette pyjamas Candice bought him. She picked up a heap of clothes in his size from the op shop, as well as buying new shoes, socks, underwear and a warm winter jacket. He looks like a different man from the one I first met. Candice gave him a haircut and his beard is now trimmed and tidy. Everywhere I look, all I see is pieces of her. *She did well for a lying, deceitful bitch.*

'I'm sorry to disturb you,' I say, looking down at my feet. I shouldn't have come here. He has enough shit to deal with, without being burdened down with my drama. 'I—'

'Don't be silly. Come in.' He moves to the side so I can enter. 'You look like you have the weight of the world on your shoulders, son.'

Am I that transparent?

I feel bad when I see the covers on the bed turned back. 'You were in bed. I should go.'

'Sit down, young man,' Brian says sternly. He points to the night-stand. The lamp is on and there's a pair of reading glasses sitting on top of a newspaper. I notice the glass in one of the lenses is cracked and there's tape keeping the arms attached. I make a mental note to get them fixed for him. 'I wasn't asleep; I was reading the paper your little lady left for me.'

I usually like it when he refers to Candice as mine, but not tonight. Just the mention of her is like a sucker punch to the chest. She's not my little lady, she's—I don't know what she is anymore. She's certainly not the person I thought she was. I don't think I'll ever get over this betrayal.

The moment I try to speak, my voice cracks.

'Sit down,' Brian instructs, guiding me to the end of the bed. Once I'm seated, he takes the brown paper bag out of my hand and shuffles across the room to grab a glass. 'By the looks of it, you need one of these.' He hands me the glass after he pours a decent amount of amber liquid into it, before sitting beside me. 'Drink, then talk,' he adds, pointing at the glass.

I down the Jack Daniels in one gulp. I welcome the burn as it slides down the back of my throat. Brian takes the glass out of my hand and refills it. I shake my head in disbelief after he passes the glass back to me. Candice's revelation rocked me to the core and still hasn't sunk in. Why couldn't I see it? How did I not know Maddie was my daughter?

'I found something out tonight,' I say as I turn to Brian. 'Remember how you said that Candice's sister had my eyes?'

'Yes.' He nods. A few seconds later his eyes widen, and I can tell he understands what I'm trying to say. 'She's your daughter?'

'Yes. Three years—how could she keep this from me for three fucking years?'

'So you and Candice's mother—'

'What? Hell, no. Candice and me.' Christ, how could he think I'd hook up with Sophia? That's all kinds of wrong. 'Apparently Maddie's her daughter—our daughter. We were only together once . . . years ago.'

'Oh.'

Yes, oh. I raise the glass to my lips. I want to feel numb. This time the booze doesn't even touch the sides. I doubt if the entire bottle will lessen the dull ache in my chest.

'Did she explain why she kept this from you?'

'She tried, but I didn't stick around to find out.'

'That wasn't a very smart move. I'm not condoning what she did for a second, but she's a good kid. I'm sure there must've been a good reason.'

I hold the glass out to him. When he refills it, I tilt my head back and raise the glass to my mouth. I drink the whiskey down, but it doesn't help. I can still feel the deceit, right down to my very core.

Brian takes the glass from me when I hold it out to him. *I need more.*

'I trusted her. I fucking trusted her,' I say as I cover my face with my hands. Devastation consumes me. I will my tears back, but it's no use; I'm powerless to stop them. I haven't cried like this since I was a kid. All the shit my family has put me through over the years doesn't even come close to how I feel in this moment. Candice is the one person I believed would never screw me over.

How could she do this to me?

I'm taken aback when Brian reaches for me, pulling me into his chest. My parents never held me like this. *Never.*

'Life has a funny way of working itself out, son,' he says as he holds me while I cry.

'I'm sorry,' I say, when I eventually pull away and wipe my eyes with the back of my hand.

'Don't apologise. I'm glad you came to me. It reminds me of the time my son had his heart broken for the first time. I held him, just like I held you.'

'You have a son?'

'I do. His name is James.'

'And he knows you live on the streets?'

'Heavens no. He has no idea. He's always been a workaholic. When his mother was alive, she was worried he'd never settle down. Thankfully, he met his wife, Alana, a few months before May passed away. It gave her some hope. James and Alana married a week after she died. They pushed the date forward, but she didn't make it. It would've made her so happy . . .' He stops. I can see the pain is still raw, even after all this time. 'They have a young family now. I'd never want to burden him with my problems. My grandson, Aiden, would be almost one. Hopefully I'll get to meet him one day.'

'Hasn't your son looked for you? Doesn't he wonder where you are?'

'I have a phone card. When I can afford to put some money on it, I call him. I always tell him I'm doing fine, and he has no reason to doubt what I say. He was transferred to Perth years ago, which makes it a lot easier to hide my predicament. He's busy with work and his family, and hasn't been back to Sydney since the funeral. He's high up in the advertising industry, you know. His job is very demanding. I'm extremely proud of him.'

'Wow.' I sit there in stunned silence. I wonder how Brian's son would feel if he knew his father was living on the streets. I can't stand my parents, but I wouldn't like to see them in his position.

He stands and walks over to the shelf to grab another glass. 'It's been years since I've had a drink, but I think I might join you, if that's okay.'

'I'd like that,' I say. I really admire this old dude. He's a good man. Completely selfless.

••••

My head is pounding when I wake the next morning. I remember stumbling home at some ungodly hour. Brian and I ended up polishing off the rest of the bottle. Well, I drank most of it—he's not much of a drinker. But spending time with him helped. He's a wise man and gave me some good advice.

I head for the bathroom. Brian made me promise I'd hear Candice out. I'm not sure if she can say anything that will justify her actions, but I at least have to give her a chance to explain.

Once I'm showered and dressed, I pour myself a strong black coffee—I don't think I could stomach any food. I reach for my phone,

which is sitting on the kitchen bench. I didn't take it with me to
Brian's; I already had two missed calls and a text message from
Candice before I left and I was in no mood to talk to her.

Turning it on, I'm not surprised to see she kept trying to contact
me throughout the night. There's fifteen missed calls and twelve texts.

8.05 pm – I'm sorry.

8.23 pm – Please pick up the phone.

8.59 pm – Please, Jax. I'm begging you. Answer the
phone.

9.17 pm – Please call me. At least give me the chance
to explain.

9.38 pm – I had my reasons for not telling you. I'm sure
you'll understand if you just hear me out.

9.51 pm – I can't believe you're doing this to me again.
Why do you always walk away from me when I need
you the most?

10.02 pm – This wasn't an easy decision for me to make.
Do you even realise how hard this has been for me?

10.46 pm – I don't want to lose you over this. Please
call me, text me . . . anything.

11.09 pm – The silence is making me crazy. Please
contact me. I need to know we're okay.

11.46 pm – I can't believe you're ignoring me. Why do
you always run from me? Thanks a lot arsehole.

I stop reading after that. I'm an arsehole? Fuck her. She should've
thought about all this before she deceived me. Was she ever going to
tell me? Maddie's been in my life for almost a year now. I feel a hollow
ache inside me when I think about everything I missed: her birth,

her first words, her first steps. I've been alone for so long, but I had a daughter. *Family.* I would've been there, for her and for Candice.

I should've made more of an effort to reach out to Candice after I left. Maybe if I had we wouldn't be in this position now.

Rising from the stool, I walk around the breakfast bar and open the top drawer, pulling out an envelope. It's the letter I sent her. I've held onto it all these years. I can't even say why, but I'm glad I did. At least I have proof that I did try to contact her.

I tuck the letter into the back pocket of my jeans. To Candice it may appear that I fucked her and walked away, but in my heart I know better. It was never about the sex. She meant the world to me, and as hurt as I am right now, she still does.

After rinsing my mug in the sink, I grab my car keys off the bench and head for the front door. I can't put this off any longer. I need to see Candice and my daughter. I want answers—no, correction: I need answers. I need something to help me understand because for the life of me, I can't wrap my head around any of this.

It's only just after eight when I pull up outside Candice's house. I doubt she'll turn up for work this morning, and I can't let this wait until the end of the day. I'll go crazy if I do.

I rub my hands down the front of my jeans before knocking on the door. It's early, but I know someone will be up. Well, I hope they are. A few seconds later, the front door flies open. Sophia is standing there in her pyjamas, and she's as white as a ghost.

'Jax. Thank God. I was just about to call you. Are Candice and Maddie with you?'

'What? No. Why?'

My adrenaline picks up when her hands cover her mouth. 'Because she's not here. Neither of them are. Oh God—she's gone.'

'Is this some kind of sick joke?'

'Do you really think I'd joke about something like this?'

When I see the tears appear in her eyes, I know she's not.

Pushing my way past her, I enter the house. 'Which room is theirs?'

'Candice's room is the first door on the right at the top of the stairs. Maddison's room is next door.'

I bound up the stairs, taking them two at a time.

'I've already checked their rooms, Jax. They're not in there,' Sophia calls out to my retreating back. I continue anyway. I need to see for myself.

When I enter Candice's bedroom, it looks much the same as her room in Canberra. With one noticeable difference: there are no trophies or beauty pageant sashes in sight. She must've left them packed away when they moved. It wasn't who she was anyway. She hated that part of her life, hence her meltdown with Sophia last night.

My heart drops into the pit of my stomach when I open her wardrobe to find her clothes gone. I find the exact same thing when I run into Maddie's room. Pulling my phone out of my pocket, I call her number, but it goes straight to voicemail.

My shoulders slump. She's gone, and she's taken my little girl with her.

'She's gone ... both my babies are gone,' I hear Sophia cry from behind me.

No kidding, Sherlock. When I swing around to face her I notice the letter in her hand.

'I just found this on the kitchen table.'

Jesus. I clutch my head in my hands, as devastation rips through me yet again.

NINETEEN

JAX

Six months later . . .

I'M SITTING ON THE END OF BRIAN'S BED WHEN HE UNLOCKS the garage door. 'Jax,' he says, stunned, as he pauses in the doorway. Maybe I should've waited for him outside, but it's cold tonight, I would've frozen my damn nuts off.

'Sorry, Brian. I didn't mean to startle you.'

He removes the scarf, gloves and beanie I bought him last week, neatly placing them on the chair in the corner then comes to a stop in front of the heater. I turned it on to warm the place up when I arrived.

'No need to apologise, son. This is your place. I wasn't expecting you to be here, that's all.' The deep wrinkles around his eyes are more prominent when he smiles.

'I just wanted to speak with you before I head home.'

'Any news on your girls?' he asks, his face lighting up with hope.

I sigh. I have news, but not the kind he's referring to. 'Nothing yet. The private eye is still searching.'

'I'm sorry to hear that, son.'

They say the truth will set you free, but in my case it didn't set me free at all—it fucking destroyed me, ripped my damn heart out and smashed it to smithereens. It's been six months and Candice still hasn't returned with my daughter. She withdrew a large amount of cash out of the bank, the day after she disappeared. Sophia opened up an account for her when she was a baby, making regular deposits with some of the money her father's been sending. It's apparently enough to keep her hidden for a few years, if that's what she chooses. Because she's using cash, it's almost impossible to find them, but I refuse to give up. If she thinks I'm gonna stop searching, then she's kidding herself. I won't rest until they're both home where they belong.

Any hope I held of sorting this mess out when Candice first left is dwindling rapidly. And the fact that she hasn't contacted Sophia makes my worries intensify. Candice and Sophia apparently had a huge argument when she went back inside after finally telling me the truth about Maddie. I'm sure that's part of the reason she fled and why Sophia fell into a deep depression.

When Brian places his hand on my shoulder, I give him a weak smile. I've really become attached to him over these difficult months. I don't know where I'd be without him. His friendship, fatherly talks, wise words, and at times stern lectures, have stopped me from going off the rails a number of times since Candice left. Carter and I have become close as well, but unlike Brian, he has no idea that Candice has run off with my little girl. He thinks she's on an extended holiday or some shit.

'So what brings you here?'

'I have a few things I need you to do for me tomorrow.'

'Anything for you. I'm happy to help.'

I'm pleased he said that. I pull an envelope out of my back pocket and watch as he opens it, revealing the cash inside. When he looks up at me, there's a puzzled expression on his face. I bet it's been a while since he's seen so much money.

'What would you like me to do with this?'

'Buy yourself a nice suit, and get a haircut. A proper one.'

'I can't take your money, Jax.' He tries to pass the envelope back.

'It's not my money. It's yours. I've been putting all the coins you've been leaving into a moneybox.' It's surprising how fast it's added up. In just over a year, that small change has amounted to almost one and a half grand.

'That money was for you. I know it wasn't much, but it was my way of trying to repay you for all the kindness you've shown me.'

'I never had any intentions of keeping that money, Brian. I was always going to give it back to you one day, and that day has arrived.'

'Why now? Do you want me to leave?'

'What? Hell, no. I have something planned for tomorrow night, but I'll need you to smarten yourself up a bit.' I quickly raise my hand when I realise what I've just said may have sounded offensive. 'Not that there's anything wrong with the way you dress, but once you find out what I have planned, you'll be thankful I asked you to do this.'

'Are you going to tell me what it is?' He's sceptical, but he has no need to be.

'Do you trust me?'

'Implicitly,' he replies quickly.

I appreciate that, because believe it or not, I trust this man with my life. He and Carter are all I have left. I still see Sophia occasionally, but not as much as I used to. I already had enough shit of my own to deal with, but I couldn't turn a blind eye to Sophia's illness. She's been more of a mother figure to me over the years than my own mother ever was. Thankfully, she's coming along fine now, leaving the depression behind and trying to get used to life without Candice and Maddison. For the time being anyway. We both hold out hope that they'll return one day.

'I'd rather surprise you, if that's okay.' I've been busting my arse all week to get this organised for him and I'm really looking forward to seeing the outcome. After the hell I've been through, I could really use this to pick me up.

'Should I be worried?'

'Not at all.' I rub my hands together to warm them. 'It's a good surprise.' Well, I hope he sees it that way. He's a good man, and he deserves great things. He shouldn't be punished for the rest of his life for trying to save his wife. 'Buy the suit, get a haircut, and meet me here tomorrow afternoon at four. Don't be late.'

He hesitates before replying. 'Okay.'

●●●●

'Hey man,' I say, answering the call when I see Carter's name on the screen. I miss having him around. He's like the brother I always wished for. He's nothing like the cocksucker I've got.

'Hey, fucker. Are you still coming up on the weekend?' Carter moved to Newcastle a few months ago. It's a two-hour drive from Sydney, and a beautiful place, with a picturesque coast line and amazing beaches. If I didn't love Newtown so much, I'd probably join him. He's living the charmed life.

I was sad to see him go, but on the other hand, I'm happy to see him flourishing. The messed-up, broody kid who came to work here is no more. He has his own studio now, and seems content. I can't ask for more than that. He deserves happiness . . . we all do.

'Wouldn't miss it.' Visiting Carter is the highlight of my week, a break from the misery and constant worry that has become my life. A chance to let loose, unwind and forget for a little while. I just wish I knew my girls were okay, and more importantly, safe. It would ease my mind somewhat.

'Make sure you bring lots of coins, because I'm gonna wipe the table with you,' he says. We never play for big money, and I usually always win. I enjoy his company more than the card night anyway. I think he enjoys mine as well. We're alike in so many ways. We have similar interests, and he's a loner just like me. I never hear any mention of his family.

'Is that so?'

'Yes.'

'Keep dreaming.'

'There's a new nightclub opening Friday night. Maybe we can check it out while you're here? There's bound to be some hot arse, just ripe for the picking.'

Carter lives the life I once lived, moving from one hot chick to the next. I haven't been with anyone else since Candice left. If I can't trust her, what hope have I got with anyone else? 'Sure, sounds great,' I say.

••••

'You got everything?' I ask Brian when he enters the shop.

'Suit,' he says, holding up a bag. 'It came with a free shirt and tie, and I have new shoes.' He smiles when he holds up the bag in his other hand.

'We're all set then. I'm liking the haircut, it suits you.' His longish grey hair is now a neat short back and sides. He looks like a different person already.

'Thank you. It's been years since I've had a proper haircut.'

'Let's get going then.'

'Can you tell me what this is all about?' he asks. He has no reason to be concerned. His life is about to change, but in a good way.

'We're heading to my place, so you can shower and change.'

'Oh.' His brow furrows. 'Are we going somewhere?'

'Enough questions,' I say, taking the suit bag out of his hand. 'It won't be a surprise if I tell you. Don't worry, you'll find out soon enough.'

'Okay.' He gives me a weak smile. 'I almost forgot, here's the change,' he says, reaching into his pocket and pulling out the envelope. 'I only spent two hundred and sixty dollars.'

'It's your money, Brian,' I reply, pushing his hand away. 'There's no way I'm taking it back.' He goes to protest, so I turn my attention to my new receptionist. 'I'm heading off now, Ana. Gus has the keys to lock up.'

She's the third girl I've hired since Candice left. Thankfully, this one seems to be working out. I used Carter as a stand-in for the first few weeks, but in the end I was left with no choice, I had to find a replacement. Even if Candice did return, there's no way we could continue to work together, and Carter's talents were being wasted on the front counter.

'Okay. Enjoy the rest of your afternoon.' She gives me a pleasant smile. I like her. She's older than the others, and married with two little boys. Let's face it, I've had my fair share of young and glamorous receptionists, and that gets complicated. Ana works hard, she's nice to my clients, and she gets along with the other staff. That's what's important.

'Thank you. Just call if there're any problems.'

'Will do, boss.'

I grab a fresh towel out of the linen cupboard when we arrive at my place, handing it to Brian. 'There's a new toothbrush, razor and a can of deodorant on the basin in the bathroom.'

'Thank you. I wish I knew what this was all about.'

'You'll know soon enough.' I place my hand on his shoulder briefly. 'It's good. Stop worrying.'

I head into the kitchen to grab a beer. In all honesty, I have mixed emotions about tonight. I'm happy, a little sad, and extremely anxious. I hope Brian doesn't get upset with me when he finds out what I've done.

'Wow, look at you,' I say when he joins me in the kitchen thirty minutes later.

'I've never liked wearing a tie,' he replies, tugging at the one around his neck.

I chuckle. 'Me either.'

'Getting to have a long, hot shower makes it worthwhile.'

I can't tell you how many times over the past year I've offered to let him come here to shower, but he's always declined. I wish I'd been more persistent now.

'I feel like the person I was before . . .' His words drift off, but I know what he was going to say, and I feel sorry for him. He not only lost the love of his life, he lost everything, including his dignity. Hopefully that will all change tonight. A new beginning.

'You don't have to wear it for long.'

'Are you going to let me in on the surprise now?'

'Soon. Do you want a beer?' I ask, holding up the one in my hand.

'Please. It might settle my nerves a bit.'

'Sit,' I say, pointing to the stools at the breakfast bar. I grab a beer from the fridge before taking the seat beside him. I take a deep breath. Expressing my feelings is something I've never been comfortable with. I know what I'm doing is the right thing, but I can't help but feel selfish. I'm not completely prepared for what tonight might bring—losing him.

'Brian, I'm glad you came into my life.'

'Meeting you has been a godsend,' he says. 'I'm not sure how much longer I would've survived on the streets without your kindness. You have a very giving heart, Jax. Your parents must be extremely proud of you.'

'Huh. My parents are ashamed of me.' The words are out of my mouth before they even register. I usually don't talk about my personal life.

'I can't imagine why. You're an exceptional young man. You're compassionate, kind, hardworking ... not many youngsters can say they run a successful business at your age. Not to mention what you've done for me.' He pauses briefly and looks down at the bottle of beer in his hand. When his eyes finally meet mine again, I'm surprised to see tears glistening in them. 'Do you know, in all the years I was on the streets, you were the first person to look past my homelessness and treat me like a human being. That's a very rare trait. I'm proud of you, and I'd be equally proud to call you my son.'

'Thank you.' Apart from Candice, he's the only person to ever say they're proud of me. 'I think you'd make a pretty awesome dad.' I think back to the first day I met him. My heart certainly went out to him that day, but I never expected to care for him as deeply as I do now. 'You may not realise it, but you've given me a lot too.'

I take a gulp of beer to clear my throat. I want to remember tonight with happiness, because it may be the last time I ever see him. Looking at my watch, I realise it's just about time. Our guest should be arriving any minute.

My heart rate accelerates when I hear a knock at the door. *Showtime.*

'Are you expecting anyone?' Brian asks as I stand.

'I am. I won't be a minute.' I rub my hands together in anticipation as I walk towards the front door. Please let this meeting go as well as I've hoped.

'Jax,' he says, when I open the door.

'Yes,' I reply, shaking his hand. 'Come in.' He's older than I thought he'd be, and looks nothing like what I pictured in my head when I spoke with him on the phone. He's dressed casually in a polo shirt and jeans. I don't know why I expected him to be wearing a suit.

'Thank you. Is he here?'

'He is,' I answer as he follows me down the hall. 'He has no idea you're coming, so don't be discouraged if he's surprised to see you.' Christ, I hope Brian's not going to be angry at me for interfering. That's the last thing I want. I did what I thought was right.

Brian's gaze is fixed on his beer bottle when we enter the kitchen. I clear my throat, and he looks up at us. The moment he sees our guest, his eyes widen in disbelief.

'James,' he says breathlessly as he rises from the stool.

'Hi, Dad.'

They approach each other, meeting in the middle of the room. As soon as he's close enough, Brian pulls James into a crushing embrace.

'I've missed you, son.'

When I hear his voice crack, a lump rises in my throat. It makes me think of my own father; I know I'd never hear those words leave his mouth. James is lucky to have a father like Brian. I exhale in relief as I watch them cling to each other like their lives depend on it, neither of them daring to let go.

'You should've told me you were in trouble, Dad. You know I would've helped out.' James was shocked and devastated when I told him about the life his father had been living since his wife passed away. He had no clue.

'I didn't want to burden my child with my problems.'

James pulls back from his father, making eye contact with him. 'We're family. That's what families do. We look out for each other. You and Mum gave me everything growing up. You were always there . . . *always*. Now it's my time to give something back. I'm taking you back to Perth with me. No arguments. I want you with us, Alana does as well. You can help her with Aiden when I'm at work. I want him to know how amazing his grandfather is.'

When Brian wipes the tears from his eyes, I look away and wipe my own. I must have an allergy that's making my eyes water, because Jaxson Albright doesn't cry.

TWENTY

JAX

'JAX,' SOPHIA SAYS WITH SURPRISE WHEN SHE OPENS HER front door. I feel bad when I see hope in her eyes. 'Is everything okay? Do you have news?'

I was going to call her before heading to Carter's for the weekend, just to see how she was doing, but after Brian and James left last night, I felt something I hoped I wouldn't feel again—complete and utter loneliness. *I despise that feeling.* Sophia is one of the few people I have left, so I felt compelled to come here.

'No news, I'm afraid.' I can't bear to see the look of disappointment on her face. 'I'm heading to Newcastle for the weekend, I just wanted to see you before I left.'

Her brow furrows as she studies my face. 'What's wrong, Jax?' she asks softly, as she runs her hand down the side of my arm.

'Nothing.'

'Bullshit. You can't fool me, I know you better than you think. Come in and have a cuppa before you leave.'

'I'd like that.'

Now that my girls have gone, I hate being in this house. It holds too many memories. This place seems so big and quiet without them. I don't know how Sophia can stand it.

'Sit,' she says when we enter the kitchen. 'I'll make the coffee, then we'll talk.'

'I'm okay, honest.'

Sophia glances at me over her shoulder, raising an eyebrow. She doesn't speak a word, but I already know she can see straight through my lie.

She places a mug of coffee down in front of me before taking the seat opposite. Reaching across the table, she puts her hand on top of mine. 'Talk to me, Jax.'

'I don't want to burden you with my problems, you have enough of your own.'

'Jax, I love you like a son. I'm here if you want to talk. Always. No matter what shit I'm dealing with.'

I exhale audibly before I speak. 'I just felt lonely,' I say, shrugging. 'Carter's moved away, Brian's gone to Perth to live with his son, and my girls aren't here—'

'The girls will be back.'

'How can you be so sure?'

'I know it in my heart. Candice just needed a little space. Letting me raise Maddie wasn't easy for her.'

'Then why did she do it?' This is the first chance I've had to ask her. When Candice ran off, I was angry and devastated, but not knowing the truth is eating away at me. If only I'd heard her out the night before she left, or at least returned her calls or texts. I've been constantly kicking myself for that.

'It's not my story to tell. When she comes home, she'll tell you why. Please know I played a huge part in her final decision. I was only nineteen when I gave birth to her. I knew firsthand how hard it was going to be. I didn't want that for my little girl. I wanted her to experience life. To do all the things I couldn't. Being a single mum isn't easy, Jax. Especially at such a young age.'

'I don't know if I can forgive her for keeping it from me. I had a right to know.'

'I'm sorry,' Sophia says, reaching for my hand again. 'She didn't do it to hurt you. There's a lot more to it. We thought we were doing the right thing at the time. You left, remember? You were studying to become a politician.'

I bring my mug to my lips. I have no response for that. Yes, I left, I get that, but I still think they should've told me.

'Listen, why don't you start coming around for dinner again? Even if it's only one or two nights a week. I could use the company as well. We have to stick together.'

'Don't you have a boyfriend now?'

'Kind of.' She shrugs. 'We're taking things slow. Like him, I haven't been on the dating scene for years. Brendan and his ex-wife divorced a few years ago. This is all new to us, so we don't want to rush it. Well, I don't. It's nice though. It's been so long since I've felt like this about anyone.' She gives a contented sigh.

'Does he make you happy?'

'Yes—yes, he does. I'll let you meet him one day. That's if things work out. We haven't even had sex yet.'

I cough and splutter. Why did she tell me that when I had a mouth full of coffee? More to the point, why did she tell me *at all*? Just the thought of her in that way makes me want to bleach my brain.

Sophia comes around to my side of the table and taps my back. 'Shit, Jax. Are you okay?'

'I will be if you stop talking about your sex life,' I reply, trying not to hack up a lung. She throws back her head and laughs. I'm glad she thinks it's funny. I must admit, being this carefree suits her. It reminds me of Candice. I hate myself for missing her so much.

'Sorry. You're the only person I have to talk to . . . Brendan's been great anyway. He said he'd wait until I was ready.'

'Again with the TMI.' This time I put my hands over my ears, just in case she feels the need to elaborate.

'I'm sorry.' She reaches for my hands, removing them from the side of my head.

'You can talk to me about anything, as long as it doesn't involve your sex life.'

'Duly noted,' she says with amusement, picking up my empty mug. 'Would you like another coffee?'

'No, I'd better hit the road. I have a long drive ahead of me.'

••••

'Two pairs,' Carter says smugly, placing his cards down on the table.

Two fucking pairs, is he kidding me? 'Huh. Full house, fucker,' I retort, equally as smug. 'Read 'em and weep.'

'Cockhead,' he snaps, rising from his seat.

I slide all the money from the centre of the table to my side. 'Glad you were gonna wipe the table with me tonight,' I say. 'You've won, like what? One game out of ten.'

'Fuck off,' he grumbles. 'Want another beer?'

'Sure.'

He comes back a minute later and places a bottle in front of me. 'That'll be ten bucks.'

I laugh. 'Keep dreamin', dickhead. I'm not paying you ten bucks for a damn beer.'

'It was worth a try,' he says. 'Wanna go check out that new club after we drink these?'

'Sure.' I grab a handful of nuts out of a bowl on the table, and shove them in my mouth. I know exactly why he wants to go, but he'll be the only one picking up tonight. I'm not interested.

••••

I groan and bury my head further into the pillow when I wake. Opening one eye a fraction, I immediately close it again when I'm almost blinded by the bright light flooding the room. My head hurts like a bitch, and my whole body aches. I feel like I've run a damn marathon. I try to swallow in an attempt to ease my parched throat.

Carter and his bright ideas. I lost count after our eighth or ninth shot last night. I'm certainly paying for it now.

My eyes spring open when I hear a soft moan. There's a naked blonde lying beside me. I raise my head off the pillow. Christ, and a fucking brunette on the other side of her. I scan the room. I'm not even sure where I am, but I'm definitely not at Carter's house. How did I even get here?

My brain goes into overdrive as I try to retrace the steps of last night. *Nothing.* I remember being drunk, that's about it. Everything is foggy. Carter and I were having fun. There were girls at our table—are these the same girls? Shit. Guilt floods me. Although I haven't seen or heard from Candice in six months, I can't help but feel like I've just cheated on her.

We aren't even together.

We'll *never* be together.

We're finished, of that I'm sure.

Despite my feelings for Candice, I can't be with someone I don't trust. Trust is everything in a relationship. Again I'm filled with sadness at the realisation that I've lost the love of my life.

I slowly try to get out of bed—I need to go. Maybe nothing happened. Who am I kidding? There are two hot chicks lying next to me, naked— of course something happened, if only I could remember what. I pause when I realise that my arm is positioned under the blonde's neck. Fuck. How am I gonna get out of here without waking her?

The moment I try to slide it out from underneath her, she stirs. Now I know what guys mean when they say they'd chew their arm off to escape, because if it meant getting out of here without any drama, I'd damn well do it. I hate awkward goodbyes. *Do you want my number? Can I see you again?* Nope and nope.

It takes a good couple of minutes before I finally free my arm, inch by inch, and slowly climb out of bed. When I see two used condoms on the floor beside the bed, my heart sinks. There's no denying it now. If I was so drunk I can't remember, I'm surprised I could even perform.

Gathering my clothes, I make a hasty retreat into the hallway to dress. I don't want to be anywhere near those girls if they wake. *Fuck. Fuck. Fuck.* I exhale a deflated breath as I slide into my jeans. I have no idea what Candice is up to, or who she may or may not be with, but it doesn't lessen the guilt I'm feeling. She could be shacked up with someone for all I know, playing happy families with my damn kid. Christ, I hope that's not the case.

When we finally agreed to make a go of our relationship, I swore she'd be my one and only. She was all I wanted. All I'd ever wanted. That was before she ripped my heart out of my chest and stomped on it.

••••

'Look what the cat dragged in,' Carter says when I enter his apartment. He's sitting at the kitchen table, nursing a coffee and looking just how I feel. I'd like to say I'll never drink again, but I know that's a lie. I will. I always do.

'Fuck off.'

'Where did you end up last night?' he asks as I grab a mug out of the cupboard.

'Fucked if I know. Some chicks' house. Well, I hope it was their house.'

He chuckles.

'Last time I ever drink shots with you, prick.'

'So it's my fault you got drunk—and laid—last night?'

'You better believe it is.'

'Well, shouldn't you be thanking me then?'

'Hardly.'

'Wasn't she any good?'

'They,' I say. 'There were two of them. And I have no idea. I can't remember a damn thing.'

'Impressive,' he replies. 'Let's just hope you weren't so drunk you couldn't perform.'

'Huh. I highly doubt it. Maybe you have that problem, but I certainly don't. I'm pretty sure I could perform even if I was comatose.'

'Whatever, cock.'

I laugh at his pathetic comeback. He can give it, but he certainly can't take it. 'Did you sleep here last night?' I ask, because again, I can't remember jackshit.

'I don't know about sleep,' he says, 'but yeah, I stayed here.'

'I bet you couldn't handle two at once.'

'Actually, there were three of them,' he says.

'Fucking liar.'

He bursts out laughing, because he knows as well as I do that he's full of shit.

After Carter cooked us some bacon and eggs for breakfast, we went back to bed. Carter has a one-bedroom apartment, right above his tattoo shop, and I stay on the pull-out sofa. He bought the building when he moved up here. Like me, he worked his arse off and saved every penny he could to put into his business. I'm so proud of how well he's doing. Like me, he's living his dream. It just proves, no matter where you come from, or what struggles you face in life, with hard work and determination, anything is possible.

It's around two pm by the time I finally leave. I love getting away for the weekend. It's a nice escape.

Well, it is while it lasts. Reality creeps back in as I head down the M1 towards home and my thoughts drift to my girls. When are we going to get some word from them? I'm not sure how much more I can take. With every day that passes, another little piece of me dies. Candice robbed me of my daughter's early years, so it infuriates me that she's doing it again. How did I not see this incredibly selfish side of her before now? If I find them, I'll be bringing Maddie home, whether Candice likes it or not. She's my daughter too.

When I arrive back in Newtown, I stop off at the local grocer and pick up a few things before heading home. Maybe it's time I sold up and moved, just like Carter did. He seems a lot happier where he is. As much as I love my place, there're too many memories here.

My mind is weighed down with all the usual bullshit when I pull up to the kerb outside my place. This is why I need my escape to Carter's. I'd go fucking crazy if I didn't.

Grabbing the bags of groceries off the passenger seat, I get out of the car. 'Jaaaax!' I hear the moment I step onto the footpath. I know that voice. My head snaps in the direction it came from, and my pulse quickens when I see Maddie running down the path towards me. I've been wishing for this moment for so long now, please don't let it be a mirage.

The excitement I see on her face as she approaches hits me right in the chest. Dropping my groceries, I open my arms, scooping her up the second she's within reaching distance. I've missed her.

'Peanut,' I whisper as I wrap my arms around her, squeezing her tight. I hold her for the longest time, breathing her in.

'You my daddy?' She leans her small body back to look at me.

A lump rises in my throat when I hear her call me 'Daddy'. It's a word I never knew I wanted to hear. Candice has obviously told Maddie the truth, which I'm grateful for. She has a right to know who her parents are. Like me, she's been deceived for far too long.

I've missed her sweet little face so much. It's only been six months, but I'm positive she's grown. Even her hair looks longer. She may look like her mum, but I can see what Brian saw now. She does have my eyes.

I love that she has my eyes.

'Yes. I'm your daddy.'

Her face lights up before her hands tightly encircle my neck. 'Daddy!' she squeals.

I try to keep my emotions in check, but no matter how hard I try, I can't stop the tears that rise to my eyes. My little girl is home.

'I wuv you, Daddy.'

The moment those words are out of her mouth I lose it and start to weep. I'm powerless to stop the tears that fall. All the anguish and uncertainty I've suffered over the past six months has finally come to a head, and all the feelings I've been bottling up rise to the surface. My heart sings with the knowledge that she loves me. Crushing her tiny body against mine, I hold her tight. I finally get to savour the wondrous sensation of being a parent. That's if Candice doesn't rob me of it again.

'I love you too,' I whisper. Before I even knew she was my daughter, Maddie had captured my heart. I finally have someone to love me just as much as I love them.

Leaning back in my arms again, she frowns as she studies my face. 'Don't cry, Daddy.'

'I'm okay,' I say, smiling. 'They're happy tears. I'm just so glad to have you back. I've missed you.'

'I miss you,' she says and her sloppy lips meet mine.

CANDICE

TWENTY-ONE

CANDICE

I WIPE THE TEARS FROM MY EYES AS I WATCH MADDIE AND Jax reunite. It's such a beautiful sight. I'm relieved that the secret is finally out, but it breaks my heart to know I won't get the same reaction from him when he sees me. I can't blame him, though. I should've brought her back sooner, but the longer I stayed away, the harder it was to return. I needed time to think, to clear my head and, more importantly, to heal. Plus, I was scared—scared he'd take my little girl away from me.

My heart shattered when Jax walked away from me again that night, and then refused to take my calls. I hope in time he can forgive me for not telling him from the beginning. I honestly thought I was doing the right thing. I had no idea we were going to reconnect, or that he was going to walk away from politics. An illegitimate child could've ruined his career before it even started. That was one of the many things I considered before agreeing to let Sophia raise Maddie as her own. That was the hardest decision I've ever had to make. Maddie was my little girl, and the only part of Jax I had left. It almost killed me to step aside the way I did.

I stand on the front porch and watch them, too scared to move. I can't see Jax's face from where I'm standing because it's buried into the crook of Maddie's neck, but I can tell he's crying by the slight jerking movements of his body. It kills me to know I've hurt him like this. I want to run to him and wrap him in my arms, but I know he wouldn't want that. If getting down on my knees to beg and plead for his forgiveness would help, I wouldn't hesitate. There's nothing I wouldn't do to make this right.

Minutes pass before he finally sets Maddie on her feet and wipes his eyes. He picks up the bags of groceries from the footpath before scooping her into his spare arm. The smile on his face as he looks at her warms my heart. He's going to be an amazing father. I want that for her. I want her to have everything I didn't.

My heart rate accelerates as they approach me. I have no idea what kind of reception I'm going to get, but I already know he's not going to welcome me back with open arms.

It's not until they're a few feet away that his eyes finally move to me. He pauses briefly and exhales visibly, but his expression remains passive. As expected, he doesn't appear to be happy to see me. I'm surprised by how much his lack of a reaction hurts. Instead of the anger I expected, all I see is pain. An awful lot of pain. I swallow hard, in an attempt to hold back my tears. I know firsthand how much his family have wounded him over the years, so I hate myself for doing the same.

'Hi,' I whisper.

'Hi.' He clears his throat as he walks straight past me. Putting Maddie on the ground, he fishes his keys out of his pocket. He scoops her into his arms again before walking inside. I half expect him to slam the door in my face, but he doesn't. I'm not sure if I'm welcome in his home anymore, but I enter anyway. I have a lot to say to him, and I refuse to leave here until he hears me out. Whether he wants my side of the story or not, he's going to get it.

Jax takes Maddie into the lounge room and sits her on the sofa. I stand in the doorway while he turns on the television, changing the channel to Nick Jr. He doesn't make eye contact as he passes me on his way to the kitchen. I'm not sure if he wants me to follow, but I do.

I find him standing at the breakfast bar, his back is to me as he unpacks the groceries. I come to a stop just inside the door, shoving my hands nervously into the pockets of my jeans. I'm devastated by the way things have ended up between us. I miss him, his friendship, his kisses, his hugs—his everything. I've spent the past six months trying to let my feelings for him go, to no avail. I'm still in love with him.

'Does Sophia know you're back?' he asks without turning around. There's venom in his voice.

'Not yet. I came here first. I wanted to talk to you, and I thought you'd like to see Maddie.'

'It's a little late for that, don't you think?' he snaps as he spins around. 'I wanted to see her six months ago, Candice. And every fucking day since. But yet again you stole that from me. Keeping my daughter from me for three years wasn't enough for you? You had to add another six months just to punish me further?' He raises his trembling hands, running them through his hair. 'If I'd known she was mine, I would've wanted to be there from the very beginning. For her birth, for her first word, her first step—for everything. But you didn't even give me a chance. I never picked you for such a selfish bitch. You really had me fooled.'

His words sting, but I guess I deserve them. 'It wasn't like that, Jax,' I say as I take a step towards him.

'Don't.' He holds his hand up. 'So you didn't keep the truth from me for years, or disappear with her for six months?'

'Yes.' I sigh as I look at the floor. I can't bear to see the hate in his eyes.

'Exactly.' He doesn't say anything else as he snatches the carton of milk off the bench and walks to the fridge. 'I'll tell you this; you try to take her away from me again and you'll be sorry.'

'So you're threatening me now?'

'You better believe I am. I won't let you rob me of one more day of my daughter's life.'

'I wouldn't.'

'Really?'

'Yes, really.' I've never seen this side of him before. I don't like it.

'And you expect me to take your word for it? I trusted you once, Candice, I'm not stupid enough to do it a second time. I'll be going to a solicitor. I want joint custody. If you don't agree, I'll fight you every step of the way.'

'Jax.' I bite my bottom lip when it starts to quiver. I don't know what to say to make this better. When the tears fill my eyes, I look away. 'I'm sorry,' I whisper. 'You don't have to do that. You can see her whenever you like. I promise.'

'Huh,' he scoffs like he doesn't believe me.

Granted he's angry, and he has every right to be, but his attitude is really pissing me off. 'You don't have to act like such an arsehole. I fucked up, I know that. You haven't even given me a chance to explain.'

He slams his fist on the benchtop, making me flinch. 'I may have walked away from you, but do you blame me? You drop a fucking bombshell like that and expect me to take it in my stride? I was shocked, angry and completely fucking devastated that you'd deceived me.'

'I—'

'Let me finish. I needed some time to process the fact that I had a daughter I knew nothing about. That my best friend—*the woman I loved*—the person I trusted more than anyone, had been lying to me and deceiving me for years. Just put yourself in my shoes for a minute. In my heart, I wanted to believe that the Candice I knew would never do something so incredibly cruel without good reason. What a fool I was.'

I know I deserve every hateful word that spews from his mouth, but it still hurts to hear them. He's never treated me like this. 'I'm so sorry, Jax.' It's a lame response, but I don't know what else to say.

'So am I,' he says, disappointment lining his voice. 'You were the best thing that ever happened to me, Candice . . . or so I thought.'

JAX

I feel like a prick when Candice buries her face in her hands and starts to sob, but as much as I want to, I refuse to comfort her. I'm incredibly hurt and angry. Those words have been festering inside me for six long months; they needed to be said. No matter what her reasons were, what she did to me was wrong. She needs to be held accountable for that.

I stand there and watch her cry, arms folded across my chest like an uncompassionate prick. Everything in me wants to hold her, but I can't bring myself to. Having her here brings all my feelings to the surface. I hate myself for still loving her when I should hate her for what she's done.

I try my hardest to soften my voice when I finally speak. 'Why don't you go home and talk with your mum? She was devastated when you left.'

Wiping the tears from her face once more, her red-rimmed eyes meet mine. There's no doubt she's lost weight while she's been gone. Her face is drawn, and there're dark circles under her eyes. I'm guessing the past six months haven't been easy for her either. She looks broken. Even after everything she's done to me, it kills me to see her hurting.

'You want me to leave? I'd like the chance to at least explain. Please, Jax.'

'I have every intention of hearing you out,' I say, even though I don't hold any hope that it'll make a difference. There's nothing she can say that will make this right. *Nothing*. 'I just want to spend some time with my daughter first.'

'You're keeping Maddie?' What colour there is in her face drains away when she speaks.

I'm not keeping her, but I'd like to spend some time with her. I've missed out on so much of her life already. 'I think it's only fair that I get to spend some quality time with my kid, since I haven't seen her in six months.'

'You're gonna give her back though, right?'

'Of course I'm going to give her back, but we'll need to come to some arrangement. I want her in my life.' As much as I want Maddie here with me, I could never take her away from her mother. I know how much she loves her.

'Okay.'

'Go see Sophia, and I'll drop her back later tonight. Maybe we can talk then.'

'Sure. I'd like a chance to explain. Please know I didn't do this to hurt you. I thought I was doing the right thing.'

'Well, you did hurt me. You hurt me a lot.'

••••

'Are you hungry?' I ask Maddie as I take a seat beside her on the sofa. She's watching a *Dora the* fucking *Explorer* marathon, but I don't care. As much as I hate this damn cartoon, I'd sit here all night and watch it if it made my little girl happy.

'Yes.'

I smile when she climbs onto my lap, her eyes never once leaving the television. 'Do you wanna go get something to eat then?'

''Kay,' she says, snuggling into me and laying her head on my chest.

I wrap my arms around her tiny waist and place a kiss on her hair. 'What do you feel like?'

'Ride rice,' she says, looking up at me briefly.

It's funny how all the signs are as clear as day now. Her eyes, her left-handedness, even her tiny fingers and toes resemble mine. *I love that.* I guess I couldn't see it before because I never would've believed that Candice could betray me like she has.

'When this episode finishes, we'll go get some fried rice.'

''Kay.'

She's such a good girl. I find myself smiling as she laughs, squeals and repeats the words Dora says in Spanish. This show is still painful, but I love how much she loves it. When it's over, I grab the cardigan Candice left for her, sliding her little arms in.

'Ta,' she says when I finish buttoning up the front. I pick her up and kiss her cheek. I'm so happy she's back.

'You're ready to go.'

'Puppy?' she says, extending her arms. I see him lying on the sofa.

'Maybe we should leave Puppy here. We don't want to lose him like we did last time.'

'Puppy come. Puppy like ride rice.'

When she pouts, I cave straightaway. I think I'm going to have a hard time denying her anything. 'Okay. Puppy can come.'

Maddie reaches for my hand on the way to the restaurant and it's the best fucking feeling ever. It blows my mind that I'm a father, but I couldn't have asked for a sweeter girl. I'm going to try my hardest to be the best damn father I can. Nothing like my fucked-up parents. My only regret is that my relationship with Candice is ruined. I don't think it's possible to get back what we had. Too much has happened.

I groan when I realise I'm singing the *Dora the Explorer* theme song in my head. That show is going to be the death of me.

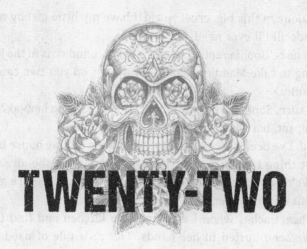

TWENTY-TWO

JAX

'PHIA!' MADDIE SQUEALS WHEN SOPHIA ANSWERS THE DOOR.
I was hesitant in bringing her back—a few hours with her wasn't
nearly enough.

'My baby!' Sophia cries, taking Maddie out of my arms and
crushing her small body against her own. 'God, I've missed you ...
I've missed you so much.'

Maddie giggles as Sophia peppers kisses all over her face.
Witnessing their reunion brings a lump to my throat. That's exactly
how I felt a few hours ago. Although there're tears streaming down
her face, Sophia is smiling when her eyes move to me.

'Our girls are home,' she whispers. She moves Maddie to her hip
and uses her free arm to pull me into a crushing hug. 'I told you
they'd come back.'

She did, and I'm so glad she was right.

'My daddy, Phia,' Maddie says, pointing to me. It makes my smile
widen. It's a wonderful feeling to be needed, wanted, *loved*. I'm no

longer alone in this big, cruel world. I have my little girl by my side, and that's all I'll ever need.

'Yes, he is,' Sophia replies, winking at me. 'Candice is in the kitchen. I'm going to take Maddie upstairs for a bath, so you two can talk.'

'Thanks.'

As I turn, Sophia grabs my elbow. 'Take it easy on her, Jax? I know you're upset, but she's very fragile at the moment.'

I nod. I've been racked with guilt since she left my house in tears. The last thing I want to do is hurt her more than she already has been. We're going to have to find a middle ground if we're going to co-parent our daughter.

My heart aches when I walk into the kitchen and find Candice with her head buried in her hands. There's a pile of used tissues sitting on the table in front of her. When I reach her side, I pull her off the chair and into my arms.

'Don't cry,' I whisper.

'Oh, Jax. I've ruined everything. Can you ever forgive me?'

When she buries her face into my chest I rest my chin on the top of her head. Her sweet apple scent envelops me. I've missed that smell. 'Shh,' I say, rubbing her back as I hold her tight. Can I forgive her? I don't know.

I don't let go until her tears finally stop. 'I'm sorry,' she whispers, wiping her eyes with the back of her hand before plucking another tissue out of the box and blowing her nose.

'This has been hard on all of us,' I say, taking a seat at the table.

'Thank you for coming over . . . and for bringing Maddie back.'

'Of course I'd bring her back. I'm not a monster. She loves you, and I'd never take that away from her.'

'Like I took her away from you?' Candice's shoulders slump and I can see she regrets what she's done. She should—her actions almost broke me.

'We need to sort this out, Candice, find some kind of common ground. We can't be fighting all the time. We have Maddie to consider now.'

'We do,' she says, giving me a half-hearted smile. She takes a seat beside me.

'Can you start by telling me why? Why did you keep the pregnancy from me?'

She shrugs. 'I wanted to tell you from the very beginning.'

'Then why didn't you?'

'The day I sent you that text message was the same day I found out I was pregnant. I was in shock, frightened and totally devastated. You were the first person I contacted. I hadn't even told Sophia. It's not something I expected, Jax, or even wanted. I was only eighteen. You were the first, and only, person I'd ever slept with.'

'I knew I should've fucking wrapped it,' I mumble under my breath, as I shake my head.

'Well, you didn't. There's no point dwelling on that now. What's done is done. I wouldn't give Maddie back for anything.'

'I wouldn't either.' She's the only good thing to come out of this mess. 'I still wish you'd told me. Why didn't you tell me?' I'm trying not to get angry at her, but I need to know.

'It had been over a month since I'd heard from you. It was really hard for me to reach out to you by then. You'd slept with me and done a runner in the middle of the night, so the last thing I wanted to do was chase after you like some pathetic loser. Your reply to my text was hurtful, Jax. So unlike the person I thought I knew, and definitely not the response I'd hoped for.'

'Your message wasn't what I'd hoped for either. I was so happy to see your name on the screen. You have no idea how much I needed to hear from you that day. And then you said I was a disappointment. All my life I've been called a disappointment.'

'I *was* disappointed. I thought our friendship meant more to you than that.'

'Well, it's what I do best. I disappoint people.' I pause, giving myself a moment to calm down. Losing my shit is not going to help. 'Regardless of my reply, there was no mention of a kid.'

'After the way you replied, I wasn't sure if you'd even want to know.'

'Of course I would've wanted to know—she's my fucking kid. I had a right to know, Candice.'

'A part of me hated you for treating me as if I was nothing. You used me.'

'I never used you. That night meant everything to me.' I reach across the table and place my hand on top of hers. 'It meant *everything*. I'm sorry I made you feel that way.'

'It meant everything to me too,' she whispers, but she can't meet my eyes. 'I was eighteen, Jax. Pregnant . . . alone. Sophia freaked when I told her. Fuck, did she freak. I guess it was a given after everything she went through with me. It was history repeating itself. She never wanted me to end up like her, young, single and pregnant.'

'I can understand that. But, it still doesn't explain why you never told me.'

'There were so many reasons, Jax.'

'Like?'

'It wasn't one thing. It was a combination of things.'

'For fuck's sake, Candice.' I feel like I'm banging my head against a fucking wall here. I need answers.

'You leaving, your lack of contact, your reaction to my messages, your potential career in politics, my age, Sophia . . . the list is endless. You always said you never wanted to have kids, Jax. That you never wanted to settle down, or commit to anyone. When Sophia first mentioned that she should bring the baby up as her own, I thought it was preposterous. The baby was a part of me—of *us*. It was all I had left of you.' Her eyes finally move back to me. 'I didn't make the decision on a whim, Jax. I took everything into consideration. That's when we made the choice to move away. I chose Sydney because I knew that's where you were. I still hoped . . . you know . . . that we'd somehow magically reconnect and live happily ever after. I was young. Delusional.'

'I'm sorry.' I feel like such a bastard. I should've made more of an effort. In my heart I already knew our friendship would never be the same; once we crossed that line everything changed. But that's no excuse for the way I treated her. 'I still wish you'd told me.'

'So many times I picked up the phone to call you. My heart was hurting. I felt like I was walking around with a thousand bricks crushing my chest. I was fragile, and unsure if I was even capable of taking another blow from you. Try to understand things from my point of view. You were never the commitment type. At school you moved from one girl to the next. After you left, I heard nothing from you, so I naturally thought that you were doing the same thing to me, moving on to your next good time. You left me feeling like I was just another notch on your belt. The further the pregnancy went on, the more I lost hope. In the end, I decided to take Sophia up on her offer. I was in a dark place, and I knew she could give Maddie the stability she needed.'

'What about when you came back into my life? Why didn't you speak up then? You had me spending time with her. Fuck, I even looked after her. How could you not tell me?' My voice cracks. I'm not even sure what I expect her to say. There are no magical words that will make this ache in my chest go away. Nothing she can say is going to fix this.

'There were so many times I wanted to tell you . . . *so many times*. It was eating away at me. Especially when I saw how good you were with her. But by then it was too late. There was no point in telling you. Maddie was happy, and I didn't want to disrupt her life. You were happy too. Your business was going well, and you seemed content. It killed me to know she was yours and I couldn't say anything, but then you'd say or do something that seemed to confirm I'd made the right decision. Having you spend time with her was my way of giving you something . . . giving you *both* something. She'd never taken to anyone the way she did to you. You bonded right from the beginning. It was like you both somehow knew you belonged together.' Pausing, she covers her face with her hands. 'I thought I was doing the right thing for all of us.' The moment she starts to cry again, I reach for her. 'I'm so sorry, Jax.'

I don't know what to say to that. I understand why she felt the way she did, but that's not how it was, not in my eyes. Candice was my *life*. I was in love with her. I would've been there if I'd known. I'm still angry. She should've told me.

Letting her go, I lean back in my chair and exhale. What's done is done, I suppose. As much as I hate it, we can't change the past. But one thing's for sure, we can't go back to the way things were. Even if her reasons hold merit, my trust in her is gone. All I can do now is move forward the best way I can. I have no choice.

'Where did you go? Why did you stay away for so long?'

'Mudgee.'

'Mudgee? That's in the middle of fucking nowhere.'

'It's only four hours away.' She lets out a small laugh. 'It's actually a really beautiful place.'

'Why Mudgee?' She doesn't really need to answer that. She probably thought that would be the last place we'd look for her, and she was right.

'When I first left we stayed in a motel for a few nights.'

I watch the tissue she's twisting around in her fingers as she talks.

'I was never going to go for so long, but I knew I wasn't ready to come home yet. My head was all over the place. So, I just got in the car and drove and drove. That's where we ended up. We stopped in the town to get something to eat, and I saw an advertisement in the window for a small cabin for rent. After lunch I went out to the property to take a look, and it was beautiful. So picturesque. I fell in love with it. I knew it was just what I needed to get my head in the right space. The cabin had 360-degree views of the countryside. The old couple who owned it, Mr and Mrs Lynch, were so lovely. They adored having Maddie around. Their homestead was on the same property as the cabin, but still far enough away to give us privacy. It didn't seem to stop them from looking out for us. They even invited us over for dinner occasionally.'

As much as I hated them being gone, I'm glad they were looked after. That's what weighed on my mind the most, not knowing if they were safe. She should have at least let us know they were okay.

A simple call or text. Was that too much to ask? I think Sophia and I would've suffered a lot less if Candice had at least done that.

My chest aches, and my head hurts. I'm still struggling to wrap my head around this bullshit. Only a few short months ago everything was perfect. I was happy. *Deliriously happy.* I had the woman of my dreams by my side. I thought I was set.

At least they're home now. I may have lost my lover, my best friend, but I have the rest of my life with my little girl to look forward to.

You've gotta take the positives where you can.

TWENTY-THREE

JAX

'HOW ABOUT THIS ONE?' I ASK MADDIE, HOLDING UP A FRILLY white quilt cover set. We've been in this damn shop for almost an hour, but every suggestion I make gets squashed immediately.

'No. Pink one,' she snaps, crossing her arms in defiance.

'Fine. Pink it is,' I reply with a sigh. I already know she's not going to give in until she gets her way. She's her mother's daughter, that's for sure. Stubborn as all hell. Pink bed, pink dresser, pink linen and pink fucking curtains. I don't want all this pink shit in my house. She's lucky I love her.

It was after midnight when I left Candice's place after we talked. We agreed that we'd share custody of Maddie. I'll be having Maddie every second weekend, and on Tuesdays. My day off. The rest of the time she'll be living at Sophia's with Candice. Technically my weekend will start next week, but Candice let me have Maddie this morning so I'd have time to set everything up for her.

I'm going to see if Gus will help me move my gym equipment out of my spare room and into the empty garage behind the shop, now that Brian's moved out. If Maddie is going to be staying with me regularly, she'll need her own room. I want her to be comfortable while she's with me.

Things between Candice and me are still strained to say the least. She has promised me she won't run again, and I think she means it. Well, I hope she does. Her word means nothing to me now. Although I'm confident we'll be able to keep things civil for our daughter's sake. Even though Maddie seems to be taking it in her stride, this is a big adjustment for her. Six months ago, she thought Sophia was her mother. Thankfully she's young, so she can't really grasp the whole concept.

Taking the pink quilt cover off the shelf, I put it in the shopping trolley. Maddie follows me down the next aisle where the fitted sheet sets are. I don't even bother asking her what colour, I know it's going to be fucking pink.

Moving further along, I reach for one of the quilts that are stacked along the back wall.

'Pink, Daddy.'

'They only come in white. Once you put the cover on it, it'll be pink.'

''Kay,' she replies, smiling. She may be stubborn like her mother, but thankfully she's also easygoing like me.

'The pillows only come in white too, but we have a pink pillow case.'

'I wuv pink.'

'Don't I know it.'

Once I've paid, I pack everything into Candice's car. I don't have a booster seat yet, so I had to borrow her car.

'Wanna get an ice cream before I take you home?'

'Ice cream!' She claps her hands.

'What flavour do you want?' I ask, lifting her into my arms before we cross the road. She better not say pink. I'm all pinked out.

'Nella and spinkles.'

'Vanilla? With sprinkles?'

'Yes, nella and spinkles.'

I smile. Vanilla is my favourite too. Another thing we have in common.

••••

Friday afternoon rolls around fast. With my long days at work, and the nights filled getting Maddie's room ready, you'd think I'd be worn out, but I'm not. I'm excited about spending my first weekend with her. She's gonna love her new bedroom. I've worked my damn arse off trying to get it perfect, so she'd better. It's very fucking pink, but I'm actually impressed by how great it looks. For a pink room that is.

I gave the walls a fresh coat of white paint, but added some pink to the architraves and cornices. I'm no interior designer, but with the pink furniture, even I knew it needed a neutral colour to break it up. The quilt cover Maddie chose is covered in pink and white butterflies, so I went with the butterfly theme for the entire room. I found some butterfly transfers online, which I've put on the wall behind her bed. I bought a pink shagpile rug, the same colour as the curtains, to cover the polished floorboards. Even the pink bedside lamp has tiny butterflies cut out of the shade, so when lit up, it projects butterflies around the room. It's pretty impressive if you ask me.

I left work a little earlier than usual so I could grab some of Maddie's favourite foods from the supermarket. Candice is going to drop her off after dinner. I bought a booster seat for my car during the week, so I can take her out. I have a fun-filled weekend planned for my little girl.

It's just after six when they arrive. 'Daddy!' Maddie squeals when I open the front door. She looks so sweet, wearing a fluffy pink robe over the top of her pyjamas, and pink slippers. Just what this house needs, more fucking pink. I chuckle when she launches herself at me.

'Hi,' I say to Candice, as I scoop Maddie into my arms. I inhale her sweet baby-powder scent, and plant a soft kiss on her hair.

'Hi.' Candice gives me an uncertain smile. I hate that things are so tense between us. We'll never get back to what we were, but hopefully in time we'll find some normality again.

'Come in,' I say, taking Maddie's small pink suitcase out of Candice's hand. I probably shouldn't invite her in, but if we're going to make this arrangement work I need to force myself to be normal with her.

'Thanks.'

As I follow her down the hallway, I try my hardest not to check out her arse, but my eyes betray me. Why does she have to be so goddamn beautiful?

'Do you wanna see your new bedroom?' I ask Maddie.

'My pink bed come?'

'Yes, your pink bed came.'

'Can I see her room too?' Candice asks.

'Sure. I've set her up in my spare room.' When Maddie squirms in my arms, I put her on the floor. Candice comes to a stop a few feet from the doorway, but Maddie runs straight past her. 'Close your eyes,' I say, reaching for the doorhandle.

''Kay.'

'Are they closed?'

She nods, placing her hands over her eyes.

I open the door slightly, sliding my hand inside to turn on the light. 'Are you ready?'

'Yes.' Her tiny body bobs up and down with excitement. I can't help but smile as she waits for me to fully open the door. My gaze moves briefly to Candice, and I find her smiling too, but she's not looking down at Maddie—her eyes are firmly fixed on me.

I quickly look away as that familiar ache settles in my chest. Again I'm reminded of everything I've lost. Things could've been so different if she hadn't deceived me for so long. Trying to push those thoughts out of my mind, I fling open the door. I worked hard putting this together for Maddie, so I want to enjoy her reaction.

'Here's your new room, Peanut.'

'My room!' Maddie squeals, running over to her bed. It takes her a few seconds to climb up, but when she does, she grabs the butterfly-shaped pillow I bought her. 'Butfry.'

'I hope you like butterflies?'

'Wow. It's beautiful, Jax,' I hear Candice say from behind me.

I glance at her over my shoulder. 'Thanks.'

'You did this all by yourself?'

'I did.'

Maddie giggles as she stands on the bed and starts to jump, but I'm drawn to Candice, who steps into the centre of the room. I hate that I'm still so captivated by her; I need to find a way to break this damn spell. It's like some kind of voodoo shit. She's not worthy of my heart anymore.

'I'm pretty impressed with it, despite all the pink,' I admit. The sweet sound of Candice's laughter hits me straight in the chest. I tear my eyes from her and go to Maddie, lifting her off the bed. I need a distraction.

'It's a girl thing,' Candice says.

'What do you want to do tonight?' I ask Maddie.

'Dora.'

I was expecting her to say that, so I'm prepared. 'Would you like to watch a movie with Puppy in it?' I bought *The Peanuts Movie* for her during the week. Charlie Brown runs rings around that Dora chick. I even bought a bag of microwave popcorn. Hope she likes popcorn. I hate that I don't know all of my daughter's likes and dislikes. A parent should know these things. That's another thing Candice has robbed me of. I'm gonna make it my mission to find out every little thing about Maddie, even the insignificant things.

'Puppy!' she squeals, clapping her hands.

I'm still holding her as I leave the room. I pause when I reach the doorway. Glancing back, I see Candice holding the framed picture I've placed on the bedside table. It's an old picture of me and her, in happier times. Things might be strained between us now, but they weren't always like that. I thought it would be nice for our daughter to have a photo of her parents together.

A small smile tugs at Candice's lips as she puts it down. When she turns to follow us out, I see tears glistening in her eyes. I'm so torn. Doesn't she realise I'm hurting too? She was my fucking world.

After getting Maddie settled on the sofa under a blanket, I walk Candice to the door. It's too hard having her around, so there's no way I'm inviting her to stay and watch the movie with us.

'Everything you'll need is in Maddie's suitcase. She doesn't wear a nappy to bed anymore, just make sure she goes to the toilet before bed and she'll be fine.'

'Thanks.' At least I won't have to suffer through one of those shitty nappies. I'm still scarred by that incident.

'If you have any problems, just call.'

'I will, but I'm sure we'll manage. I'll drop her off Sunday night.'

She looks at the floor. 'I guess I should get going then. Enjoy your movie.'

'Thanks, we will.'

'You can stay for dinner if you like . . . you know, on Sunday, when you drop Maddie off.' She's stalling. I can tell she doesn't want to leave, but I can't have her around me for long periods of time. I just can't. How awkward we've become hurts.

'Sure. Sounds good.' I went over there for dinner one night last week—I was missing Maddie, and Candice has said I can come over anytime I want to see her. The nights I was busy getting her room together, I talked to her on the phone instead. Only having her on Tuesdays and every second weekend is going to take some adjustment. I want her with me all the time.

'Oh, I almost forgot. Here,' Candice says as she riffles around in her bag, before pulling out a set of keys. 'The keys for your shop. I guess I won't be needing them anymore.'

She brought up her old job when we had our big talk and I made sure to tell her that I'd already replaced her. You can't walk away from your job and expect it to still be waiting for you when you return, six months later. I can't have her working there anymore. The less I have to see her, the easier it will be.

I hold out my hand and she places them in my palm. 'Fuck,' I say, immediately dropping them to the floor and rubbing my hands down the front of my sweats. 'Seriously, you have a damn cock on your keyring.'

'Oh.' She laughs, like it's funny. It's not. 'Maybe I should've taken that off first.'

'You think?' I bet she left it on purposely. 'You need fucking help. Have you ever considered attending Cocks Anonymous?'

'What? I don't need therapy. I doubt there even is such a group.'

'You sure about that? Because I'm starting to see a disturbing pattern emerging here.' I see her trying hard to suppress her smile as she bends down to pick up the keys. 'Can you remove that—that thing?'

'Fine.' I hear her mumble '*Pussy*' under her breath as she removes the plastic cock from the keyring.

I'm no fucking pussy.

••••

I bolt upright when something wakes me.

'Daddy!' There it is again.

Shit—Maddie.

Leaping out of bed, I frantically slip into my sweats. I can't go to her wearing only my boxer briefs.

'Daddy!' she calls out again. Christ, she sounds distressed.

My heart thumps in my chest as I run down the hall to her bedroom. 'Peanut,' I say flicking on the light. 'Are you okay?'

I see tears in her eyes. 'I scared.'

'Oh baby,' I say, sitting down on the side of the mattress. 'There's nothing to be scared of.' I suppose this is all new to her. She's in a strange house, a strange room. It's the first time she's slept over. I'd lie down with her, but there's no way I'd fit in that tiny pink bed. 'Do you want me to sit with you until you fall back to sleep?'

She shakes her head. When her bottom lip starts to quiver, my heart is torn in two. This whole parent thing is going to be harder than I thought. I want her to be happy here—to feel safe. I'm not prepared for this. I thought I was. I have no idea what to do.

'Do you wanna come sleep in my bed, with me?'

She nods.

'Come on then.' I slide my hands under her arms.

'Puppy come. He scared too.'

'Okay, Puppy can come.' I scoop him up off her pillow and pass him to her before heading back to my room.

Once I have her settled, I climb in beside her. Pulling her closer to me, I tuck the blankets up around her chin. 'Is this better?'

'I not scared now,' she answers with a yawn.

I kiss her forehead. 'That's good.'

'I wuv you, Daddy,' she whispers as her eyes drift closed. Hearing her say that makes my heart sing. I'm pretty sure it will never get old.

I'm smiling as I close my eyes as well. 'I love you too, Peanut.'

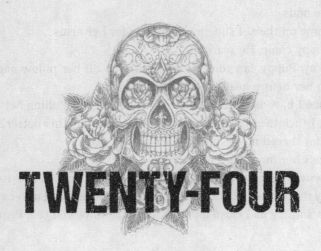

TWENTY-FOUR

CANDICE

I PLASTER A SMILE ON MY FACE WHEN I WALK THROUGH THE front door. Sophia is worried about me. I've put her through hell the past six months and she probably thinks I'm going to fall back into the hole I was in when Maddie was born. At the time, I was still struggling with the loss of Jax, so stepping aside to let Sophia raise Maddie sent me spiralling out of control. She was a piece of us. All I had left. Yes, I got to live with her and see her every day, but it wasn't the same.

When she was born, I breastfed her for the first two weeks, but then Sophia suggested that we wean her onto a bottle. She said it would keep me from getting too attached. She was probably right, but I was already attached. I was the one who experienced every kick, every movement as she grew inside me. She was part of me. How could I not be attached to a life I created? I knew Sophia was doing what she thought was best for me, but there was a part of me that resented her for it.

I wish Jax could understand how hard this has been for me, how much I suffered from the decisions I made. How his treatment of me led me into years of heartache and regret.

In time I'll get through this, I know I will. This is a walk in the park compared to what I've already been through. I have my little girl back, and I now get to be the mother I always craved to be. I wish things were the way they used to be between me and Jax, but I have to accept that they're not, and probably never will be. Seeing him is going to be a struggle, as well as a continual reminder of what I've lost. But being able to witness the relationship he's trying to have with his daughter is beautiful. As much as it hurts me to see him, I don't want to miss that. He's already proven he's going to be a wonderful father, and I'm happy that Maddie is going to have that, as it's something I wished for all my life: a father to love me.

I freeze when I enter the kitchen and see my mum wrapped in the arms of a man—something I've never seen before. This must be the guy she told me about. God, what's his name again? Bruce? Brock? Bryce?

I stand there bewildered, unable to look away. He's humming some song in her ear as their bodies sway. A smile tugs at my lips when he twirls her in his arms before dipping her. It's a beautiful sight. Sophia deserves happiness. She's sacrificed her whole adult life to care for me, then Maddie. It's time she got that back.

'Candice,' I hear Sophia say as I spin around to leave the room. 'I didn't realise you were back.'

'I just got back now.'

'Come,' she says. 'I want you to meet Brendan.'

Ah, Brendan, I was close. He looks to be in his early fifties, and very handsome. His thick, dark hair is greying at the sides, and he has the most beautiful green eyes. They kinda twinkle. The way Sophia looks up at him and smiles when she says that warms my heart. I hope he feels the same way about her—I don't want to see her get hurt. As far as I know, there's been nobody since my father. He really did a number on her. I've never seen her with anyone.

Although my sperm donor has provided for us financially all these years, he's wanted nothing to do with me. I hate him for that, but especially for the way he's treated my mother. She didn't deserve to be treated so poorly. She didn't ask for me, but I'll be forever grateful she stepped up and took responsibility for the life she helped create. God knows where I would've ended up if she hadn't.

'Hi,' I say. 'I'm Candice.'

He shakes my hand. 'It's lovely to finally meet you, Candice. I see you inherited your mother's exquisite beauty. You two could pass as sisters.'

He's a charmer, I'll give him that. He's right though, we could. Although she's in her early forties now, thanks to Botox and her plastic surgeon, Sophia doesn't look a day over thirty.

Sophia filled me in on Brendan's entire life story when I first came home. He's some hotshot criminal lawyer. He was married for twenty-six years. He and his wife were both very career minded and didn't have any children of their own. Their divorce was amicable—apparently they drifted apart over the years. Now he lives in a penthouse apartment in the city. He's a sensational kisser. A total romantic. A die-hard footy fan. He's close with his family. He has two brothers and one sister, or was it two sisters and one brother; I'd kinda tuned out by then.

'Thank you. It's nice to meet you too,' I reply. 'I'll leave you two alone, I'm going to my room.'

'Wait,' Sophia says, grabbing my arm. 'How did things go at Jax's?'

'Okay.' I shrug. 'Maddie's new room looks amazing. He did such a good job.'

'How was he with you?'

'Fine. You know . . .' I don't really feel comfortable talking about this in front of Brendan. 'They were settling in for a movie night when I left.'

'He didn't ask if you wanted to join them?'

'No. I think he was looking forward to spending time with his daughter.'

'Oh, sweetie.' Sophia rubs her hand affectionately down my arm. 'Give him time. It's a big adjustment for him.'

'I know.' I plaster on a smile again. 'Where are you off to tonight?'

'Dinner and dancing,' Sophia says, smiling up at Brendan all goofy-eyed again.

'You're more than welcome to join us,' Brendan says. He slides his arm around her waist, and pulls her into his side before placing a kiss on the top of her head. It's very sweet. I envy them.

'Thanks for the offer, but I don't want to be the third wheel.'

'You won't be. Come with us,' Sophia says. 'I hate the thought of you being here all alone.'

'Honestly, I'm fine. I have some things I want to do anyway.' I kiss her on the cheek. 'Have a great time.' I glance at Brendan. 'Look after my mum, she's pretty special.'

'She is. And I will,' he says, his eyes never once leaving her. The way he looks at her has me feeling somewhat relieved. It's pretty obvious he's just as smitten as she is.

••••

'Maddie!' I cry as she lets go of Jax's hand and leaps into my arms. I'm impressed that she's already bathed and dressed in her pyjamas. He's a good dad. 'I missed you, baby girl.'

It's only been two days, but it felt like an eternity. I know Jax needs his time with his daughter, but I struggled without her this weekend. That six months we spent alone together really bonded us. It strengthened what we already had and finally gave me the chance to do what I'd craved since her birth: to be her mother in every sense of the word. Yes, I helped raise her, but our time away was different.

'Mummy,' she says, squeezing me tightly around the neck. Hearing her call me that makes me smile. She occasionally slips up and calls me 'Sissy', but mostly it's 'Mummy' now.

'Did you have fun at Daddy's house?' It feels weird yet liberating to say that.

'Daddy fun. We had cake.'

'Wow, cake. You're a lucky girl.' Jax smiles as he shoves his free hand into his pocket, showing me that vulnerable side I've always loved. But his smile seems forced, and I hate that he now sees me in a different light. I'm still the same person I always was. I made a mistake. Hopefully in time we'll at least get back to a fraction of what we were. I miss him so much I ache inside.

'Chocwit cake.' Maddie gets her sweet tooth from him.

'Mmm, my favourite.' After burying my lips into her soft cheek, I put her on the ground. 'Sophia is in the kitchen, why don't you go and say hello?'

''Kay. I home, Phia,' Maddie screams as she runs down the hall.

'So, how did you go with her?' I ask, taking the suitcase from him.

'Good. We had a great time.'

'I'm glad.'

'Her dirty clothes are in a plastic bag inside. I'd planned on washing them for you, but I didn't get time. She can be a little full-on.'

I laugh. 'They say terrible twos, but I swear three-year-olds are worse. She's like the Energizer Bunny, she just keeps on keeping on.'

'Exactly.' He chuckles. 'But she's good value.'

'She is.'

'I loved having her, she's—'

'Amazing,' I say.

'Yes.'

It's good to see that we still have that uncanny knack of knowing what the other is going to say. I put Maddie's suitcase at the bottom of the stairs before following Jax into the kitchen. When he comes to an abrupt stop just inside the doorway, I hastily step to the side to avoid crashing into his back. That's when I see Sophia singing and dancing around the kitchen with Maddie in her arms. It reminds me of what I saw last night between Sophia and Brendan. She's been floating ever since she returned from their date. He sent flowers this morning, and this afternoon they talked on the phone for over two hours.

Jax turns his head slightly, making eye contact with me. 'Has she been drinking?' he whispers.

'No. She's on a Brendan high,' I reply, rolling my eyes. 'I think she's in love.'

'Oh.' I see his smile widen as he turns his attention back to them. 'Being in love suits her.'

Being in love suited me too, until I messed everything up and lost the other half of my soul.

Jax focuses most of his attention on Maddie during dinner. I'm flooded with guilt for the inkling of jealousy I feel. I was the one he used to shower his attention on. It hurts to suddenly be on the outside. To know he's only here for Maddie. I should be grateful he wants to keep things amicable for our daughter's sake. I suppose things could be worse.

I wipe Maddie's hands and face when she's done. 'It's time for you to go to bed.'

'Daddy read Caterpiwa.'

'Sure. If he wants to,' I say, looking at Jax. 'Do you want to read to her before bed?'

'Of course.'

I stand in the doorway of Maddie's bedroom and watch the two of them together. Jax is lying beside her on the bed, reading *The Very Hungry Caterpillar*. I know the words off by heart. I'm sure Maddie does too. Is it wrong that I use the time to pretend that this is my life? That this is our house, and Jax is my husband? That we're a happy family? Because that is exactly what I'm doing. From the moment I found out I was pregnant, I wished for this. I wished that he'd find out about the pregnancy, and we would be together. Happy and in love, raising our child together. In a way, I got my wish. We are raising her together now, but it's nothing like I'd dreamt it would be.

After he tucks her in and we both kiss her goodnight, I follow him down the stairs. 'I have something for you,' I say, when we reach the landing. 'I'll just grab it.'

When I return I pass him a large gift box. 'I spent the weekend putting this together for you.'

'Really,' he says as he begins to remove the lid.

'Don't open it now.' I put my hand on the box to stop him. 'Wait until you get home.'

JAX

My eyes keep drifting to the box sitting on the passenger seat of my car. I have no idea what's inside, but it makes me feel uneasy for some reason. I can see that Candice is remorseful about what's happened, and she's trying hard to make things right. I need to remember that. Can you ever right a wrong, though? That's the million-dollar question. I have my doubts.

When I arrive home, the first thing that hits me is how quiet it is. I miss my little girl already. Placing the box on the coffee table, I stare down at it as my fingers run through my hair. I'm pretty certain there's nothing bad inside, but the betrayal is still raw. Maybe I should have a beer first.

I twist the top off a beer bottle, tossing it into the trash as I leave the kitchen. Entering the lounge room, my eyes immediately land on the box again. It's just a damn box, why does it have me on edge?

I sit on the sofa and take another pull of my beer before putting it on the table. I exhale loudly as I pull the box closer, and remove the lid. The first things I see are a few ziplock bags. I pick up the one that contains a pair of tiny pink shoes. *Maddison's first shoes* is written on the front. Opening the bag, I take the shoes out and lay them in the palm of my hand. I'm grinning as I look down at them. They're so small. I feel a pang in my heart. My gaze moves back to the box. It's full of things from Maddie's short life. Am I ready for this? I'm hurting already.

Placing the shoes back into the bag, I pick up the next bag. Inside are a few blonde curls and the bag is labelled *Maddison's first haircut*.

When I pull out the hospital band from her birth, I slide it over my finger. It amazes me to think her wrist was not much thicker than that.

I find a small frame that has a plaster cast of her tiny hands and feet mounted inside. A lump rises in my throat as my fingers skim over the surface. This must've been done shortly after her birth.

In the bottom of the box I find two more things: an album and a DVD, which has *Maddison* written on the cover. I pop the disc inside the player in my entertainment unit. I grab the remote from beside the television and pick up my beer, settling back into the sofa.

I'm smiling the moment Maddie's sweet face comes into the frame. She's so small. Her hair is a lot shorter, and when she smiles I see she only has a few teeth in her mouth. 'Sis-sis,' she says, holding her hands out in front of her and wiggling her small fingers.

'Oh my God!' Sophia squeals. 'Did you hear that? Her first word. She said "sis-sis". Yes, Candice is your sissy, Maddie . . . Good girl.'

Maddie laughs and claps her little hands when Sophia praises her.

'I wish I didn't have to be her sister,' I hear Candice say in the background.

'Oh, baby. I know how hard this has been for you,' Sophia says. She must lower the video camera, because all I can see now is the sole of Maddie's foot, her cute little toes, and part of the rug she's sitting on. 'You may not think so, but you made the right decision. This way you get the best of both worlds: you get to spend time with your daughter, but by having me raise her, you can still live your life to the fullest. I don't want you to miss being able to go out with your friends, to travel the world, and to conquer all your dreams. Whatever your heart desires. You can never get those years back. Trust me, I know.'

My heart hurts as I listen to their conversation, and even more so when I hear Candice start to sob in the background. I have to take some of the responsibility for all this.

'Don't cry, baby girl.'

'I don't have any friends to go out with, and I hate that my birth ruined your life,' Candice sniffles.

'Oh, sweetie, don't ever think that. You're the best thing that ever happened to me. You and Maddie both. My career doesn't even compare to the happiness I found after you were born. You're my world . . . you both are.'

As the home video moves to another time in Maddie's life, Candice's words continue to play in my mind. I've been so wrapped up in my own feelings of betrayal and loss, I haven't really thought about how hard this decision must've been for her. It's obvious she loves her daughter; giving up her parental rights and handing Maddison over to Sophia to raise wouldn't have been easy. I'm still angry at her for keeping this from me, but I regret acting so harshly towards her now. She has suffered as well. *Next time my resentment rears its ugly head, I need to remember that.*

The video goes for over an hour, giving me snippets of Maddie's early life. As well as her first words, I got to see her take her first step, and her first, second and third birthday parties. Well, they weren't exactly parties, but Sophia and Candice went out of their way to make them special. Candice was right when she said it wouldn't make up for everything I've lost, but it has given me pieces of my daughter's past that I thought I'd never get, so I'm thankful for that.

I grab another beer from the fridge before I pick up the album. The first photo I see when I open it is Candice and her very pregnant stomach. I smile as I run my hand over the image. She looks breathtaking, especially because she's carrying my child inside her. That familiar feeling of being cheated creeps to the surface. I never got to run my hands over her stomach, or feel the baby moving inside.

It's after midnight by the time I finish flipping through the album and studying every photo. Unlike the home movie, this covers every phase of her life, from the day she was born until now.

After gently packing everything back into the box, I pull my phone out of my pocket. It's late, and she's probably already asleep, but I send a message anyway. I'm grateful she went to the trouble to do this for me.

Me: Thank you.

I'm startled when the phone dings a few seconds later.

Candice: You're welcome. Hope it helps give you back
a little of what you've lost.

Me: It was nice to see the special parts of her life that
I've missed.

What else can I say? I'll never get those moments back, but I do
appreciate what Candice has done. It's also helped me see a little of
what she's gone through as well.

Candice: I'm glad. I wish I could give you more, but
that's all I have.

I sit there and stare at my phone, unsure of how to reply. We
wouldn't even be in this position if she had just told me from the
beginning. As much as I try, I can't seem to let go of the anger. But
she did a nice thing by putting all this together for me, and I don't
want to spoil it by being negative or angry. A minute or so later, my
phone dings again.

Candice: Night, Jax. x

I look down at the tattoo on my arm, the one I got especially for
her. *A moment of patience in a moment of anger saves you a hundred
moments of regret*. It's my constant reminder to pull my head in
when needed. We'll never be what we were, but that doesn't mean
we can't try to be the best of who we are now. For our daughter's
sake if nothing else.

Me: Goodnight, Candice.

TWENTY-FIVE

JAX

Eighteen months later . . .

I SMILE WHEN I HEAR MADDIE'S LOUD FOOTSTEPS BARRELLING down the hallway to my bedroom. For someone so petite, she sounds like a baby elephant.

'Wake up, Daddy,' she says excitedly as she jumps onto my bed and shakes my hip. 'Wake up.'

I lie perfectly still as she moves up the bed towards my face. My eyes remain closed and I try to suppress my grin when I feel her warm breath dance across my cheek. Today is her fifth birthday, and I was lucky that it fell on my weekend. I can't believe how fast she's growing up. She'll be starting big school in a few months, and I'm not sure how I feel about that.

'Daddy,' she whispers as she clasps my shoulder and shakes me once more.

I can't hold back my smile any longer when her lips connect with my cheek. I adore this kid. She enriches my life so much.

When she's least expecting it, I roll over and capture her in my arms, flipping her over. 'Happy birthday, sweet girl,' I say, burying my face into the crook of her neck.

'Daddy!' she squeals as my fingers tickle her sides. The sweet sound of her laughter warms my heart.

'Are you ready for your presents?' I stayed up half the damn night putting her dollhouse together. She has a small one at Candice's house that she plays with a lot, but it doesn't compare to this one—it's the mother of all dollhouses. I want her to have nice things here, for when she stays over. She's going to love it. It's a three-storey wooden one. I bought all the tiny furniture to go with it, and a family of dolls.

Maddie's slowly pulling away from Puppy as she grows. He still sleeps with her every night, but he no longer accompanies her everywhere. It's kinda sad.

'Yes,' she says, her face lighting up.

'After breakfast, I'm going to take you somewhere special.'

'Where?'

'To Luna Park. It has rides and lots of fun stuff.'

'Yay. I love you, Daddy,' she says, kissing me on the cheek.

'I love you too, Peanut.'

I sit back on the sofa and watch her play with her birthday present. My ears are still ringing from the loud, high-pitched squeal she made when she saw her dollhouse for the first time. There were even a few tears in her eyes as she threw her arms around me, and thanked me. I love her so much, and I love having her here. I miss her when she's with her mother.

I can't help but smile as I listen to the different voices she uses for each of the dolls. She's so fucking adorable.

Turning to me, she holds up two of the dolls, one in each hand. 'This is the daddy dolly,' she says. 'And this is the mummy dolly. Where can the daddy dolly sleep?'

'In the dollhouse with Mummy dolly,' I say.

Her brow furrows as she gives me a confused look. 'But mummies and daddies don't live in the same house.'

Her words tug at my heart. She must think her situation is the norm. I guess she's too little to know otherwise.

'Some mummies and daddies live together.'

'Why don't you live with my mummy? She's nice.'

'I know she's nice.' Christ, I totally walked into that one.

I stand and head towards the kitchen. 'Do you want a soft-boiled egg with the toast cut into fingers, so you can dunk them?' I ask as I pass her. It's my pathetic attempt at changing the subject. I'm not getting into this conversation with her.

'Yes please, Daddy.'

After we eat, I get her clothes out. She's little miss independent now, and likes to dress herself. Grabbing the brush off her dresser, I pull her hair back into a ponytail. I've got this shit down pat now. When I'm done, she sits on the bed so I can put her shoes on. Pink Converse sneakers, just like her mother's.

'I was thinking,' I say as I tie her shoelaces, 'since we're going to be out all day, we might call past your mum's on the way to the amusement park, so she can see you for your birthday.'

'Okay. That means I'll get more presents today.'

I chuckle when she rubs her hands together. *Kids*. I remember feeling like that when I was a boy. My parents always went out of their way to give us over-the-top birthday parties, and the best presents money could buy. It was never done to please us though, it was to try to outdo all the other showy and pretentious parents in the neighbourhood.

While Maddie brushes her teeth, I head into my room to get dressed and send Candice a text.

> Me: I'm taking Maddie to Luna Park today. I thought if
> you were home, we'd call past so you could see her.
> We won't be back until later tonight.

By the time I'm dressed and washing up our breakfast dishes, there's still no reply from Candice. I notice Maddie sitting by her dollhouse again, getting in a little more play time before we leave.

When I wipe the last of the dishes and put them away, I pull my phone out of my pocket. There's still no reply. My mind goes into overdrive. Although our friendship has improved over the past year or so, I have no idea what Candice gets up to in her free time. No matter how hard I try not to love her, I still do. I often wonder if she has a boyfriend, even though I don't really want to know. My philosophy is what I don't know won't hurt me. Maddie has never mentioned any other guy, but that doesn't mean there isn't one.

Picking up my car keys from the bench, I call out to Maddie, 'You ready to go?'

'Coming, Daddy, I'll just grab my hat.' I love that she still wears the *Princess* cap that I bought her.

I open the car door so she can climb in. It's a warm November day. The sky is a beautiful rich shade of blue, and there's not a cloud to be seen. Once she's seated in her booster seat, I lean in to fasten her seatbelt.

'I can do it,' she says, pushing my hand away. Again I'm reminded of how fast she's growing. I love—and hate—that she's becoming so independent.

'Okay.'

My phone dings as I walk around to the driver's side. Candice has finally replied.

> Candice: Sorry, I was in the shower. If you haven't left yet, I'd love it if you could bring her by. It feels weird not having her here on her birthday.

I push away the thought that she's gotten to spend every birthday with our daughter. Last year it fell on Candice's weekend, but I can't complain. She invited me over for dinner and birthday cake, so I could spend some time with Maddie on her special day. This visit is just repaying the favour.

> Me: Great. We're leaving now. We'll be there in ten.

The first thing I notice when Candice opens the front door is her wet hair and a face totally devoid of makeup. She still takes my breath away. I inhale her sweet apple scent, it's prominent today. I wish I wasn't still so affected by her.

'Happy birthday, baby girl,' she cries, lifting Maddie into her arms.

'Daddy bought me a dollhouse.'

'Wow. Lucky girl.' Candice smiles sweetly when she looks at me.

'Daddy is taking me to Luna Park.' Maddie looks at me too. 'Can Mummy come?'

Fuck.

Candice must see my reaction because she quickly comes to my defence. 'It's your special day with your dad.'

'But you can come too. Can't she, Daddy?'

'Of course she can come.' How can I say no to her? I try my best not to make my answer sound forced. It kills me to be around Candice for long periods of time.

'Only if you're sure,' Candice says hesitantly. The uncertainty on her face is mixed with a dash of hopefulness. It has me nodding. I'm such a sucker when it comes to these two.

'Come. It'll be fun,' I lie. Torture more like it, but it's Maddie's birthday. If she wants both her parents with her, then who am I to deny her that? I want to give her everything I never had: love, affection and most importantly, security.

••••

'There's Mummy,' Maddie yells as she points to Candice in her dodgem car, only a few metres away. 'Get her, Daddy.'

Making a sharp turn of the wheel, I head straight for Candice. I burst out laughing when I see the horror on her face as we collide roughly with her.

'Oh, you want to play dirty,' she growls. She straightens her car and does a loop around the outside. I give chase, but she's already got a clear lead on me.

'Catch her, Daddy, catch her,' Maddie squeals with excitement. I'm so focused on Candice, I don't see the other car coming until it smashes into us, jolting us sideways.

'Shit. Are you okay?' I ask Maddie, looking down at her.

She laughs. 'Yes, Daddy.'

'I've got my little girl in the car, you idiot,' I say when I turn my attention to the fool who just crashed into us. Before I get a chance to say anything else someone careens into the back of us, catapulting us a few feet forward. I turn in my seat, ready to shout abuse, only to find Candice laughing behind us.

'Payback's a bitch,' she mouths.

'Game on,' I mouth back and stomp my foot on the pedal.

After lining up for another turn on the dodgem cars, we head over to one of the outdoor cafés for some lunch. I was wrong about not wanting to bring Candice—the three of us are having a great time. Maddie manoeuvres between us, taking our hands in hers. It's not hard to see she's enjoying having both of us here.

We spend a few hours in the old-school Coney Island funhouse after lunch. My jaw aches from smiling and laughing so much.

Candice insists on watching Maddie as I take on some of the scarier rides. I get the feeling she's chickening out on me, but she'd never admit it.

'Can we ride on that one next?' Maddie asks, pointing to the Ferris wheel.

'I'll wait down here,' Candice says.

'Nice try,' I reply, grabbing her elbow and guiding her towards the line. 'You're not getting out of this one.'

'But—'

'No buts.'

I start rocking the carriage when we reach the very top. The view of Sydney Harbour is spectacular from up here. Maddie laughs—she's a daredevil like me.

'Please stop rocking the carriage,' Candice says. She has her eyes clenched shut and her fingers are gripping the seat with such force her knuckles have turned white. She looks petrified.

'Are you okay?'

She shakes her head vigorously.

'Mummy's scared,' Maddie declares.

'Hey,' I say, nudging Candice's leg with my foot. 'The view is amazing from here, open your eyes.'

She shakes her head again, so I move to sit beside her. 'It's okay,' I say, prying her fingers from the seat and wrapping them in my hand. Her eyes immediately spring open and they take in our linked hands. I see a smile tug at her lips. 'I won't let anything happen to you, I promise.'

Her grip on my hand tightens. 'Thank you,' she whispers.

We stop at an Italian restaurant for dinner on the way home later that evening. Spending long periods of time with Candice is something I've avoided for the last couple of years, but now I'm trying to drag the evening out as long as I can. I don't want it to end.

Maddie is sound asleep by the time we pull into Candice's driveway. 'Thank you for letting me come today,' she says. 'It's been fun. Just like old times.'

'Like old times,' I reply as I look away. I miss those times, but we can never get them back.

I turn back to her when she wraps her fingers around my hand. 'I miss you, Jax.'

I close my eyes and release a long, drawn-out breath. I fucking miss her too, but that ship sailed the moment she betrayed me. When I reopen my eyes, she's watching me. We sit there in silence just staring at each other. It feels like an eternity passes but it's only minutes. Then the inevitable happens—that damn shift, the one that always happens when we're together like this. My face inches towards hers.

Just before our lips connect, everything that has happened between us flashes through my mind. This is a bad idea. I close my eyes again, as I rest my forehead against hers.

'I can't do this,' I whisper.

She sighs just before she pulls her head away. 'I understand.' I can hear the hurt in her voice. 'Good night, Jax.' Without looking at me, she reaches for the doorhandle and gets out of the car. I see her wipe a finger under her eye as she closes the door, and I know she's crying. She runs across the front lawn and towards the house.

'Fuck,' I say, banging my hand down on the steering wheel.

Two months later . . .

'Daddy, you came,' Maddie cries as she runs towards me, leaping into my arms.

'Of course I came. I wouldn't miss your first day of big school for anything.' After kissing her cheek, I put her back down. I sigh—she looks so grown up in her school uniform. Candice and I put in a lot of effort last year, trying to find the perfect school for our little girl. A place where she'd be happy and looked after. It was tough, because neither of us were prepared to let her go. I've been dreading this day for months.

When we finally settled on a school we both liked, we attended the parent interview together. I'll never forget that day. *Never*. The moment Candice got in the car when I picked her up, she handed me an envelope.

'I hope you don't mind that I went ahead and did this,' she said.

'Did what?'

'Open it.'

I still remember all the feelings that ran through me as I looked down at the piece of paper in my hand that said, *Maddison Albright*. Happiness, pride, gratitude, just to name a few.

'It's all legal. It was done through Births, Deaths and Marriages,' Candice said, reaching across the centre console and placing her hand on top of mine. 'She's your daughter, Jax, she should have your name.'

She was my daughter regardless of her name, but it was now official. I now have the piece of paper to prove it.

'Morning,' I say with a nod, looking over at Candice, Sophia and Brendan. It's great that Maddie has so much support. I only wish she had it from my family as well. I've never told my parents about her, but maybe it's time I did. They may have turned their backs on me, but surely they'd want to be part of their granddaughter's life?

Pulling my phone out of my pocket, I hold it up as I take a picture of Maddie.

'Do you want one together?' Candice asks.

'Sure. That'd be great,' I say, passing her my phone. Things have been weird between us ever since we almost kissed after our day at Luna Park. We've avoided each other as much as we can. Apart from the drop-offs, pick-ups and occasional dinners at Candice's place, we don't go near each other. We did spend Christmas Day together with our daughter. After seeing how happy Maddie was on her birthday, having both of us with her, we made a pact that every special occasion—birthdays, Easter and Christmas—would be spent together as a family.

Crouching down beside Maddie, I wrap my arm around her and look up at my phone.

'Say cheese,' Candice says.

'Cheese,' Maddie calls out.

When the school bell rings, a lump rises in my throat. I'm not ready to let her go. Candice picks up Maddie's backpack, and helps put it on her back—it's almost as big as her. Everything in me wants to bundle my little girl into my car and take her away from this place. She's not ready—correction: I'm not ready.

She makes her way along the line, starting with me. 'Bye, Daddy,' she says, wrapping her arms around my waist. When she releases me, I crouch down in front of her, tucking a blonde curl behind her ear.

'Have a great day.' That's all I can manage to say without getting choked up.

'I will, Daddy. I love you.'

'I love you too, Peanut.'

She smiles. She seems excited and happy to be here, so I need to accept that.

'Bye, Mummy,' Maddie says, moving to Candice.

'Bye, baby girl.'

When I see the tears welling in Candice's eyes, I have to look away. I don't dare look again until Maddie moves to Brendan. Even then I avoid making eye contact with Candice.

'Bye, Poppy,' she says, hugging him. She's been calling him that for a while now. She adores him just as much as he adores her.

'Have a great day, sweetheart.'

'Bye, Sophia.' Of course Sophia's crying too, but it doesn't seem to affect me like Candice's tears do.

Brendan bends and whispers something in Maddie's ear.

'I mean, bye, Nanny.'

We all laugh when Sophia elbows Brendan in the ribs. Brendan proposed to her a few weeks ago. They're even talking about moving in together soon. It's great to see them so happy.

Maddie runs back to me and gives me one last hug before she joins the rest of her class. I swear if I see one tear fall from her eye, I'm going to take her home with me. But I don't. She looks so proud standing there in her uniform, smiling. The sight only seems to break my heart a little more. I enjoy watching her grow, but I need it to slow down a little. It's all happening too fast.

We stay until she disappears around the corner. Walking away and leaving her here is hard. The moment we're out of the gate, Candice breaks down beside me. Christ, doesn't she realise how hard I'm trying to keep it together? Sophia and Brendan are a few metres in front of us, oblivious to what's just happened.

'Come here,' I say, pulling Candice into my arms. She slides her hands around my waist, clinging to me as she cries softly into my chest. I need this just as much as she does.

'I'm not sure if I can leave her here, Jax,' she whispers.

'I feel exactly the same way.' My voice cracks as I speak.

Who knew parenting could be this hard?

TWENTY-SIX

JAX

I READ OVER THE LETTER IN MY HAND ONE MORE TIME.

Dear Mother,

I hope this letter finds you well. I know it's been a few years since we've had any contact, but I thought you might like to know that you have a granddaughter. Her name is Maddison. She's five years old. If you're wondering why I've taken so long to inform you, I only found out she was mine a few years ago. She has become a huge part of my life since then. She's beautiful, smart and has such a sweet nature. I'm extremely proud of her. I'm writing this letter because I'd love for her to meet my family. She has her mother's family in her life, and it would be nice if she had some contact with you all as well. I'm enclosing a photo of her. It was taken last week on her first day of school.

As for me, if you're the least bit interested, my life is going well. I own and run a successful tattoo parlour in Newtown. I'm currently looking into buying another one. I know it's not the career you envisioned for me, but I'm happy.

Tell Father and Brent I said hello.
Take care,
Jaxson

The letter seems formal at best, but it's all I've got. My family don't do mushy anyway. I hate even having to write this, but I'm doing it for Maddie. No other reason. I'm in two minds about even subjecting her to them, but she should be given the opportunity to meet them. Although I'm not expecting miracles. Look how they've treated me.

My gut churns as I fold the letter and put it inside an envelope. I hope I'm not going to regret this.

I'm pulled from my thoughts when my phone dings. It's a message from Carter.

> **Carter:** Hi fucker. Are you coming up this weekend? I bought a Jet Ski yesterday. You've gotta try this baby out. It's wicked.

This weekend I have Maddie. I haven't even mentioned her to him yet. He's never asked why I've gone from visiting him every weekend to only every second. He just presumes I'm busy with work. It's not like I'm ashamed of my situation, I love my daughter and I want the world to know she's mine. But as close as Carter and I are, we don't talk about personal shit. Chicks do that, not guys.

> **Me:** Hey cocksucker. I'm busy this weekend, but I'll definitely come up next weekend. I need to talk to you about a business proposition anyway. Looking forward to taking your Jet Ski for a spin. I can give you lessons if you like.

> **Carter:** I don't need lessons, arsehole. I know how to ride it.

He bites every damn time.

••••

'Jax, it's Candice,' she says the moment I answer the phone. 'I just got a call from the school. Maddie's in the sick bay. She fell and hit her head in the playground.'

'What?'

'She's okay. Don't panic, but they've asked me to come and get her. It's school policy with any type of head injury.'

The moment she says head injury, I go weak at the knees. 'I'm coming with you,' I blurt. I need to see Maddie with my own eyes.

'I was going to get Sophia to go pick her up.'

'We're her parents, Candice, not Sophia.'

'I'm at work, plus my car is in getting serviced. I can't pick it up until this afternoon.'

'Text me your address.' I have no idea where she works—the less I know about her life, the better. 'I'll pick you up on the way.'

'Okay,' she says with a sigh.

Fifteen minutes later I pull up outside her work. I find her waiting for me by the kerb. The first thing I think is how beautiful she looks, which annoys me. I read the sign above the shop and see she's still working in the beauty industry. I know this isn't the career she wants. She was happy when she was working for me.

'Hey,' she says once she's seated in the passenger seat.

I glance at her as I pull onto the road. 'Hey.' Maddie's school is only five minutes from here, so we should be there soon enough. I'm trying hard not to work myself up into a state. You don't send your kids to school to get hurt. 'Have you heard anymore from the school since we talked?'

'No. Stop panicking, the lady in the office said she seemed fine.'

'I'm not panicking,' I say defensively.

'Yes, you are.' She chuckles.

She's right, I am, but I'm not about to admit that to her.

The office lady, Pam, ushers us into the sick bay. Maddie is sitting on a chair in the corner, holding an icepack to her forehead. Rushing over, I crouch down in front of her. She has puffy eyes from crying. It tears me up inside.

'Are you okay, Peanut?' I scan her body as I speak. Apart from the icepack and a scraped knee, I can't see any other injuries. That calms me slightly.

'I hit my head, Daddy. I tripped over Thomas.'

'Oh,' I say, pulling her into my arms. 'It's okay, Daddy's here now.' Drawing back, I remove the icepack to inspect her forehead. There's a small lump there, but it's not as bad as I expected. 'We're going to take you home. I think we should get a doctor to check you out.' I lift her off the chair, while Candice chats with Pam.

'I'm okay, Daddy.'

'We're still going to see the doctor. Just to be sure.'

I swear I see Maddie look at her mother and roll her eyes, but I ignore it.

'That school has a lot to answer for,' I say to Candice once we have Maddie in the car.

'What? Why? She was playing, Jax. She was in the playground.'

'I don't care. They should've been watching her.'

'There's over four hundred kids at this school, and maybe two teachers, max, on playground duty.'

'Well, that's not good enough. I'm going to call the principal when I get back to work. No, better still, I'll write him a letter. At least we'll have something in writing then.'

'You will not,' she snaps. 'You heard what Pam said. She was running on the concrete and tripped over another kid. How is that the school's fault?'

'They should've stopped her before she got hurt.'

'You can't wrap her in cotton wool. She needs to be a kid. Kids run. It's what they do.'

'We do, Daddy,' Maddie says from the back seat.

I'll never win with these two.

I'm relieved when the doctor gives Maddie the all-clear. At worst she has a mild concussion, but he's given us a list of things to look out for just in case. That does nothing to ease my mind.

'She can come back to work with me,' I say to Candice when we're in the car.

'It's okay, my boss gave me the rest of the afternoon off. I'm going to work back for Thursday night trading to make up for it.'

'All right. Well, make sure you keep an eye on her. You have the list the doctor gave you, right?'

'Yes, Jax.' This time Candice rolls her eyes. 'When did you become so overbearing?'

'Why, because I care about our daughter's welfare?'

She goes quiet. I guess she has no comeback.

'You're right,' she murmurs a few seconds later. She says it so softly, I barely hear her.

'What was that?' I say, bringing my hand to my ear.

'You're right. Maddie's lucky to have a father who cares about her. I wouldn't know what that felt like.'

My smugness immediately disappears when I glance at her. She looks so sad as she picks at an imaginary piece of fluff on her trousers.

'Hey,' I say, placing my hand on hers. 'Your father's an idiot. He's the one who's missed out on something amazing, not you. He'd adore you if he took the time to get to know you.'

'You think so?' she asks as a smile tugs at her lips.

'I know so.'

TWENTY-SEVEN

JAX

'I'M DEFINITELY BUYING ONE OF THESE,' I SAY TO CARTER AS
I help him hose down the Jet Ski after our day on the ocean.

'It's pretty sick, hey?'

'It is. How much did this baby set you back?'

'Eighteen grand. They usually go for around twenty-two. This guy I inked did me a good deal. We can go see him tomorrow if you like.'

'Sounds like a plan.' I seriously want to own one now. I've had the best afternoon. I knew coming here would help. It always does. It's my escape from all the bullshit back home.

After we shower and change, Carter cooks up a mean dinner. I wish I knew how to cook as well as he does.

'How'd you learn to cook like that?' I ask, as we set the table for our card game.

'My mum worked a lot when I was a kid. I had to grow up fast.'

I've always suspected he had a shitty family life like me. You could tell—well, I could. It was like looking in a damn mirror the first day I laid eyes on him. Trouble always finds trouble. But I still know nothing about his life before we met. Like me, he holds his cards close to his chest.

'What about your dad?'

He shrugs, taking a long pull of his beer. I get the feeling he's doing that to avoid answering me. 'I've never met my dad—I'm a bastard.'

'Just because you never met your dad doesn't make you a bastard.' I chuckle.

He gives me a look telling me there's nothing amusing about what he just said.

'I'm an illegitimate child, dickhead. You know, my parents weren't married when I was born? Technically, that makes me a bastard. It even says so in the fucking dictionary.' The anger in his voice is clear. This is obviously a touchy subject.

My mind instantly shifts to Maddie. Candice and I aren't married. That technically makes her a bastard as well.

'People don't really think like that anymore, do they?'

'The narrow-minded ones do.' The torment I see on his face has me feeling bad for him.

'Heaps of people have kids out of wedlock these days.'

'Well, they shouldn't.'

It's now my turn to take a long pull of my beer. 'So it was just you and your mum growing up?'

'Yeah. She more than made up for me only having one parent. She was great.'

He's lucky he at least had one good parent, it's better than two shitty ones. 'I grew up with a father, so believe me when I say you didn't miss much. It's seriously overrated. My dad is a cock.'

'So that's where you get your cocksucker side from?' he says, chuckling.

'Fuck off, arsehole.'

He throws back his head and laughs. He thinks he's a comedian. 'Seriously, man,' he says when he finally stops. 'I'm sorry your old man was a prick.'

I shrug like I don't give a shit, but I do. 'You can't choose your family.'

'I'll drink to that,' Carter says, raising his bottle.

'Cheers,' I reply, clinking my bottle with his. 'Who invented parents anyway?'

'They're not all bad. I would've been lost without my mum. Fuck, I miss her.'

What does he mean by that? Please don't tell me she died. 'Is she like . . . you know?' I can't even bring myself to say the word out loud.

He frowns. 'No. I don't know—what?'

I tilt my head to the side and roll my eyes back in my head, hanging my tongue out the side of my mouth for extra effect. It's my pathetic attempt at playing dead.

'Is my mother crazy? No, she's not fucking crazy,' he snaps. 'You know I'd punch you in the head right now if she was?'

'I wasn't trying to look crazy.'

'Well, you did.'

'Fuck off. I did not.'

He shakes his head and laughs. 'What are you trying to say then? Are we playing fucking charades now? FYI, I hate charades.'

'No we're not playing charades, cock. You probably hate charades because you suck at it.'

'I don't suck at anything. Just say it.'

'It just doesn't feel right to come out and say it.'

'Say what? You're starting to get on my nerves with all this cryptic shit.'

'Um . . . is your mum, you know . . . pushing up daisies?'

'Pushing up daisies? You mean dead?'

I nod, still hoping it's not the case.

'What the fuck? No, she's not dead. And why couldn't you have just said that? Pushing up fucking daisies. Who even says shit like that?'

'Me apparently.'

'Right. That's enough alcohol for you,' he says, reaching across the table for my beer. I snatch it and slap his hand away.

'Fuck off. This is my first one.'

Placing my lips around the top of the bottle, I take a drink. I make sure to keep it in my hand when I'm done so he can't confiscate it from me. He narrows his eyes at me, so I reach into my pocket with my free hand and grab a few dollar coins to distract him, putting them on the table in front of me. I actually have a pocketful, but I know he's going to bite.

I see him look at the coins, so I put my beer down and start dealing the first hand. Getting this card game underway will avoid any further conversation. That's why guys don't do deep and meaningful, we suck at it.

'Where's the rest of your coins?'

'That's all I brought with me.' I shrug, trying to act casual.

'What? Three fucking coins. They aren't going to get you far.'

'I cleaned the floor with you last time I was here, and the time before that. Come to think of it, every time I leave here my pockets are so weighed down with all your cash, I can barely walk.' I try hard to keep a straight face. 'I thought I'd travel light this week. It was the sensible thing to do.'

'You're a cock. You know that right?'

'How can I forget when you keep reminding me?' I take a sip from my beer. 'Does your mum live up this way? Is that why you moved here?'

I don't know why I keep bringing up his family. Maybe because that damn letter I sent my mother is weighing heavily on my mind. It's been almost ten days, and I still haven't received a reply. Even though I didn't hold out much hope that I'd get one, it still hurts that I haven't. My family can reject me all they want, but I'll be damned if I'll let them reject my little girl.

'What's with all the damn questions? My mum lives in Sydney with my cocksucker stepfather. Maybe he's related to your old man.'

'Maybe.' I chuckle. I'm a private person too, so I can understand his hostility.

He picks up his beer. 'I moved up here to get away from the kid next door.'

'To your apartment?'

'No. She lived next door to my mum and the fuckwit.'

'So you let a kid drive you away. Pussy.'

'Technically, she isn't a kid. Far from it.' He sighs, and I can tell by the look on his face that he's thinking of her, and not in a friendly way either, if you catch my drift. 'She's short, so I used to call her "kid" to annoy her.'

'Was she a stalker?'

'No.' He laughs. 'She was a pain in my arse, but pretty cool. I moved up here to put some distance between us.'

'Ah. So you're in love with her, and you're running away from your feelings instead of facing them.' I only know that because that's exactly what I did with Candice.

'Hardly,' he scoffs. 'I don't do love.'

I've said the same thing a thousand times, so I know he's lying. His words say one thing, but his body language says something entirely different.

'Right. Keep telling yourself that.'

'What's that supposed to mean?'

'You love her.'

'Fuck off.'

He exhales a deflated breath before going quiet. I know I'm right. He starts to pick at the label of his beer bottle before his eyes finally meet mine.

'So what if I do?'

See, I was right. He's full of shit. The more I get to know him, the reasons I was so drawn to him in the beginning become clearer. We're so alike it's uncanny.

He goes quiet again, so I decide to cut him some slack. 'You know how we talked about one day possibly going into business together, by starting our own franchise?'

'Yeah.'

'Well, I think I have our first shop, if you're still interested.'

He nods. 'Tell me more.'

'Remember how I told you about my first part-time job? The one I got when I moved to Sydney? Working at that parlour in Surry Hills on weekends.'

'Yeah.'

'I kept in contact with my old boss, and he wants to get out of the game. He's buying a boat and moving to Queensland. It's an established business in a prime location. We were always flat-out when I worked there. When I told him I was possibly interested in taking over, he let me go over the books. It's a fucking winner—he does really well. A few of his artists are interested in sticking around and we can find someone we trust to run it.'

'How much is he asking for it?'

'Believe it or not, the market value of the building and the price of the shop fittings.'

'That's it?' he asks. 'What about his clientele? That's gotta be worth a bit.'

'He's looking for a quick sale, and like I said, he's a friend of mine. That's all he's asking for, but we need to give him an answer soon. I've already talked to the bank. With the equity in my shop alone, I can get a loan no problems. I'm sure you'd be in the same boat. We'd be able to make the repayments—it pulls in some big bucks.'

'Fuck, yeah. I'm keen. Let's do it.'

We bump fists. 'Awesome. I'll call him in the morning and we can get the ball rolling.'

Looks like Carter and I are going into business together.

I have a really good feeling about this.

••••

I have to leave work early on Monday so I can pick up Maddie from school because Sophia has a modelling job this afternoon. She does a lot of catalogue work for the department stores. Maddie still stays with me on Tuesdays, even though most of her time is spent at school. I've come to resent the fact that I have to give her back when our time together is over. I want her with me always.

I called in briefly to see her on Sunday night on my way home from Carter's. But for some reason, the moment I saw her, I became racked with guilt. Carter's words kept circling in my mind: *I'm a bastard, an illegitimate child.* I could tell he was burdened by this label, and it made me wonder if Maddie would ever feel that way about herself. Christ, I hope not.

I can feel a few of the mothers' eyes on me as I wait outside Maddie's classroom, but I try to ignore them. I'm not going there. No fucking way.

'Daddy!' Maddie squeals as she exits the classroom.

'Hey, Peanut,' I say, giving her a hug. I always feel like my time with her is so limited. When I let her go, she puts her school bag on the ground, opening the zipper.

'I made you something today.'

'You did?' I'm grinning like a fool as I wait for her to retrieve it out of her bag.

'It's a painting. Of you, me and Mummy.'

'I love it,' I tell her as my eyes skim over the stick figures. Our heads are fucking huge. The one in the black cap must be me, and she's painted pink hair on Candice. The small figure standing between us is obviously Maddie. Our hands are linked. She seems well adjusted with our situation, but again I wonder if she really is.

We stop for vanilla ice cream and sprinkles on the way home. It's become our after-school ritual.

The first thing I do when we get back to my place is check the letterbox. I always check it, but not as religiously as I have been the past week. I sling Maddie's school bag over my shoulder as I sift through the pile of envelopes in my hand. Bill, bill—and then I freeze. I recognise the handwriting straightaway—it's my mother's. Well, fuck me, she actually replied. Why does that make me smile?

'Daddy, hurry. Unlock the front door,' Maddie yells. 'I need to pee.'

I look up and find her bouncing up and down by the front door with her legs crossed. Jogging over, I quickly unlock the door and she runs down the hallway to the bathroom.

'Don't forget to wash your hands when you're done,' I call out as I head into the kitchen.

'Yes, Daddy.'

I place the mail and Maddie's school bag on the breakfast bar. The moment my eyes land on the letter again, the smile drops from my face. Maddie's little emergency had distracted me. I stare down at the envelope for the longest time. It's funny how I've been hoping for a reply, but now it's here, I'm not sure if I want to open it.

I take the coward's way out, picking the letter up and shoving it into my back pocket. I go about unpacking Maddie's bag, taking the painting she made and sticking it proudly to the fridge with a magnet.

When I hear the television turn on in the lounge room, I pour Maddie a glass of milk and place a few Oreo cookies on a plate. Dinner won't be for a few hours, and she's always hungry when she gets home from school.

••••

I rinse the last of the shampoo out of Maddie's hair as she sits in the bath. 'Are you ready to get out, or do you want to play with your bath toys for a while?'

'Play,' she says, looking up at me with a smile, as she squeezes a small amount of shampoo on her doll's hair

'Ten minutes, okay? Any longer and the water will be cold.'

As I head into her bedroom to get her pyjamas out of the drawer, my mind drifts back to the letter. I feel like it's burning a hole in my pocket. I've managed to avoid opening it for the past few hours but I suddenly can't put it off any longer.

My hands tremble slightly as I sit down on Maddie's bed next to her pyjamas and pull the envelope out. Again I stare at it. This is my family we're talking about. This letter is liable to contain anything. I take a deep breath as I tear it open and unfold the piece of paper inside.

Dear Jaxson,

I hope this letter finds you well. You're right, it has been years since you've made contact. I'm surprised you even bothered after all this time.

I wasn't completely shocked to hear you have a child, or that you chose to pursue such a menial and degrading profession. Your father and I spent a fortune on your education, and this is how you repay us. As usual you have little or no concern for this family or our reputation. At least your brother doesn't continually disappoint us. Where did we go wrong with you?

I haven't enlightened your father or brother about your news. I'd appreciate it if this dirty little secret is kept between us. If this was to become public knowledge, it could severely damage our good name. An illegitimate child, Jaxson—really? When are you going to grow up? Your poor brother and his lovely wife, Jennifer, are struggling to conceive, and here you are popping out babies to every Tom, Dick and Harry. Do you have no self-respect?

Your daughter however, is very cute. I can see some of my mother in her, God rest her soul. But I'm afraid under the circumstances, any formal introduction will not be possible. Please tell her I said hello though.

Sincerely,

Your mother

I screw the letter up, trying to swallow the golf ball-sized lump in my throat. *Dirty little secret.* How dare she refer to my daughter like that. I take a deep breath, trying to control the rage that bubbles up inside me.

The only positive thing in that letter was the mention of the similarities between my grandmother and Maddie. I adored that woman. She'd love my daughter if she was alive, I know it.

A dull ache settles in my chest as I go over her words in my mind. *Tell her I said hello.* Is she fucking kidding me? I will never tell Maddie about her. It's my job as a father to protect her. There's no way I'd ever tell my precious daughter that her own flesh and blood want nothing to do with her. Like my mother said in the letter, I shouldn't have even bothered.

I suddenly have a whole new understanding of Carter's situation. I felt for him when he spoke about his childhood, but even more so now. My daughter will hopefully never know such rejection. Not if I have any say in it. Going by my experiences with my family, Maddie's better off without them in her life anyway. But even that doesn't seem to lessen the sting of my mother's rejection. It hurts way more than all the other times. She's just an innocent child. But she's part of me, so why would they want anything to do with her? I guess I'm not surprised they aren't even giving her a chance.

'I'm ready to get out of the bath, Daddy,' Maddie calls out.

'Coming.' I take a deep breath as I stand, shoving the screwed-up letter into my back pocket. I need a minute to pull myself together. Maddie can never know about this.

Grabbing a clean towel from the linen cupboard, I head into the bathroom. I hold the towel open for her when she stands, wrapping it around her as I lift her out of the bath.

After I help her into her pyjamas, I kneel in front of her so I can run a brush through her hair. She gives me a serious look, like she's studying me. I smile when she lifts her hand, placing it softly on my cheek.

'Are you okay, Daddy? You look sad.'

'Sad? Why would I be sad? I have my little girl here, and in a few more days, I'll have you for the entire weekend.' When I tickle her, she laughs and squirms in my hands. I love the sweet sound of her laughter. 'Don't you know how happy I am when you're with me?'

She wraps her arms around my neck, placing a kiss on my cheek. 'I love you, Daddy.'

Holding her against me, I clench my eyes shut to stop the tears. She's all I'll ever need. 'I love you too, Peanut. So much.'

When her hold on me tightens, I get the feeling she can see straight through my lies. She's smarter than I give her credit for. My heart is breaking for her, and she has no idea why. My family may not want her, but I can tell you one thing, she'll always have me. *Always*.

'I wish you could live with me and Mummy all the time. I miss you when I'm at Nanny's house.'

I chuckle. Sophia thought being called 'Mum' made her feel old, so I can only imagine how the new 'Nanny' label is making her feel.

'I miss you too. Always. I count down the days until you're here again.'

'Shelby's mum and dad live in the same house.' She draws back and makes eye contact with me again. 'They even sleep in the same bed.' Her eyes widen when she says the last part, like it's a huge scandal. It makes me smile.

'Who's Shelby?'

'My friend, silly. She's in my class.'

'Oh, her.' I have no clue who Shelby is.

'Nanny said when her and Poppy get married, they're going to live together. You should marry Mummy, then we can all live together too.' She gives me a serious look, like it's something I should really consider.

Fuck! Where the hell did that come from?

TWENTY-EIGHT

CANDICE

I'VE BEEN WORKING AT THIS JOB FOR ALMOST A YEAR NOW.
It's the seventh one I've had in the last three years, but I've finally
found one where I feel almost comfortable. It's a far cry from the glory
days of working with Jax at Wicked Ink, but it's a job nevertheless.
I really miss working there. After trying my hand at a few different
professions, I decided to go back into the beauty industry. It's never
been my career of choice, but it's what I know. Sophia spent a small
fortune when she sent me to the most reputable beauty school in
Sydney, and it would be a shame to waste it. At least my new boss,
Naomi, is lovely, not like the cow I used to work for.

'Morning,' Naomi says when I push through the front door of the
salon. She's in her early fifties and bought this place six years ago
when her husband left her for someone younger. She needed to work
to help provide for her two daughters.

'Morning,' I reply, with a smile, as I walk past her to stow my
handbag in the back room.

'How was your weekend?' she asks, when I return to reception.

'Lonely,' I say with a shrug. 'It was Jax's turn to have Maddie, and my mum spent the weekend with her fiancé.'

Sophia and Brendan's relationship is coming along in leaps and bounds. It's nice to see her so happy, she deserves it. Brendan is the perfect man for my mum. He loves her just as much as she loves him. He's fantastic with me and Maddie as well, and we adore him.

Sophia has been on my case for months about finding a boyfriend, or at the very least a friend to spend my free time with. I did join a dating site briefly. What a nightmare that turned out to be. The first guy wasn't too bad—he was cute and seemed nice enough. But ten minutes into our date he reached across the table to grope one of my tits while he whispered, 'I can't wait to titty fuck you later.' I calmly picked up my glass of water and threw its contents in his face. I vaguely remember hearing a few gasps from the other diners in the restaurant before I stood and left without a word.

The second guy, well, that was an entirely different story. He was easily sixty in the shade, even though he claimed to be only twenty-eight on his online profile. The moment I saw him waiting in our designated meeting spot, holding a flower that looked half dead—like him—I turned around and hightailed it out of there. When I got home, I permanently deactivated my account and made a mental note not to listen to any more of my mother's suggestions.

To be honest, I'm not ready for a boyfriend anyway. Not when my heart still belongs to Jax. It wouldn't be fair to jump into a relationship with someone else if my heart wasn't completely in it.

'Aw, sweetie,' Naomi says, running her hand down my arm. 'You should've called. We could've done lunch, or a movie.' Naomi doesn't know the ins and outs of my situation, just that Maddie's father and I aren't together.

I laugh. 'I'm sure you have better things to do than hang around with me.'

'Not really. Kylie has just taken up a second job on the weekends. She's saving for her European holiday. And Amanda is busy making all her wedding plans. I would've enjoyed your company, so next time call. Okay?'

'All right. I will. Thank you.'

'Good girl.'

When she opens the cash drawer and starts counting out the day's float, I pick up the appointment book to go over my client list. I silently groan when I see Joseph Pentecost's name down as my last appointment. Just thinking about him makes all the hairs on my neck stand on end. He is a major creep. He's one of those types who think they're God's gift to women, but let me tell you, he's not. He has a nice body, and he's not what you'd call ugly, but he has shifty little eyes, and the way he flirts and stares at me gives me the heebie-jeebies. His mere presence makes your vagina dry up, your womb retract and your clit hide for its own safety. No kidding.

He's a self-confessed gym junky and he never stops talking about himself or his damn physique. I have the misfortune of seeing him once a month—he comes in regularly to get his arms, legs, chest and back waxed. He has a disgustingly hairy back. I presume he waxes his body so he can oil himself up and admire his muscles in the mirror. *Puke.*

My eyes move over to Naomi's schedule. I see only two appointments for later today, so her afternoon is pretty much free. My first instinct is to fake another illness and go home early, but I can't do that again. Plus, Naomi let me leave early last week when Maddie hit her head at school. I contemplate asking her to take Joseph's appointment for me, but I can't do that either. He always insists on me being the one to do it anyway. One day I actually went home, pretending to be sick, only because he was coming in later that day. To my displeasure, he rescheduled his appointment for when I was back.

One hour tops, I remind myself. I can suffer through it, just like I always do.

Putting the diary back down on the front counter, I head into my cubicle to turn on the wax pot and get prepped for the day. When I feel my phone vibrate in my pocket, I pull it out. Naomi lets me keep my phone on me while I work, as long as it's on silent. When I see Jax's name on the screen, I'm instantly smiling. He rarely messages me these days. I miss his friendship so much.

> Jax: Hey. Are you free for lunch? I need to talk to you about something.

It would have to be something about Maddie—she's all we ever talk about. He never mentions the tattoo parlour, or asks me about my job or my life outside of being the mother to his daughter. I hate that he no longer has any interest in me or what I do.

> Me: Sure. My break's at one. Is everything okay?

> Jax: One's perfect. Everything is fine. I just want to talk to you about something Maddie said. I'll pick you up out the front.

Way to leave me hanging.

> Me: What? No hint?

> Jax: Nope. See you at one.

I growl when he sends me a smiley emoji. I'm tempted to send him the middle finger emoji in reply, but I don't.

My mind is on our lunch date all morning. I'm excited to see him, even though I'm concerned about what he has to say. By 12.55 pm, I have butterflies in my stomach. I spend the next few minutes fixing my hair and makeup. I know it's not a real date, but I still want to look nice for him. I long for him to look at me the way he used to.

I pop my head into Naomi's cubicle before I leave. 'I'll be back by two.'

'Okay, sweetie.'

There's definitely a bounce in my step as I emerge onto the footpath. Jax has been distant from me for months, ever since our almost kiss on Maddie's birthday. That night I finally realised we were definitely over, but here I am again, hoping that this lunch will lead to something more. There's nothing wrong with carrying a little hope around in your heart. It's all I have, and none of us know what lies around the corner.

'Hey,' he says when I open the passenger door and climb in. He gives me a genuine smile when my eyes meet his. It's been a while since he's graced me with one of them. It takes my breath away when he smiles at me like that.

'Hey. How's the parlour going?' I ask, as he pulls away from the kerb.

'Good.'

I smile, even though I hate the one-word answers he gives me.

'That's good. Is Gus still working there?'

'Yep.'

'Can you tell him I said hello?'

'I will.'

Wow, I got two words that time. Lucky me.

'I miss working there.'

He glances at me briefly, before focusing on the road again.

Right. Okay then. The old Jax would've said, '*You're welcome to come to the shop whenever you want.*' It hurts that he doesn't want me there anymore. I gaze out the window. My hope is fading fast.

'Where are we going for lunch?'

'Just somewhere local. I got Ana to make reservations for us.'

'Ana?' Please don't tell me that's his girlfriend. Maddie has never mentioned her.

'My receptionist.'

'Oh.' The person who stole my job.

We're quiet for the rest of the drive. I have so many questions I want to ask him. I hate that he's become virtually a stranger to me.

My eyes scan the small but elegant restaurant when we enter. Ana did well, I'll thank her if I ever get to meet her. I'll be telling her to give me my damn job back while I'm at it.

'So, are you going to tell me what this is about? I think we both know that it's not because you wanted to see me.' I don't mean to sound so cold, but his lack of enthusiasm when he's around me hurts.

'Can we order first? You've gotta be back by two, right?'

'Yes.'

I pick up the menu and pretend to read over it. I've suddenly lost my appetite. When the waitress comes over to take our order, I order the same as him. I'm only going to pick at it anyway.

'Does Maddie ever say anything to you about our situation?' he asks the moment the waitress walks away.

'What do you mean by "our situation"? The fact that you hate me?'

'I don't hate you,' he says, his brow furrowing.

'Well, you don't like me.'

'Of course I like you. Why would you think I don't?'

'I'm not blind, Jax. I have eyes.'

'Really?' he says, sarcastically. 'I didn't notice.'

'What we were and what we are now are miles apart. You're always so ... distant.'

'It's called self-preservation, Candice.'

'Oh, you find it hard to survive when you're around me? Wow. Thanks. That makes me feel a lot better.'

'No, smartarse.' He looks at the table briefly, then back to me. 'I find it hard not to feel when I'm around you.'

'What's that supposed to mean?'

'Look, do we really need to have this conversation right now?' He removes his baseball cap and runs his hand through his hair. He always does that when he's nervous or uneasy. I can read him like a book.

'Yeah, we do,' I say, crossing my arms over my chest. I get annoyed when his gaze darts straight to my tits. I should lean across the table and rub them in his face, so he can get a better look. 'My eyes are up here, Albright.'

'Right.' He chuckles, moving his eyes back to my face. 'What do you want me to say, Candice? That I avoid being around you because I still have feelings for you?'

A tiny piece of hope returns. 'Yes, if that's how you feel.'

'I'm not a robot. You were my life. I can't just turn my feelings off like a tap.'

'So you still have feelings for me?' I ask, sitting up straight in my seat.

'Can we change the subject? This is not why I brought you here.'

I deflate the instant he says that. He's going to fight this thing between us with everything he has.

'I'm worried about Maddie.'

He has my undivided attention now. 'What? Why?'

'Something Carter said got me thinking. About him being a bastard . . . you know, illegitimate—like our daughter. I don't want her to ever feel burdened by a label like that.'

'She won't,' I say, placing my hand on top of his.

'Has she said anything to you about mums and dads living together?'

'No, why? Has she said something to you?'

'Yes. She told me last week that you and I should get married, so we can live together.'

I clear my throat, and do an inner fist pump. *That's my girl.* I try hard to suppress my smile. 'Did she?'

'She was deadly serious. I didn't know what to tell her.'

'Well maybe we should just get married then.' I shrug like it's no big deal. I know I'm being brazen, but he just admitted, in a round-about way, that he still has feelings for me. That was the green light I needed. *Hello, glimmer of hope.* If he's not going to fight for us, then I sure as hell am. *Game on, Mr Albright.*

'Christ, not you too.'

'Why not?' It's time to pull out the big guns. I should've told him years ago exactly how I feel. If this is the only chance I'm ever going to get, I'm taking it. 'I think I've been in love with you from the moment you bombed your stupid brother and his idiot mates, and drenched me.'

His eyes widen at my confession, but he remains silent.

I reach for his hand again, and when he tries to pull away, I hold tight. 'I was in love with you the night we made Maddie. I was in love with you when you came back into my life a few years later. And I'm still in love with you now, Jax. I've never stopped . . . I'm not sure I ever will. I know you're still upset with me about the whole Maddie incident. I get that. But please believe me when I say I thought I was doing the right thing at the time. For her, for you, for all of us.'

He opens his mouth to say something, and then closes it again.

'Say something, Jax. Anything.' *Please say you love me too*.

When he goes to speak again, the stupid waitress approaches the table and places our food in front us.

When he stares down at the food in front of him, I release his hand. I get the message loud and clear. As if things between us aren't already awkward enough. I may be feeling humiliated right now, but I have no regrets about finally telling him exactly how I feel. It's been a long time coming.

••••

Jax didn't say another word to me over lunch. We ate, we left, and he dropped me back here. The silence was deafening. I was on the verge of tears when I stepped out of the car, but I sucked it up. I wasn't going to give him the satisfaction. Stupid jerk.

My crappy afternoon gets even crappier when creepy Joseph arrives for his waxing.

'Hey gorgeous,' he says when I walk into my cubical where he's waiting. He removes his shirt and flexes his muscles before lying on the bed. He's such a tool. Doesn't he realise how pathetic he looks when he does that?

'Hi,' I reply dryly, turning my back on him to stir the wax in the pot. The quicker I get this done, the quicker he can leave.

Once I've laid out the fabric strips on my work tray, I turn to face him again. When I find his eyes firmly fixed on my arse, I get chills up my spine. I'd like nothing more than to pour the entire pot of hot wax over his face and wax those beady little eyes right out of their sockets. 'The usual?' I ask with disdain.

'Mmm,' he says as his eyes move down the length of my body. 'I don't know, I might require some extra pampering today. What's on offer?'

He says shit like this all the time—his lame attempt at flirting. *Dream on, buddy.* I wouldn't touch him if he was the last man on earth.

'Well, we have a special on castrations today. Interested?' I have to suppress my smile when he squirms on the table. Hopefully now he'll get the message and shut the fuck up. I'm in no mood for his creepy shit.

'Someone's wearing their bitch suit today.'

I bite my tongue and let him have that one. He's a client, and I need to remember that. If he calls me a bitch again though, he's gonna have a lap full of hot wax.

His death grip on the side of the bed tightens with every strip I pull from his body. I smirk to myself when I look up at his face and see his eyes clenched shut, a tear running down the side of his face. *Pussy.* Call me spiteful, but I'm savouring the thought of making him hurt. Usually I feel bad about causing my clients pain.

'I'm not hurting you, am I?' I ask in the sweetest voice I can muster.

'Nope,' he replies in a voice that is so high-pitched, it's almost a squeak.

I bite my lip in an attempt to hold back my laugh. *Liar.*

I stop what I'm doing when Naomi pops her head around the privacy curtain. 'I'm done for the day. Would you mind closing up when you're done? Amanda has her first fitting for her wedding dress tonight. I'd really love to be there.'

My first instinct is to scream, 'No! Please don't leave me alone with this twat-waffle,' but I can't say that. This is her daughter; she should be there. I'd want to be there if it was Maddie.

'Sure,' I say, with a sigh. I don't feel comfortable being left alone with this douche.

'Thanks, sweetie.'

'Make sure you take a pic for me. I'd love to see the dress.'

'Of course. I can't believe in a few short months my little girl will be getting married.' She blows me a kiss before disappearing behind the curtain.

'So it's just you and me now, babe,' Joseph says with a wink.

'Don't get any ideas,' I grumble.

'You can deny it all you want, but you know you want me. I see you checking out this fine specimen of a body. Get in line, sweetheart.'

I can't help but laugh at his comment. He's so full of himself. 'The line of women running away you mean?'

'Very funny,' he spits. 'No. The line of women who want a piece of this.' He grabs hold of his crotch, and it makes me shudder. 'See. You're trembling with need.'

'Repulsion more like it.'

'If I got the python out, you'd be all over it.'

Python? I highly doubt it. Worm maybe.

'Yeah. With a razor. Keep that thing in your pants.' I give him a look that tells him I'm not joking, but being the cocky shit he is, he slips his thumb into the waistband of his workout shorts, pulling them down slightly. 'I'm warning you.'

'You're sexy when you're feisty. You turn me on.' He pulls his shorts down further, until his teeny-tiny half-erect penis is fully on show.

I swear I throw up in my mouth as I quickly turn my head in the other direction. 'You've got two seconds to put that thing away, or I won't be held responsible for what I do.'

'Loosen up, babe,' he says, reaching out to grope one of my tits.

I jump back, slapping his hand away at the same time. 'Get out!' I scream, pointing to the curtain.

'Stop being such a bitch,' he spits, sitting up. My eyes dart to his waist, where his now fully erect penis is still exposed. It turns my stomach.

'Take your stuff and get out. You're no longer welcome here.' I pick up his T-shirt from the chair and toss it at him.

His hand comes out of nowhere, grabbing a chunk of my hair. I thrash around as he roughly drags me towards him, putting up a good fight. But no matter how hard I try, I'm no match for his strength.

'I should just fuck you. Show you what a real man feels like.'

'Just try it,' I challenge. He's twice the size of me, but I refuse to back down.

'My cock is too good for you anyway. Stuck-up bitch.' His hand is still gripping my hair as he pushes my head down towards his waist. He doesn't say another word, but I know exactly what he's trying to do.

I clench my eyes shut when his pathetic excuse for a penis comes into my line of sight. 'If you had a dick, this is where you'd tell me to suck it, right?'

He reefs my head back, making me stumble. The murderous look in his eyes makes my heart drop into the pit of my stomach. My mind instantly goes into survival mode when he raises his arm and backhands me across the face. This time when I stumble backwards my work tray digs hard into my lower back, causing me to groan from the pain. I reach for the small cupboard by the wall to stop myself from falling.

When I regain my footing, I stand tall, wiping the back of my hand over my bottom lip. I already know it's bleeding, because of the metallic taste in my mouth. I square my shoulders and take a step towards him. I may not be as strong as him, but what he fails to realise is my hands are lethal.

He's messed with the wrong chick.

TWENTY-NINE

JAX

BY FOUR PM I DECIDE TO CALL IT A DAY. MY MIND ISN'T ON the game anyway. All I can think about is Candice, and what she confessed over lunch. I'm gonna fuck up someone's tatt if I stay. 'Can you cancel my last two appointments?' I ask Ana, when I walk out into the reception area. 'I'm going home.'

Candice has loved me just as long as I've loved her. How could I not know that?

'Are you okay?' Ana asks as I remove my cap and run my fingers through my hair.

'I will be,' I reply, giving her a half-hearted smile. 'See if you can move them to tomorrow.'

'But tomorrow is your day off.'

'That's fine. I don't have any plans, so I can come in.' Maddie's at school during the day anyway.

'Okay. I'll organise them now and text you with the details.'

'Thank you.' I push through the front door and into the street. I need some fucking air. No, I need a damn cigarette. I have a packet stashed in my car for just such an occasion.

I rub my hand across my chest in an attempt to relieve the dull ache that's settled there. I'm not sure if it's indigestion or Candice. My guess is Candice. I'm angry that we've both fought these feelings for so long. Look where it's got us ... fucking nowhere.

I've waited my entire adult life to hear her say those words, but now that she has, I'm so torn. I'd be lying if I said I didn't feel the same way about her, but she lied to me and tore my fucking heart out. How can I get past that? Then there's that million-dollar question: Am I capable of spending the rest of my life loving her from afar? I doubt it. Trying to act like I don't care is tearing me apart.

The moment I get home, I head straight for my car to grab a smoke out of the glove compartment. I take a long drag as I flip open the lid on my letterbox. I no longer have to worry about my family contacting me, I'm going to treat them as they treat me—like they don't exist. It's the only way. They're dead to me.

I pick up the hand-addressed envelope inside. I don't recognise the writing. Flipping it over, I smile. It's a letter from Brian, all the way from Western Australia. We spoke at length on the phone after Candice returned, but I haven't heard from him since.

I go into the kitchen and grab a bottle of Jack out of the cupboard and a shot glass. My titty cup, the one Candice bought me. Maybe not the best cup for this situation. Placing them on the breakfast bar, I pick up Brian's letter and open it. I could use a pick-me-up.

Hello my dear friend,
I'm sorry it's taken me so long to write. James bought me a
mobile phone not long after I moved here, so we could keep in
touch, but I've yet to master how to use the darn thing.
      Life for me is good. I've been busy helping Alana with Aiden
and the baby, while James works long hours at his job. Being

a full-time grandfather is exhausting, but I love it. It keeps me young.

I have you, and only you, to thank for that. Your kindness and compassion to an old man has changed my life. I'm not sure where I'd be now if you hadn't taken me in and helped me reconnect with my family. Don't ever let anyone change who you are, son. You're an honourable young man, Jax, and I'm blessed to have someone of your stature in my life.

My granddaughter, May, was born six months ago. Yes, they named their daughter after my sweet May. God rest her soul. Little May has her grandmother's eyes and sweet nature. I'm not ashamed to admit that I worship the ground she walks on. It's like having a piece of my wife back...

I stop reading when my phone rings. Placing the letter on the breakfast bar, I pull my phone out of my pocket. I see Sophia's name on the screen and my first thought is for Maddie.

'Hey. Is everything okay?' I ask the moment the phone is to my ear.

'Jax, it's Candice. She's been attacked.'

'What? What do you mean "attacked"?' I stand, grabbing my keys. 'Where is she?'

'She's at work. One of her clients attacked her. She said she's okay, but she was probably just saying that so I wouldn't worry.'

I'm already jogging to the car by the time she's finished speaking. 'I'm heading there now.'

'I was going to see if you would watch Maddie, so I could go.'

'You stay with Maddie. I'll go to Candice.' My hand shakes as I try to put the keys in the ignition.

'Okay. Please call me as soon as you've seen her.'

The moment she starts to cry I freak out even more.

Please let Candice be okay.

I swear I break every speed limit on the way. There are two police cars and two ambulances parked out front of her workplace when I arrive. The sight has me feeling sick to my stomach. I park behind one of the cop cars, running straight to the officer standing by the door.

'I'm looking for Candice, the girl who was attacked.'

'Are you family?'

'Yes.' That's not really a lie. Hypothetically, she's always been like family to me, and she is the mother of my daughter.

He opens the glass door, flicking his head to let me know she's inside. My heart beats furiously against my ribcage as I enter. I have no idea what I'm going to find. My eyes scan the reception area and relief floods through me the moment I see her sitting in a chair, alert and talking with one of the officers. I make a beeline straight for her. I have her wrapped tightly in my arms almost before she even realises I'm here.

'Jax,' I hear her whisper as her fists clutch the front of my shirt.

'Thank Christ you're okay.'

'I thought Sophia was coming.'

'I told her to stay with Maddie. I wanted to come. I needed to see for myself that you were okay . . .'

'I'm glad you're here,' she says, resting her head on my chest and sliding her arms around my waist.

I hold her for the longest time before stepping back to see her face. Tears rise to her eyes when I tenderly cup her face in my hands. When I notice the mark on her cheek, and the cut on her swollen bottom lip, I see red.

'Who did this to you?'

'I'm okay. Honestly. He came out of this a lot worse off than me.'

'He? A guy hit you?' My blood pressure spikes to a dangerous level. I look at the cop standing beside me.

'Once he's been treated for his injuries, he'll be charged,' the officer says. The cop has a smirk on his face, but there's nothing amusing about this situation.

Dropping my hands from Candice, I turn to leave. I don't care what injuries he has, nobody hits my girl and walks away from it.

'Jax, don't,' Candice pleads, reaching for me.

'I'd advise you to listen to your wife,' the officer adds. I want to tell him she's not my wife, but for some reason I don't.

'Can we have a few minutes alone?' she asks him.

'Sure. We'll be right outside.' He gives me a look as he passes, a warning not to do anything stupid.

The anger is just rolling off me as I run my fingers through my hair, trying to calm the hell down. For Candice's sake, nothing else.

'I appreciate you coming here,' she says once we're alone. 'And I love that you want to protect me, but hurting him will only get you in trouble. I don't want that.' She laces her fingers through mine. Her touch, like always, seems to have an immediate soothing effect. Nobody has ever come close to making me feel the things she does.

••••

'Stop fussing,' she says when I pass her a clean towel, a pair of my sweats and a T-shirt. She smiles, but I can tell it's forced. She's trying to play this down, but I felt her body trembling in my arms when I first arrived at her work. She's barely said a word since we left there. I'm not stupid, I know she's affected by what happened.

'I'll be right outside if you need me.'

'Thank you.' She reaches for my hand, giving it a small squeeze before I turn and leave her to shower in peace. I called Sophia while the paramedics checked her over. Of course Candice refused to go to the hospital. She's so stubborn. Sophia protested when I said I was taking Candice back to my place, but when I mentioned that I didn't want Maddie to see her mother like this, she agreed. That was only part of the reason. I wanted to be the one to take care of her. It meant I'd be giving up my night with my daughter, but Candice needs me more.

I promised Sophia I'd bring Candice home later tonight, after Maddie has gone to bed.

When I hear the spray of the water, I rest my forehead against the wood and try not to think of Candice naked on the other side of the door. She's been through a traumatic experience. The last thing she needs is me lusting after her.

A few minutes later, I swear I hear her crying. I feel an over-whelming compulsion to go to her and my hand instinctively moves to the doorhandle. But after everything that's happened today, I think better of it. I don't want to traumatise her further.

A good twenty minutes pass, but I continue to wait outside the bathroom just like I promised. She can take all the time she needs, I'm not going anywhere. My primary concern right now is her.

I'm leaning up against the wall in the hallway with my arms crossed over my chest when she finally emerges. Her hair is wet, her face is free of makeup, and she looks sexy as fuck in my shirt. She has her dirty clothes in her hands, so I take them from her.

'I'll put these in the laundry.'

'Thank you.'

'Are you feeling better after the shower?' I ask as she follows me to the lounge room. It's a stupid question really. A shower isn't going to help erase what she's been through.

'I guess,' she replies with a shrug.

I hand the throw blanket from the sofa to her. 'Wrap yourself in this. I'll be right back.' I hold her dirty clothes up, so she knows I'm only going to the laundry.

When I walk back through the kitchen, I see the bottle of Jack I got out earlier still sitting on the breakfast bar. I grab it, bringing it into the lounge room with me. A stiff drink may settle her nerves.

'Here. Drink this.' Filling the glass, I pass it to her. 'It's not Sambuca.' I hold up the bottle of Jack Daniels. 'This is all I have.'

'You're letting me drink out of your titty cup?' she asks, taking the shot glass out of my hand.

'Yes.' I sit down next to her. 'This glass I'm happy to share with you.'

She lets out a small laugh. 'But you won't share my cock cup?'

'Never.'

She downs the shot like a pro and passes the glass back to me. I pour her one more. It should help take the edge off.

'Thank you,' she says as she drinks her second shot.

'Want another one?' When she shakes her head, I pour one for myself before placing the empty glass and the bottle on the coffee table.

Turning my body to face her, I notice there's a small bruise forming on the side of her mouth. I run my thumb softly over her cut lip. Everything in me wants to kiss it better.

'Are you going to tell me what happened today?' She needs to talk about it. Bottling it up won't help.

'There's not much to tell,' she says. 'He's one of my regular clients. He's always creeped me out. I was in the middle of waxing him when Naomi popped her head in to say she was leaving.'

I had no idea she had male clients.

'This guy has said inappropriate things to me in the past, but that's as far as it's ever gotten. I guess the fact that we were alone ... he decided to take it to the next step.'

'He didn't ... you know ... do anything to you?'

'He tried. When I told him to leave, he grabbed me by the hair.' She clutches the blanket and wraps it tighter around herself. 'He pushed my face towards his waist, and when I insulted him by saying he had no dick, he backhanded me.'

My body goes rigid when she says that. I roll my head from side to side, trying to keep my anger at bay. 'I want to kill him for laying his hands on you.'

'I got my revenge, don't you worry.'

I don't doubt that for a second.

'After he hit me, I regained my footing and stepped forward.' She pauses for a few seconds. 'I wrapped my hand around his dick. It was already hard. The stupid idiot smiled when I did that. He actually thought I was going to get him off. I held it as tight as I could and using all my strength, I flicked my wrist until I heard a sickening pop. He went instantly limp as he fell back onto the bed ... when he started screaming, I knew I'd snapped it.'

'Fuck.' My face screws up just thinking about it. My hand instinctively moves down to my crotch. My ball-busting ninja strikes again. 'You snapped his dick?'

'I think his exact words were, "You broke my dick, you fucking psycho bitch." I didn't stick around to find out. He was screaming in agony as I ran from the room and out into the street. A passer-by saw I was distressed, so he stopped and asked if I was okay.' Her gaze moves down to the floor. 'When I told him what had happened, he called the police.'

We sit there in silence for a few minutes. I'm trying hard to remain calm after everything she's just told me. I honestly have no words right now. I'm angry at myself that I wasn't there to protect her.

When she finally lifts her head and looks at me, I see tears in her eyes. 'It was awful, Jax. All I could think about was not seeing you and Maddie again.'

I pull her into my arms, and she cries softly into my chest.

'I'm sorry,' I whisper as I stroke my hand softly over her wet hair. *I'm sorry for so many things.*

I draw back from her when there's a knock at the door.

'Are you expecting anyone?' she asks.

'Nope. I'll just see who it is, I'll be back in a minute.'

'Okay.' She smiles up at me.

I'm really glad she's here.

'Brendan,' I say when I open the door.

'Hi Jax. I'm sorry to come here unannounced, but Sophia called me and told me what happened to Candice. Can I see her? I won't stay long.'

'Of course.' I move to the side so he can enter. 'She's just through there,' I say, pointing to the lounge room.

'Brendan,' I hear Candice say. 'What are you doing here?'

I stand in the doorway and watch, giving them some space.

'Your mum called and told me what happened,' he says, pulling her off the lounge and into his arms. 'I'm sorry for dropping in like this, but I needed to come and make sure you were all right. I would've come earlier, but I was in court.'

'I'm glad you came,' she says, sliding her arms around his waist.

He pulls back slightly, looking down at her face. 'Are you okay?'

'I will be,' she answers as she looks at me. 'Jax has been looking after me.' Placing his hand on the back of her head, he pulls her face into his chest.

I can't help but smile as I watch them together. It's obvious he cares for her. I know how much her own father's absence has hurt her over the years, so this is nice.

He continues to hold her for a short time before letting her go. 'Your mother has invited me over for dinner, so I best be going. I just needed to see you.'

'I'm happy you came,' Candice says, smiling up at him.

He pulls a business card out of his pocket. 'Call me if you need anything.'

'Okay,' she says, taking it from him.

'I mean it, sweetheart. I'm here if you need me. Always.'

'Thank you.' A smile tugs at her lips, but I can also see the tears in her eyes from here.

He places a tender kiss on her forehead. 'Take care of yourself. I'll call in and see you tomorrow once you're back at home.'

I follow him to the door when he leaves. He's a good man. I really like him.

'I'm gonna make that bastard pay,' he says as soon as Candice is out of earshot. 'The police prosecutor is a friend of mine.'

'I'm pleased to hear that. I want to kill him for laying his hands on her.'

'Makes two of us.'

••••

'Hello,' I say quietly, when I walk into the kitchen to answer my phone.

'It's almost ten, Jaxson Albright,' Sophia screeches. 'When are you bringing Candice home? I need to see her.'

'She's fallen asleep on my sofa. I don't want to wake her. I think it's best if I bring her home in the morning.'

'The morning? You said you were going to drop her home once Maddie was asleep. That was almost two hours ago.'

I exhale a frustrated breath. I know Sophia's upset, and I know she's concerned about her daughter, but there's no way I'm waking Candice up. She's my first priority at the moment. She's doesn't need her melodramatic mother watching her every move. She'd hate that.

'As I told you earlier, she's fine. Upset, but you know as well as I do that she won't dwell on what happened today. She'll deal with it and move on, like she always does.'

'I just need to see her with my own eyes. I've been a mess all afternoon. She's my baby, Jax.'

I roll my eyes. She's twenty-four years old, far from a baby. 'Hold on,' I say. I walk back into the lounge room and snap a quick picture of Candice asleep on my sofa. I attach the image to a text. I tried to take the picture from an angle that made Candice's bruised cheek and cut lip look less prominent. Otherwise, Sophia's liable to get in the car and come over.

'You have a photo coming through now.'

'It's just come through. Let me take a quick look. Aw, she looks so peaceful. Thank you for that. How has she been since we last spoke?'

'Okay. Better than I thought she'd be. How's Maddie?'

'She's fine. I didn't tell her what happened. I didn't want to worry her.'

'Thank you.'

'Naomi, Candice's boss, has been calling all afternoon. She's so upset that this happened. She's tried calling Candice, but she won't answer.'

'I haven't heard her phone ring. It might be on silent, or switched off. I'll let her know in the morning when she wakes.'

'Thank you. As much as I want to see her, I'm glad she's with you. I know you'll take care of her.'

Guilt floods me when she says that. I've been such an arsehole to Candice lately. But Sophia's right, I will.

Once I end the call, I head back into the lounge room and stand beside the sofa looking down at Candice. My mind's been all over the place since she confessed her love for me. But if anything positive is to come out of the attack, it's made me realise just how much I need her. It's time to put this hurt and betrayal aside and move forward. We've already wasted too much time fighting the inevitable. I can't do it anymore.

Sliding my hands underneath her, I lift her effortlessly into my arms.

'Jax,' she whispers, as her eyes flutter open.

'Shh,' I say. 'I'm just carrying you to my room. I want you here with me tonight.'

She smiles as her arms slide around my neck. 'There's no place I'd rather be.'

I pull back the blankets and lay her down on the mattress then pull the covers up around her chin. I smile when I straighten to full height. I've missed seeing her in my bed.

'You're not sleeping in here?' she asks. The disappointment is visible on her face.

'Yes. I'm just going to jump in the shower. I won't be long.'

'Okay.' She's grinning as she closes her eyes and snuggles into the mattress.

Sharing a bed with her probably isn't a wise move, but I'm not leaving her alone tonight.

••••

Light's streaming into my room when I open my eyes. I look over at the clock on the bedside table—it's only 6.42 am. Candice is still wrapped tightly in my arms. I have a few more hours before I have to give her back.

When I climbed into bed after my shower last night, she'd already fallen back to sleep and I had to fight the urge to pull her into my arms. Instead, I just lay there and watched her, all the time wondering what the future held for us.

Around midnight, she became restless, and started whimpering in her sleep. It was only then that I gave into the temptation and pulled her into my arms. It seemed to work, because she settled straightaway.

I pull her tightly against me and savour the feeling of having her in my arms. Who knows if, or when, I'll ever get to hold her like this again? I place a soft, lingering kiss on her hair.

'Morning,' she mumbles against my chest.

'Morning. I thought you were still asleep.'

'I've been awake for a while. I was just pretending to sleep so I didn't have to let you go. I felt you kiss my hair, by the way.'

'Did you?' I chuckle.

She lifts her head off my chest and smiles. The first thing I notice is that the bruise on her cheek has darkened overnight. 'How are you feeling this morning?' I ask, to divert the conversation away from the kiss.

'I'm with you, so I feel great.'

I'd be lying if I said I wasn't happy to have her here as well, because fuck me, I am. My eyes keep wandering down to her injured lip. I run the pad of my thumb gently across it. I'm still angry that this happened.

'Does it hurt?'

'A little. Maybe if you kiss it better, it won't hurt so much.'

'Candice,' I breathe. I've missed her, and I know I want her—I've never stopped wanting her—but I can't rush into anything with her right now. For both of our sakes, I need to be sure.

'I'm sorry,' she says, sighing. 'It was worth a try.' She untangles her body from mine and lies on her back.

'Hey.' I roll onto my side and face her. The moment I do, she shuts her eyes, refusing to look at me. 'Look at me. Candice.'

'It's okay, Jax. Honestly.'

'No, it's not.' She opens her eyes, and turns her face towards mine. Without saying a word, I place a soft kiss on her bruised cheek and then on her cut lip. 'Does it feel better now?' I ask.

'My lip still hurts; you may need to kiss it again.' She's smiling as she speaks.

Sliding my arm around her waist, I turn her body to mine and draw her closer. My eyes close when our mouths meet again. I've missed her sweet lips. She moves her hand up to cup my face as my lips linger against hers. Neither of us take the kiss any further. It's just a simple peck, but my cock is so hard right now it aches.

When she finally pulls back, she rests her forehead against mine. 'I love you so much, Jaxson Albright, it hurts.'

THIRTY

JAX

I DROP CANDICE HOME JUST BEFORE NINE. I ALMOST CALLED
in sick so I could spend the day with her, but not only do I have a
business to run, I need space to think. To process everything. There's
no denying how I feel, but can I really let the past go? Are we strong
enough to get through everything that has happened? I have Maddie
to think of as well. If things don't work out between Candice and me,
where does that leave the whole co-parenting thing?

We timed it so Sophia had already left to take Maddie to school.
Maddie is still unaware of the attack on Candice, so we didn't want
her spending her day worrying about it. Candice can talk to her
about it tonight. Sophia looks after Maddie while we're at work, but
other than that she leaves the parenting up to us. She's taken on the
grandmother role now instead. That's how it should've been from
the very beginning.

I try hard throughout the morning to focus on the job, but Candice
remains at the front of my mind. Around lunchtime, I pull out my
phone and shoot her a text.

Me: Hey. How's things?

She replies almost immediately.

Candice: Good. Sophia is fussing over me like a mother hen.

I chuckle at her reply.

Me: I bet she is.

Candice: She just asked who I was talking to. She said to say hi, and asked if you want to come over for dinner tonight?

Me: Sure. Tell her thanks. And hi.

Candice: Great. I'll see you tonight then. I know I already said it, but thanks again for taking care of me last night. x

Me: You're welcome. See you tonight.

Putting my phone back in my pocket, I walk towards reception.

'What are you looking so happy about?' Gus says as I pass him in the corridor.

'What?'

'You're smiling, like you just got lucky or something.'

'Or something,' I reply.

He gives me a sceptical look as he passes me and pops his head inside the door of my studio.

'What are you doing?'

'Just making sure you don't have a hot babe hiding in there.'

'You're an idiot.' I chuckle, shaking my head.

He returns and places his hand on my shoulder. 'Well, what put that smile on your face then? Come on, you can tell me.'

'Do you really want to know why I'm so happy?' I raise one of my eyebrows.

'Fuck yeah.' He rubs his hands together like he thinks he's about to hear a juicy secret. He's so gullible.

Leaning forward, I whisper, 'I'm heading out to lunch, so that means I won't have to see your meathead for the next hour.'

I throw my head back and laugh when he punches me in the arm.

'Very funny, arsehole,' he calls out to my retreating back.

••••

Sophia offers to bath Maddie after dinner. I'm not stupid—she wants to give Candice and me some time alone. Candice has applied some makeup over her bruised cheek and lip, but the injuries are still visible.

'What did you tell her?' I ask.

'That I fell,' she replies, shrugging. 'She doesn't need to know the truth.'

She's right, telling Maddie the truth will do no good. She's too young to understand. 'Fair enough.'

'Naomi has given me the rest of the week off.'

'What? Who's Naomi?'

'My boss. She called me this morning. She actually said I can take as much time off as I need, but I told her I'd be right to come back Monday.'

'Like fuck. You're not going back there, Candice.'

'Excuse me? You can't tell me what to do.'

'There's no way in hell I'm letting you work there, Candice, and that's final.'

'Fuck you, it's *final*. I know you help me out financially with Maddie, but I need to work. I'm not letting that twat-waffle who attacked me stand in my way.'

I chuckle. *Twat-waffle*.

'It's not funny, Jax.'

'I'm not laughing at that.' Then it hits me, the perfect solution. 'Hold on a minute.' I grab my phone. She gives me a peculiar look when I dial a number and put the phone to my ear. 'Hey twat-waffle,' I say when Carter answers.

'Twat-waffle? What the fuck is a twat-waffle?'

'My new favourite word.'

'It's very fitting,' he replies. 'It describes you perfectly.'

'Fuck off it does, cock,' I say when he bursts out laughing.

'Did you just call to insult me? I'm busy, what do you want?'

'Of course I did. It's fun.' We both have a bit of a laugh before I continue. 'You know how we were looking for someone to run our new tattoo parlour?' My gaze moves to Candice as I speak.

'Yeah. Did you find someone?'

'I did. Candice.'

'Really? She'd be perfect. She not only knows what she's doing, but we can trust her.'

'Exactly.' Although I'm still working on the trust bit. 'So are you cool with that?'

'Definitely.'

'Great. I'll see you next week when you come down.'

'Okay. See you then, twat-waffle.'

'Hey. I told you that's my word.'

'Not anymore, fucker.'

The line goes dead before I get a chance to reply.

I shake my head as I put my phone on the table. 'All settled. You can manage our new shop. We sign the papers next week. We're hoping to be open for business in three weeks.'

'Do I even get a say in this?' Candice says, but she's happy. I can tell by the smile she's trying hard to hold back.

'Nope. It's a done deal, sweetheart.'

She narrows her eyes when I wink at her, but within seconds she's smiling. 'I didn't know you and Carter were buying another shop.'

'This guy I used to work for is getting out of the business, so we're taking over. It's already established, so it makes perfect sense.'

'Wow.'

'If everything works out, Carter and I are planning on starting up a Wicked Ink franchise. Our dream is to have our shops all over the country.'

'You'll do it,' she says confidently. Her belief in me never wavers.

••••

I stay long enough to read Maddie a bedtime story. 'Night, Peanut,' I say as I tuck the blankets up to her chin and kiss her forehead.

'One more story, Daddy,' she pleads.

'You have school tomorrow, you need to get some sleep,' Candice cuts in from the doorway, where she's been standing, watching us.

Maddie rolls her eyes so only I can see, and I have to try hard not to smile.

'Your mother is right.'

'Fine.' She shifts onto her side, tucking Puppy into her chest. 'Night, Daddy.'

'I love you,' I say, leaning down to kiss her one more time. It's getting harder and harder to walk away. 'Sweet dreams.'

After Candice says goodnight, she follows me out of the room and down the stairs. 'I'll walk you out.'

'You don't have to. It's cold outside.'

'I want to.'

She opens the small drawer of the hall table as she passes and pulls out an envelope, before opening the front door.

'Bye, Sophia,' I call out.

A few seconds later, Sophia appears through the doorway that leads to the kitchen. 'Night, Jax,' she says as she wipes her hands on a tea towel.

'Thanks for dinner.'

'You're always welcome here, you know that.'

I smile and nod before turning to follow Candice out the door. We come to an abrupt stop when we reach my car, standing there in silence. I don't know what to say to her.

'Thank you for the job offer,' she finally says.

'I don't want you going back to the other place. You'll be safe working for me. I'll make sure of it.'

'I know. I'm actually looking forward to working there,' she says, wrapping her arms around herself.

'You can come with me and Carter next week and check out the place if you like.'

'Really?'

'Of course. You're going to be running it. It makes sense that you see it.'

'I'd love to come. It'll be great to see Carter too. I've missed him.'

'He's doing well. He's living in Newcastle now.'

'Really? Why did he move so far away?'

'Some chick.'

'Indiana,' she says.

'You know about her?'

'Yeah. She lives next door to his parents.'

I scratch my head. Why am I always the last to know these things? I suppose I've never told Carter about Candice or Maddie either.

'Well, I guess I should let you get back inside, out of the cold.'

'Sure.' She smiles briefly. 'Here, this is for you.' She's offering me the envelope I saw her grab a few minutes ago.

'What is it?'

'Just a card.'

I take it from her, but when I go to open it, she places her hand on top of mine to stop me.

'Open it when you get home.'

'Okay. Thank you.' I slide it into the back pocket of my jeans, curious as to why she doesn't want me to open it now.

I pull my keys out of my jacket and unlock the driver's door.

'Goodnight, Jax.' There's a hopeful look on her face when I glance at her over my shoulder.

Turning, I wrap her in my arms. 'Goodnight, Candice.' When I rest my chin on the top of her head, I inhale her apple scent.

I pull the card out of my pocket and put it on the passenger seat once I'm in the car. I find myself glancing at it all the way home. Curiosity gets the better of me when I pull up outside my place, and I reach for it. I turn on the interior light and tear open the envelope. Removing the card, I hold it out in front of me.

'Jesus Christ,' I mumble, flicking my wrist and letting the card go at the same time. It flies onto the passenger seat. Candice and her damn cock fetish. No wonder she told me to wait until I got home. I swear she does shit like this just to taunt me. She can deny it all she wants, but she definitely needs therapy.

Leaning across the centre console, I smile as I look down at the card. There's a cartoon drawing of a dick with these giant, gross-looking, hairy balls on the front. That's not what I'm smiling at though. It's the caption underneath: *I'm nuts about you.*

Pulling my sleeve down over my hand, I use it like a glove so I can flick the card open and read what's written inside.

Dear Jax,
Thank you for caring for me last night. You helped more than you'll ever know. Whether you want to be or not, you'll always be the sun in my day, the wind in my sky, the waves in my ocean, and the beat in my heart. I'll forever be lost without you by my side.
Yours always,
Candice xxx

A lump rises in my throat as I lean back into my seat. I know what I need to do. I leave the card where it is, because I'm not picking that fucker up again. I'll come back out later with a pair of kitchen tongs or something.

When I unlock my front door, I head straight into the kitchen and open the top drawer. I pull out the envelope that contains the letter I wrote to Candice when I first moved to Sydney. The heart in a bottle necklace is still enclosed. Things would've been so different if she'd gotten this back then.

Pulling out a fresh envelope, I put the original one inside it. I grab a pen and write her name and address on the front. Tomorrow morning I'm going to do what I should've done a long time ago—resend it.

It's time she knew the truth—that I've loved her just as long as she's loved me.

THIRTY-ONE

JAX

'MORNING, BOSS . . . ANA,' GUS SAYS WHEN HE COMES THROUGH the front door.

'Gus,' I reply with a nod. 'Have you got a minute?'

'Sure, what's up?'

My gaze moves from him to Ana. I haven't mentioned any of this to her yet. 'Can I speak to you in private?'

I don't wait for his reply as I head to my studio. When he enters a minute later, I can see the apprehension on his face.

'Is everything okay?'

'Sit.'

He rubs his hands nervously down the front of his jeans as he does.

'I . . . I, um.' Christ, I didn't think this would be so hard. He's one of my best workers, and I don't want to lose him. But, after many hours of consideration, this was my best option. 'I'm going to be moving you.'

'What? What do you mean?'

'Carter and I are opening a new parlour in Surry Hills, and I want you to go and work there.'

'You don't want me here anymore?' He slumps in his seat.

'It's not that I don't want you here. It's just that I need you there.'

'Oh.'

I can tell he's not happy about this. When he goes to stand, I hold my hand up to stop him.

'Hear me out. Candice is going to be running the new place, and I need someone there I can trust . . . someone to keep an eye out for her.'

His face lights up when I say that. He looked out for her when she worked here. And I know how much he missed her when she left—he was constantly asking about her. That's why I know he's perfect for this job. If I can't be there to keep an eye out for her, I know he will.

'Pinkie's coming back?'

'Yes. Yes, she is. This wasn't an easy decision for me, Gus. Please know that.'

'I like working for you, you're a good boss.'

I smile. 'Even though you annoy the shit out of me sometimes, I like having you here.'

'Then why do you want me to go to the other place?'

'It's like this, Gus.' I need to tell him what happened, so he understands why I'm doing this. 'Candice was attacked at her other job a few days ago.'

'What do you mean?' His body goes rigid and he sits up straight in the chair.

'She's okay, but one of her male clients roughed her up a bit.'

'I'll fucking kill him,' he spits.

'No need for that,' I say. 'Although I'd like to do just that myself. Can you see why I need you at the new place? I have to know she's going to be safe.'

'It's that fucking obsession of hers. I knew that would get her in trouble one day.'

'What obsession?'

'You know, with cocks.'

His comment instantly gets my back up. 'How the fuck do you know about that?'

'Calm down. One day when we were locking up, I saw the cock on her keyring.' He shakes his head before continuing. 'She told me about her cock collection.'

'She needs therapy.'

Gus chuckles. 'It could be worse.'

'Like how?'

'Well, she could have a collection of old toenail clippings or belly-button lint.'

I laugh. 'I guess. Do people really collect that kinda thing?'

He nods. I fucking hope he's not one of them. 'You care about her a lot, don't you?'

I look at the floor and sigh. 'I love her, Gus.'

'I fucking knew it.' When he slaps his leg and laughs, I want to kick myself for admitting that to him.

'Shut up, fucker. You knew jackshit.'

He throws back his head and laughs harder and I want to punch him.

'You breathe a word of this to anyone and so help me . . .'

'Your secret is safe with me,' he says smugly as he draws a cross over his heart with his finger, like a five-year-old would do.

'I mean it, Gus.' *What was I thinking by telling him?*

'You have my word. This will stay between us, boss. But I'm gonna give you shit about it, you know that, right?'

'You better not.'

He chuckles, so I know he's gonna do it regardless of what I say. 'So when am I leaving?'

'Three weeks.'

'I'm gonna miss working here, but I'll enjoy working with Pinkie again. She's a top chick.'

'I spoke with Carter last night, and we're going to give you a pay rise to compensate you.'

'There's no need for that.'

'It's already been decided. You'll be the head artist there.'

Standing, he shakes my hand. 'I won't let you down, boss. Keeping Pinkie safe will be my first priority.'

'You're a good man. Thank you.'

When he turns to leave he starts to sing, 'Jax and Candice sitting in a tree K-I-S-S-I-N-G.'

'I take that last statement back,' I call out to his retreating back. 'You're not a good man, you're a cock.'

He roars with laughter as he walks down the hall towards his studio.

••••

I pull on a pair of sweats and a T-shirt when I get out of the shower. Heading into the lounge room, I grab the remote off the coffee table before settling down on the sofa. Another night of dreary solitude.

I called Maddie when I got home from work this afternoon, something I always do. It's not the same as having her here with me, but I like to hear her voice, and to see how her day went. She always gives me a blow-by-blow description, which I love. My mind drifts to Candice. For the last two days, thoughts of her have consumed me in a way I haven't let them for years. She hasn't mentioned the letter yet, although she should have it by now.

As I flick through the channels, there's a knock at the door. It's almost eight, so I have no idea who it might be.

I'm pleasantly surprised when I open the door to see the object of my thoughts standing on my front porch.

'Candice. Hey. Is everything okay?'

'Everything's fine. I just wanted to see you.' She smiles nervously as she twists her fingers together in front of her. 'I . . . um . . . would've come earlier, but I waited until Maddie went to bed. I got your letter today.' She lifts the heart in a bottle pendant that's around her neck. 'I love this, and everything it symbolises.'

I lean against the doorframe. 'The moment I saw it I had to buy it. It reminded me of you, and your hair.'

'It's beautiful, just like the letter that came with it. Your words made me cry.'

I sigh. It's been so long, I'm not even sure what I wrote. But I do know I poured my heart into that letter. 'I'm sorry it took so long to get to you. Things would've been a lot different if I hadn't waited.'

'I wish I'd known back then how you felt, Jax. It would've changed everything.'

I can hear the hurt in her voice. We've wasted so many years fighting the inevitable. What the heart wants, it wants. There's no changing it, no matter how hard you try.

'You said in the letter that you knew you'd disappoint me. But the only way you could ever do that is if you didn't follow your heart.'

We both stand there in silence, neither of us knowing what to do, or say. Her beautiful blue eyes lock with mine before she takes a step forward, and her scent invades my senses. It's like a drug. She's my kryptonite. My heart starts to hammer in my chest when she gets up on her toes and fists her hands in the front of my T-shirt, pulling my lips down to hers. The moment our mouths connect, I lose all my resolve. I slide my arms around her waist and draw her body flush with mine. Burying my hand into her hair, I tilt her head back. I'm powerless. I can't fight this any longer. I need her, I want her . . . I crave her.

'Jax,' she moans.

'Candice.'

I bring her with me as I take a few steps backwards. I kick the door closed with the heel of my foot, and push her up against the wall.

I groan into her mouth when she lifts one of her legs and anchors it around my waist. The sweetest sound falls from her lips when I push my cock against her.

'I miss you, Jax. I miss you so much.'

'I miss you too. I miss you like you wouldn't believe, but I think we should take this slow. So much has happened—'

She places her finger over my lips. 'We can take it slow, right after you fuck me.'

A primal growl erupts from deep inside my chest. How can I say no to that? I've longed for that connection with her again. I've never felt as close to anyone as I do when I'm buried deep inside her.

'I need this, Jax . . . *we* need this.'

My hands move down to her arse and I lift her off the ground. She wraps her other leg around my waist as my lips crash into hers. I groan when she grinds her pussy against my cock. We've done hardly anything yet, and I already feel like I'm on the edge. She has no idea how much she turns me on.

'Oh, Jax,' she moans. 'I've missed the way you make me feel when we're together . . .'

I know exactly what she means. I may have been fighting this, but deep down in my soul there was a part of me missing.

Manoeuvring my hand between us, I slide it down the front of her pants. I need to touch her, taste her . . . be buried balls-deep inside her. It's been far too long. I groan when I feel how wet she is for me.

'Oh God,' she whimpers when I slip two fingers deep inside her tight pussy. She tilts her head back as her lips form a perfect 'O'. A long, drawn-out moan escapes her as she pushes her hips into my hand. 'Don't stop,' she pants. 'It feels so good.'

I have no intentions of stopping.

My cock starts to ache with need as she rides my hand with a fiery passion. 'Yes, fuck my fingers,' I whisper into her ear, as I suck her earlobe into my mouth. I'm not sure how much longer I can hold out.

She reaches for the hem of her shirt, pulling it up and over her head. 'I need to feel your skin.' When she drops it to the floor, she slides her hands under my shirt, bunching it under my arms so the skin of our torsos is touching. My free hand cups one of her tits as I pinch her nipple through the thin lace fabric of her bra. 'Oh God,' she whimpers.

I groan when I feel her clamp tightly around my fingers. I love the sounds she makes when she comes undone.

I don't stop my assault until she goes limp in my arms. She sighs when I remove my fingers and her eyes follow my every move as I suck them into my mouth.

'Mmm.' She still tastes as sweet as honey.

'You could not get any sexier right now,' she breathes.

Her lips trail a path up my chest as she removes my shirt. When she suddenly pauses, I know she's seen it.

'Jax.' Her head snaps up and I see she's smiling. 'You have a little peanut tattooed over your heart, next to the pink candy.'

'Carter did it for me a few weeks after you left. I didn't tell him what it symbolised, so he now thinks I have a freaky food obsession. He always has a bowl of nuts out on the table when we play cards.' I chuckle just thinking about it. He gave me so much shit when I asked him to ink the peanut on me, even more so when he saw the candy.

'And the candy?'

I see the hope in her eyes as she asks that. When we were together a few years back, she'd stare at it a lot—so many times I wanted to tell her I got it for her, but I never did. I probably would've after we became official, but two days later she ripped my heart out and fucked off with my kid.

I try to push those thoughts out of my mind. I don't want to ruin this. It's time I let the hurt go. 'That's you,' I say, smiling. 'My Candylicious. It was the first tattoo I got. I had no idea if I'd ever see you again, but this way I knew I'd have a little piece of you with me always.'

'That's so beautiful,' she whispers as tears fill her eyes. She places a soft kiss on the peanut, and another on the pink candy. 'I love these so much.'

And I love her. *Fuck, do I love her.* I love both my girls.

I untangle her legs from around my waist, and she puts her feet on the floor. 'I need to be inside you,' I say. 'I can't wait another second.'

She draws her bottom lip between her teeth as she places her hand on my chest, slightly pushing me back. 'We're going to fuck hard, and then we're going to make love.'

Her words make my cock jump in my pants. This bossy side of her is a turn-on.

She steps away from me and turns, giving me a sexy look over her shoulder. My pulse quickens as I watch the hypnotic sway of her hips. She slowly removes the remainder of her clothing, leaving a trail as she heads to my bedroom.

I'm glued to the spot, watching her hot-as-fuck striptease. The moment she's out of sight, I unbutton my jeans and strip off, leaving my clothes in a heaped mess by the door. I grab a condom from the bathroom as I pass, and I'm already rolling it on by the time I enter my bedroom.

I almost swallow my damn tongue when I find Candice on all fours on my bed, her luscious arse proudly on display for me. 'Jesus,' I growl. I swear I almost blow my load then and there.

'Do you like the view?' she asks, glancing back at me.

'Very much.' I close my eyes briefly, trying to snapshot this vision of her. I don't ever want to forget this moment.

'Oh God, hurry, Jax,' she whimpers. I grab hold of my dick and stroke it as I saunter towards her. Grabbing her arse cheeks, I groan when I part them, opening her up to me. She's so beautiful.

I trail a line from her wet pussy all the way up her arse with my tongue. She pushes her hips at my face and arches her back. My mouth takes over as I devour her . . . consume her . . . own her. She's mine. There's no way I'll let her go again.

'You taste like heaven,' I murmur as I stand and wipe the back of my hand across my mouth.

Without a second thought, I line myself up with her opening as my hands grab her hips and draw her body to me. In one swift motion, I drive my rock-hard cock deep inside her.

'Yes,' she moans. My grip on her hips tightens, and my fingers dig into her soft flesh. Throwing my head back, I close my eyes and allow the feeling of my girl to consume me. I'm fucking home. That's what she feels like. *Home.*

As the minutes pass, the urge begins to overtake me. I need to fuck her badly. 'I can't go slow,' I say as I continue to pump into her.

'Fuck me harder, Jax,' she breathes.

That's all I need. Stilling her, I pick up the pace.

'That's it,' she moans. 'Oh God, Jax.'

My balls slap up against her, and the sound of skin on skin drives me wild. The sexy little noises she's making have me teetering on the edge.

Her breath catches as I lean forward and wrap her hair around my wrist, tugging her head back. My other hand slides towards her tits.

'I want to do this all night long, but fuck, you're too much. It's too much. I'm head over heels in love with your pussy. I've been in love with it since I was nineteen.'

I see her lips curve up into a smile, as my mouth trails a path across her jaw and down to her neck. 'I'm head over heels in love with you—I mean, your cock, too,' she pants. 'I love every delicious inch.'

I chuckle at her words, but I think we both know there's a deeper meaning to what we're both saying. She knows how I feel about her, my letter said it all, but I'm not ready to say the 'L' word out loud just yet. But I'm gonna blow if she keeps talking like that. And I'm not ready for this to end.

Letting go of her hair, I quickly withdraw and flip her onto her back. Hooking my arms under her knees, I lift her legs and place them over my shoulders. 'Sweet Jesus,' I mumble, when I slide back in. I'm so deep. Her pussy is so tight it feels like a vice around my cock.

'Oh God, Jax, I'm coming.'

I can't hold back any longer. I chase her there, pushing deeper inside her at a fevered pace. My body shudders as my own climax tears through me and I tilt my head back and come so damn hard only incoherent noises fall from my lips.

Sex with her is so good. *So fucking good!*

••••

'Morning,' I say when she snuggles closer.

I feel her smile against my chest. 'Morning.'

I swear I haven't slept this good in years. One night with her and my whole world feels like it has finally aligned again. I know in my heart I've made the right decision. I'm not a whole person without her.

Lifting my head off the pillow, I seek out her lips. We have so much lost time to make up. When she shimmies her body up further and deepens the kiss, I flip her over and settle between her legs. 'I want to go to bed with you every night, and wake up with you beside me every morning.'

'I want that too,' she says, threading her fingers in my hair.

'Move in with me, Candice. I want you and Maddie here with me.'

'Really?'

'Really.'

'But you said last night you wanted to take it slow.'

'Fuck what I said. I'm an idiot. I think we've wasted enough time apart.'

'Oh, Jax.' Tears fill her eyes.

I study her face. Doesn't she want to live here? 'We can wait if you're not ready.'

'What? Of course I'm ready.'

'Then why are you crying?'

'You're right, you are an idiot,' she says, slapping my chest. 'They're happy tears.'

'So you and Maddie are going to move in then?'

'Yes. Maddie is going to be over the moon.'

'She's dropped enough hints.' I chuckle. 'She want us to be a family.'

'I thought about what you said the other day, and you're right. She's always saying, "I wish Daddy was here with us." I just didn't put two and two together.'

'And I'm the idiot?' I say, raising an eyebrow.

'Fuck off.' When she goes to playfully punch my arm, I capture her wrist, drawing it above her head.

'Put your other hand above your head,' I command. She does as I ask and I reach over for one of the condoms that I left on the bedside table after our marathon sex session last night. Once I've rolled it on, I wrap the fingers of my right hand around both her wrists, grab my cock with my left hand and rub it against her pussy. She wraps her legs tightly around my waist as I slide the tip inside. She feels so damn good.

'Jax,' she breathes as I lace my fingers through hers.

I place a soft kiss on her lips before drawing back. My heart thumps furiously against my ribcage as our eyes lock once again. 'I love you, Candice,' I say as I slowly push all the way inside her, filling her completely. 'I've loved you from the beginning, and I'm going to love you to the very end.'

THIRTY-TWO

JAX

One year later . . .

'HEY TWAT-WAFFLE,' CARTER SAYS WHEN I ANSWER HIS CALL.

'I don't know how many times I have to tell you—that's my word, fucker.'

'Was.' He chuckles. 'It's mine now.'

'Did you call just to be a cock, or do you want something?'

'I need your help.'

'With what?' He rarely asks for anything, so I'm immediately concerned, especially because he sounds stressed out. 'Is everything okay, man?'

'Yes. Sort of. I have . . . um . . . a date tonight. I need you to help me out.'

'You have a date?' I laugh, because I think he's pulling my leg. I know him well enough to know he doesn't date. 'And you want my help with that? I think you're asking the wrong person.'

'I don't need pointers, fucker . . . I'm capable of dating. *Fuck*. Well, I think I am. I just need someone to set up a few things for me. You know, so it's all ready for us when we arrive.'

'Like what?'

'A table and chairs, maybe a candle.'

'A candle? Have you been drinking?'

He exhales a frustrated breath. 'Look, just forget it. I'll work something else out.'

Christ, he's serious. 'Hold on,' I say. 'So you really have a date, with a real chick?'

'No. I'm taking your blow-up doll out on the town. Dickhead. Of course it's with a real chick.'

'Wow.'

'Why do you find that so hard to believe?'

'Come on, Carter. We've been friends for what, five, six years? Tell me how many dates you've been on in that time. And bringing random chicks home to bang doesn't constitute a date either.'

'Fair enough. But this isn't just anyone. It's Indiana. I want it to be special.'

'You mean the girl next door, Indiana? The one you've been in love with for all these years?'

'I'm not fucking in love with her, cock. I just like her . . .'

'You love her. Stop lying to yourself. You moved almost two hundred kilometres away to try to forget her. That, my friend, speaks volumes.'

'When did you become such an expert in love?'

I run my hands through my hair. I'm not going there with him right now. 'Look, I'm in the middle of something,' I lie. 'When do you need me to set up this table and . . . candle?'

'Tonight. I'm sorry for the short notice, but it was a last-minute decision.'

'I can't come to Newcastle tonight. I might be able to make it up there on the weekend.'

'I'm not in Newcastle. I'm in Sydney.'

'Since when?'

'Since yesterday.'

'Right. Thanks for popping in to say hello.'

'I've been flat-out since I got here. Are you on your period or something?'

'What? No.'

'Well, stop acting like a bitch then.'

'Fuck off, I'm not acting like a bitch.'

'You are. Quit whingeing and help me out. Oh, and by the way, I need you to order the food and bring it with you. Nothing fancy. Just burgers.'

'Burgers? Wow. You're really pulling out the big guns. And FYI, I'm not being your damn waiter.'

'You don't have to serve us,' he says. 'Just bring the food. I can do the rest. I don't want you hanging around cramping my style.'

'Why? Are you worried that your girl will see I'm the better-looking one?' Ribbing him will never get old.

'Dream on, dickhead.'

'Where's the date supposed to be taking place?'

'I'm thinking on the grassed area under the Harbour Bridge, overlooking the harbour.'

'Nice. You may win her over with the view, but seriously, dude, fucking burgers?'

'Burgers are our thing.'

'Fair enough.' I want to throw in a smart remark, but I think I've said enough. Honestly, I'm happy for him. The love of a good woman can do wonders for the soul. 'Text me all the info and I'll get it sorted.'

'Thanks man,' he says. 'I owe you one.'

'I better be best man at your wedding,' I throw in to piss him off. He's gonna bite, he always does.

'How many times do I have to tell you? I'm not in love, and there isn't going to be a fucking wedding.'

Hook, line and sinker. 'Keep telling yourself that, buddy.'

He mumbles something under his breath as I end the call, but I can't quite make it out.

'Who was on the phone?' Candice asks as she slides her hands around my waist, placing a soft kiss on my back.

'Carter.'

'Is everything okay?'

I turn in her arms and pull her soft body to mine. Life is good, so fucking good. Being with her is easy, just like breathing. She's my air. We fit perfectly. I can't even put into words what having my girls—*my family*—living here is like. It has changed me, in so many ways. I finally feel complete . . . I'm no longer empty or alone.

'Everything's fine,' I reply, tucking a strand of her apple-smelling pink hair behind her ear. Sometimes when I'm in the shower, I hold her shampoo bottle to my nose and inhale. 'He wants me to help him set up something for his date with Indiana tonight.'

Her eyes widen. '*Indiana* Indiana? He has a date with her?'

'The one and only.'

'Get out of town,' she squeals, slapping my chest.

'There's no need to get violent,' I say, rubbing the spot.

She's beaming as she places her hand over her mouth. 'I can't believe it. He actually has a date with her?'

'He does.'

She lets go of me and takes a step back. I chuckle when she rolls up her sleeves and rubs her hands together like she's preparing for battle.

'Okay, what do we need to do?'

'Settle down there, Rambo. I have to wait for him to text me all the info.'

'I can't believe he's finally doing this. We've gotta make sure it's a kickarse date.'

Her eagerness to help makes me smile. I'm glad she's on board, because I have no clue about this shit. I know I gave him a hard time about it, but I want tonight to go well for him.

I pull her back into my arms. 'Have you met her?'

'Indiana?'

I nod.

'No, I haven't, but that night I went to Carter's house, he told me all about her. They kinda remind me of us.'

It's funny, when Carter first mentioned her, I thought the exact same thing.

'It almost killed me that night when you went to his house,' I say. I've never had the guts to ask her about the details.

She gives me a sad look as her hands move up to cup my face. 'I only went because I was trying to move on . . . to get over you. As it turned out, Carter only invited me over because he was trying to do the same with Indiana. We ended up just talking.'

'Your reasons for going sound awfully familiar.' I hate that there were so many other women in between. Especially now that I know she felt the same way about me all along. 'Please know all the others meant nothing to me. It's only ever been you. They were just my pathetic attempt at trying to forget you. It never helped. You still held my heart. You always will.'

She smiles, but it doesn't quite reach her eyes. I hate that my past indiscretions have hurt her.

'It's all in the past now, Jax. What is important is the future . . . *our* future.'

She's right. I brush my lips against hers. 'If Carter can find even a fraction of what we have now, with Indiana, I'll be happy.'

'You really care about him, don't you?'

'I do. He's like a brother to me. Underneath all that attitude, he's a great guy. I'd swap him for Brent in a heartbeat if I could.'

'Oh, Jax,' she says as she squeezes me tight. 'I totally get that. It's like my relationship with Brendan. If I could swap my real dad for him, I'd do it too.'

'I'm glad that you have him. He adores you and Maddie.'

'And we adore him. I can't wait until he and Mum are married. I've come to realise that the special people in our lives don't have to be blood related to be classified as family. It's how you feel about them in here that counts.' She places her hand over her heart.

'I love you.'

Her fingers tenderly stroke my face. 'And I love you too, Jaxson Albright. So much. It took a while, but we finally got our shit together. Let's hope Carter and Indiana do the same.'

I gently kiss her, groaning when she tilts her head back and deepens the kiss. My hands slide down to cup her arse as I push my semi-hard cock against her.

We pull apart quickly when Maddie enters the kitchen. It's like she has a cock-blocking radar or something.

'Ew,' she says. 'Do you two ever stop kissing?'

I chuckle when Candice's face turns a light shade of pink.

'We're in love,' she says, looking at our daughter. 'That's what people in love do.'

'Yuck.' Maddie turns and leaves the room. 'I'm never falling in love. Kissing is gross.'

I can't help but laugh. I know she's happy that we're a proper family now, because she cried tears of joy when Candice and I told her that they were moving in with me. But I think she's still coming to terms with seeing us being affectionate with each other because we were apart for the first six years of her life. It's something I never had to witness growing up either. My parents don't do affection. Not even with their kids.

••••

'I think that's everything,' Candice says as I pack the last of the things in the boot of the car. I hope so too. She went above and beyond, making sure we had everything just right for Carter and Indiana's date. The list of instructions she's given me is a fucking mile long. I even had a lesson on how to set the table properly. I'm a damn Albright—doesn't she realise that the proper placement of cutlery was imperative in my house growing up? My mother thrived on that shit.

By the time I climb into the car and fasten my seatbelt, I'm a damn mess. I make a mental note to stop off on the way and grab a packet of cigarettes. I need to make sure I get this right, not just for Carter, but for Candice. She'll bust my balls if I stuff this up. Thanks to her, the simple act of setting up a table and lighting a damn candle has now turned into a major fucking event.

When I reach the park under the bridge, I begin to set up. After I place the rose in the vase and light the candle, the finishing touches, I start to pace back and forth. I stop and pull out the list Candice made me, going over it one more time. I need to make sure I haven't forgotten anything.

> Table – check
>
> Chairs – check
>
> Tablecloth – check
>
> Vase – check
>
> Rose – check
>
> Candle – check
>
> Plates – check
>
> Cutlery – check
>
> Wineglasses – check
>
> Thank fuck this night is nearly over – check

I pull the zip up on my jacket. It's damn cold tonight. As the minutes tick past, my gut churns. It's not even my date, so I have no idea why I'm the one who's nervous. I look down at my watch. Carter should be here by now. Pulling out my phone, I call him.

'How far away are you, fucker?' I say when he answers. 'I'm freezing my nuts off here.'

'I'm just parking the car.'

'Good. Hurry up, pussy, so I can get the fuck out of here.'

'We'll be there in a minute.'

I breathe a sigh of relief when I see them. They look good together and Carter looks happy. I smile smugly at him as they approach.

I may be happy for him, but I'm still gonna give him shit about tonight. It's my job.

'Hey,' he says with a nod.

I examine his date. She's a looker. Not as beautiful as my girl, but close. She has long dark hair and pretty green eyes. I see what he means about her being short. She's like four foot nothing. Carter towers over her.

'Hey.'

'Indiana, this is my friend, Jax. Jax, Indiana.'

I reach for her hand and bring it to my mouth. I suppress my smile when I hear a slight growl come from Carter. 'So, I finally get to meet the elusive Indiana. Carter never shuts up about you.'

I try not to laugh when I hear him mumble, 'Motherfucker.'

This is fun.

'He·talks about me?' Indiana asks. There's a huge smile on her face as her eyes dart to Carter.

'All the damn time,' I lie.

'I do not, arsehole,' he snaps. I bet he's wishing he didn't involve me in his plans tonight.

'I'm just messing with you, mate,' I say, slapping his back. He gives me a look that tells me I'm gonna pay for what I just said, but I'm not worried. He may not realise it, but chicks dig that shit, so in a roundabout way, I'm actually helping him.

'Is this all for us?' Indiana asks, looking at the table.

'It is,' Carter replies, draping his arm over her shoulder. He can deny it all he wants, but he's in love with her. 'Do you like it?'

'I love it.' She slides her arms around his waist, and when she looks up at him and smiles, I can see she's in love with him too. It's the same expression I see on Candice's face when she looks at me. 'Thank you, Jax,' she says to me.

'Don't thank me. Just doing what the big fella asked.' Her smile widens as her gaze moves back to Carter. I'm truly happy for them both. 'I'm gonna duck off and pick up the food,' I say. 'Then I'm out of here.'

I watch as Carter pulls out a chair for Indiana and places a kiss on her hair once she's seated. 'I just need to speak to Jax for a second,' he says.

I take a few steps away from the table, and he follows. 'Thanks for all your help,' he says shaking my hand. 'I appreciate it. You did well for an arsehole.'

I laugh. 'No problem. I aim to please.' I pull out a cigarette and light it—now that part of tonight is over, I can breathe a little easier. The pressure isn't off yet though. I still have to get their food. 'For the record, I'd probably turn pussy for her too.' I whisper it softly enough so only he can hear.

'Keep your eyes off her, she's mine,' he snaps.

I shake my head and laugh as I walk away, heading for my car.

He bites every damn time.

••••

It's around 10.30 pm when I finally arrive home, but I'm not surprised to find Candice waiting up for me.

'How did it go?' Candice asks excitedly, the moment I walk through the front door. She rubs her hands together as she bounces with anticipation.

'It was a hit,' I say, pulling her into my arms and crushing her body against mine.

'Jax, I can't breathe,' she says, trying to wiggle out of my embrace.

'Sorry.' I loosen my grip as I rest my chin on the top of her head. I don't have the heart to tell her that when I went back, Carter confessed that Indiana is sick, really sick, hence all the trouble he went to tonight. I feel like a prick for ribbing him about his date now. He tried his best to play it down, but I could see he was traumatised by the news. Surely life couldn't be that cruel, to take her away from him when he's only just gotten her back?

Who am I kidding? I know firsthand what a fucking bitch life can be sometimes. For their sake, I pray that's not the case.

'What's she like?'

'Nice. Pretty. They're good together.' I try my best to sound enthusiastic, but fail miserably.

Drawing back, her eyes meet mine. 'Are you okay?'

'Of course,' I lie, forcing out a smile to try to hide my true feelings. Candice cares about Carter as well, so I know this news will upset her. It's my job to protect her from stuff like that. I pull her to me once more. I'd be lost without her. I can only imagine how Carter is feeling right now.

When I finally release her, I lace my fingers through hers. 'Come on, let's go to bed.'

I need to make love to my woman.

THIRTY-THREE

CANDICE

'GOD, NO,' I EXHALE IN A PANIC AS I OPEN THE LID OF THE washing machine and pull out Maddie's bedsheets. My heart beats furiously in my chest when I realise what I've done. There's stuffing and tiny fragments of fake fur all through the machine. 'Shit . . . not Puppy.' He must've got caught up in the bed linen when I stripped her bed this morning. She's going to be devastated—*I'm devastated*. She's had that toy since she was a baby.

I pull out my phone. My hands are shaking as I dial Jax's number.

'Hey, babe,' he says when he answers.

'Jax.' I start to cry the moment I hear his voice. 'I've killed Puppy.' I reach into the machine and pull out one of Puppy's ears, holding it up in front of me as I speak.

'Puppyyyyyy!' I hear Maddie scream at the top of her lungs. I look over to find her standing in the doorway. 'You killed my Puppy!'

'Fuck. What in the hell is going on?' Jax asks.

Maddie runs towards me with tears streaming down her face. She gets up on her toes and looks inside the machine. As soon as she sees her beloved stuffed toy in a thousand pieces, she starts sobbing hysterically. When those big brown tear-filled eyes look up at me, I swear my heart breaks in two. Her eyes have always been my weakness because they're just like Jax's. When she notices Puppy's ear in my hand her face screws up and she snatches it from me, clutching it to her chest.

'I'm not your friend anymore!' she screams as she runs from the room. Hearing her say that makes my already broken heart shatter into tiny pieces.

The phone is still against my ear, and I vaguely hear Jax say, 'Christ, I'll be there in a few minutes.'

'Maddie,' I call as I drop the phone and chase her.

She runs straight to her bedroom, closing the door and locking herself inside.

'Maddie, please. Open the door. It was an accident.'

She doesn't reply, but I can hear her crying on the other side.

'Baby, please let me in. I'm so sorry.' The tears are flowing freely down my face now as I rest my forehead against the door. My heart is hurting for my little girl. She loves that damn toy.

Within minutes, Jax comes bursting through the front door. He's breathless, so he must've run home from his shop. I'm still working Monday to Friday at the other place, but only nine am until 2.45 pm. Jax wants me to be here for Maddie after school.

'Jesus,' he pants, when he sees the state I'm in. He pulls me into his arms and I can hear his heart beating rapidly as he holds me. I'm so glad he's here. I can't deal with this on my own.

'It was an accident. Puppy must've been tangled in the sheets when I put them in the machine.'

'It's okay,' he says, tenderly stroking my hair. 'I know you wouldn't do it on purpose.' He cups my face in his hands and wipes my tears away with the pad of his thumbs. 'Don't cry. We'll get it sorted. Maybe it can be sewn back together.'

'It's in too many pieces.'

'Fuck. Where's Maddie?'

'In there,' I answer, pointing to her bedroom door. 'She's locked me out. She told me she's not my friend anymore.'

He pulls me into his chest again. 'She's just upset. She doesn't mean it. She probably picked it up from school. You know what kids are like.' He kisses the top of my head before releasing me. 'Let me talk to her.'

He steps in front of the door and knocks. 'Peanut, it's me. Can I come in?'.

She doesn't respond, but a few seconds later we hear the latch unlock before she opens the door. Her tear-stained face rips me apart. 'Daddy,' she cries as she collapses into his arms. 'Puppy is dead.'

'I know, princess, I know.' He wraps her tightly in his arms while she sobs.

My hand covers my mouth to muffle my own sob. I hate myself for breaking my little girl's heart. I should've been more careful.

••••

'Goodnight, baby girl,' I say, tucking the blankets up around Maddie's chin.

'Night.' Her voice is so soft, it's barely audible. She's hardly spoken a word all night. Jax had to go back to work after he settled her down—he was in the middle of a job when he ran out. She hasn't cried again since he left, but she's still heartbroken, her sombre face tells me that. She didn't even eat any of her dinner, just pushed it around her plate.

A lump rises in my throat when I notice Puppy's ear still clutched in her hand. It's all she has left. She's never gone to sleep without him.

My eyes move to the butterfly-shaped clock beside her bed. It's just after eight. I was hoping Jax would be back by now. When he finished work he came home to pick up his car. All he said was he had somewhere he needed to go, and that he'd be home as soon as he could.

'Would you like me to lie with you until you fall asleep?' My hand runs over her hair as I speak. She nods. 'I know I've said it a hundred times already, but I'm really sorry about Puppy.'

'It's okay,' she says. 'I'm sorry I said I'm not your friend, Mummy . . . you are my friend.'

'I'm glad.' I tuck a stray curl behind her ear. 'I'd hate it if we weren't friends. I'll go to the store tomorrow and buy you another Puppy.'

'I don't want another Puppy,' she says as her eyes fill with tears. 'I just want *my* Puppy.'

'Oh baby.' I pull her tiny body into mine. 'I know. I wish I could fix this. I hate to see you hurting.'

'He was my best friend,' she whispers as she softly cries into my chest.

••••

I wake with a start when someone gently shakes me.

'Candice, wake up.'

Jax's handsome face is illuminated by the lamp beside the bed. I sit up and look at the clock. It's eleven pm. Maddie is sound asleep beside me.

'Are you just getting home?' I whisper as I get out of Maddie's bed slowly, careful not to wake her.

'Come, I have something I want to show you.' He reaches for my hand as he leads me out of the room.

What is he up to? 'Where have you been?'

'Shh.'

'Oh my God,' I say, when he opens the flaps of a cardboard box that's sitting by the front door. 'You bought her a puppy?'

'Not just any puppy.' He beams. 'It's a beagle, the same breed as Snoopy.'

Tears fill my eyes as he reaches in and gently lifts the sleeping puppy out. 'He's so cute.' I gently run my hands over his fur and he opens one of his eyes. He has the cutest little face. He's mainly white with some black markings on his back and head. There's a tiny patch of tan over one of his eyes. 'Where did you get a puppy at this time of night?'

'I picked him up a few hours ago. I had to drive to a property three hours away. I had Ana search online for me this afternoon, before I left work.'

'You're amazing,' I say as I slide my arms around his waist. 'She's going to love him.'

'Can I take him in there now?' he asks. He's like a big kid. I don't want to wake her since it took her so long to fall asleep, but he's gone above and beyond for our little girl tonight, so I'm not going to ruin this for him.

'Of course.'

He brushes his lips against mine before walking towards Maddie's room. I follow closely behind him.

He places the puppy gently down beside Maddie. 'Peanut,' he whispers, softly shaking her.

'Daddy,' she murmurs, opening her eyes. As soon as she speaks, the puppy rises from beside her and moves towards her face. Maddie giggles when he starts to lick her. 'A puppy!' she cries. 'A real puppy.'

'I know he'll never replace *your* Puppy, but Mummy and I got him for you. We hate seeing you so sad.'

She sits up and hugs the puppy to her chest. 'I love him. He's so cute.' She giggles again when the puppy licks her chin.

After the afternoon we've had, hearing her laugh is like music to my ears. I can already tell they're going to be the best of friends. I never thought I could love my man any more than I already do, but right now my heart is close to bursting.

'I'm glad,' Jax says as he runs his hand over her hair.

She puts the puppy down beside her and reaches for her dad. 'I love you, Daddy,' she says as she hugs him.

'I love you too, Peanut.'

When she lets him go, her gaze moves to me. She extends her arms, so I step towards the bed.

'I love you, Mummy.' She gives me a hug too.

'I love you too, baby girl.' My voice cracks as I speak. 'I love you so much.'

When she lets me go, she picks up the puppy again. 'Can he sleep with me?'

'Of course he can,' Jax says, 'but put him on the other side so he's close to the wall. We don't want him to fall out of bed in the middle of the night.'

'Okay.' She does as he asks.

'In the morning you can think of a name for him.'

'I want to call him Snoopy,' she says without hesitation.

'That's a great name,' Jax replies, ruffling her hair. 'Now lie down and get some sleep. Tomorrow we have to go shopping and get all the things Snoopy will need.'

'Good night, Daddy.' She yawns as she lies down and snuggles the puppy to her. 'Good night, Mummy.'

Jax drapes his arm over my shoulder and smiles. Thanks to him, all is right with the world again. 'I love you, Snoopy,' we hear her say as we leave the room.

Jax pulls me against him when we step into the hallway. 'Are you okay?' he asks.

'I am now. You're an amazing father. We're both so lucky to have you.'

He holds me tight as he places a kiss on the top of my head. 'I'm the lucky one.'

••••

'I now pronounce you husband and wife.' I wipe the tear that leaks from my eye. 'You may now kiss the bride.'

The look that Brendan gives my mum when he pulls her into his arms makes my heart sing. It's not hard to see how much he adores her. I know he's going to spend the rest of his life looking after her and making her happy. Like I said to her this morning when we were getting our hair done, 'Good things come to those who wait', and it certainly feels like my mum's waited a lifetime for him.

They opted for a small, private, garden wedding. It's nothing fancy, but beautiful nevertheless. They picked the perfect day to exchange their vows: the sun's shining, and all the colourful flowers are in full bloom.

Jax, Maddie and I are here, and Brendan's parents, siblings and their partners are in attendance as well. Mum and Brendan asked me and Brendan's older brother to be their witnesses. Maddie and Snoopy were in charge of looking after the rings. Snoopy goes everywhere with Maddie—except to school, of course.

'Congratulations,' I say, wrapping Mum in my arms and squeezing her tight. 'I'm so happy for you. You sacrificed everything to raise me and I'll always be grateful for that, but it's your time now. It's your time to be *you*, and to do what makes *you* happy.'

'I've always been happy,' she says. Tears fill her eyes as she runs her hand tenderly down the side of my face. 'From the moment I held you in my arms when you were born. You changed my life for the better. I loved you then, and that will never change. Even though you're all grown up and a mother now too, you'll always be my baby girl.'

'I love you too, Mum.'

She's finally come to terms with being called 'Mum', and 'Nanny' by Maddie. She's even let go of her obsession with aging. I think she realises that Brendan will love her no matter what. It's funny how the love of a good man can change you. Things that once seemed so important suddenly aren't anymore.

She kisses my cheek before releasing me, and I go over to my new stepfather. The thought makes me smile. It also appears that I now have step-aunts, step-uncles and step-grandparents as well. They're all as lovely as he is. I'm thrilled that our little family is growing.

'Congratulations, Brendan,' I say, when he hugs me. We've become really close. 'I couldn't ask for a better man for my mum.'

'I was hoping, once your mother and I finally got married, that you'd start calling me "Dad".'

'What?' I say, drawing back so I can see his face. I can tell by the look he's giving me that he's serious.

'Only if you want to, of course. No pressure. I know I'm not your real father, but I love you like you were my daughter.'

'You love me?'

'Of course I love you. I love you and Maddie both.'

I tighten my hold on him, resting my head against his chest. Closing my eyes, I fight to hold in the tears. He has no idea how much this moment means to me. He's just given me something I've always been missing, something I've wished for since I was a little girl.

'I love you too, Dad,' I whisper. Those words are something I never thought I'd say in this lifetime. 'If I could choose any man on this earth to be my father, I'd choose you.'

••••

'You haven't stopped smiling since we came home,' Jax says as he strips off and climbs into bed beside me.

'I know. My cheeks actually hurt.'

'Are you gonna tell me why?'

I roll onto my side to face him, and he slides his arm around my waist, pulling me to him. 'I'm just happy for my mum. She deserves someone like Brendan.' His lips trail a path along my jaw and down my neck as I speak. As soon as I feel him hardening, I'm pretty sure he's stopped listening, but I continue anyway. 'Their wedding may not have been elaborate, but it was still beautiful. I think that's the type of wedding I'd like.'

His head snaps back. 'You want to get married?' Okay, he was listening. 'I didn't think that kind of thing was important to you.'

'I think every little girl dreams about finding her Prince Charming and getting married one day, Jax.'

'Oh.' He moves his body on top of me and settles between my legs. 'I didn't pick you for that kinda girl. You may not get the husband, but would you settle for your Prince Charming?' I laugh when he wiggles his eyebrows.

'Are you saying we're just going to live in sin forever?'

He lifts my right leg, wrapping it around his waist. I bite down on my bottom lip to suppress my moan as he slowly slides inside me.

'There's nothing sinful about the love I have for you,' he says as his lips brush against mine. 'You're all I've ever wanted.'

'You're all I've ever wanted too.'

'My sinful thoughts though . . . that's a whole other story.'

I laugh. I know all about his sinful thoughts. I love them almost as much as I love him.

'My thoughts about you are pretty sinful too, Mr Albright,' I say, burying my hands in his thick brown hair.

'Oh, yeah? Enlighten me.' He pushes his hips forward and slides all the way in, filling me completely. The pure ecstasy that only he can bring me takes over and I'm incapable of answering him. My eyes flutter shut as a long, drawn-out moan falls from my lips.

When I finally open them, Jax is giving me that look he reserves for only me, and it's so sexy, it makes my stomach do flip-flops. Sliding my hands into his hair, I pull his face towards mine.

'Let me show you,' I whisper against his mouth.

••••

'If you really want to get married, we will,' he says as I lie in his arms, still coming down from our post-coital bliss. 'There's nothing I wouldn't do for you, you know that.'

'It's gotta be something we both want, Jax.'

'It's not that I don't want to marry you, it's just that I don't need a piece of paper to prove how much I love you.'

'I don't either,' I say, snuggling into his side and placing a soft kiss on his chest. 'As long as we're together I'm happy. We've never been conventional types anyway.'

'That's right, we haven't.' He chuckles. 'We had a child when we weren't even together.' He kisses my hair. 'If it's meant to be, babe, it will happen at the right time, and for the right reasons. Not because society says it's what we should do.'

'That's right. In my heart I know our best is yet to come. In the meantime, just keep loving me, and I'll keep loving you. The rest will fall into place.'

'I'll never stop loving you, Candice,' he says, brushing my hair from my face. '*Fucking never.*'

EPILOGUE

JAX

Five years later . . .

'WE DON'T TURN HERE,' CANDICE SAYS.

'I know, I'm just making a quick detour.' I wink at her when she eyes me sceptically from the passenger seat.

A few minutes later when I put my indicator on to turn into the parking lot, I hear her growl.

'Really, Jax. You're gonna stop and buy donuts now? We're already running late.'

I hear Maddie snicker from the back seat.

'Come on, babe, I've been craving donuts all day.'

'You're not the one who's pregnant, Jax, remember?'

'It's not uncommon for fathers to get cravings you know.'

'Is that right?' She laughs. 'And I suppose you read that in one of those baby books you always have your head in.'

'It's written in black and white, so that makes it a fact.'

'I call it bullshit,' she says. 'People make up stuff like that all the time. You're obsessed with those damn books.'

'There's nothing wrong with being prepared. Don't forget, this is the first time for me.'

I look at her when I shut off the ignition. When her eyes narrow, I know she's misconstrued what I've just said. Damn baby hormones. I'm not stupid enough to intentionally insult her when her emotions are all over the place. I like my balls exactly where they are. I read up about this when I first noticed that some crazy woman had possessed my fiancée. Lately she's been normal one minute, angry the next, and more often than not, crying a few seconds later.

'I didn't mean it like that,' I say, reaching across the centre console and wrapping her hand in mine. 'I'm sorry. I just want to be the best support I can be, to you—to you both.' My hand comes to rest on her stomach. 'I hate that you went through it without me last time. I just want to be prepared—I wanna be your rock.'

Her face relaxes and her lips curve into a smile. 'You say the sweetest things sometimes.' Seconds later I notice tears pooling in her eyes, and she sniffles.

'Come here.' This pregnancy is making her an emotional wreck.

'I love you,' she whispers.

'I know you do. And I love you too, even when you're acting all psycho.' Drawing back, I gently wipe her tears away with my thumb. 'Do you forgive me?'

She nods. 'Always.'

'That's my girl.' Leaning forward, I place my lips on hers.

'Gross,' I hear Maddie say from the back seat. 'Do you two ever give it a rest? You're going to scar me for life, you know that right?'

'I can't help it if I'm head over heels in love with your mother,' I say as I turn towards the back seat. Maddie rolls her eyes, but it's quickly followed by a smile. This kid still knows how to turn my heart to mush in the blink of an eye. She has me wrapped around her little finger.

My baby girl is growing up way too fast. She'll be starting high school next year. As much as I love seeing her blossom into the young lady she's becoming, I'd be lying if I said it didn't scare the hell out of me.

'You better hurry up and get those donuts you're craving,' Candice says. 'Carter's waiting.'

When she reaches across the centre console and grabs a chunk of skin on my stomach, I slap her hand away. I know exactly what she's implying. 'I'm not putting on weight.'

'Nobody said you were. If you keeping eating all these donuts though . . .'

Candice doesn't finish her sentence, but there's no need. *It will never happen*, I reassure myself. I work out every day. In the bedroom, and with my home gym.

'You are what you eat, Daddy.'

'Hey, who asked for your opinion?' I chuckle.

'Well, if that's the case, your father must've eaten a sexy beast for breakfast,' Candice says, placing her hand on my thigh. In an instant, all is forgiven. Christ, I love this woman.

'Puke,' Maddie mumbles, and Candice and I laugh. 'I have the grossest parents ever. Jessica's parents never smooch like you two.'

'That's because Jessica's dad doesn't have a hot wife like I do.'

'Daddy,' Maddie screeches. 'Ew.'

When I wink at Candice, she mouths, 'I love you.'

'Mum, can you pass me my earphones? I'm gonna listen to music so I don't have to hear you two.' Snoopy lets out a bark from beside her. 'Do you want me to cover your ears too, boy?'

●●●●

'You finally made it,' Carter whines when we pull into the driveway of Indiana's father's house. 'You should've been here an hour ago.'

'He had some make-believe cravings on the way,' Candice replies.

'You're an idiot.' Carter chuckles, shaking his head at me.

'Fuck off, arsehole, they're legit,' I mumble as I get out of the car. Why doesn't anyone believe me? I'm not making this shit up.

'Uncle Jax,' Carter's sons, Jaxson and Levi, scream as they come bolting out of the house, heading straight for me. Indiana is following close behind with their youngest, Eve, in her arms. Carter named his first born after me—it was up there with the best moments of my life.

After kissing Indiana, I take Eve from her. 'How's my second favourite girl?' I ask, planting a kiss on her chubby cheek. My gaze moves to Maddie, and I wink. She'll always be my number one. Eve giggles, squirming in my arms when I bury my face in her neck and blow a raspberry. Seeing her always makes me wish my own little girl wasn't growing up so fast. I'm in no way ready for that.

Like Candice and me, Carter and Indi went to hell and back to get to where they are today. But sometimes the fight we go through is worth it in the end. It makes you appreciate everything you have so much more. It's like winning the ultimate prize. Something you'll cherish for-fucking-ever.

'Are you nervous about tomorrow?' I hear Carter ask Candice, as he gives her a quick hug. Even though my attention appears to be on Indiana and his kids, I'm listening intently for her answer.

'Not at all. I feel like I've waited my whole life for this.'

Of course I'm grinning like a fool when she says that.

Carter takes Eve out of my arms and passes her to Indi, before following me around to the back of my car so I can collect my suitcase out of the boot.

'We should hit the road,' Carter says, taking the suitcase out of my hands.

'Okay. Just let me say goodbye to my girls.'

Maddie is the closest, so I pull her into my arms first. 'I'll see you tomorrow, Peanut. Have fun at Nan and Pop's tonight.'

'I will,' she says, wrapping her arms around me tightly. It's only one night, but I'm missing my girls already.

'Look after your mum for me.'

'Of course.' When she looks up at me, I'm surprised to see tears in her eyes.

'Hey,' I say, cupping her face, 'what's with the tears?'

'I'm just happy.'

'Happy to be getting rid of me?' I ask.

'No, just happy that you and Mum are finally getting your shit together.'

'Watch your mouth,' I say, trying not to laugh. She's got spunk, just like her mum.

'I've wanted this for so long.'

'You have?' That surprises me. Sure, she mentioned it a few times when she was young, but once they moved in with me, it never came up again. I just presumed Maddie was content with our situation. 'Why didn't you say something?'

'I knew in my heart it would happen one day.'

'Jesus.' I pull her face into my chest. 'I'm sorry we made you wait so long.' I always said I never needed a piece of paper to prove my love for her mother, but I would've married her years ago if I'd known that's what my little girl wanted. There's nothing I wouldn't do for her.

'It's okay, Dad. Honestly.'

'I love you,' I say, placing a kiss on her hair.

'I love you too.'

Candice steps forward and puts her arms around my waist.

'I'm gonna miss you tonight,' I whisper. We haven't spent a night apart since we started living together.

'I'm not sure if I'll be able to sleep without you beside me.' When I hear her sniffle, I know she's crying again. These next five months are going to be the death of me.

'I know what you mean.' I draw back and cup her face in my hands as my mouth bears down on hers. *It's only one night*, I tell myself. Tomorrow she'll be my wife and we'll never have to be apart again. 'Call me if you're having trouble sleeping. Maybe we can have phone sex.' I wiggle my eyebrows and she laughs.

'I'd like that.'

'I love you. I'll be counting down the minutes until I see you tomorrow.'

'Me too.'

I open the driver's side door and close it once she's seated inside. 'Drive carefully, and call me when you get there,' I say through the open window.

'I will.'

'Tell your parents I said hello.' I reach into the car and run the back of my hand down the side of her face. I'm finding it hard to walk away.

'Come on, you two,' Carter calls out. 'There's plenty of time for that on your honeymoon.'

'Remind me why I'm friends with him again.'

'Because you're like long lost twins.' She laughs.

She's right, we are.

'I can't wait to become Mrs Jaxson Albright tomorrow.' Christ I love the sound of that.

In my heart she's always been mine, but tomorrow it becomes official.

'I know it's none of my business,' Carter says on the drive to the hotel, 'but I'm glad you're finally doing the right thing. You know . . . before this kid is born.'

'Things aren't like they used to be, Carter. I know you had a hard time growing up without your father around, but lots of people have kids out of wedlock these days. The stigma doesn't really exist anymore.'

'I guess, but I'm still glad you're getting married. You're doing the right thing for Candice, Maddie and the baby. My life was shit because of my circumstances. I'd hate for any child to go through what I did.'

'In my defence though, Maddie was almost three before I even knew she was my daughter.'

'I know, but she's what . . . fucking twelve now?'

There's not much I can say to that, except Candice and I were always content with how things were. All we cared about was being together, and being great parents to our daughter. But things changed when we found out Candice was pregnant with our son. I can't even put it into words, but something shifted inside me that day, and I knew then and there I wanted more. We did everything arse-about with Maddie, and this was our chance to do it right.

When I dropped Candice back at work that morning, I headed straight to a jeweller to buy her an engagement ring. That night, the three of us went out to dinner to celebrate the news about the baby. Maddie was over the moon that she was going to get a little brother or sister.

Candice had no idea what I had planned, so I had no clue how she would react. I was a bundle of nerves when I got down on one knee and proposed to her in front of the entire restaurant. To my relief she didn't hesitate with her answer, launching herself into my arms with a very confident *yes*.

'You've made your point, cock. You can shut up now,' I say to Carter.

'I always knew you were a bit slow,' he retorts, punching me in the arm.

'Fuck off.' I rub my arm. I'd punch him back, but he's driving. 'My family means everything to me.'

'Mine too,' he says, smiling. 'I don't know where I'd be without them.'

I chuckle as I shake my head. 'Would you listen to us two, we sound like chicks. When did we become such pussies?'

'Speak for yourself, arsehole.'

After Carter and I check in at the Harbour View Hotel in North Sydney, we take our bags to our room. We chose to stay here because it's close to Luna Park. After much debate, Candice and I decided on a theme park wedding instead of the conventional church one. Our trip to Luna Park for Maddie's fifth birthday was the first time the three of us went out together, officially as a family, so it made perfect sense for us to get married there. We may not have realised it at the time, but that day planted a seed in us both: it reminded us of the importance of family and togetherness. Every major event that we spent together with Maddie after that day only helped to mend what had been broken for so long.

I can't help but smile when I think about how wonderful my life is now. My only regret is that we waited so long to be together. We let our minds rule, even though our hearts knew what they wanted from day one.

Carter and I take a seat at the bar on the ground floor of our hotel. When the bartender approaches us, I order two beers, the good imported shit. We have plenty to celebrate. It's been a while since we've had a quiet drink together, and I'm looking forward to spending the evening unwinding, in preparation for one of the most important days of my life—the day I say 'I do' to the only girl who's ever held my heart. My soulmate.

'We found out last week that the baby's a boy,' I say to Carter after taking a long pull of my beer.

'A son, hey?' He lifts his bottle, clinking it with mine. His smile tells me he's genuinely happy about my news. 'Congratulations. My boys can be terrors, but they're great fun.' He's a fantastic dad. It just proves you don't necessarily need a positive male role model in your life to be a good father. I'm proof of that as well. I strive to be nothing like that cocksucker who raised me.

'Candice and I were talking,' I say, picking at the label on my beer bottle. 'We want to name him Carter.'

'Really?' His face lights up. 'You don't have to do that, but I'd be honoured if you did.'

'I know you named Jaxson after me, but that's not why I'm doing this. You mean a lot to me. You're like the brother I always wanted.'

Carter goes quiet as his eyes move down to the bottle in his hand. 'Same,' he whispers, his voice slightly cracking.

'You're not getting all emotional on me, are you?' I say, punching him in the arm.

'Fuck off,' he grumbles. 'My sinuses are playing up.'

I laugh when he wipes his eyes with the back of his hand.

'Well, I'm glad I didn't tell you I loved you or anything. You'd probably be sobbing your heart out right now.'

'Whatever, cock, I'm not a pussy.'

We both laugh briefly, before an awkward silence falls over us. He clears his throat.

'If you did say that,' he finally adds, 'I'd probably say I feel the same way about you.'

My gaze darts around the bar in a slight panic. I hope nobody can hear what we're saying. The fact that we're sharing a room tonight only makes our conversation sound even dodgier.

'Yeah, well, lucky I didn't say that then.'

'Who are you kidding?' He chuckles. 'You love me.'

'Less talking and more drinking,' I mumble as I sit up straighter in my seat. 'I already feel like I've lost a piece of my manhood this afternoon.'

Carter releases a boisterous laugh. 'I hear ya, man. I think we've broken every damn man code there is.'

'Candice and Indiana have a lot to answer for,' I say, shaking my head.

'They've made us soft.'

'Speak for yourself, arsehole.' I laugh.

Carter raises his beer. 'To brotherhood.'

I smile and I clink my bottle with his. 'To brotherhood.'

CANDICE

Butterflies churn in my stomach as Mum zips up my wedding gown. I can't believe it's finally happening. Today I become Mrs Jaxson Albright. I feel like I've waited an eternity for this day. Even though I've been content with Jax and me just living together, in my heart I've always yearned to become his wife.

I've learnt over the years that life isn't always the fairy tale we wish for, and not everyone gets a happy ending. I'm one of the lucky ones though. The path Jax and I took to get to where we are was bumpy to say the least, but I not only got my Prince Charming, I got the husband too. That's all that matters.

'Look at you,' Mum says as she turns me to face her and pulls me into her arms. 'I can't believe my baby is getting married today.'

'I'm not a baby anymore, Mum.' I laugh.

'You'll always be my baby,' she says, drawing back and running her hand affectionately down the side of my face.

When I notice the tears brimming in her eyes, I have to look away. If I don't, she's gonna make me cry as well, and it'll ruin my makeup.

'I know you and Jax have been living together for years now, but believe me when I say that actually being married will make a difference.'

'I know. I can't wait,' I reply. 'He says it's just a piece of paper, but to me it's so much more. I've wanted to be his wife for as long as I can remember.'

When my own eyes cloud with tears, she hugs me tighter. 'A wise person once told me good things come to those who wait.'

I let out a small laugh as I wipe a stray tear from my cheek. I said those exact words to her before she married Brendan.

Our moment is broken when Maddie comes bounding into the room. 'Look how cute Snoopy looks, Mum,' she says with excitement in her voice. 'Poppy helped me put his bowtie on.'

I take a few seconds to admire my beautiful girl. She's growing up before my eyes and it scares me to think that not too far in the future, I'll be helping her prepare for her own wedding day. I'm not sure how Jax will cope with that. He almost hyperventilates if I mention the possibility of Maddie dating one day.

'Here're my three favourite girls,' my dad says as he enters the room. I adore this man so much. Not only for the way he treats my mum, but for loving Maddie and me like we're his own flesh and blood. 'The limo has just arrived downstairs.'

A smile explodes onto Mum's face as she looks at him. She does that a lot these days. Married life certainly agrees with her. She and Dad are going to look after Maddie while Jax whisks me away for a week-long romantic honeymoon at the Four Seasons Resort at Bora Bora. We're staying in a water bungalow. We were going to wait until after the baby was born, but we knew it would probably never happen if we did.

'You ready?' Mum asks me.

'Yes,' I answer with a smile, as I run my hand over my stomach. I'm so ready I think my heart might burst.

'Come help me carry the bouquets to the car, Maddie,' Mum says as she leaves the room, giving me a moment alone with Dad.

'You look beautiful, sweetheart,' he says as he closes the distance between us.

'Thanks, Dad.' Saying that will never get old.

'I'm honoured that you asked me to give you away today. You have no idea what it means to me.' Tears fill my eyes when I hear his voice crack.

'I'm honoured that you accepted. There's nobody else I'd rather have walk me down the aisle.'

No more words are exchanged as he pulls me into his arms. I savour this feeling. Growing up with Sophia was always enough, but I'm so blessed I now have him as well.

'I love you, Dad,' I whisper.

'I love you too, sweetheart.'

JAX

'Do your parents know you're getting married today?' Carter asks as we arrive at Luna Park.

Maybe it's the big kid inside me, but I fucking love that we're getting married here. It wasn't cheap to hire out the entire park for the morning, but you can't put a price on what today means to Candice and me. After we tie the knot, we're going to change clothes to let loose and have fun. We have the rides to ourselves until midday, before the park opens to the public. Then we're heading to Watsons Bay for a beautiful lunch overlooking the water.

'Nope. They wouldn't give a shit anyway.' I didn't even bother asking them. I knew they wouldn't come, and there was no way I was gonna set myself up for another rejection. It kinda sucks that I don't have any of my family here, but I have Carter. *He's family.*

'How's all that shit going with your brother?'

I shrug. 'No idea. I don't have anything to do with them.' Last year my brother's name was splashed on the front page of every newspaper, not for the reasons he'd hoped for either. He was embroiled in some kind of sex scandal with his secretary and another politician's wife, and subsequently forced to step down from his position in parliament. Even though Brent was the golden child in my parent's eyes, I know them well enough to realise they would've distanced themselves from him after that—possibly even disowned him, like they did me. Even Brent's wife left him after a few other women came forward—one even claimed to be carrying his child. I felt bad for him, but you reap what you sow. Karma's a bitch.

'Can we change the subject?' I ask. Today is my wedding day, and I refuse to let those fuckers put a dampener on it.

I didn't anticipate feeling this nervous. I shake out my hands as I try to calm the hell down. I need a damn cigarette, but I promised Candice I wouldn't smoke anymore. The night I planned on proposing to her, I was a mess. While Candice and Maddie were inside getting ready for our dinner date, I snuck out the back to have a quick smoke. I needed something to take the edge off. She wasn't angry when she busted me, just upset. She asked me to stop, and I haven't had one since. She's never been one to tell me what to do, but her reasons made perfect sense: she wants me around for her and the kids.

I tug at the bowtie around my neck. 'I feel like a fucking penguin in this get-up.'

'You look like one too,' Carter chuckles. Does he not realise he's also wearing a tux? Dickhead.

'Jax,' I hear someone say from behind me. Without even looking I know who it is. It's been a while, but I'd recognise that voice anywhere.

'Brian,' I say as I spin around. I can't believe he's here. How?

I guess the look on my face says it all. 'Your little lady called me.' Of course she did. My pink-haired angel.

Brian looks great, nothing like the man I remember. Words can't convey how happy I am to see him again. I've missed him.

'I'm so glad you've come.'

He ignores my extended hand, opting to pull me into a hug instead.

'I wouldn't have missed it for the world, son.'

A lump rises in my throat. Why would I need my family here? Everyone who's important to me is present. This is all the family I'll ever need.

As we stand there and chat, a pretty blonde approaches. She's short even in her sky-high heels.

'Hi,' she says, coming to a stop in front of us.

'Hi.' I have no clue who she is.

'Which one of you is Jax?'

She has an English accent, but all I can think is, *how the fuck does she know my name?* I have a mini freak-out, and my eyes dart to Carter. He better not have ordered me a damn stripper on my wedding day. I'll knock him out if he did. The blonde doesn't really look like a stripper, but she has that sexy secretary/librarian thing going on.

'My name is Michelle . . . Michelle McGinty.' Her greens eyes sparkle as her gaze moves from me to Carter. It only seems to heighten my concerns. 'I'm the marriage celebrant.'

'Oh.' Relief floods through me. Of course that's who she is. 'I'm Jax,' I say, shaking her hand. I'm not up to speed on every detail of today—I only played a part in choosing the venue. The rest of the details were left to Candice and Sophia.

'And I'm Carter, the best man,' Carter says, as he winks at her. I shake my head. He's such an idiot.

Carter leaves us when Indi and the kids arrive, and Michelle spends the next fifteen minutes going over the details of the service with me. She's already discussed it at length with Candice when they met. I couldn't make it, because I had some issues at work. Candice did give me a run-down when I got home from work that night, but I'm pretty sure I tuned out after a few minutes. The only words that were important to me were the 'I do's.

'Hey, boss.'

I spin around when someone clasps my shoulder. 'Gus,' I say, smiling. I'm glad he's here. He's the only guest we invited, other than our family.

'This is Gina.' He puts his arm proudly around a brunette, puffing out his chest. 'Gina, this is my boss, Jax.'

He brought a date? Wow.

'Hi,' she says.

'Hey. It's nice to meet you,' I reply.

When I shake Gus's hand, I lean my body in. 'How much did you pay her to be your date today?' I whisper.

'Very funny.' He chuckles, playfully punching my arm. 'She's my girlfriend. Pinkie set us up.'

'Really?' How come I didn't know anything about that?

When the time comes, Carter, Michelle and I move into place. I rub my sweaty palms down the front of my trousers as the nerves kick in.

A red carpet has been laid out for the girls to walk down. A few chairs have been placed either side for our handful of guests: Sophia, Brendan, Carter, Indi and the kids, Brian, Gus and his date, Gina.

There's a small piano set up left of the chairs, with a woman sitting in front of it. I guess she's in charge of the music. As soon as she starts playing, Maddie comes into view. Candice is right behind her. *My girls.* A lump rises in my throat. I hate to think of how miserable my life would be without them by my side. When our son finally arrives, our family will be complete. I can't wait to experience all the things I missed with Maddie.

I'm smiling as Maddie makes her way down the aisle towards us. She has Snoopy on a leash, and I chuckle when I see the bowtie he's wearing around his neck. I can't even put into words how much I adore my little girl. She looks so grown up in her long pink gown. Her blonde curls are piled up on top of her head, and there's a touch of makeup on her face—she looks so beautiful. She reminds me so much of Candice when we first met all those years ago. It won't be long before the boys come knocking. I think I'll need to invest in a shotgun when that happens.

'I love you, Daddy,' she murmurs as she comes to stand with me and Carter under the iconic smiling mouth of Luna Park. Candice and I chose this exact spot to exchange our vows because that's all we seem to do these days—smile.

'I love you too.'

The moment I see Candice in all her glory, I swear all the air leaves my body; she still takes my breath away after all this time. Her stepfather stands proudly beside her, ready to give her away.

My eyes drink her in, as I try to imprint this image in my mind forever. It's a moment I don't want to ever forget. Once upon a time it was something I only dreamt about. Never in my wildest dreams did I think one day this would be my reality. Her small belly is visible in the elegant white strapless gown she's wearing, which only makes her look even more gorgeous to me. I can't tell you what an amazing feeling it is to go through this pregnancy with her. Attending all the doctor's appointments, seeing the first ultrasound of our son. Soon I'll be able to feel him moving inside her.

I place my hand over my heart as I return her smile. She lifts her dress slightly, and I chuckle when I see she's wearing pink Converse sneakers underneath. She looks every bit the beauty queen today, but the real Candice, the one I'm hopelessly in love with, is ever present.

Tears fill my eyes, as she starts walking towards me. I'm surprised how emotional I feel in this moment. For a long time, I never thought I'd get the one thing in life I always wanted—*her*. I'm so glad I was wrong. She completes me.

'Here,' Carter says from beside me. When I briefly pull my gaze away from Candice and turn my head in his direction, I see he's holding out a tissue to me. 'You might need this.'

'Fuck off, cock,' I grumble under my breath, pushing his hand away at the same time. 'I'm not crying. A bug flew into my eye.'

'A bug. You're such a liar,' he says, chuckling. He can be such a smug prick sometimes.

Ignoring him, I seek out my girl again. My heart thumps furiously against my ribcage when she's within reaching distance. I extend my hand to her, and she takes it willingly. 'You look stunning,' I whisper as I wrap her in my arms.

'And you look totally fuckable in that tux,' she growls, soft enough that only I can hear.

I cup her beautiful face in my hands before my lips bear down on hers. I hear the celebrant gasp from behind us. I know the kiss is supposed to come after, but like I said, we don't do conventional. I need to taste her. It's been almost twenty-four hours and I'm having withdrawals.

'Get a room, you two,' Carter leans over and whispers, so I flip him the bird.

When I finally pull out of the kiss, my eyes lock with Candice's. She's glowing. 'Are you ready?'

'I've never been more ready.'

•••

'Flight eight-two-nine to Tahiti is now boarding at gate sixty-three,' the flight attendant says over the loudspeaker.

I bring my wife's hand up to my mouth, placing a chaste kiss on her knuckles. 'That's us.' The full smile she gives me hits me right in the chest. She looks as happy as I feel. Standing, I help her to her feet.

'As much as I'm gonna miss Maddie, I can't wait to have you all to myself for a whole week,' she whispers in my ear as we line up behind the other passengers waiting to board.

Just the thought of it has my dick jumping in my pants.

Sliding my arms around her waist, I pull her to me. I inhale her apple scent as I kiss her hair. *My kryptonite.* I'm suddenly doubting whether I can wait until we get there to have her again. 'Have you ever thought of joining the mile-high club?' I practically groan into her ear.

She doesn't answer, but the look she gives me has all the blood in my body rushing straight to my cock.

'Do you have any idea how much I love you, Mrs Albright?' I say as my lips brush against hers.

'I love you more, Mr Albright.'

'Not possible,' I reply, smiling, and that's the truth. *I'm so fucking happy it's ridiculous.*

Our wedding day turned out to be everything I'd hoped it would be, and so much more. There's something pretty cool about getting married at a theme park. For years our life was like a damn roller-coaster ride; way too many ups and downs to count. We went through some pretty hard times, but when we finally stopped fighting the inevitable and let go of all the demons from our past, our lives became nothing short of majestic. The heart wants what the heart wants, no ifs or buts. It's as simple as that.

Apart we were hollow.

Together we are whole.

I look forward to my future with her by my side.

From the author of the #1 bestseller *Bastard*

HOOKER

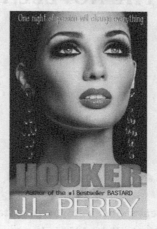

**One night of passion with a sinfully hot stranger will
change everything.**

Jade's young life was tough. She grew up feeling unloved and unwanted
as she was passed around from one screwed-up foster home to the
next. Things began to look up for her when she was adopted by a
wealthy socialite at the age of eleven. Jade didn't know it at the time,
but her new adoptive mother had big plans for her . . .

Brock grew up with everything going for him. Money, looks and an
endless array of beautiful women. He wasn't interested in commitment.
Then he met Jade. Their one night together ignited a burning desire
to own her, possess her. But Jade had other plans. Nobody says no to
Brock Weston, nobody.

When fate brings them together again, will Brock get what he
wants? Or will Jade's secrets ruin everything?

Join Carter and Indiana once more in

LUCKIEST BASTARD:
THE NOVELLA

Available now in ebook!

It's been two years since reformed bastard Carter and his treasured wife, Indi, had their happy-ever-after in the #1 bestselling *Bastard* . . .

Contains:

Luckiest Bastard, a novella with a HEA
First White Christmas, a bonus story

Two years and two children after their happy ending
in *Bastard*, **Carter** and **Indiana** have settled into
married life after their tumultuous pasts. But a shocking
event will threaten everything they hold dear.

If you enjoyed *Jax*, you'll devour Carter's story.
Read on for a preview.

BASTARD

Available now!

The #1 bestseller. A heartbreakingly beautiful love story by Australia's favourite new romance author, J.L. Perry.

My name is **Carter Reynolds**. I was born a bastard and I'll die a bastard. I learnt it at a young age, and nothing and nobody can change that. I'm on a one-way path of destruction, and God help anyone who gets in my way. That's until I meet the kid next door, Indi-freakin'-ana. My dislike for her is instant. From the moment I lay eyes on her, she ignites something within me. It freaks me the hell out. She's like sunshine and rainbows in my world of gloom and doom.

I'm **Indiana Montgomery**. My friends call me Indi. Despite losing my mum at the age of six, I have a wonderful life. My dad more than makes up for the fact that I only have one parent. I'm his little girl, the centre of his world. When Carter Reynolds moves in next door, things take a turn for the worse. He's gorgeous, sinfully hot, but he seems hell-bent on making my life miserable. He acts tough, but when I look into his eyes I don't see it. I see hurt and pain. I'm drawn to him for some reason. Whether he likes it or not, I refuse to give up on him.

PROLOGUE

CARTER

the past . . .

REACHING OUT, MY MUM WRAPS HER LONG, DAINTY FINGERS around my small hand. "Jump, baby." She smiles as I launch from the bottom step off the bus, landing on the sidewalk. We both laugh. I love my mum. She's fun.

"Brrrrrr, it's cold today," she says.

Looking up, I find her shivering. I smile at her as she zips up her coat to keep warm. Digging through her bag, she takes out my favourite Spiderman beanie and scarf, holding them up for me to see.

"Put these on, sweetie," she says smiling as she crouches down in front of me, placing my beanie on my head and wrapping the scarf around my neck. "Let me get your gloves," she adds, reaching into her bag again. "I can't have my little man getting sick." I stand and watch as she pushes my small fingers into my blue gloves, one by one. "There, all snug."

"Snug as a bug in a rug," I add. This is something she says to me every night when she tucks me into bed.

"That's right, baby," she says leaning forward, giving me a soft kiss on my nose. Rising to her feet she reaches for my hand. "Come on."

As we walk down the street, my eyes take everything in. I don't think I've ever been here before. There are shops on one side of the street, and big houses on the other. "Where are we, Mummy?" I ask while looking around. The loud roar of a motorbike passing makes me jump.

"This is my hometown. I grew up here." I look up at her. Wow. Mummy lived somewhere else before our home?

She gazes down at me, but she looks sad. "You lived here when you were little, like me?" I ask.

"Uh huh. This is where your grandparents live."

"I have a grandma and grandpa?" I didn't know that either. I feel my eyes widen and I smile. I hear the kids at school talk about their grandparents all the time. I've always wondered why I didn't have any of my own.

I've never asked my mum why. Once I asked her how come I didn't have a daddy like the other kids, and it made her cry. I don't like seeing my mummy cry.

"I'm taking you to meet them now. They've never met you before." I'm getting so excited, like I did a few weeks ago when I turned five, and my mummy bought me a big chocolate cake. My friend, Josh, was allowed to come over. He even bought me a present. Nobody but my mummy has ever bought me a present before. I met Josh's grandparents once, when I was playing at his house. They were really nice. I hope my grandparents are like his.

I start jumping along because I'm so happy. Mummy stops in front of a big, white house. It's really, really big, like the houses you see in movies. It's so much bigger than where mummy and me live.

My mum's hand starts shaking as she holds mine. I look at her. She looks mad, like the time I drew on the wall at home. Her eyes are doing funny things.

"Your hands are shaking, Mummy."

"I'm okay little man, I'm just cold." She looks down at me and smiles. Her eyes look happy when she looks at me.

"Do you want to borrow my gloves?"

"No, baby," she says as her smile widens. She crouches down, placing her hands on either side of my face. "No matter what happens when we go in here, just remember how much I love you, and how special you are."

"Okay," I say. I love my mummy. I know I'm going to love my grandparents too.

"Good boy." She leans forward and kisses my cheek before standing up and reaching for my hand again. "Let's do this."

As we walk down the long driveway, my mum's hand continues to shake. I wish she'd put my gloves on. I hate how she's cold.

"One . . . two . . . three . . . four . . . five." I count the stairs in my head as we climb them before we stop in front of the big yellow door. I hear my mum let out a big breath. Letting go of my hand, she makes a fist as she raises her arm, but she stops mid-air. Looking down at me, her lips turn up before finally knocking on the door. I can't wait to see my grandparents. I hope they have chocolate. I love chocolate.

Reaching for my hand, she gives it a squeeze. When the door opens, I look up at the man who stands there. He doesn't look happy when he sees Mummy.

"Elizabeth," he says sternly.

"Hi, Daddy," she replies nervously. He relaxes when Mummy says that. The corners of his mouth turn up slightly. I feel my own big smile. Wow, this must be my grandpa. He looks so strong.

"What are you doing here?" he asks.

My mum doesn't say anything for what feels like one hundred years. "I wanted to see you. I . . . ummm, wanted you to meet your grandson, Carter." She gives my hand another squeeze as she looks down at me.

"Hello, Grandpa," I say. I'm seeing my very own grandpa. I want to hug him.

He looks angry again as he stares down at me. Then his head snaps back up to look at my mummy. "Why did you bring that little *bastard* here?" he asks really, really meanly. "Get him out of here. Don't you ever bring him here again." Stepping back, he slams the door in our faces.

My mum makes a strange sound and I feel like crying. I'm sad because my mummy is sad. She only makes that noise when she's upset. I don't like my grandpa. He's mean. "Come on, baby," she says. When her eyes meet mine, I see her tears are already falling. I don't like seeing my mummy cry.

I'm almost running behind her as she tugs on my hand. She hurries down the driveway and back out into the street. "What's a bastard?" I ask. I've never heard that word before. The way my grandpa said it, it doesn't sound like a nice word.

My question stops her walking. Wiping her eyes with the back of her hand, she squats down in front of me. "You're not a bastard," she says sadly. "Pay no attention to what he said. You're a beautiful boy." She gives me a kiss on my forehead. "I'm sorry I brought you here."

"It's okay, Mummy," I say trying real hard to be brave. When my bottom lip starts to quiver and the first tears fall, I know I've failed. I'm not brave.

"Oh, baby." She opens her arms, pulling me tightly against her as I cry into her chest. "You're not a bastard," she whispers.

I want to believe her, I do, but why would Grandpa say it if it's not true? *I hate that I'm a bastard.* Even though I don't know what it means, I know that this moment and that horrible word are going to stick with me for a long time. Maybe even the rest of my life.

••••

bas·tard
1. *Offensive* A person born to parents not married to each other.
2. *Slang*
    a. A person considered to be mean or contemptible.
    b. A person, especially one considered to be unfortunate.
3. Something that is of irregular, inferior, or dubious origin.

It's funny how one fleeting moment in time can change you. One stupid, crazy, fucked-up word can define you. I didn't know it at the time, but after that day things changed—I changed. I was only five years old the day I learnt I was a bastard, and sadly as the years progressed, that's exactly what I became.

ONE

CARTER

present...

PACKING THE LAST OF THE BOXES INTO THE TRUNK OF THE CAR,
I turn and take one final look at the only place I've ever called home.
The place I've lived for the last seventeen years of my life. Sure it's
just a shitty old apartment block, but it's my home. It's all I've ever
known. I'm fucking pissed they're forcing me to leave here. I've been
dreading this day. I hate that I'm going to have to live with that
fuckwit my mum now calls her husband.

Thank God it's only for six months. That's when I'll be turning
eighteen; finally becoming a legal adult. You can be sure as hell the
first thing I do, is blow this godforsaken place. My mum has that
cocksucker to look after her now. She doesn't need me anymore.

She started dating John Shepard six months ago. It was a whirl-
wind romance you could say. I guess she's been alone since I was
born, so I can't really blame her for wanting a companion. It's
always been just the two of us. At first I kind of liked the idea of
having a father figure around, but my hopes were soon dashed

when I got to know Fuckwit. That's my pet name for him. It suits him perfectly.

I saw the difference in her when she'd come home from being out with him. She was happier. Lighter. Like she was floating or some shit. I liked seeing her like that. She deserved happiness.

They'd been seeing each other for a few months before she brought him to the house to meet me. I was on my best behaviour the first time we met. I did it for her. He was very pleasant until she left the room for a few minutes to get us some drinks. The way he looked me up and down with disdain instantly had my suspicions rising. As time wore on, those looks turned into hateful remarks. In the beginning I'd done nothing to provoke them. I guess he just took a disliking to me for some reason. Maybe because I was a bastard. Who knows? I was used to rejection. I'd faced it my whole life.

My mum's love has always been unconditional. Even when I acted up, she still loved me, still cared. I'll be forever grateful for that. She's been through a lot with me over the years, but her feelings for me never wavered. *Not once.* I was nothing to Fuckwit, I guess. Just a thorn in his side. Someone standing in the way of him being with my mother.

I was shattered when he proposed and she accepted, but I didn't let her know that's how I felt. I wasn't about to burst her bubble. She deserved happiness after all the sacrifices she'd made for me over the years. I wasn't about to stand in her way.

The day he finally put the ring on her finger was the same day he made his true feelings for me be known. They had some lame-arse civil ceremony at the registry office. It was my mum's first marriage. She deserved so much more than that. I didn't even want to attend, but she wanted me there, so for her sake I had to grin and bear it.

Afterwards, the three of us were heading to a nice restaurant for a celebratory lunch. Well, they were celebrating. I sure as hell wasn't. My mum asked Fuckwit to stop off at the local patisserie so she could buy a nice cake to take with us. The minute she was out of the car he gave me a hateful look through the rear vision mirror.

"I love your mother," he told me. "But don't think for a minute that any of that affection extends to you, because it doesn't. In my eyes, you're the unwelcomed part of the package." I hate to admit it, but his hurtful words stung. It only served to make me feel even lower about myself.

Why was I such a hard person to love?

Before I get a chance to close the trunk, my stepfather leans out of the driver's side window. "Hurry up, *son*. I haven't got all day," he sneers in a sarcastic tone. I swear he does shit like this to bait me. My head snaps in his direction.

"I'm not your son. You best remember that, old man," I retort, my eyes narrowing. "If you got off your arse and helped instead of sitting there barking orders at me all afternoon, we would've finished hours ago."

Throwing back his head, he laughs at my comment. He acts so sweet in front of my mum. She falls for his pathetic shit all the time. Truth is, he's a fake-arse prick. As soon as my mum's back is turned he treats me like dirt. She might love him, but I don't. *I fucking hate him*. This is going to be the longest six months of my life.

Slamming the trunk shut, I make my way around to the passenger side of the car. "Wipe your damn feet before you get in the car," he barks. I swear if there were some dog shit nearby right now, I'd tread in it just to spite him.

Sighing, I do as he asks before seating myself in the passenger side. *"Prick,"* I mumble under my breath.

"Watch that smart mouth of yours, boy. I won't tolerate you speaking like that in *my* house, and especially in front of your mother." *I'd never speak like that to my mum.* Him though, that's a whole other story.

Ignoring him I turn my head, gazing out the window, taking one last look at *my* home as he backs out of the drive. Christ, it hasn't even been twenty-four hours and I already want to punch him.

Not a word is spoken on the drive to his place. I'm thankful for that. My stomach is in knots. Living with this arsehole is going to be pure fucking hell. I have no idea what my mother sees in him, but surprisingly he makes her happy. That's the only reason I'm going along with this bullshit. I'm doing it for her, no other reason. After everything she has sacrificed for me she deserves to be happy.

It's about an hour's drive from my old neighbourhood to the gates of *hell*. Fuck, I need a cigarette. As soon as we pull into the street I'll now be calling home, my heart rate picks up. The street is lined with perfect houses, with perfect lawns and fancy manicured gardens.

I hate it here already.

"This is your new home, *my* home. Remember that," Fuckwit says when we pull into the driveway.

"Whoop-de-fucking-do," I reply as I exit the car before he has a chance to say another word. I make my way around to the back of the vehicle to unpack the boxes. Of course that lazy fucker heads straight inside. I guess I'll be doing all the work again.

Figures.

As I go to open the trunk, I'm stopped when I hear laughter. Pure, sweet, sickening laughter. My head snaps in the direction it came from, and that's when I see her. Well actually, the first thing I see is her tight little arse. She's bending over patting a dog, wearing these sexy little shorts. Tearing my eyes away from her, they land on the dog. It's a long-haired German Shepherd.

The perfect dog.

Growing up I always wanted a dog like that, but living in an apartment building that didn't allow animals made it impossible.

When the girl stands up straight my eyes move up to her long, dark hair that now cascades down her lean back. The sun's beaming down on it, illuminating its shine. I find myself wishing she'd turn around so I can see her face. She doesn't, so my gaze moves back down to her arse. Fuck me, what an arse.

Images of me wrapping her hair around my wrist as I bend her over, pounding her from behind enter my mind. It makes my dick stir. Jesus, why did I let my thoughts go there? Her body might be rockin', but that doesn't mean her face is. I guess, if I was giving it to her from behind, that wouldn't really be a problem anyway.

I watch as she raises her arm, throwing the ball across the yard. She's got a pretty good throw for a girl. The dog turns, galloping towards it. When he makes his way back he almost bowls her over in his excitement. She starts to laugh again, and I feel the corners of my lips turn up in a smile as I watch them.

"Good boy," she says in a sweet voice as she scratches him behind the ears. "Who's a good boy?" When the dog notices me standing there watching, he drops the ball from his mouth and trots in my direction.

"Hey boy," I say holding my hand out for him to sniff. He seems friendly so I reach down, running my fingers through his long mane. I can feel my smile widen. Smiling is something I don't usually do.

"Lassie," I hear her call out, making my smile instantly turn into a scowl. She's got to be fucking kidding. *Lassie?* She had the audacity to name this cool dog Lassie. What in the hell was she thinking? He looks more like a Rambo or Butch, definitely not a fucking Lassie.

"You poor thing," I whisper as I scratch him behind the ears. "She'll probably be cutting your balls off next and putting a fucking bow in your hair."

My head snaps up and my brow furrows as she makes her way towards us. Fuck me if her face isn't as beautiful as that luscious body of hers. I swear my jaw goes lax as she approaches. *She's a fucking babe.* Her long dark hair frames her angelic face. Her large eyes are surrounded by thick, dark lashes. Her creamy skin is flawless, just making me itch to touch it. My eyes drift down to her tits. They're kind of small, but more than a mouthful's a waste, I suppose. She has a cute little button nose that makes me want to throw up in my mouth.

Okay, maybe that last comment was a bit over the top. That's just my bastardry rearing its ugly head. It's a defence mechanism I've developed and mastered over the years. A barrier I've put in place. I hate that she's already making me feel things I don't want to feel. I've learnt over the years if you can't feel, you can't hurt. If I'm going to be seeing her daily, I need to nip this shit in the bud right now before it gets out of hand.

"Hey, you must be Carter. Your mum told me you'd be moving in today." Her beauty has rendered me speechless. *What the hell?*

Pulling myself together I straighten up to full height, towering over her tiny frame. Her sexy-as-fuck plump lips curve up into a smile as her beautiful green eyes meet mine. "I'm Indiana. Your new neighbour," she says sweetly, extending her hand to me.

Game on.

It's time to push her away before she gets too close. It's called self-preservation. I learnt a long time ago, it lessens the sting if I reject someone before they get a chance to do that to me.

My gaze moves down to her extended hand then back up to her face. "You called your dog Lassie?" I snarl. "What were you fucking thinking? That's a pussy name for a dog like this. You do realise he's a boy, right?"

Her sweet mouth opens in shock and her pretty green eyes widen before narrowing into slits. "The dog that played Lassie in the movies was a boy too, you know," she retorts, folding her arms over her chest. If she's trying to look tough she's failing miserably. Crossing her arms only manages to push her perky little tits up further. I feel my cock grow at the sight, and that pisses me the hell off. I hate how she's having this effect on me.

Opening the trunk, I reach in to retrieve a box and place it in front of me. The last thing I want her to see is the damn hard-on she's just given me.

"What's your problem anyway?" she asks, her eyes meeting mine again. "You're not exactly making a great first impression."

I almost want to smile at her fucking attitude, but there's no way in hell I'll be giving her that satisfaction. "I don't give a fuck what you think of me, *kid.* Why don't you run along and go play with your dolls like a good little girl?"

I'm really struggling not to smile now as her eyes widen in disbelief at the way I'm speaking to her. When her lips open, forming a perfect little O, all I can think is she has the most fuckable mouth I've ever seen. That thought only makes my cock even harder.

Sweet Jesus, what is she doing to me?

I'm surprised I almost feel bad for the way I'm treating her, but riling her up is way too much fun. I'm not about to stop now.

"Well that's just plain rude. Something pretty shitty must've happened in your life to give you such a bad attitude." She hit the nail right on the head. It sure did I want to say, but I don't. My brow furrows. Why does her saying that piss me off even more?

I hate that in less than a minute she has already seen through my facade. What is she, some kind of crazy clairvoyant or something? My eyes lock with hers again, and the sympathetic look I see on her face makes me dislike her even more.

"Nope. I'm just a bastard, and stop fucking looking at me like that. You're creeping me the hell out."

"Like what?" she huffs, placing her hands on her hips.

"Like you feel sorry for me. I don't want or need your sympathy. The sooner you learn that the better off we'll all be, Princess. Do yourself a favour *kid*, stay the fuck away from me." She gasps at my words and a satisfied smile crosses my face.

Mission accomplished.

"Later, Larry," I say to the dog, giving him one last scratch behind the ears before walking away.

"His name's Lassie, arsehole," she snaps to my retreating back.

"Not to me it isn't," I chuckle as I walk towards the house. "You won't catch me calling him that pansy-arse name." Maybe living here isn't going to be as bad as I thought.

"Come on boy," I hear her say, exhaling an exasperated breath.

As I walk up the porch stairs to my new hell, I hear her front door slam shut. Surprisingly, this makes the smile instantly drop from my face. I actually feel shitty for the way I just treated her. I don't often feel remorseful for my actions.

Why am I such a bastard? That's right, I was born one.

J.L. PERRY

J.L. Perry is a mother and a wife. She was born in Sydney, Australia in 1972, and has lived there her whole life. Her other titles include *My Destiny*, *My Forever*, *Damaged*, *Against All Odds*, *Hooker*, *Bastard* and the novella *Luckiest Bastard*, which follows *Bastard*. J.L. Perry's standalone novel *Nineteen Letters* will be available in 2017.

For updates and teasers on all my future books,
you can follow or friend me on:

Facebook Profile
www.facebook.com/JLPerryAuthor

Facebook Page
www.facebook.com/pages/J-L-Perry-Author/216320021889204

Goodreads
www.goodreads.com/author/show/7825921.J_L_Perry

Twitter
www.twitter.com/JLPerryAuthor

Amazon Author Page
www.amazon.com/author/jlperry

Destiny's Divas Street Team
www.facebook.com/groups/323178884496533/

JL Perry Fan Page
www.facebook.com/groups/667079023424941/